Praise for *Days o*

"Watch out for this new write...   ...r
territory. Man Martin has all of O'Connor's deadpan hilarity and
smarts, but O'Connor never had a '53 Corvette ('If you've ever sat in
one, it's like a red velvet cake'). Only 300 of these were ever made, but
that's still 299 more than the one-of-a-kind concoction that is *Days of
the Endless Corvette.* Delicious guilty fun, and cerebrally fattening."

–Nancy Zafris, author of *The Metal Shredders*

"Ladies and gentlemen, please welcome to the stage Man Martin, a
wholly original writer whose voice will linger in your mind. This is a
wonderful novel—a tenderly shaded love story and a deliciously inti-
mate portrait of human beings seeking answers to all the hard questions. *Days of the Endless Corvette* casts a spell that is memorable,
painful, and sweet."   –Mark Childress, author of *One Mississippi*

"*Days of the Endless Corvette* was an absolute hoot, yet I wondered
why I had shed a tear over it. Because character Earl Mulvaney was a
loser? No, he was also the town's hero. Was I saddened by Earl's infat-
uation with a dead '53 Corvette? No, with replacement parts, he had
almost given that car eternal life. I guess Earl was so noble, he was
simply worth crying over. All the folks of Humble County, Georgia,
were so sweet that I couldn't bear to leave them behind, so I'm rereading *Days of the Endless Corvette.*"

–Peter Brown, author of *Ruthie Black*

"Man Martin's tall tale stretches truth until it squeaks and gives up
small moments of such perfect beauty that more than once I found
myself grinning through tears. It's smart and funny and quirky and
deeply imagined, and at its heart is a gorgeous faith in the potency of
human connections. Martin crafts a rich feast from love's leftovers and
smallest pieces, delivering a wonderful book, wonderful, in every
sense of the word."   –Joshilyn Jackson, author of *Between, Georgia*

"If a reader could coax Earl Mulvaney to slip from these pages and
mentor the dismantling of Man Martin's *Days of the Endless Corvette*,
there would be more than enough comedy pathos, tenderness, excitement and pure d magic left over to populate a dozen lesser novels."

–Sonny Brewer, author of *The Poet of Tolstoy Park*

DAYS OF THE
Endless Corvette

MAN MARTIN

CARROLL & GRAF PUBLISHERS
NEW YORK

DAYS OF THE ENDLESS CORVETTE

Carroll & Graf Publishers
An Imprint of Avalon Publishing Group, Inc.
245 West 17th Street
11th Floor
New York, NY 10011

AVALON
publishing group incorporated

Copyright © 2007 by Man Martin

First Carroll & Graf edition 2007

This book is a work of fiction. Names, characters, places, and incidents either are products of the author's imagination or are used fictitiously.

Library of Congress Cataloging-in-Publication Data

Martin, Man, 1959-
  Days of the endless Corvette : a novel / Man Martin. — 1st Carroll & Graf ed.
    p. cm.
  ISBN 978-0-7867-1987-7 (trade pbk. original)
  1. City and town life—Fiction. 2. Self-actualization (Psychology)—Fiction.
  3. Automobiles—Conservation and restoration—Fiction. 4. Georgia—Fiction.
  I. Title.

PS3613.A7833D39 2007
813'.6—dc22

                                                                    2007005657

ISBN-10: 0-7867-1987-7

9 8 7 6 5 4 3 2 1

Interior design by Maria Fernandez

Printed in the United States of America
Distributed by Publishers Group West

To Mur

DISCLAIMER

Those curious enough to check an atlas may be nonplussed to find that while there is a Deepstep, Georgia, there is no Humble County. The reason for this is that I selected the names Deepstep and Humble purely for their euphony and with disregard for reality. The street names and locations I largely took from Deepstep's neighbor, Sandersville, where I spent much of my halcyon childhood. Anyone requiring a more specific geographical location should imagine that Deepstep is the seat of Humble County, which lies somewhere in the nexus of Washington, Hancock, and Baldwin Counties. Everything else in this story is moon mist and wood smoke.

PART
I

CHAPTER ONE

We never came to complete agreement about Earl and the Endless Corvette: whether it kept him from going crazy or proved he was crazy from the get-go. Had he lived someplace else, there would have been no doubt, but because of Humble County's history, we have a higher tolerance than most for craziness.

During the Civil War, the story goes, the local leaders buried our most valuable possession to keep it out of Sherman's hands. Exactly what that possession was, I couldn't say; some claim it was the courthouse tower bell; others that it was the pipe organ from First Baptist; others that it was a chest filled with those lumps of gold and silver people call "pigs." All accounts agree on two particulars: that whatever it was, it was valuable and metallic. When the war ended without so much as a whiff of

Sherman's army within twenty miles, people figured it was safe to dig the treasure up. Sadly, the papers telling where it was had been burned for safety's sake. Worse, all the people who were in on the plan in the first place had died or been lost in the war.

Ever since, the county has conducted an intermittent search—issuing bonds to pay for workers, metal detectors, and backhoes. No sign has turned up yet of the missing bell, organ, or pigs, but this has not deterred the city fathers. It is not surprising, therefore, that we are relatively patient with even the most farfetched schemes.

The Endless Corvette came to Earl during his senior year of high school, in the fall of '73, between the time his dad left home for good and Ellen Raley got engaged.

It was an August evening right before his senior year that Earl spoke to his father, Roy Mulvaney, for the last time. Roy came out of the house, letting the screen door slam behind him, shutting off his wife's protest, "Don't let that screen door—" The family Buick, once midnight blue, now faded, sat parked on the gravel driveway, its hood open like a patiently gaping hippo. Earl leaned inside its maw, his shoulder shifting as he pushed and pulled on his socket wrench. Roy patted his son's shoulder and gazed in the direction of Ellen Raley's house, across the street from the Mulvaneys'.

"How's the car doing, son?"

"Just fine," Earl said, looking up from the engine.

Roy didn't know it, but the car was only half the reason Earl was out; Ellen Raley was the other half. Just before twilight she always sat out on her stoop to read a book. Earl made a point of coming out when she was there to try to make her look at him but not seem like he was trying. Over many nights, the sight of Ellen reading in the glow of the yellow bug light with her baby-oiled legs, together with the smell of wood smoke and the lonely baying of the town dogs in the distance, had combined on Earl, and he'd fallen for her. When he noticed she'd started bringing a Dr Pepper out with her, he began drinking Dr Pepper, too. He admired her for the solemn and beautiful expression on her face as she read, he admired the way her long red hair fell over her shoulders, and he imagined how perfectly his arms would fit around her waist. But Earl had not spoken to her, hopeful that proximity, Dr Pepper, fragrant air, and canine lamentation would have the same effect on her as it had on him.

"Getting the timing fixed?" Roy asked. He tried setting one foot on the bumper and resting his elbow on his knee to seem casual and self-confident, but the Buick's bumper was an inch too low to bring it off, so he stepped back down and just stood there.

"Yes, sir."

"You going to have her ready before I come back?"

"It'll be ready for you. It always is."

Earl loved and pitied his father, but it was hard for them to talk. Both of them retreated into their private thoughts. From his pants pocket Roy pulled a pencil and a notepad. He studied the numbers written in it, then licked his pencil tip and began to add, subtract, and multiply, running a hand through his thick brown hair when his calculations momentarily stumped him. As his father calculated, Earl pushed his taped-together glasses back up his nose and kept his eyes on the bolt he was tightening. In the amber twilight, dirty Quaker State outlined his fingernails as if they'd been drawn on. Earl wondered if across the street Ellen were looking at him.

Ellen could have seen the Mulvaney men, standing side by side for the last time, if she'd looked over the top of her book, but she didn't do it. If Earl got his ideas on love from car repair and listening to dogs on pleasant August nights, Ellen got hers from reading. At the time Ellen's favorite book was about a girl named Jane who loves a millionaire who loves her, too, and even wants to marry her, but it turns out he's got a crazy wife locked up in the attic already. It comes out all right in the end because the house burns down with the crazy wife inside, so Jane and her millionaire live happily ever after. Ellen just loved that story, and, well, who wouldn't? But it made ordinary boys like Earl suffer by comparison since he didn't have a mansion or a crazy wife, and as far as Ellen knew, his little frame house didn't even have an attic.

"Do you want to hear a riddle?" Roy asked. Earl said he would, and Roy said, "Okay. There's fifty-two bicycles on the floor and a dead man. What happened?"

"I give up."

"He was caught cheating at a poker game," Roy said. Then, "Bicycles are a kind of cards, son," unnecessarily. A long pause. Roy put the pencil and pad back in his pocket, took out a pack of Fruit Stripe gum, peeled the foil off a stick, and stuck it upright in his mouth. He held out the pack to Earl's shoulder, but Earl was looking in the engine, so Roy nervously withdrew it. "You're pretty much a grown man now, Earl," Roy said finally.

"Yes, sir," Earl admitted.

"We have to look after your mother. We're the men, you know."

You'd have never known it to look at her, how sick Ruby Mulvaney was. She had high cheekbones, a glowing complexion, and rich auburn hair, but Earl's mother was in such decline, it seemed like she'd been remanufactured instead of born, as if someone else had worn out her parts before she'd gotten them. She had no specific illness, just a way of breaking down in one place or another. At the time of this conversation, her hip was degenerating, young as she was. It hadn't gotten to the point the doctor would put a new one in, but getting out of bed got harder every day. Before that, there'd been a prolapsed valve, and before that, a glass eye. Earl's delivery had culminated in a total hysterectomy. And as far as anyone could remember, she'd always had that plastic hand. Ruby Mulvaney was a foot-washing Baptist, but she didn't get to church as often as she liked because she could barely get down on her knees—her kneecaps were none too sturdy, either—and it seemed selfish if her own feet got washed every time.

"Yes, a grown man." Roy studied the smiling multicolored zebra on the gum pack; he wanted to get out his pad and pencil again, but now he had to contend with not only the pack of gum but also the foil wrapper from the stick he was chewing in addition to the pad and pencil. He fumbled with everything before he finally got the pad and pencil out again. Roy Mulvaney was a man afflicted with an inability to hold on to things. "Time sure does go by. Time." He seemed to think of nothing more profound to say about the subject than just the word itself. Meanwhile across the street Ellen closed her book, stood up and stretched. "Lordamighty! That Raley girl sure blossomed, didn't she?"

That summer Ellen had come back from Vacation Bible School with more than just Scripture. There's a Bible verse about mustard seeds and mountains, the precise wording of which I can't recall, but it'll give you an idea of the proportionate change that had taken place. Her breasts were not enormous, but astonishingly full to be placed on such a slim frame.

"Yes, time," said Roy returning to his subject. Ellen had gone inside, and Earl began reassembling the car. In a greasy aluminum bucket by his ankle he dropped the leftover pieces—a seal and a clamp. After many nights of tinkering in the Buick, Earl had filled the bucket a quarter of the way up with such odds and ends. "You can't stop time going by, so you got to use it," Roy said. "Life's like a game of roulette. Now I don't hold with gambling, you understand. This is just an analogy."

"Yes, sir."

"Say you bet five dollars on black and lose. Now the thing to do is to come right back and bet black again, but this time ten dollars. And if you lose then, come right back and bet twenty. You see where I'm going?"

"I think so, sir."

"Sooner or later, black is bound to come up. You just got to believe in your dream. It might take twenty times, it might take a thousand, but every time it comes up red, it's just that much more certain it'll be black next time. Eventually you're bound to win, ain't you?" Roy chewed his gum wetly between words, chasing the vanishing ghost of sweetness.

"Yes, sir." The logic was indeed unanswerable.

"Bound to. Can't help it. Now when you do win, as long as you been doubling your bets every time, even though you lost all those times before, if you subtract all your losses from your winnings, you're going to be exactly five dollars ahead. And all those people you let down up to then would be relieved to see how it finally paid off. Bet black and double your bets. Everything's bound to balance out in the end. You can do the math for yourself."

"I'll take your word for it, sir."

"Then, of course, you can go back to just betting five. That's it." Roy paused to consider the moral behind his hypothetical gambler. "You got to make time work for you, you got to believe in your dreams. And you got to be patient." A mud-spattered Pontiac pulled up, driven by Mort, one of Roy's friends from the kaolin mine. Earl's dad seemed to be about to add something else, but just ripped a sheet from his notepad and pasted it to the Buick in the wet circle where Earl's Dr Pepper had been; then he got in the Pontiac and rode off.

When Earl finished up and went inside, he found his mother on the couch stuffing envelopes and watching former stock-car racer and tall-tale spinner Junior Samples deadpan his way through a skit about a used-car salesman. The house was warm and close compared to the outside; a box fan buzzed in an open window to stir the air. Earl threw away his Dr Pepper bottle, and kissed her on the head, smelling her sweet flowery pin curls. "You got a new shipment."

"Yes. Two hundred gross," she nodded to the cardboard boxes by her ankle. "They'll pay an extra half cent per if I can get them done by Thursday." Using her good hand to fold, and her plastic hand against her leg as an iron to smooth out the crease, Ruby folded a letter crisply and put it in an envelope. She wore a long-sleeve shirt, but she'd pushed the sleeves up to work, revealing the strap that held on her plastic hand.

"I'll help." Earl sat beside her and began to stuff, too.

"Do you want me to make you a grilled cheese for supper?"

"No, thank you."

Ruby gave unusual attention to the next letter as she folded it and stuffed it into its envelope, "Has your father gone off to do some of his research?"

"Yes, ma'am."

"Oh," she sighed, and turned her eyes away from Earl toward the TV. "Well, bless his heart." A kaolin miner by profession, by avocation Roy Mulvaney was a scientist. The laws of probability had proven to him that he must draw 1.915 times to fill a flush for every 8.085 times he drew to a busted one. He added up the number of busted flushes he'd had through the years and determined he was owed approximately two hundred successful flushes. Although on moral grounds he felt opposed to gambling, Roy Mulvaney judged those odds simply too good to resist for anyone of a purely rational frame of mind, and therefore was frequently away from home on field research. "How's the Buick?" Earl's mom changed the subject to a happier one. "Did you get the timing adjusted to suit you?"

"Just about." Earl leaned over and grabbed another handful of envelopes.

On the TV, Buck Owens introduced the special guest to a roar of recorded applause, and Johnny Cash appeared on the screen singing "How High's the Water, Mamma?"

Earl did not notice the paper slip stuck to the car until the next afternoon when his dad still had not come home. Earl went out as usual to tinker on the Buick and saw it there, curling up, ruffling slightly in the warm breeze, and held down by one corner.

On one side Roy had written, "Some things you just can't help. Please understand." On the back was "52 × 51 × 50 × 49 × 48 = ~~311,785,200~~ 311,875,200."

His father's disappearance worried Earl, of course, but then again, Roy Mulvaney had disappeared so many times before, Earl had some practice coping with it. What to say to Ellen Raley when they met at school mostly occupied his mind. The first student to arrive in Mrs. Price's science class, Earl sat up front, just to left of center. Resting his elbows on a notebook full of virgin Blue Horse paper, Earl rubbed his hands together. The air was fragrant with the smell of chalk dust, mimeograph paper, and hope.

My head will bob up. Hey, Ellen. A thought just came to me. Why don't I give you a lift home? The head bob is crucial. It will show I just had an idea and give me a reason to speak. Offering a ride is the main thing, but the head bob guarantees to put it over and not make it seem like I practiced it.

Albert, the full-size human skeleton in the front of the room, gave an unwavering smile that seemed to confirm this was a good plan.

The Humble Tigers' fullback, Troy Badcock, came in, interrupting Earl's reverie. Troy dragged around the desk right of center and straddled it backward. Then he piled his book bag and letter jacket on the center desk, the very one Earl had counted on Ellen's taking. Being in Troy's company—he was nearly as broad as he was tall, and all muscle—always made Earl feel self-conscious of his own skinny frame, the way, for example, his ankles stuck out over the sides of his old tennis shoes. In a yellow raincoat and a red pillbox hat, Earl could have gone trick-or-treating as a pencil.

Earl pondered the new obstacle to offering Ellen a ride; in every class since first grade, she'd always sat front row, center, but now she wouldn't be able to take her customary seat if it were filled with Troy Badcock's stuff. Earl reconsidered and

11

revised his plan. Arnold grinned eager encouragement from his stand.

"Hey, Mulvaney," Troy said. "How's it going?" Anyone else asking such a question would be making mere glib chatter, but not so Troy Badcock. Troy had a gift, which later served him quite well when listening as tearful customers described septic tank implosions, of leaning his big square head forward and training his hazel eyes on yours as if the next words to drop from your lips just might uncork the inmost mystery of his own life, and that he had lain in bed staring at the ceiling the entire night anticipating what you might say.

The little red needle in Earl's heart wavered, and he was just on the point—I mean the very point, the tip end—of confiding in Troy that he intended to ask out Ellen Raley, but before he could speak—

"Mr. Badcock," Mrs. Price looked up from the names she'd been recording in a green ledger book, "That is not the way we sit in school."

"I can't sit the other way," Troy said, "The doctor says it's bad for my back. Honest," he raised his index and middle fingers, taking the Boy Scout's oath.

"I see. How sad. And did this doctor write a note?"

Troy laughed and turned his desk back right way round. There was no pulling wool over Mrs. Price's eyes: she'd read every book there ever was and knew everything.

More students came in, and Earl turned his attention back to his private thoughts. Barbara Allen stood in front of Troy, a hand on her outthrust hip, her mascara still sticky from having just applied it in the girls' restroom moments before. "What did you do this summer, Troy?"

"Nothing much. Swam, I guess." Troy leaned back and folded

his hands behind his head. Troy had dated Barbara, but it went against number three of his unspoken rules to say much to her now. He looked away impatiently from Barbara and caught Earl's eye as if to say, "The things men like us have to put up with, huh?"

"Hello, Ellen," Mrs. Price said.

Troy and Earl turned. A flash of red hair at the door, the swish of a cotton skirt, the scent—or did Earl just imagine it?—of sweet shampoo. Ellen Raley had come in. Earl opened his notebook, and studied a table of weights and measures the manufacturer had thoughtfully printed inside the cover, bracing himself to bob his head up as if at a sudden thought.

Troy was the next to speak, letting loose a long low whistle, first. "If them things are speakers, they ought to be at least six to eight feet apart." Troy always did have a way with a compliment; Ellen's face clouded, then she turned red and got mad. "I'm just kidding," Troy laughed. "Here, you can sit next to me if you want to." And he cleared his letter jacket and book bag from the center desk. Ellen took the seat, to Earl's relief.

"Hey, Ellen," Earl said. His greeting went unnoticed in the general business of Troy's giving Ellen a seat, but it was just as well because Earl'd forgotten to bob his head anyway. Only now the opportunity had passed. Earl poised himself for the next good chance to tell Ellen he'd thought of riding her home.

After taking roll, Mrs. Price, who was a no-nonsense veteran of the public school system, dispensed with the other formalities of the first day of school, and launched right into education. "The earth was formed around four point five billion years ago." Mrs. Price paused to allow the students to measure this length of time against the four hours remaining until lunch. Earl tried to get his mind off Ellen by concentrating on the sound of Mrs. Price's voice; however, he could not keep his gaze straight on the Blue Horse paper; the gravitation of Ellen's face in profile kept drawing his eyes.

Days later, sitting in the hospital, Earl remembered from Mrs. Price's lecture a comment about time that seemed somehow significant. Something about the age of the earth being like a mountain range, and the time humans had been on it like the thinnest side of just one of its fingernails. But mountain ranges don't have fingernails, so that couldn't be right. He looked at the notes he'd written that day, but they just said, "Pada ata lane pad not ogo old wart alan ther tale feur far rant lant tal told."

Earl didn't have Ellen in any other classes, meaning he had to wait for lunch to see her. He reworked his script, taking out the head bob, which he decided would have complicated his performance too much anyway. The revised plan seemed much more natural. He wouldn't have to pretend getting the idea on the spot, but, brown bag in hand, would sidle up to her table and say, "Hey, Ellen, I had an idea."

But the new script didn't work out either. Earl had counted on her sitting all alone at lunch as Earl himself always did, and as she had every year before. But today, probably to make up for his joke about the speakers, Troy had invited Ellen to sit at the football players' table, and no one but an athlete or specially invited guest had best approach.

Troy and the other football players always ate lunch together. In the cafeteria line they loudly and comically flirted with and berated the lunch ladies, who shook their heads in mock fury, but nonetheless piled their trays with extra scoops of mashed potatoes and double helpings of banana pudding.

Most of the other students sat with their friends and talked exclusively to each other, and some, like Earl, preferred to sit at tables by themselves, meditatively chewing the fluff and peanut butter sandwiches their mothers made for them and saving their Ho-Hos for last. But anyone crossing within a three-foot radius of the football table was fair game. The teammates accosted pretty girls with personal inquiries about dimensions. Homely girls they greeted with appropriate barnyard sounds. Any straight-A student was called over, and while the quarterback solemnly asked about class work, the placekicker surreptitiously taped a sign to his back, reading, "Will you be my friend?" Known churchgoers were surveyed on a variety of topics on moral character, such as "How many times would you say you've kissed your mother, on the whole?" or "If Jack helped you off your horse, would you help Jack off his horse?" And everyone had better dodge the fusillade of green peas, corn niblets, and bread balls that the players loaded onto makeshift fork catapults and fired across the cafeteria and at each other. The victims of the football table never complained, and even the principal, who was unforgiving when it came to tardiness or being in the hall without a pass, looked on with an indulgent eye.

People forgave the lunchroom misbehavior because it was the football team's duty to uphold the honor of the Humble Tigers every game day. The team had to be aggressive in the lunchroom if they were expected to be aggressive on the field. Coach Fuller made no pretense about the importance of character or sportsmanship in football; for him it was all about tackling, running, and passing. Every day after school he had his men on the field practicing these arts, often until after dark.

And so Earl did not get to make Ellen his offer until that afternoon. After school he saw her walking home through the

15

grassy margin of West McArthy, holding her books against her chest, and he pulled his Buick up beside her. "Hey, Ellen," Earl leaned across the passenger seat and called through the open window. He strained to get her fragrance, but got nothing except the smell of his own vinyl seats. "I had an idea. Why don't I ride you home? We live right next to each other and all." As soon as he said it, he knew he'd over-rehearsed; his voice sounded unnaturally cheerful and false, like a Sunday school teacher about to tell her students the story of the Good Little Boy who learned all his Bible verses and even paid a tithe out of his allowance.

"No, thanks," Ellen said, giving him a smile. "I'd rather walk."

It was a short distance, Earl had to admit to himself, barely worth driving. Since she was already on West McArthy, it was maybe a quarter mile past Humble Elementary and the football field, then another mile at most down Warthen Street to her house, with pecan trees lining the road for shade.

—

All during Mrs. Price's class Ellen had stared at the chalkboard, her face hotter than a skillet lid, swearing to herself she'd never speak to that Troy Badcock again. She couldn't bear to look around, and couldn't bear not to look, for fear of seeing Troy grinning at her, but then he'd asked her to sit with him at lunch, and even made his friends not throw niblets and bread balls. That afternoon before turning onto Warthen Street, Ellen stopped to rest at the football field on her way home. She took her book to the top bleachers at Humble Stadium, where there was plenty of light and she could watch Troy run scrimmages down on the field and practice passes with a squad of sweaty boys, hurling themselves grunting against the tackling dummy, pushing it as far downfield as they could while Coach Fuller blew a silver whistle and shouted musically, "Hus-tle! Hust-le!" She imagined the millionaire in her book sometimes might wear a football uniform and those tight football-player pants, and she pictured Jane watching him from her window high up in the mansion as he hurled himself again and again against a tackling dummy on the estate's private football field.

After practice, Troy waited for her at the bottom as she walked slowly down from the bleachers, carefully watching each step she took, holding her books against those same breasts he had been so rude about.

Troy asked her how it was going, and Ellen told him she'd seen him practicing.

"Yeah," Troy said. It did not come as news to him that girls watched him practice. "What's your book?"

Ellen told him, but Troy didn't comment. "I know all the plays better than Brad, but Coach Fuller says he can't afford to waste me as quarterback. I'm too quick and strong to be anything but a fullback."

Ellen studied Troy in the failing light. Did she like him? Troy was an uncomplicated boy who lived by four unspoken rules, rules so unspoken that Troy himself didn't know he had them. But anyone who'd been around him for any length of time could have told you:

1. Jesus is your Personal Savior.
2. Never do it with any girl you're going to marry.
3. Never marry any girl you already did it with.
4. Stay low, knees bent, legs wide, and drive forward from the back foot.

Ellen had always liked skinny boys, but Troy was not skinny. He'd gotten an early growth spurt and hadn't stopped. Troy could have told her, if she'd asked, how he'd already been a Junior Midget when all his friends were still just Mitey Mites. Ellen would never have told him so to his face, but he looked to her a little like an orangutan; he had a towering upper body perched on surprisingly short, but powerful legs. Still, he had been the first boy to remark on her late but sudden breasts, a subject in which she had developed considerable interest herself.

"You can ride home with me if you want to," Troy offered.

Ellen thought about what it would be like sitting in a truck next to this boy who smelled of sour pigskin and bruised grass. "Okay," she said.

~

When Earl got home from school that day, he saw his mother hadn't brought the mail in yet, but there was nothing too strange about that.

"Momma, I'm home," he shouted, letting the screen door slam behind him before he remembered to stop it. He stood just inside the doorway and looked through the mail: two bills and a letter from someone named Holton. A box of Ruby's unstuffed envelopes lay on the couch.

"I'm in the kitchen, sugar," Ruby called.

"I'm going out to work on the Buick."

"Actually, could you come in here for a second?"

"Momma?" Three letters fell in a patter to the floor.

"My hip gave out right after you went to school," she said, stretched out like an overturned chess piece on the checkerboard linoleum, hands across her chest. "I told myself there ain't no use to get worked up, you'd be home sooner or later. So I just made up my mind to wait it out and make myself as comfortable as I could."

"We got to get you to the hospital."

"I think that's a good idea, son."

"I'll call an ambulance." Earl looked around for the phone book. This was before they had 911, and if you had an emergency, you had to look it up.

"No, lord, no," from the floor she waved the suggestion away. "You know what them things cost? We can't afford no ambulance. You know that little dolly you made to roll you under the Buick? Get it, and use it to push me around to the car."

"You mean my creeper? No, Momma. We need to call an ambulance."

"I told you we can't afford no ambulance."

"I'll pick you up and carry you to the car, then."

"I don't think that's a good idea, honey."

"It's better than a creeper." Earl tenderly cradled Ruby's shoulders in one arm and slid the other beneath her knees and began to lift.

"Nope, nope, nope!" Ruby said in pain and alarm as she began to leave the floor. Earl set her back down. "It hurts too much that way, honey," she explained.

"Then we'll just have to call an ambulance," Earl said, and got the phone book down from the counter.

As Earl knelt beside her, flipping through the A's, Ruby reached up and held his arm. "Earl, because your daddy ain't shown up for work all this time, the chalk mine gave his job to someone else. We ain't got no insurance. It's going to be hard enough paying for the hip, without throwing in a fancy ride in a glorified sedan. Some things you just can't help. Now go get that creeper."

19

"I'm calling an ambulance." Humble County's phone book, white and yellow pages together, had about as much heft as a good-sized comic book, and it hadn't taken long for Earl to find the ambulance service, which was actually a Milledgeville listing, all the way over in Baldwin County, since in those days Deepstep still didn't have its own hospital.

"You and me got to depend on each other," Ruby said, "By the time that thing gets out here, you could've run me to the hospital and back a dozen times." Earl bit his lip. She knew she'd loosened him. "That creeper you made is as long as any stretcher and it's going to be firmer and more comfortable to me. The longer you take to make your mind up, the longer I got to lie here on this floor."

Earl went outside. The creeper lay leaning against the yellow siding, the shadows of the Mulvaneys' little sassafras tree falling in cool blue stripes against its back. He brought it into the kitchen, braced it against the dinette legs, and as gently as he could, helped roll his mother up on it. Ruby Mulvaney was well acquainted with all varieties of pain, but even so the pain of twisting made her grunt. After she was on, Earl gave her a few moments to sweat and catch her breath. Earl had made the creeper from an old linen-closet door, so it was narrower than a regular door, but there was more than enough room for Ruby's small frame.

"Wouldn't you rather be lying on your back?" he asked.

"No, my stomach's fine." After the spasm passed, the pattern of the linoleum came into focus, and she smelled the reassuring fragrance of Pine-Sol. "I think it's more natural this way. I can see where I'm going and help steer with my hands." With her good hand she lifted her skirt where it touched the floor and tucked it under her thigh. Earl slid off her shoes to make her more comfortable. Her bare feet, toes pointed off the backside of the creeper, were as delicate and pretty as a ballerina's.

"I'll have to start you out backward, though. Your feet are pointed to the door."

"That's fine."

"I'll wheel you around when we get to the living room."

"Thank you."

Earl pushed hard to start off, but after that she glided easily over the linoleum until she jolted still.

"What's the matter, honey?"

"It's the threshold, Momma, the creeper don't want to cross it." Earl went around the back of the creeper to study the situation. "We're going to need a running start."

"Let's do it, then," she said. He rolled her to the back wall. "Oh, lord!" she cried out.

"What's wrong?" Earl asked, thinking she needed an ambulance after all.

"All the dust bunnies under that stove!"

"I'll sweep them out later, Momma. Now this thing wants to pull left, so I need you to lean right to balance it."

"Like this?"

"Yes, ma'am, just like that." Earl said nothing for a while.

"What's wrong?"

"When you hit that threshold, you'll be going pretty fast. It's liable to hurt something fierce." Hunkered down in front of his mother, Earl studied the geography of the kitchen, using the longitude and latitude of the linoleum squares to line up his mother with the door. The creeper was narrow enough to go through an ordinary doorway, but the Kenmore refrigerator reached all the way to the doorsill, leaving little clearance. "And I'm worried about you hitting your elbows on the doorframe."

"I tell you what. Just before I get there, you say 'now,' and I'll push the front down with both arms. That'll heft the back wheels over the threshold a little. Then right away I'll stretch my arms out front like Superman. That way my elbows will clear the frame."

Earl considered her suggestion and could not find a flaw in it. "Let's try it one time," he said, "okay? When I say 'now,' push down and stretch out your arms. Now!"

Ruby stretched out her arms like a diver. "How was that?"

"Perfect, Momma. Are you ready? Don't forget to lean right. Let's go." They started off. First slow, then rapidly faster, with a noise like grumbling thunder or a dozen bowling balls, then, "Now!" she pushed down, stretched out, and scooted through the kitchen door.

"You did perfect, Momma."

"Did I look like Superman?"

"Just about. Superman don't fly feetfirst or that low to the ground, but if he ever did, you'd look just like him."

"What was that crash?"

"You knocked the floor lamp down. I don't think you hurt it none."

Earl turned her front ways and piloted her through the slalom of living room furniture, then to the front door, where he paused. "We can't send you through the front door like we did the kitchen. You need room on the other side to stop. The stoop's too short."

"On top of that, the first step's a six-inch drop," she pointed out.

"It's no good, Momma, I'll have to call an ambulance."

"How are you going to explain to them drivers what your momma's doing on a creeper on the living-room floor? We got

22

this far already. I don't expect them ambulance drivers could do better."

Earl realized he'd let his mother outmaneuver him. "I expect I'll have to bring the car around to the steps. If I park right in front, I might be able to pull the creeper out to it. I'll rest the back end on the threshold and maybe the front can reach all the way to the backseat. Then you can just slide down off it into the back."

"That's a good idea, honey. But be careful not to drop me off it when you're pulling the front end of the creeper out to the car. Don't you have something to strap me on?"

"That's a good idea." Earl had a long red canvas strap with a cam buckle that he fed under the creeper and tightened over Ruby's back. "Tell me if I get it too tight," he said, ratcheting up the cam buckle.

"Tight's good. Better safe than sorry."

Earl parked the Buick beside the front stoop and opened the back door to have it ready. "That way you can just go directly in." He'd been reluctant to do things Ruby's way, but now they'd gotten this far, he rose to the challenge. He lifted the front end of the creeper and tugged it partway through the door. When it was resting like a ramp down to the backseat, Earl and Ruby rested, too.

"Let me get my breath. I think if you get behind and push me just a little bit further and then unstrap me, I can crawl into the backseat on my own."

He did as she suggested, and with his help, and a few cuss-words, she hauled herself down into the backseat. Sweat made dark brown stains under her arms and on her back. Earl was sweating, too. He rolled down the windows front and back, and pulled a stray brown curl away from her eye to make her comfortable.

After he'd driven for a little while, Earl looked at his dash and said, "Uh-oh. Momma?"

"Yes, honey?"

"We ain't got enough gas to get all the way to Milledgeville."

"Well, I guess you'll just have to stop and get some then."

Tooley's Texaco had just gone to self-service, but Edgar Tooley himself wasn't used to the concept, so when customers pulled in, he still walked out in his green coveralls to the pumps as if he were still needed to operate them. When he walked out that day, Earl Mulvaney was apparently having a conversation with his Buick.

"Would you like me to turn on the radio?" Earl asked the back window as he put two dollars of regular into the tank to the ding-ding-ding of the pump.

"That'd be nice," Ruby said, speaking with one side of her mouth into the vinyl seat.

Edgar Tooley found himself staring through the rear window at Ruby Mulvaney stretched out barefoot in the back seat.

"And how is that precious granddaughter of yours, Ed?" Ruby asked.

"She's fine, Ruby. Growing like a weed."

After paying Edgar, Earl set off again, and there was only one more bad moment, when the car went thu-bump over the tracks of the old Nancy Hanks, and Ruby cried in sudden pain.

"Momma, are you all right?" Earl asked.

"It'll feel better as soon as it stops hurting," Ruby said.

In spite of everything, Earl had to laugh. You can say what you like about Ruby Mulvaney, but she was one tough nut.

"Now when we get to the hospital," she reminded him, "you got to remember we can't go spending much money. Don't let them take me in until you find out how much it's going to cost."

Earl drove into Milledgeville, and turned left at Hatcher Square Mall to go to the hospital. A blue H sign pointed the way. Inside the green and white emergency room, amid the comforting medicinal smells and the dinging of the hospital's paging system, Earl's questions about the cost nonplussed the hospital staff, a petite black nurse and two orderlies, one white and one black. They could not believe anyone would keep his mother waiting in the car with a broken hip while he negotiated with the staff.

"My mother's hip is broken," Earl explained, "but we don't have much money."

"What do you want us to do?" the nurse asked. "Shoot her?"

"I just want to know how much it'll cost to fix a hip and what's the least expensive way to do it."

"This isn't a body shop," the nurse said. "We don't have a sign that says how much for a broken hip and how much for an appendix."

The black orderly, whose name was also Earl, thought the situation was very funny. "My name is Earl Schweib!" the black orderly said. "I'll fix that hip for twenty-five dollars!"

The nurse gave the orderly an angry look, but before she could speak, the physician, Dr. Gilmore, came out. After hearing the situation, he went out and examined Ruby in the car. "Sounds like your hip's broken, all right," he said. "We won't know for sure until we get you X-rayed."

"We can't pay for nothing we don't need," Ruby said.

"Well, you need this," Dr. Gilmore explained. "And you're going to need a doctor to come in from Macon to do the surgery. I know just who to use."

"Before you go to a bunch of trouble," Ruby said, "you need to know we don't have much money."

"We'll work something out," Dr. Gilmore promised kindly. "We never turned away a patient yet because they couldn't afford it."

"We don't want charity either," Ruby said. Earl Schweib and the other orderly came through the automatic glass doors rolling a stretcher with squeaking wheels onto the concrete and then the blacktop parking lot.

CHAPTER TWO

For the whole next week the thought of speaking to Ellen did not occur to Earl; his mother's hip left no room in his head for anything else. Every day after school, he drove to Milledgeville to see his mother, not coming back until late at night. He made himself eggs and bacon for supper, watched Andy Griffith on TV, and wondered how to get in touch with his father to let him know about Ruby. But Saturday Earl came home and saw a thing to make him forget about his mother, if just for a little while. Turning onto Warthen Street in his Buick, Earl saw a pickup truck parked in the Raleys' driveway. For a moment he thought, when did the Raleys get a pickup truck? It was a cloudy night, and Earl had just passed the shadow of the big magnolia that darkened the corner of Mrs. Smith's yard, but even so he recognized the truck as Troy Badcock's.

27

Earl had an impulse to put his car in reverse, pull back into the magnolia shadows, and retreat around the corner. His pounding heart warned him he didn't want to see what Troy Badcock was doing in Ellen Raley's driveway. But he couldn't turn his eyes. Ellen sat all the way over in the center next to Troy, leaning against him. The dome light of the truck cast a yellow glow over them, lighting up Ellen's red hair, the red leather of Troy's letter jacket, so Earl could see quite clearly, like watching a TV screen in a dark room.

They kissed.

Sunday Earl drove into Milledgeville to see his mother, just like he'd been doing up to then, and he would have given his soul and two fingers from one hand if only he could have just stayed over at the hospital the night before. He knew by now the way to his mother's room: through the automatic doors, down the hall, left at the nurse's station, and then on the end to the right.

"Hey, son," Ruby said when she saw him in the door. "Come give me some sugar."

He gave her some. Her hair smelled like sweet hairspray and hospital disinfectant. The big ruddy-faced nurse who was in the room to give Ruby her pain pills said, "Doctor says your mamma's going home soon. I have to talk to him about that. I don't want her to leave. Me and her have too much fun. Don't we, sugar?"

"That's right, Dot," Ruby said. "I might just have to go and bust something else so I can come and see you. Now could you help get me in my wheelchair? Mr. Thigpen's coming, and I want him to see how good the surgery came out." Mr. Thigpen was the minister at Ruby's church, Sanctified Tongue True Gospel out on Ridge Road.

Earl and the nurse helped Ruby slide off the bed and steered her body into the seat. Then he helped her with the assortment of other things that lay on the Formica top of her nightstand: her eye, her partial plate, and her plastic hand. This was before she lost her hair, so they didn't have to bother with a wig. Ruby felt at ease letting her son and Dot see her any which-way, but in front of company, she always made an effort to pull herself together.

Dot left when Ruby was fixed up. "Now don't you go busting something just to come back," Dot said.

"I won't," Ruby promised. "I was just kidding." When the door closed, Ruby became serious. "Son, you know," with her hands, the plastic one and the real one, she smoothed her gown out over her knees, "it's starting to look like your daddy ain't coming back."

"Yes, ma'am. I guess I knew that."

Ruby sighed and looked at Earl with brimming eyes. "Between your daddy's research and the way my parts keep wearing out, we spent what little money both sets of your grandparents left us on top of every cent your daddy brought home, plus we've yanked the chain as far as it will go when it comes to borrowing. Stuffing envelopes don't pay too good, and even that I can't do lately. Sugar, the only way we'll be able to borrow enough to get by is if you get a job to start paying back some of what we already owe."

"Yes, ma'am."

"Sugar, unless your daddy shows back up, I'm afraid, you're going to have to quit school and go to work."

"Yes, ma'am." Earl's voice sounded like it came back to him from underwater.

"I'm so sorry. I love you, son."

"It's okay, Momma. I love you, Momma." Earl hugged his mother's slim body. She ran her real hand through his hair, thick like his father's, with a tendency to stand straight up on end. It might not be such a bad thing, Earl told himself; I can go back at some point to finish up, and at least I won't have to be around at school to see Troy Badcock and Ellen Raley. He imagined seeing them laughing together at the football players' table in the cafeteria, or even worse, kissing in the hall on the way to class. As soon as he imagined that, he wished he hadn't.

"I swear, son, your time is going to come to be happy. Things are bound to balance out sooner or later. I won't let you miss it. You're all I got in the world now. I'd do anything for you, son, you know that."

Then they sat and watched the TV weatherman. Knowing the weather was about as much use to Ruby right after her surgery as training wheels to a goldfish, but she always took a polite interest in it for other people's sake.

There was a soft knock, and Mr. Thigpen came in. "Why, you're looking fine, Ruby." He put down a big case he'd brought, and hugged her in her wheelchair. Mr. Thigpen was the approximate size of a brown bear standing on its hind legs. The hair on his head was pure white, but his bushy eyebrows were pure black. In spite of being such a big and bristly-looking man, he always spoke and moved around quietly and meekly, as if once he'd swatted someone by accident and was resolved on never doing it again.

"I learned something interesting today," Mr. Thigpen said. He sat in a chair and patted his thighs twice. He was curious about every subject under the sun and always learning something new. "You know the word 'amen'? Well, it means 'so be it.' So at the end of the prayer when everyone says 'amen,' what they mean is 'so be it.' It's like we're seconding the motion of the prayer. It's like putting it to a vote."

"Well, I'll be," Ruby said.

"You know what I got in my case here?" Mr. Thigpen said with a twinkle in his eye like he'd smuggled in a suitcase full of Christmas presents. "I've got my Bible, and a basin."

"Oh, that's wonderful," Ruby said.

Earl said he'd like the honor of washing. "Why, sure, son," Mr. Thigpen said, his fingertips tenderly touching the Bible's black leather cover, "but what say we start off with a Bible verse, first?" Mr. Thigpen liked to let God choose the verse by letting his old black Bible fall open to whatever page it wanted. Only his Bible had gotten so much use, and the spine was so cracked, it always fell open to the same place.

"To every thing there is a season," Mr. Thigpen began, "and a time to every purpose under heaven." He went on to read the rest of the passage, only leaving out the "Turn, turn, turns," that Earl, who'd never gotten around to reading it for himself, thought belonged in there. After the verse, Mr. Thigpen got out the Dove dishwashing liquid and filled the basin with warm water, and Earl got down and washed his mother's feet. He knelt in front of her wheelchair, took her white slippers off, and dipped her feet in the basin, lathering up the tops of her arches and between her toes. Her feet were smooth and soft and already clean because lately she hardly got to use them.

"You know where this comes from," Mr. Thigpen said. "Washing feet like this?"

Earl, having a scientific mind like his father's, did not go in for religion much, but said he knew.

"Mary Magdalene," Mr. Thigpen said, ignoring Earl's reply. "She washed our Savior's feet. Now some people say Magdalene was a prostitute, only there's nothing in the Bible that says she was the same Mary who was a prostitute mentioned somewhere else. Lots of Marys in the Bible."

"Yes, sir." Earl scooped up soapy water from the basin and poured it over his mother's feet.

"But even if she was a prostitute, she stopped being one when she met the Lord. That's the point. Sin is something you can leave behind you. No matter what you done, you can leave it behind you and start fresh. And do you know why she washed His feet?"

"No, sir. Yes, sir."

"Because she loved Him, and love makes you humble. That's what it's all about, love. Jesus took all those complicated laws the Jews had and boiled them down to just two. We have to love our Lord with everything we've got, and we've got to love each other every bit as much as we love ourself. Do that and every-thing else will be taken care of."

"Yes, sir."

"So that's why Mary Magdalene washed His feet. She loved Jesus, and she was humble. And also because his feet were dirty; in those days they mostly walked around barefoot."

Earl wrapped his mother's feet in a soft white towel to dry them, pressing his own face into the cotton to cool his eyes and somehow soothe the scorching in his throat which he felt every time he was about to cry. He put her slippers back on and emp-tied the basin in the sink. Before he left, Mr. Thigpen gave a prayer. He prayed in his soft solemn voice that the metal hip the doctors put in would help out Ruby, that all the metal and plastic and ceramic parts she already had would serve her well for many years to come, that all the parts she still had made out of meat and bones would hold up, and lastly that the part that wasn't plastic, metal, ceramic, meat, or bone would out-last all the rest with God's grace. Ruby added a line to remember Earl, who was such a good son.

The three of them put the prayer to a vote, and it came out unanimous. Mr. Thigpen packed up his case and left.

The next day, Monday, Earl didn't go to school, but applied as a mechanic at Jimmy Wiggins' Used Cars. Maybe you remember his commercials from the radio; "What's that name? *Wiggins'* Used Cars." The lot sat across the street from Miller's Grocery, a cluster of quality pre-owned cars, festooned with strings of flapping red, yellow, and blue triangle flags that waved overhead like a fiesta.

Earl asked the first man he saw on the lot, a gray-haired hunchback smoking a cigarette that looked soldered to his lower lip, where he could find Mr. Wiggins. The salesman decided Earl didn't look likely to buy a car, but couldn't figure out another reason he would have come. So he pointed to the long blue sheet-metal building at the back of the lot that housed the service center on one side and the sales office on the other. He told Earl to go inside and look for an open door with a sign on it that said, "My door is always open."

Earl found the open door, which had a cardboard clock with adjustable red plastic hands that said, "I had to step out! I'll be back at." A stocky red-faced man with a gray buzz-cut looked up from his desk with a questioning smile when Earl came in.

The September Clik-Tite Auto Parts Girl on the wall had chosen a hot-pants jumpsuit for her pose with a Carolina Blue Chevrolet. Beside the calendar hung a plaque: "Jimmy Wiggins.

For Meritorious Service. 1970. The Humble Volunteers."
Beneath that hung two more plaques, the same except the year.
Sitting on the desk, a picture of a pretty woman whom Earl
guessed was Jimmy's niece faced outward. An unlit cigar,
ignored but with spit still glistening on the tip, dozed in an ashtray that read, "Ft. Lauderdale." Placed beneath the ashtray, to
keep the oscillating fan from blowing it off the desk, lay a contract, the blue ballpoint signature, *Jimmy Wiggins*, still fresh.
Awestruck to be so close to the very throne of business, Earl
could not find his voice for several seconds.

"Mister, if you want a mechanic, then I'm your man." Gary
Cooper had given a similar speech in a movie about a Hard-
Working Young Man with a Dream, which was just the sort of
image Earl wanted to craft for himself.

I myself have dickered enough with Jimmy over car prices to
picture how he must've squinted those honest blue eyes of his
and cocked his square head in puzzlement. One thing he certainly did not need, and that was a mechanic, and even if he
had needed a mechanic, he sure wouldn't have gone looking
for a skinny kid with a home-done haircut and taped-together
glasses. But the legendary tenderness and generosity of a car
dealer's heart hate letting a soul walk off until a deal's been
struck, and Jimmy's heart surpassed most car dealers' when it
came to tenderness and generosity. "We ain't so far apart,"
weren't just negotiating words to Jimmy Wiggins; they were a
proverb on the universal brotherhood of man.

Jimmy thought solid nearly fifteen seconds, rubbing his
chin. Then he said, "Come here." Earl followed him out of the
office and to the rear door, which opened onto an unpaved and
scarcely mowed dandelion patch, at the far end of which sat a
large shed with double doors, a corrugated tin roof, flaking red

paint, and warped boards that parted from each other at the top and bottom. With difficulty Jimmy opened one door, dragging it through the tall weeds as he swung it wide and let sunlight in. Inside sat a dusty white sports car up on blocks.

"That there's a genuine classic. Fifty-three Corvette, but she ain't run since the day we got her," Jimmy said. "Hell, even before that. The original owner towed her in and said he never got a day's good use out of her. As far as I know, she came off the *line* not running. My mechanic can't do nothing with her. If you can get her going, you got a job."

"I appreciate it, sir," Earl said. "But—is there any way I could get my first week's salary in advance?"

Jimmy raised a hand to shield his eyes from the bright sunlight outside the shed and said, "Son, you ain't hired yet."

Now Earl was stumped. He needed the money at once to start paying bills, and couldn't afford to leave the lot without it. Earl explained his mother's situation to Jimmy.

"What is it?" Jimmy asked. "Brittle bones?" Jimmy imagined Earl's mother must be flabby, fair-skinned, and fifty-five. It came as a surprise to him when he played cards with her some time later how young and slim she was and that she had attractive auburn hair—still hers—a Cupids-bow mouth and a dimple on one cheek.

"No, she just breaks down a lot," Earl said. "Her parts ain't good just in general. It's like they made her on a Monday." Earl pondered his dilemma and let his gaze wander. "I got an idea," he said. "See that Buick over there?" Earl pointed in the direction of Miller's Grocery and the Deepstep water tower, and around the side of the sales office Jimmy could just see the nose of the Mulvaney family car parked beneath a string of flapping red, yellow, and blue flags. "Give me a week's pay now as an advance, but if I can't fix your Corvette, that Buick will be yours."

"Well," Jimmy temporized and stroked the gray bristle on his chin that his Norelco had left behind.

"Can't you think of something I can sign, a paper or a contract? There's got to be a way to make this legal."

Earl had touched a point of pride; when it came to writing, Jimmy Wiggins was to contracts what William Shakespeare was to tragedies. What that man could not do with a clause or an addendum simply could not be done. Jimmy rubbed his chin, squinted his eyes, cocked his head, and drew on his cigar. It was a gamble, but the sort of gamble Jimmy liked: the kind he couldn't lose. The Buick was worth a lot more than a hundred bucks, and a Corvette that worked was worth even more than that.

"OK, son, you got one week."

Earl didn't need to hear another word. He stayed all that Monday and worked on the Corvette. Jimmy didn't see him come in bright and early Tuesday but only because by then Earl was at Vernon Lice's salvage yard on Old Eighty-Five, prowling that kudzu-ridden graveyard of wrecked and half-cannibalized rusted and busted cars looking for parts.

When Jimmy went to the shed Thursday to check on Earl's progress, the cigar fell out of his mouth and the blood drained from his face. Earl didn't notice because he was sitting Indian-style, busy scrubbing a rusty valve with a wire brush. By this time Earl had so disassembled the Corvette, it looked as if it had collapsed into piles of chrome and fiberglass. White side panels leaned against the back wall of the shed; forlorn head-lights near Earl's knee stared up from the floor like the missing eyes of a giant frog; greasy black cylinders, belts, and hoses were everywhere; only the axles and the merest skeleton of the driveshaft remained on the blocks. "Now, you know, I can't afford to buy you any parts for that car," Jimmy stammered as he watched Earl work on the valve. Four days had passed since Earl had started on the Corvette. "I'd like to, and I don't want to trim your chances short, but—Well, I just don't want you laboring under no misconceptions."

"Jimmy, you don't need to buy me no new parts," Earl explained confidently, and wiped the rusty flakes off his hand onto his jeans. Associating with the tycoon had made Earl easy in his company. "My way of fixing things ain't replacing stuff, just rebuilding. I put in a new hose or belt here and there, which is why I got to spend so much time at the salvage yard, and of course once I get the motor running, you'll need to get some new tires, but mostly all I need to do is take a car apart— I mean all the way apart, so the only thing left whole will be the four cinder blocks it's been sitting on—and put her back together piece by piece."

Jimmy could think of nothing to say, so he said it. He picked his cigar up, put it back in his mouth, and left Earl to his work. It so happened that later that afternoon, Jimmy got on to Wayne, his regular mechanic, whose apparently bottomless need for new parts suggested he was feeding them to a twenty-foot tall billy goat out back. Finding an invoice for a new oil filter on his desk, the third one in as many months, Jimmy stomped from his office to the service center to confront Wayne with the bill. Jimmy could not understand why, for the love of God, in a car lot, which was filled with cars of every description, anyone would ever need a new part trucked in. Wayne patiently explained that when a customer requested a new filter and paid for a new filter, it wouldn't do to get it from another car; nothing less than a fresh, never-before-used, brand-new, oil filter virgin would suffice. This overscrupulousness on the part of his mechanic struck Jimmy as wasteful, possibly sinfully so.

"You know how that kid fixes things?" Jimmy asked, jerking his square head toward the shed in back. "He just rebuilds them. He says he don't need new parts!"

Wayne irritably rubbed grease from his hands with a chamois. Wayne had one of those faces that's unpleasant to look at, but you can never quite figure out why. He was a little shorter than average, but no dwarf. He had thick blond hair, a regular face, and a clean jawline. He should have been downright handsome, but he wasn't somehow, and you could stare and stare at him trying to figure out what was so unappealing, but never find anything. His nose wasn't too big or small or high up or low down, and his eyes weren't on crooked, and his ears lined up, but when you saw him, you'd have to say he was the ugliest good-looking guy you'd ever met.

"You can't get something for nothing," Wayne said quietly.

"Something for nothing? You say it like it's something to be ashamed of," Jimmy said. "What's wrong with something for nothing? What's a mother's love if that ain't something for nothing? What's heaven and forgiveness and Jesus Christ?" Jimmy paused and bit his cigar. He studied the invoice in his hand as if it reminded him of something. "Let me tell you a story."

"I really ain't got time."

"It's a Bible story, about this man and his two sons."

"The Prodigal Son?"

"Maybe. In the story I'm thinking of, one son's an optimist and one's a pessimist."

"I don't think that story's in the Bible."

"Well, it ought to be. So anyway, the father decides he's

going to even out his two boys' outlooks by getting them these unusual presents for their birthday. These boys were twins, I forgot to mention. So he buys the pessimist the most expensive gold pocket watch he can find—it's shiny with Roman numbers and a big long chain—hoping to cheer him up, and for the optimist, he just has a load of manure delivered, thinking that will bring him down a peg.

"The morning of their birthday," Jimmy continued, "the pessimist unwraps his pocket watch and gives it a look like a rotten oyster. 'I bet I just end up losing it,' he says, 'That is, if I don't break it first.' Meanwhile—"

"Meanwhile the optimist is digging through his steaming pile of shit with both hands," said Wayne, who'd heard the story before, "looking for the pony."

"Exactly," Jimmy said triumphantly, and shoved the invoice in his back pocket. "That's my point exactly. I *told* you it was in the Bible. You'll probably say the pessimistic boy makes a good point, and the optimistic boy is just foolish, but anyone'll tell you the optimist is the lucky one. See, you're like that pessimist, nothing don't satisfy you. But Earl—and me—we're the optimists, and we can be tickled pink with a pile of shit—in fact, the more of it the better! We don't give up just because people say we can't get something for nothing. We know, just know, with so much shit around, there's got to be a pony in it somewhere!"

With that Jimmy went back to his office, leaving Wayne in the cool dimness of the garage to contemplate the Bible lesson. Hearing the story did not budge Wayne one way or the other except to make him begin disliking Earl, but telling it did have an effect on Jimmy. Friday came; it had been a full five days since Earl had shown up on the lot, and in that time Jimmy mulled over what he'd said to Wayne, until finally he made up his mind to tell Earl he had the job and never mind about the Corvette. Jimmy went to the shed. He found the Corvette reassembled and the dust and cobwebs lovingly wiped away. She gleamed like a pearl, and Earl was sitting in the driver's seat, a wide grin on his face. Beside her lay a bunch of leftover parts, and as Jimmy stepped across the threshold, Earl reached down and started her up.

Naturally Earl couldn't drive anywhere; the car was still on blocks, but Jimmy climbed in beside him, and they sat there listening to that motor hum, while Jimmy lit up one of his big cigars, and the car filled up with smoke. A '53 Corvette, if you've ever sat in one, is like a red velvet cake: creamy white exterior, but inside the dash and upholstery are luscious red. They sat and talked for about an hour, and it's a lucky job the shed door was open, or they'd have died for sure, from carbon monoxide or Jimmy's cigar smoke. The smoke and exhaust fumes must've overcome them a little bit because they talked about things that day no mechanic and car dealer ever discussed before or since: politics, God and the devil, true love.

Jimmy told Earl, "Boy, I won't tell you that you got a future. Every damn thing on earth has a future; hell, that's nothing special; the future's just time. But you're going to *make* something of yourself." Jimmy rubbed the dashboard with one hand. "Fifty-three Corvette. Only three hundred ever made, and they say GM tore apart two of *them* before they even left the factory. That engine is a six-cylinder Blue Flame Special. You know how many colors this particular model comes in?" Earl, a virtual encyclopedia when it came to cars, knew full well, but he politely shook his head, no. "One. You're sitting in it. White. That's the only color they made the first year. The windshield leaks when it rains—don't bother trying to fix that;

it does that on all the Fifty-threes. She ain't even got side windows, just plastic flaps. But listen." Jimmy punched a button on the dash, and the unmistakable chords of a Johnny Cash song mingled with the smoke. "A signal-seeking radio. That music's pure AM gold." Jimmy turned to look at Earl in the two-seater, and Earl could see the car dealer's eyes shining with tears, but whether from some heartfelt emotion or because cigar smoke was scorching them, Earl wasn't sure. "I'm telling you, Earl, a boy like you, he can do anything he's a mind to. You've just got to decide on what you want."

As soon as Jimmy got tires on the Corvette he brought his wife out to the lot to take her for a spin. Earl recognized Donna Wiggins from the photo on Jimmy's desk, a beauty ten years Jimmy's junior. Jimmy left the lot in high spirits; "Boys," he said to his staff, as he pulled on some leather driving gloves he'd bought specially for the occasion. "Mind the store, we ain't stopping 'til the wheels fall off."

The call came ten minutes later.

"Jimmy's on the phone. He wants to talk to you," Mr. Moss, the hunchbacked salesman said, finding Earl in the garage.

"Dang thing broke down," Jimmy said. "Barely got to the square. I had to walk to Tooley's to use the pay phone. Come on out here and bring your tools. She's on the square, the 10:15 side."

The Deepstep Courthouse, which sits in a green square of clover and crabgrass, has four clocks, telling four different times. The western side says 10:15, the eastern 12:05, the southern, which faces the library—where I work—says 8:17, and the northern 6:30. There's an old saying that even a busted clock is right twice a day, but the Deepstep Courthouse can multiply that by a factor of four. An additional advantage is that anyone in sight of the courthouse can instantly tell which side he's facing. One time when the northern clock unexpectedly began running, it caused such confusion, the city fathers had to stop it and set it back to 6:30 to prevent pandemonium from breaking out.

When Earl arrived, he found Jimmy unperturbed and more understanding than he might have hoped. "Donna walked over to the drug store for a Coca-Cola," he explained as Earl looked under the hood.

Earl examined the battery cables, loosened one, and scrubbed the post with a wire brush. "I'm sorry, Jimmy."

"These things happen," Jimmy said. "Classic cars ain't windups. You can't just point them and run. They need constant attention, like a woman." Jimmy put his cigar to his lips and drew on it, looking across the square at the bleak gray sky in the direction of Deepstep Drugs. Intermittent drops of moisture fell, not so much rain as liquid spite. "I should have remembered that."

Earl finished his ministrations to the car, and said, "Start her up." The engine cleared its throat and came to life at once, and, satisfied, Earl put the leftover pieces in his pocket before he closed the hood.

Thereafter, Donna did not come along when Jimmy wanted to drive his Corvette. Even if Donna had agreed to ride "that car" again, there wouldn't have been room for her, Jimmy, and Earl. Jimmy had to have a mechanic along in case the car stalled out, and Earl was the only one who could get it going again.

On slow business days Jimmy'd take a long lunch break, and he and Earl would drive off with bacon and mayonnaise sandwiches and Dr Peppers, and explore Humble County until the car broke down, which usually didn't take too long. Then wherever they found themselves, they'd get out and eat a picnic lunch, after which Earl got the car going again, putting the leftover parts in the pocket of his red coveralls, and they'd return to the lot. Earl found repairing Jimmy's car brought some relief from thoughts of Ellen, and when he found his imagination wandering to her and Troy, he would shake his head and concentrate on the inner workings of that Corvette. It was on one of their outings when the car broke down near a kaolin mine that Earl first broached the subject of the Endless Corvette to Jimmy. They'd been eating bacon sandwiches Donna Wiggins had wrapped in wax paper for them, and Earl tore apart a sheet into bits, and fitted it back together to demonstrate the leftover pieces.

"—and once you had two of them," Earl concluded, "you'd have breeding stock, and the third one would come even faster."

When Earl had finished explaining his idea, Jimmy sat sucking on his wet cigar for a minute and didn't say anything. He sat in the grassy margin at the edge of the road, leaning against the Corvette and looking at a white clay mountain that rose above a sinkhole of sky-blue water. A chalk truck rumbled by on the highway behind them and the breeze lifted bits of wax paper and swirled them around in the air. Privately, Jimmy suspected that Earl wasn't firing on all cylinders, but no car dealer will crush the dream of a fellow human by calling it foolish. If you'd made an offer on the old Fairlane painted dog-shit brown, convinced it was an engineering masterpiece, Jimmy wouldn't have had the heart to tell you otherwise, although he knew it for the biggest lemon on the lot. Jimmy's high regard for other people's dreams prevented him from dashing Earl's hopes now.

Besides which, there was just the chance, just the off chance, that Earl could actually do it—build a Corvette out of spare parts from another Corvette and still leave the original behind. He was that good.

"Well, Earl," he said at last, "I won't tell you it can't be done, especially since I just got through saying you could do anything you want. Hell, it's already a miracle you got this Corvette running without needing any parts. I do see obstacles —big ones—in your way. But if there's anyone could make a thing like that work, it's you. And if you want to start with this Corvette right here, be my guest."

Then Jimmy shared his own idea, why cars look the way they do. According to him, it was because gasoline came from fish and rotten kelp that had decayed a half a billion years ago. Ever since the Model T, people had been feeding their motor-cars a diet of composted fish, so over time cars were turning into fish in the same way that a man who eats cat food and nothing else will begin resembling a cat, or a person who eats a lot of birdseed is bound to have more birdlike qualities than is common.

"You take fins," Jimmy said, "that ain't just decoration on a car, that's e-vo-lution." The way that he explained it, it was the same with two-tone paint jobs. "With most two-tone paint jobs, the cars are lighter on the bottom than the top. There ain't no reason for a car to look that way, but that's the way a fish looks—light on the bottom and darker on top. That can't just be a coincidence!"

When this conversation took place, the only thing remaining of fins and two-tone paint jobs were relics like that old Corvette; Earl reasoned Jimmy had gripped one era with sucker cups and couldn't let it go. But to hear him talk, gesturing with that cigar and leaving clouds of smoke like fog in some primeval swamp, it seemed to Earl that Jimmy had a point. He could picture Stingrays scuttling through asphalt creek beds like the trilobites in Mrs. Price's class, almost aware of drowsy humming overhead from helicopter dragonflies, their wingspans thirteen feet across and pilots watching in their big glass eyes.

Then, when to the spell of his boss's strange philosophy, and to the smell of car exhaust and lit cigar, time condensed to just one moment, so '53 Corvettes and dinosaurs, and fishlike cars still undesigned, and whatever dinosaurs were still to come— when all these things not only could but did exist, and all at the same time, and when Earl saw for a moment that all those different things were just one thing—he told Jimmy Wiggins about Ellen Raley.

Jimmy hadn't much more than a stub by that time, and took it from his mouth and looked at it like he was measuring how many puffs remained. "You got to do something about her," Jimmy said. "You got to go up to her, Troy Badcock or no."

But Earl knew what heavy competition Troy would be; not only was he the Humble Tigers' running back, his daddy was about as rich as King Solomon from his plumbing business. Troy had his pick of girls, and Earl was just a skinny hick with busted glasses. But what was worse, Troy was fun. Troy Badcock could make you laugh. Earl could be amusing, too, but in a different way. Earl's ad-libs took careful thinking out ahead exactly how to word. And even then half the time people didn't laugh, so Earl kept most of his planned-out off-the-cuff remarks inside. Troy Badcock, on the other hand, was just funny automatically.

"You got to talk to her," was all Jimmy said. "See what she says about it. Maybe you two ain't that far apart."

After he and Jimmy talked that afternoon, Earl did not go up to Ellen right away. He should have, and later he often regretted that he hadn't, but he waited nearly four full months before he said another thing to her. He kept busy in the meantime working as mechanic and a sometime firefighter; Jimmy enlisted him in the Humble Volunteers, Humble County's volunteer fire department. Fires are rare in Humble County, but the ones we do have—mostly at the county line, where houses are as sturdy as balsa wood and just about as fireproof—require fast response. Earl also had his hands full taking care of Ruby. She moved back from the hospital, but wasn't on her feet for weeks after that. And then, whenever things in the garage were slow, he'd sneak off to the shed out back with its gaping boards, tin roof, and blistered red paint, and work on that white Corvette.

CHAPTER THREE

I've told you how Jimmy came to hire two mechanics, but I need to explain what he wanted with two salesmen. A fisherman will keep a type of bait on hand for every situation; days when mayflies swarm, he'll use a mayfly; if fish are biting poppers, he'll use one of them—in just that way, Jimmy had two salesmen. In '73 racial tensions boiled high; the schools had integrated just the year before, and Lester Maddox—who once, brandishing a pistol, chased black patrons from his restaurant and into the street—was Lieutenant Governor, so in those days a car dealer needed to have a black salesman for his black customers—a tall, elegant man named T. J., who always wore a vest and a precisely trimmed Afro and goatee—and a white salesman for the whites—the gray-haired hunchback Earl first talked to, Mr. Moss. Jimmy himself never directly sold cars.

47

Selling cars, unless it's done the most amateurish way imaginable, is theater. When you make an offer on a car, the salesman, who up to then has seemed totally self-confident, suddenly becomes unsure and hesitant. He expresses fear at bringing Jimmy such a lowball sum. Won't Mr. Wiggins take it as an insult? It wastes the paper to even write it down. Nonetheless, the salesman draws the contract up, and swallowing his fear with a manly gulp, he takes the offer in his trembling hands to the boss. You can see you've won your way into the salesman's heart, and although he might lose his job to even tender such an offer, he does it for your friendship's sake.

Minutes later the salesman reappears, plainly shaken from his ordeal, and yet relieved at Jimmy's boundless generosity and wisdom. Jimmy has not fired him on the spot for incompetence, but taking into account the salesman's pleas on your behalf, penned a new price on the bottom line, subtracting every dollar possible off the asking price. In almost every case, you'll take the deal, but maybe you decide to counter. The salesman disappears again; when he returns, Jimmy Wiggins himself comes with him, trailing clouds of fragrant cigar smoke and sincerity. Jimmy shakes your hand, and patiently explains he just can't go as low as you want him to, because, frankly, he's taking a loss on this car as it is. But studying the figures, he chews on his cigar and cocks his head, and declares that you and he ain't that far apart. So just to get it off the lot, he knocks an extra fifty off and throws in a free fill-up, but that's as low as he can go.

At this point, if your nerves hold up, you might try countering again, but this time Jimmy just won't budge; he can't afford to, he explains, and looking in his honest eyes, you can see he's made his Final Offer. And so the deal is closed; you may have paid more than you planned, but you also got some fine dramatic performances chock-full of pathos and suspense thrown into the bargain.

The week after Earl got the Corvette running was a slow one, and the salesmen—you now know why there were two— leaned against cars under the blue, red, and yellow flapping flags, and talked. Under the shade of the open garage door, Wayne the other mechanic looked up from the fender he'd been hammering back into shape. Wayne could see that Mr. Moss was doing all the talking and knew well what the topic would be. Other than pressing a car's merits on a customer, Mr. Moss had just one topic for discussion. Years ago, just hours before their wedding, Pam Marshall, his fiancée, said she was taking his golden retriever, Digger, for a walk. She never returned. It came out later that she'd run off to Nevada, and gotten married to the best man, Dwayne Moss, Mr. Moss's first cousin.

Though intervening years had grayed Mr. Moss's hair and curved his spine, he'd never gotten over the loss of that good dog.

Mr. Moss told the story to everyone who cared to listen and many who did not. He's even come in the library to bend my ear a few times, and for the life of me, I could never tell if or when he would have ever actually gotten around to mentioning the dog. He'd start off in a promising direction and then veer into every alleyway and cul-de-sac along the way, never getting any closer to the meat of his story than Sherman got to Deep-step. Mr. Moss seemed to think that if, just once, he could make someone listen to the whole story of Digger's abduction com-pletely through, while he omitted no detail, however slight or apparently unrelated to the main theme, he could solve the mystery of his private grief and lay it to rest.

From his darkened vantage point, Wayne studied T. J.'s pos-ture as the salesman shifted his weight impatiently from one foot to the other. He could read T. J.'s increasing boredom as easily as if he had a gauge on his forehead that measured boredom in pounds per square inch.

In the short time he had known Earl, Wayne had conceived a dislike for the new mechanic as pure as it was strong, and now he wished to bring his coworkers around to his way of thinking. No easy matter, for if T. J. had one fault, Wayne knew, it was his tendency to like other people even before they had given him any reason. But Wayne also knew well the dullness of listening to Mr. Moss, and he judged that if he bided his time until just before T. J.'s valve blew from sheer exasperation, the salesman would welcome an interruption and willingly hear a few home truths about Earl Mulvaney. Timing was everything.

Finally T. J. snapped his gaze eastward to look at the Humble County water tower framed against the blue sky, then gave a fast westward look toward the courthouse clock that always said 10:15, a desperate back-and-forth sweep of his head like a trapped rat seeking an escape route. That was Wayne's cue. He put down his ball-peen hammer and strode into the glare of the car lot.

". . . the Marshalls lived on Alfred C. Carson Street," Mr. Moss was saying as Wayne approached. Mr. Moss did not raise his eyes to T. J.'s face, but looked with an unfocused stare at the distorted reflection of the world in the chrome of a pickup's wheel well, which at that moment represented Mr. Moss's window into the past, "you know, which is just off Warthen, but they lived on the end closer to West Haynes. Alfred C. Carson, if you don't know, was mayor of—"

"Do y'all know anything about that new mechanic?" Wayne asked.

"No," T. J. said. "What do you know?" T. J., who was the

50

third member of the Humble Volunteers, did know a thing or two about Earl, but felt grateful for any change of subject; getting a word in edgewise with Mr. Moss required a stellite wedge and fifteen-pound sledge.

"If you ask me, he's half a bubble off," Wayne said. "He spent the last few days working on that old Corvette Jimmy's got out in the shed."

"Like I was saying, Pam's family lived on Alfred C. Carson Street," Mr. Moss put in insistently, hoping to revive his fiancée and her family, but too late; they'd already flatlined.

"I thought he had her running already."

"He did. But now he's working on her again."

"Old sports cars ain't something you can fix just once," T. J. said, pulling at his goatee thoughtfully. "They ain't like them New York taxis where you can just unbolt a bumper and put on a fresh one. They need constant attention."

Wayne shook his head. "He ain't maintaining her. He's taking her apart. This is the second time he's done it."

"He might be practicing," T. J. ventured.

Wayne gave him a dismissive look. "Wake up and smell the coffee." The world for Wayne was full of drowsing people and unsmelled coffee. "There's something going on that ain't quite right. Something Jimmy and that new mechanic have. It's fishy. A secret project or something."

The next day, another slow one, Wayne had more to say on the subject of Earl. Again Wayne waited in the shadows of the garage until just before the pounds per square inch of boredom seemed likely to exceed T. J.'s capacity. This time, though, Mr. Moss saw Wayne coming and rushed to supply a few last details on the never-finished saga of his loss. "Anyway, Pam's father was big in the chalk mines, except it ain't really chalk, you know. It just looks like it; it's kaolin, from a Indian word, 'kay-ole-in.'" But before Mr. Moss's story could get any closer to the missing dog, Wayne was upon them.

"Here's the latest thing," Wayne said. "Earl's putting that Corvette together now, and saving all the parts left over. He's got them labeled, stacked and sorted on a shelf."

"That is strange," T. J. admitted.

"It's a Cherokee word for 'looks like chalk,'" Mr. Moss threw in bitterly. He shot his Camel butt down with a flick of his finger, and crushed it into the concrete with a twist of his heel.

"Maybe he wants to take the car apart again, and put the leftover parts back where they go," T. J. suggested.

"No one ever puts the leftovers back," Wayne said. "They won't go anywhere. They're just left over. There's always leftover parts. It's something you'd know about if you worked on cars."

"Why can't you just be careful, and put it back together with no leftover parts?"

Wayne huffed. "It can't be done. There's always parts."

"But if you took the car apart again—"

"There'd be leftovers every time."

"But if you took kept taking her apart long enough, you'd just run out."

Wayne shook his head. "You don't never run out. There's always more parts."

That might seem astonishing, but it's something every good mechanic knows, though how black rubber gaskets and galvanized wing nuts manage to produce themselves ex nihilo remains a mystery. An example of this strange phenomenon occurred after World War II, when the English army took over a Volkswagen factory. The factory, Kraft durch Freude, (Strength through Joy), you understand, had not produced a bug in a coon's age because the Nazis had retooled it to make Schimmwagens—German jeeps that could go from land to water like an amphibian—and it hadn't even been making those because the Allies had bombed the tar out of it, so it wasn't much more than a Swiss cheese of holes and craters by the time the British got there. Nevertheless, an English officer, Major Hirst, who never until then so much as turned a monkey wrench, built two thousand VWs from nothing but *leftover parts*. This is an historical fact, and if you don't believe me, you can check up on it for yourself.

Neither Jimmy nor Earl had told anyone about the Endless Corvette; that was top secret. But Wayne, who already figured Earl's gears were slipping, would have thought him touched for sure if he'd known that while he broke down gearboxes and unscrewed nuts, and took the fiberglass outsides apart and stacked them piece by piece in a corner of the shed, he was composing poetry to Ellen Raley in his head.

You might think that practically being weaned on thirty-weight, any poem Earl would write would have cars all mixed up in it, like: "Ellen, your beauty is to me like those nice clean cars of Ford." But it wasn't like that at all. One day working on the carburetor and thinking about Ellen, Earl came up with four real pretty lines of poetry, just like that.

Looking in your two green eyes,
I can see to my surprise,
Open fields and open skies,
Of beauty.

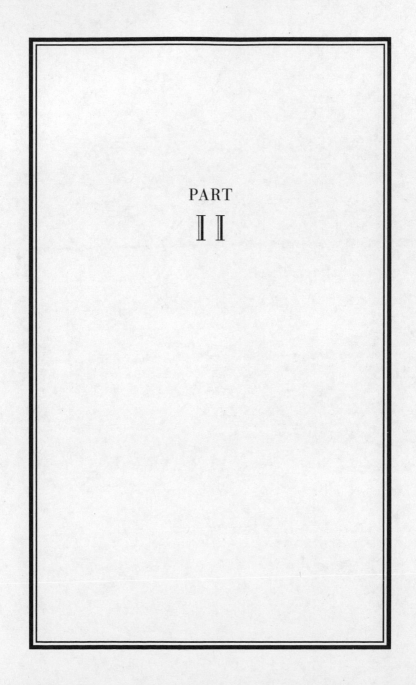

PART

II

CHAPTER FOUR

Ruby Mulvaney returned from the hospital deeper in debt, but otherwise in improving condition. Ellen and Troy continued seeing each other, and Troy helped lead the Humble Tigers to their first undefeated season in living memory. Business picked up at Wiggins' Used Cars, and it was all Earl could do to squeeze in a few spare moments to work on the Corvette, daydream about Ellen, or write her poetry. The Humble Volunteers, the three of them, practiced every Wednesday afternoon in the vacant lot next to Tooley's Texaco. Mostly they dug trenches.

"It's all about firebreaks, Earl," Jimmy explained sternly but not unkindly, using the butt end of his cigar as an added finger to point at Earl's chest. Earl held the handle of a pick loosely in his gloved hands, which despite their leather covering, were raw and sore. Jimmy had read in Earl's glum expression that fire-fighting had not proved as glamorous as he'd hoped. "You might have your heart set on being a big hero, busting down doors and hauling out babies, but that ain't real firefighting. Usually by the time we get there, the fire's already done its damage. Our job is first to keep it from spreading, then to put it out."

Jimmy gave Earl a fat coffee-stained manual missing its front cover, which the young mechanic studied sitting at the dinette, long after darkness pressed itself against the kitchen windows and all the town dogs had fallen silent, learning about the causes and treatments of the three main kinds of fires. Class A is your regular garden-variety fire. That's just regular stuff burning, like wood. Class B is electrical. It's harder to put out because you can't turn a hose on it since water's a conductor. Lots of fires start out Class B and then turn into Class A. Class C is a liquid fire, like with oil; it's the trickiest of all because if water gets to it, the burning liquid's likely to just float on top and spread even faster.

After practicing digging firebreaks, chopping through kudzu vines and the hard-packed Georgia soil with picks and shovels and quizzing each other on different classes of fires, the Volunteers, smelling of sweat and red clay, usually went to Daisy's Diner. Earl soon felt at home at Daisy's, but that was not always the case.

"You look nervous, son," is what Jimmy had said the first time he'd taken Earl to Daisy's. It would be an exaggeration to say that as he walked up railroad ties to that unpainted wood shack with faded red lettering spelling "Daisy's" on the roof, Earl's eyes were as wide as supper plates, unless we're talking about very small supper plates, so I'll keep to the strict truth and just say they were as wide as silver dollars. Though certain his mother wouldn't approve, Earl had found his mentor's kind invitation coupled with the mysterious lure of the place irresistible. "I expect you must've heard some stories about Daisy before."

"Yes, sir, uh,—I heard when the police frisked her one time, they found she'd hidden all around her body in rolls of fat, and under her—and in her—crevices—enough twenty-dollar bills, loose change, ammo, and weapons to cover an entire table. I heard she'd concealed on her body all sorts of guns and pistols, and two bowie knives."

"That's the sort of thing people pull if you believe everything you hear," Jimmy said, placing his hand on Earl's shoulder, as he led him through Daisy's front door. "That's a big exaggeration, I can tell you. You got to use your sense with stories like that. In the first place, what would anybody be doing with *two* bowie knives? And secondly, there are some places that ain't no policeman going to search."

On entering, Earl looked around, expecting to see stuffed deer heads or velvet Elvis posters on the walls, but there wasn't any such thing. Daisy served beer and her famous chili sausage dogs and onion rings from a counter at the rear, and customers seated themselves at tables covered with brown kraft paper that Daisy changed daily. Daisy was too proud to go dressing up her place with a lot of pretentious atmosphere. Plain sheetrock walls, kraft paper tablecloths, and a drain in the center of the floor to wash the garbage down were good enough for her. She believed good food, reasonable prices, and legal beer could speak for themselves.

Many legends have grown up about Daisy's, most of them untrue. You might have gotten the impression that Daisy's was a will-o-the-wisp kind of establishment, since from one story to the next it drifts from south Alabama to North Carolina to

Tennessee, but the one true original Daisy's was a two-room shanty that had been hauled intact on a flatbed and balanced on an abandoned trestle over Gumm Creek just before it crosses under Prosser Road, precisely on the border between three dry counties; the front door opened into Humble County, and the back door into Hancock, and the window looked out over Baldwin. The diner itself spanned the gulley, which formed the boundary line, which meant that as long as you stayed inside, you were in no jurisdiction and had the right to buy as much beer as you cared to. Sad to say, Daisy's is no more; the creek changed course, the banks collapsed, and the trestle fell through. Stories differ about what happened to Daisy herself, whether she got married or buried, but in either case, she never reopened.

Jimmy was not democratic about whom he invited to join the Volunteers; he had two mechanics and two salesmen, but he did not cherish enough warmth for the other mechanic, Wayne, nor the white salesman, Mr. Moss, to invite them.

Jimmy's two salesmen, T. J. and Mr. Moss—no one called him anything but Mr. Moss—were as different in their approaches as night and day. A hungry snapping turtle will sometimes anchor himself in the pool at the very base of a dam and catch any unwary little fish that wash over the spillway; that's just the way Mr. Moss waited every day at the lot's entrance to nab the customers as they entered. T. J., by contrast, substituted likeability and charm for Mr. Moss's reptilian persistence; in time even the white customers had come to prefer him.

"Well, it's really pretty simple," T. J. said one afternoon at Daisy's, leaning back in his chair and gesturing easily with his long graceful hands. A smear of brown chili and two cold uneaten onion rings lay on T. J.'s plate, and an easy peace settled like a mist over the afternoon. Through the hole in the floor the diners could hear the lullaby of a breeze blowing under the trestle and the occasional roar of a pulpwood truck along Prosser Road. After drilling for the day, the age-old question had arisen among the Volunteers over which came first, the chicken or the egg. T. J., an ordained minister as well as a car salesman, brought theology to bear on the question. "If you take the Bible, then the chicken came first. It says in the Bible that God made the birds of the air and told them be fruitful and multiply." Jimmy took a sip of beer and considered T. J.'s position. "So God made the first chicken and there it was."

A lesser man would have quibbled that, strictly speaking, a chicken is not a bird of the air, but Jimmy was too fair-minded for such tactics. "You got to take into account science," Jimmy said, leaning forward, his chin just inches above his beer mug. "If you take an e-vo-lution perspective, which is the way I see things, not saying a word against the Bible, but I'm just naturally scientific that way, then what came first was the egg. The first chicken, see, hatched out of an egg, but that egg was laid by something that wasn't quite yet a chicken. Almost but not quite. Like maybe half a bubble off chicken. Maybe it had ears, or teeth, or fur instead of feathers. Maybe it had three feet and only one wing, but this thing that wasn't quite a chicken, e-volved, it a-dapted to its environment, and it laid an egg and out of that egg came the first real chicken like we know today."

Earl, who for weeks had drilled as a Volunteer without seeing his first real fire, listened, but did not venture an opinion. Privately he had begun to wonder if there were anything more to being a fireman than digging trenches and discussing philosophy at Daisy's. "Do the Volunteers ever really get called out?" Earl asked at last. Digging practice firebreaks had callused his hands and then torn the calluses back off the tender pink skin underneath, and his eardrums buzzed with A's and B's, foaming agents, and flash points.

"You better believe it," T. J. said.

Jimmy nodded. The two might differ when it came to eggs and chickens, but they agreed on this. "One night the phone's going to ring," Jimmy said, "and we'll be doing this for real."

Earl didn't quite believe him, but later that very week the call came. It happened in the middle of the night, as these things do. The phone rang, waking Earl from a dream that he was on a picnic with Ellen.

"Get your uniform," Jimmy's voice came over the line. "I'm on my way." Earl got his fireman's boots and raincoat from the closet and pulled them on in darkness and clopped out on the front stoop to wait, his helmet in his lap. Underneath the fireman's raincoat, which hung on his skinny body like a sack, Earl felt hot and clammy, but the night air was cool against his face, and the silence was lovely to listen to. The silhouetted houses along Warthen Street slept on in the darkness. Even the crickets slept. Growing excitement prickled the hairs on his arms. After a few minutes Ruby, who'd also gotten up, came out on the stoop in her chenille robe and brought Earl a warming cup of sweet black coffee.

"It's quiet," she said, handing him the cup.

"Thanks, Momma," said Earl, and blew on the coffee before tasting it.

"You make me proud," Ruby said. "I don't do near enough for you."

When Jimmy's truck came by, Earl sprinted to it and climbed in the cab, beside T. J.

"It's on Kaolin Road. We don't know yet if this is a Class A fire or a Class B," Jimmy said as they drove off. The dashboard light lit up his face from underneath. A partially unfolded county map lay in T. J.'s lap. Outside the bumping truck, in the glowing headlights, white lines on the blacktop sped underneath them.

"I wish a fire could happen in downtown Deepstep now and then," T. J. said, "where we have that fire hydrant handy."

"Earl ought to equip this truck with its own water tank and pump," Jimmy said. "Cars and trucks naturally adapt to hauling water, being more or less aquatic to start with." His voice became eager at the thought.

"What?" T. J. asked.

"Never mind," Jimmy said, remembering T. J. did not know the theory of car evolution. "Now, remember, boys, I don't want to see no heroics until we find out what kind of fire we got here. There ain't nothing more useless or dangerous than treating a Class B or C fire like it was Class A. And don't go running into no burning buildings thinking you're going to haul out a baby or something. Main thing we got to do is start a firebreak and make sure the fire don't spread. That's what the shovels are for. Then, if need be, we can go smashing down doors and hauling out babies."

"Did you bring the fire axes?" T. J. asked.

"Dang it!" Jimmy slapped the steering wheel. "I clean forgot! I hope we don't have to smash no doors down."

Jimmy needn't have worried; it turned out to be a garden-variety Class A, a brush fire on the margin of the road. As Jimmy called out instructions, the men began chopping a trench around the perimeter to contain the flames, tamping out the fire as they went, covering the burning weeds with shovels full of dirt. T. J. and Earl started on the downwind side and moved in opposite directions around the fire; Earl's friends were only shadows across the burning weeds, but he could hear their shouts of triumph, frustration, or occasional command. "Earl, you missed a spot!" "Hurry, Jimmy! This end's making a break for it!" Earl shouted in return. They worked by firelight, by Jimmy's headlights, by starlight. In the wavering blackness, Earl watched his gloved hands grip the pick, the blade's sharp tooth bite the black loam and tip it over onto the grass. Just before daybreak the job was all but done. Blackened clumps smoldered here and there, flavoring the fresh morning fog with smoke. Earl put down his pick, but his blistered hands could not seem to forget holding it; he could only uncurl them by pulling the fingers of each hand against the other.

"I am tee-eye-ar-dee, tired," Jimmy said and reached into the glove compartment of his truck for a cigar.

"So, Jimmy," T. J. said. "Class A fire, don't you think?"

Jimmy nodded in confirmation. "Yep. Cigarette butt, that's what did this," was Jimmy's verdict. Sweat streaked the smoke stains on his face. Earl rubbed his own face; his ungloved hand came away black. "Some Kaolin trucker threw one out his window yesterday, I bet. It sat there without doing nothing all day, but finally by evening it caught some little piece of weed and there you go." Jimmy spit out the tip from a cigar, lit it in three white puffs, and shook the match vigorously before tossing it aside. "Number one cause of brush fires: cigarette butts."

CHAPTER FIVE

No one except for Ellen and Troy could have told you why they broke up, and even they really couldn't have explained it clearly. Mainly it was because Ellen ran afoul of Troy's third rule.

It happened the night of the Regional Championship. Third quarter, third down and nine; the Warthen Wildcats ahead by five. The sun had set hours a o and under the stadium lights the grass glowed a strange livid green. The Humble spectators, restless and edgy, rustled like dried leaves in the bleachers. Out of the east, from the direction of the Old Nancy Hanks and a mound of dirt where the city fathers had been digging up a vacant lot in their interminable search for the missing Confederate loot, a black storm cloud moved implacably across the sky toward the stadium, the smell of a winter downpour preceding it. From the sideline Coach Fuller called his squad out for a talk.

"They'll be looking for a pass," he told them. "But we ain't going to give them one. Troy," sweat flashed on Coach Fuller's clenched jaw, wind from the approaching storm blew through his white hair; his bright eyes locked on the fullback's. Troy leaned forward to catch the words, "take the ball straight up the middle. Run low, run hard. Hit the hole hard. It may not be a big hole, but you got to hit it hard as you can."

Later Troy could never clearly remember that triumphant play. He recalled the rough touch of the football as Brad pushed it into his hands, and one leap as he cleared a downed blocker and then nothing but a kind of blurry hurricane of grunting, sweating, and clawing until there he was, standing under the goalposts on the other side of the field, listening to the screaming of the spectators, and the preliminary popping drops of rain hitting his helmet.

At first there'd been a startled silence when the crowd saw the handoff instead of the pass they'd expected, but the silence had broken into scattered shouts as Troy cracked through the line, and as he'd pulled away from the tacklers, the scattered shouts had coalesced into a rhythmic, "Go, go, go!" By the time Troy reached the end zone, the goalposts were vibrating with the screams. Ellen even put down her flashlight and *Jude the Obscure* to watch her boyfriend's green uniform move like an irresistible force through the red Wildcats.

After the game (Tigers, 16; Wildcats, 9) Troy and Ellen parked down by Gumm Creek. Troy, too exhilarated after the game to bother with a shower, still wore the jersey in which he'd run that triumphant play, and even though Ellen wasn't much for football—she always brought a book to the games for something to read—her heart pounded when they kissed and she tasted the triumphant smell of sweat and shoulder pads that clung to him. She kissed him again and felt his foot-ball-player hands undoing the buttons on her blouse. She buried her face in his neck and kissed him there. His hands were on her breasts. The rain fell harder, splattering the truck's windshield with big drops, pounding the roof. Her hands were up under his jersey, feeling his muscular naked back. Wind buffeted the privet bushes along the banks. Part of her warned *this isn't right*, but that part was just a passenger. The part of her that was steering didn't care whether it was right or not. Some things you just can't help. Then he was on top of her. She held him close and kissed him.

Shortly after Ellen broke up with Troy, Earl saw her on her front stoop and went up to her. It was a winter dusk in late December—the smell of wood smoke in the air, and the sun-light shifting down from yellow to red.

"Ellen Raley," Earl came right out and said it, "I'm in love with you."

The two of them just idled on the porch a little while after that, but Earl could feel the red needle on his heart jump all the way to the right side of the dial. He couldn't tell if Ellen felt the same. She looked at him square in the eye for a full five sec-onds, then said, "Just a minute," and went back inside. When she came out, she had two Dr Peppers with her. She gave Earl one, and they sat down on the stoop to talk.

Ellen didn't tell Earl that she loved him, and she didn't try to make him take back what he'd said. She didn't even ask him to repeat it or explain himself for saying it. And once Earl had said it, and the red needle in his chest had settled back to normal, he figured he had no need to say it again right away. Instead, he stared over the tops of the pines behind his house at the distant hump of the Humble County water tower and listened as Ellen described the book she was currently reading, about a town a lot like Deepstep, except in England. There's a boy who wants to go to college where he plans to study Latin, but before he can get there, he ends up getting married to a local girl. Ellen hadn't gotten very far in it, but had figured out already the boy's life wouldn't go at all the way he planned it. Earl said he'd seen a show a lot like that, called *It's a Wonderful Life*, and expected the two stories must be pretty much the same.

Then Earl told Ellen about the Endless Corvette. He felt about as skittish mentioning that as he had telling Ellen he loved her because he knew it sounded like a wild idea, and you had to have a lot of car know-how to understand how a thing like that might work. The air grew colder as they talked, and they scooted next to each other on the porch, their shoulders, hips, and knees close to each other, and Ellen found herself staring at the way his ankles stuck out over the tops of his worn-out tennis shoes.

Ellen felt more than just a little skeptical, but Earl described for her the mound of nuts, bolts, and whatnots accumulated from the Corvette, now stacked and labeled in Jimmy's shed, which he believed proved his theory true. Although Ellen didn't think that Earl was crazy, she could not make out if he were altogether serious. She sometimes entertained herself by dreaming up far-fetched ideas, and she thought Earl might be doing the same. Earl's expression of earnest kindliness was impossible to read behind his smudged glasses; it was just the sort of face her uncle wore when spinning one of his famous tall tales.

They sat and talked for hours. After sunset a winter wind began to blow, and the moon came out and lit the bare treetops. The conversation drifted to the subject of time. Paleontology had fired Ellen's imagination, and recently it had come to her that how we look at time was because of the way that we'd evolved.

"You see," Ellen said, "we're chordates; we've got a spinal cord. So we're in the same phylum as fish, reptiles, amphibians, and birds."

"Uh-huh." Earl was trying hard to listen, but his mind kept wandering to things like the shape of her lower lip. He noticed that the underside of her ear's arch was bumpy. He wanted to run his finger lightly along it and feel the bumps.

"But it's more than that that makes us different, there's something just about everybody else overlooks. We've got a mouth and an anus."

"Beg your pardon?"

What she was saying was very important to her but a little embarrassing to talk about, so Ellen spoke in a whisper. Earl had to sit closer to hear, the fragrance of her shampoo hypnotizing him; he wondered what it would be like to cover his face in her hair. "We've got a mouth at one end, and a butt at the other. The food goes in one place and comes out somewhere else. We're just about the only phylum that does that. For jellyfish and sponges, food just kind of floats around them and through them. And there's a certain kind of worm that the waste goes out the same hole food goes in.

"But the thing is that the way we think about time is because of our—digestive system," Ellen explained. Earl noticed her hands as she gestured. He imagined they would be smooth and cool to touch. "The present and the future is what we put into our mouth. The past is what comes out the other end when we're done with it. Everything we're about to eat is the future. Everything we've already eaten is the past. We think time moves in a straight line because that's what our food does, and because our mouth is on the front of our bodies, we think time is always moving forward."

"Instead of backward or sideways," Earl finished her thought. "Like if we were sponges instead of us, we'd see time swirling round and round, or if we were those worms you were talking about, time would just go back and forth. Or in and out."

"That's it, that's it exactly," and Ellen, excited that someone understood her theory, leaned over and nudged Earl's shoulder with hers. Earl wished he were a sponge right then so he could let that first sweet pressure swirl and swish all around inside him instead of just being over all at once, chordate fashion.

When he finally walked across the street back to his house, his shoulder glowing from the warmth of Ellen's touch and his heart's red needle quivering, he had the unfamiliar feeling of looking forward to tomorrow.

—

At breakfast the next day, Earl's day off, Ruby noticed but didn't call attention to the way he kept one eye on the front window during breakfast, nor did she mention he had on his nicest jeans and his favorite shirt. She added Earl's alertness to his wardrobe; it equaled Ellen Raley. When they'd finished their grits and sausage, she volunteered to get the dishes even though she'd cooked and they always split the chores.

"This new hip is making me so spry, I don't want to waste

my energy. Why don't you go out—" Earl was too old to tell "go out and play," so she just let the preposition hang in space. "Why don't you go out—?"

Ten minutes later, the dishes done, Ruby went outside to stuff some envelopes and enjoy the sunshine. Across the street Earl and Ellen stood in the Raley's front yard talking.

"Thank you, Lord," Ruby hummed and rocked as she stuffed her envelopes, "for giving my boy something to look forward to. Things are finally balancing out for him. It's his turn to have some happiness."

She clucked her tongue as she recalled how considerate of her feelings he'd been when he rolled her out of the house on his creeper. Even as a boy Earl had never gotten the good things he deserved, she thought. Things always seemed to turn out like Santa Claus.

The people who laid out Deepstep had no sense of zoning; the most fabulous split-level in the county stood catty-cornered across Deepstep Road from a row of unpainted shanties heated by wood-burning stoves. The differences on Warthen Street were not that stark, but if you knew a family lived there, you could roughly estimate how well-off they were by which side they lived on. And the Mulvaneys, not to put too fine a point on it, lived on the poor side. Christmas in the Mulvaney household never meant store-bought presents. Earl was vaguely aware that in late December other kids seemed to get new sweaters, toy trucks, red wagons, and tricycles, but the only toys Ruby and Roy could afford for Earl were screwdrivers and adjustable wrenches, and those were hand-me-downs. Then when he was in the first grade, he heard his classmates talking about Santa Claus, and the letters they would write him, and the presents they would get.

To Earl, it was as if a new planet had been discovered. That's the secret of the presents, he thought, Santa Claus! You had to write a letter! His poor mother, he couldn't blame her, really; she had never known the secret!

It is not an exaggeration to say that after school Earl ran all the way home. Even when he stopped for breath, his mind was still running. What would he ask for? Lincoln Logs, an Erector Set, a Mr. Potato Head. He promised himself, hugging his sides at the hilarity of the thought, that at least once he'd try putting all Mr. Potato Head's parts in the wrong holes to see how he'd look with his mouth on top, nose on the side, and eyes on the bottom. When Earl came in the front door, letting the screen slam behind him, in spite of his mother's warning not to, he said, "Momma, I need you to help me write a letter!"

Ruby, being a professional envelope stuffer, always had letter-writing materials handy. She went to their unsteady dinette, pen in hand, judging by Earl's flushed face that he wanted to send a note to a girl he was sweet on.

Earl pondered how to word this very important letter. Did you go right into what presents you wanted, or did you start with general questions about health and weather? In any case, he knew the first two words he would dictate.

"Dear Santa."

He stopped to think what should come next, and then he noticed how strangely his mother sat at the table, humped over as if all the bones had gone out of her back. Her shoulders shook, and she dropped the pen on the paper. Why was she crying? She turned and squeezed Earl to her. He smelled her sweet hairspray and felt her wet eyelashes against his face.

Slowly the truth sank in.

I think it shows what a thoughtful boy Earl was, that the

next day he didn't go right out and tell the other kids at school about Santa. I guess he figured for them there was one.

All those years later, as Ruby watched Earl and Ellen walking down the street, she made up her mind right then to do absolutely everything in her power to further their romance.

Earl and Ellen strolled down Warthen Street to Main and near the courthouse they got a soda at the pharmacy. Then, it being ideal walking weather, a sunny day in winter, they kept on walking right past the courthouse on the 8:17 side, to railroad tracks of the Old Nancy Hanks to Good Hope Cemetery overlooking Sloppy Floyd Lake, a place not many boys would have taken a girl. Troy Badcock, for example, would not have dreamt of taking Ellen to a graveyard, but Ellen didn't have a very wide experience in dating so didn't think it odd. As for Earl, he didn't know a place so pretty in the county except the golf course, and they were not allowed on that.

Holding hands they walked a grassy hill to look across Sloppy Floyd Lake, which bounded the graveyard on the eastern side. They studied glossy marble tombstones in the newer part and pondered the rectangular sinkholes in the older part. They put together family histories by noticing the Smith twins died before their mother, Mrs. Breedlove buried two husbands before a third one buried her, and Johnny Haynes died in World War II.

When morning settled into afternoon, they found convenient resting places—Earl on the first Mr. Breedlove and Ellen on the second. "I'm glad you're not a sissy-type girl," Earl said. "I didn't think of it at first, but most girls wouldn't want to see a graveyard."

"It's pretty here," Ellen said simply. From where she sat she could see the cool grassy hill roll down under a sky as blue as glass, to Sloppy Floyd's copper-colored water, where a few ducks paddled and complained in low quacks to one another.

A heron, losing interest in one spot, tucked its head down and flapped its huge wings to try its luck on the other side of the lake, as silent, graceful, and unearthly as a pterodactyl. From Earl's vantage point, had he stood on tiptoe, he might have been able to just make out the top of the water tower, or if Ellen had stood on his shoulders, perhaps, she might be able to see the 10:15 on the courthouse clock. Earl pushed his busted glasses back up his nose and tried, fruitlessly, to comb down his hair with one hand. Earl is not like Troy, Ellen thought, I wonder what would have happened if I'd gone out with Earl first. "I'm glad we came," was all she said.

She leaned back, hands stretched out in the grass behind her; Earl sat Indian-style. He wondered if he should kiss her. To do so, he would have to move across to her; that seemed awkward, so instead he just said, "Do you want to see a movie tonight? They got a new James Bond, Roger Moore. He's supposed to be pretty good."

"Sure," Ellen said.

In Earl's skin, heat built up. "Can I kiss you?"

Ellen thought about it. "You're not supposed to ask for a kiss, Earl."

"I didn't want to be rude," he said. It shamed Earl not to know the kissing rules. He wondered how to kiss a girl without getting permission first.

"So, do you want to kiss or not?" Ellen asked. Eagerly Earl hunkered down beside her—Ellen did not move, and even the Sloppy Floyd ducks fell silent—and tried to brush her parted lips with his, leaning forward until he met her head.

Earl returned to Mr. Breedlove. "I guess that was probably the second worst kiss in the history of the world," he said apologetically.

"It wasn't so bad," she said.

"It's hard to keep steady when you're hunkered down," he said. "My aim was off. I hope I didn't hurt you."

"It was fine."

"Do you want to try again?" Earl offered.

"Not right away," Ellen tenderly touched her upper lip and wondered would it swell. Dating Earl would require very different expectations than dating Troy.

They didn't talk for a little while, and silently Earl cussed himself for his clumsiness. Ellen after a little while said, "When does the movie start?"

"I don't know; I expect we better head back so I can check the times."

Before he went to Ellen's house that night, Earl brushed, re-brushed, and flossed his teeth, then drank a tumbler of ice water to make his breath as fresh as possible in preparation for further kissing opportunities. The ice-water chill would not have lasted more than two seconds ordinarily, but lavish brushing had virtually paved the inside of Earl's mouth with spearmint, making it almost as good as a thermos for keeping things cool; that night had Ruby thought to check the tooth-paste inventory, she'd have come out about a quart low.

"Hello, ma'am. Is Ellen in?" Earl said when Mrs. Raley answered the door.

"Yes, uh, come in. Sit down," Mrs. Raley said. Accepting her hospitality, Earl went through the foyer into the living room and sat on a plaid couch by the TV. An upright vacuum cleaner stood nearby, its cord snaking to an outlet. He'd apparently interrupted her cleaning. Mrs. Raley, a small woman with large eyes in a pointed face, for some reason had always reminded Earl of Mrs. Cleaver on *Leave it to Beaver*, even though she looked nothing like her. Maybe it was because in spite of the fact her house was spotlessly clean, she always seemed to be in the act of cleaning it more. Mrs. Raley called out, "Ellen!" while keeping both eyes on Earl.

"Hi, Earl," said Mr. Raley, who'd come into the room. Mr. Raley sat in the chair catty-cornered to the couch with an iced tea and a *Time*.

Ellen came into the living room, "Mom, have you seen my book?"

"Honey, Earl Mulvaney's here," Mrs. Raley said in a strange bright voice.

Ellen gave him a curious look, as if mushroomlike he'd sprung up on the couch unexpectedly. "Oh, hello, Earl."

"Hi, hello, Ellen," Earl said, tempted to get up but reluctant to disobey Mrs. Raley's instructions to have a seat.

"Have you seen my book, Momma?"

"If it's the book with the church on the cover, try beside the sink in the pink bathroom," Mrs. Raley suggested.

Ellen disappeared down the hallway in search of her book, while Earl sat on the plaid sofa and marveled at the Raleys' wealth. On the west side of Warthen Street were just wood-siding houses like the Mulvaney's; he'd never been in one of the brick houses on the east side, which had so many bathrooms, they had to be identified by color.

Mrs. Raley said, half apologetically, "I don't think Ellen expected you so early." The movie started at 7:30, so Earl'd arrived promptly at 5:45; he wanted to create a good impression by not being late. Mrs. Raley turned to address her husband, "Are you going to do anything about the vacuum? It still isn't sucking. You have to go over the same piece of trash four times to pick it up."

"I changed the bag," Mr. Raley said from his chair without looking up. He flipped through the magazine's bright photographs, waiting for one to catch his eye, "and I cleaned off the beater bar. What else am I supposed to do?"

"I don't want to go ordering another one from Sears, this one's only five years old," Mrs. Raley gave a high-pitched sigh of exasperation, then said to Earl, "Piece of junk. They don't make things like they used to. Have you eaten supper, Earl? I've got a pot roast."

"No thanks, ma'am. It smells good, though," he said honestly. "I'll just sit here until Ellen's ready."

Earl sat patiently on the couch in the living room while Mrs. Raley put out supper in the dining room. He knew the Raleys were high class, so it did not astonish him that they ate in a different room than they cooked or even a different room than they watched TV. Earl was impressed by the decorum of the Raleys as they dined in the next room; their conversation was so soft, softer than the occasional clack of flatware against a plate, it was as if they were speaking to each other in whispers.

"Do you want to turn on the TV, Earl?" Mrs. Raley called out to Earl from the dining room. It sounded to Earl like her voice was frayed with nervousness.

"No thank you, ma'am," he replied. "I'm just sitting here reading."

Earl was not much for reading, and who could blame him, since the only letter he'd ever gotten was a good-bye note from his father. But Mrs. Raley had sewn fancy-lettered quotations on pillows all over the house, and some of them were quite thought provoking. The one he found most intriguing went, "Keep your head when all about you are losing theirs and blaming it on you."

Uncomfortable at the image of himself, the only person left intact, facing the accusations of decapitated neighbors, Earl turned his attention to the vacuum cleaner, which now sat in a corner of the room.

When the Raleys finished supper, and Ellen went to her room to get ready, Earl told Mrs. Raley he'd fixed the vacuum.

"What?"

"While you were eating supper," Earl explained. "I always carry a couple of screwdrivers and a needle-nose. I took it apart. The hose was all plugged up." Earl showed her the floral-patterned wastebasket where a long tube-shaped dust bunny, a dust bunny snake, lay coiled. "And here," Earl dropped a tiny bolt and a washer in her open hand. "These parts were left over."

"Well, I'll be," Mrs. Raley said in grateful surprise.

"Well, thank you, Earl," Mr. Raley said, also pleased. "So what are you kids going to see?"

"Live and Let Die."

"Ah! I've been wanting to see that myself," Mr. Raley said. "But I don't think Ellen's mother would want to go with me."

"Why don't you come with us?" Earl asked, always polite.

"I'd love to," Mr. Raley said, and then clamped his mouth shut, afraid to let out another word. The invitation had sounded so genuine that he'd answered without thinking.

"Are you going with them?" Mrs. Raley asked her husband.

"Well, sure," Earl said generously. And the plan was set in cement.

"That sounds fun," Mrs. Raley said. She did not sound convinced of her own words.

Maybe the kid doesn't have enough money to get into the movie, Mr. Raley thought; this is just helping him out. "I'll get my sweater," he said.

Ellen came out after the three of them had waited for several minutes without talking. "I'm ready," she said. She'd gone Earl's best sweatshirt and jeans one better by wearing an actual dress. It was long and dark blue and set off her red hair falling on her shoulders. She was lovely inside it. Her feet were pretty in her strappy shoes.

"You look great," Earl said. "Oh, by the way," he added, trying to sound casual, but not sure how she'd take the news, "your dad's coming."

Ellen's jaw did not actually drop, but it certainly slackened. She said nothing as the three of them went outside and got in the Buick, Mr. Raley in the back, and Earl and Ellen in the front. When they got to the theater, Earl rushed up to the window and bought three tickets before Mr. Raley had fairly gotten out of the car.

If he didn't need ticket money, Mr. Raley thought, then why did he—? Good Lord, I have gone and ruined this kid's date. Heartsick, Mr. Raley insisted that he at least be allowed to buy the popcorn and sodas, which Earl consented to. Accepting popcorn and a Dr Pepper from Mr. Raley was pure etiquette on Earl's part; anything he would have eaten at that point would still have been toothpaste-flavored.

I don't think anyone ever watched a James Bond movie with closer attention than those three. Earl sat on the aisle next to Ellen, and on the other side of her sat Mr. Raley. Mr. Raley kept his gaze fixed forward so rigidly, he got a neck cramp, and Earl kept his hands on his knees as if they'd been bolted there. Earl's face got hot during the sex scenes. Early in the movie, 007 unzips a lady's dress using a powerful electromagnetic watch Q had given him, and Earl shriveled up inside from shame. What kind of movie is Mr. Raley going to think I took his daughter to? Earl wondered. But mercifully there were enough chase scenes that Earl figured Mr. Raley would forget the sexy parts. In Earl's favorite scene, James Bond escaped from a deadly swamp, using that same electromagnetic watch to pull a rowboat close enough to run to it over the backs of hungry alligators that snapped at him in useless indignation.

After the movie Earl walked Ellen and her father to the door, and Mrs. Raley came out to meet them. "Earl, the vacuum cleaner works like a charm! It hasn't sucked this good since it was new!"

"Let's go inside," Mr. Raley said putting a hand on his wife's shoulder, "and give these kids some time alone." For the first time that evening Earl and Ellen were by themselves.

"You aren't like any boy I've ever known," Ellen laughed. She laid a hand lightly on his chest, and he could feel the warmth of her fingertips all the way through his cotton shirt.

"Oh."

"I mean I really like you."

Fighting back the urge to ask permission, Earl took Ellen's chin in his fingers, just like he'd pictured himself doing that afternoon, and tilted her head back to kiss her. He didn't have to ask her how it was; he knew there'd been a big improvement. After they'd kissed, Ellen said, "Just a second," and ran inside. When she came out, she brought a little photograph of herself for Earl's wallet. On the back she'd drawn a heart—the sight of which made Earl's own heart swell. He went home that night in a glow, and when he went to bed, he couldn't sleep, but lay awake with his hands folded behind his head, thinking about James Bond and that magnetic watch, imagining how great it would be to carry around a piece of equipment that would save the day in an unexpected predicament and simultaneously help him get the girl.

CHAPTER SIX

T he Wednesday following Earl's date, after T. J. and Jimmy got their chili sausage dogs and beer, and Earl got a chili sausage dog and Dr Pepper, Earl passed around Ellen's snapshot to everyone, and they all dutifully admired it. Jimmy and T. J. sat across from Earl, and Daisy stood between them, a white dishrag in one hand. They all appreciated the significance of the drawing of the heart. "Not as good as the actual word 'love,'" was Jimmy's judgment, "but a whole lot better than 'friends always.'" But as Earl narrated the events of his first date, Daisy, T. J., and Jimmy became increasingly perturbed. Jimmy shook his head in disgust and disappointment as he drank his beer, T. J. slapped the table in indignation, and Daisy, who hovered around the table after bringing their orders, repeated "Oh, Jesus" at intervals.

At first controversy arose over the wisdom or unwisdom of taking a girl to a cemetery. Daisy and Jimmy disapproved strongly, but T. J. held there was some strategic value in it. "Scaring a girl makes her want to snuggle up close. Nothing like a drive-in movie about some crazy guy running around with a chain saw to get some sugar."

"She wasn't scared," Earl protested. "I wasn't trying to scare her."

"Still," T. J. said, "it's not a bad idea." Aside from visiting the cemetery, however, everything about Earl's conduct was greeted with unanimous consternation.

"Never, never show up early for a date," T. J. said. Being an ordained minister, T. J. was an expert on many subjects. "You've got to keep a girl waiting. People don't appreciate nothing they don't have to wait for. Remember that. When you go on a date, make the girl—what? Wait." T. J. leaned back in his chair. "You see what I did there? I made you wait for the last word, didn't I? You appreciated it more that way."

"And I don't even know what to tell you about asking the dad along," Jimmy said, disgustedly. "I mean, hell."

"Oh, Jesus. And what'd you go fixing that lady's vacuum cleaner for?" Daisy asked. "Who are you dating, the girl or the momma?"

Earl sank lower into his seat. His onion rings were ashes in his mouth. He hadn't guessed love had so many rules, any one of which might be ruinous if broken, and all of them contrary to his innate sense of politeness.

"Girls don't like boys that are too nice," Daisy admonished him. "They take one look at that and just go out and break your heart. You got to be a little meaner." Her black fist clenched the dishrag until it dripped droplets of dirty dishwater, and she made a stern face to demonstrate the meanness so attractive to women.

"I can't be mean," Earl said miserably.

"He's right, he can't be," said Jimmy, who'd come to know Earl well. "It ain't in him."

"He could try being a little mean," T. J. suggested.

"Every time that boy tries being mean," Jimmy predicted, "it's just going to come out nice."

"Next time before you go on a date," T. J. said, "you need to ask us—make sure in advance you don't do nothing stupid."

"I will," Earl promised. He nodded his head.

"That girl's going to break his heart," Daisy predicted and slapped the dishrag over her shoulder, turning back to the kitchen.

But Ellen, not a girl whose heart was likely to be won with drive-in movies about chain saw killers, had found the visit to the graveyard charming. And being a girl in love with ideas, she was drawn to Earl's inventive mind. And the sweetness of his kisses—so different from Troy's—made her feel a nostalgic twinge for a sweetness in herself she'd thought she'd lost.

As for Ellen's parents, they were divided on the subject of Earl. Mrs. Raley, though pleased by the repair of her vacuum cleaner, retained grave reservations about the relationship, and was not shy about sharing them. Standing in line at the Miller's Grocery behind a fat black lady with an entire shopping cart full of ten-pound Dixie Crystal bags, Mrs. Raley told her husband, "I never interfere with her life, but why can't she get back together with Troy? What was wrong with him? I just don't like seeing her waste herself."

"He's a nice kid, that's all I say. It's nice she's seeing someone so nice." Normally Mr. Raley's response would have been a noncommittal "hum," but intruding so clumsily into the first date had made him more solicitous of Earl's happiness than most girls' fathers would have been.

"I'm not saying anything bad about him. Did I say anything bad about him? He is a hard worker, dropping out of school to take care of his sick mother like that. I don't see how he makes ends meet. I just worry it's not fair to make him spend so much time and money on Ellen when he's got so much else on his plate. Ellen's got straight A's. If she's going to UGA in the fall— well, I mean, he is a dropout. There's just no future in it. Not that I'd say anything against Earl Mulvaney—"

"She better not go breaking his heart!" The woman spun around to face them with sudden fury and shot a bright-eyed glare at them, "That's all I got to say about it," she said, shaking her finger at Mrs. Raley, her jowls trembling with rage, "She better not go breaking his heart!" and then stormed out of the store with her rattling grocery cart of sugar, leaving the astounded Raleys thinking that the angels themselves had planted Earl's advocates among random strangers.

Earl would later see these as the best days of his life. Between his mother's envelope-stuffing and his weekly paycheck, he had enough not only to hold the creditors at bay but also to spend on pleasant fripperies like taking Ellen to the Pastime Theater and even getting buttered popcorn at the concession counter. He enjoyed a growing reputation for mechanical ability surpassing that of common man. Jimmy made Wayne the other mechanic take care of all the cars on the lot and put Earl in the garage to work on cars people brought in for repairs. It is an unheard-of thing for people to get their cars fixed at a used-car lot, but Earl was that good.

"Selling used cars and having a garage too is like having a hospital and a funeral parlor rolled into one," Jimmy said proudly. "I wonder why I didn't think of it before."

And best of all, Earl had won the love of pretty Ellen Raley.

Because there was no waiting room on the lot, Jimmy dragged a comfortable saggy old couch with torn brown upholstery into the garage. He set up a little table beside it with a Mr. Coffee, cups, sugar, and nondairy whitener. Then he put a soda machine on the back wall. That way, customers could make themselves at home while they watched Earl work. OSHA had not yet decreed customers could not be allowed in garages, or if it had, it hadn't gotten around to telling Jimmy.

It might surprise you the highly personal things that people told Earl as he worked on their cars. Other good places to spill your soul didn't hold a candle to that garage, musty and oily-smelling as it was. Unlike talking to a barber, hairdresser, or bartender, who have numerous customers to serve at once, when you were with Earl, you had his undivided attention. And there is something strangely confidential-feeling in talking to someone when all you could see are his legs sticking out from under your car.

Mr. Moss, who had to crank and crank his Rambler to get it to turn over, and then could not shut it off once it got going, bent Earl's ear by the hour pursuing every byway and off-ramp of the missing retriever story as Earl rebuilt his starter. Earl learned about the street the Marshalls lived on, the Marshall family tree, the Moss family tree, the spot in the high branches when a Moss and Marshall had married once before, the dangers of consanguinity—all without ever catching sight of faithful Digger, but without Mr. Moss's ever losing hope the next bend in the narrative might bring them to him.

"This county don't have no one else like him and me," Mr. Moss said to himself in almost prayerful admiration as he turned the Rambler's ignition, which came to instant life with a happy growl thanks to Earl's rebuilding. The night before he had even dreamt of Earl. He and the mechanic were searching for Digger together, and somehow their quest had brought them to Australia. Throughout his dream, Mr. Moss had explained to Earl many interesting facts, such as the origin of the word "kangaroo," the kangaroo's relationship to the native possum, and the probable Irish derivation of the word "o'possum." Although Mr. Moss and his companion saw neither hide nor hair of Digger in their travels, something in the patient doglike expressions of the kangaroos told him they were closing in, and he'd woken up feeling oddly hopeful and reassured. "No one else but him's got so much understanding when it comes to dogs," Mr. Moss told himself regarding Earl's character.

Daisy also found in Earl an understanding ear when she brought in her truck, which had four flat tires, some front-end damage, and bent axles, and not from hitting a deer, either. She'd ridden on flat tires fifteen miles over dirt and gravel roads.

Daisy sat and poured herself coffee while Earl walked around the truck, studying it from all sides. Daisy's size made the weary couch cushions wrap up around her thighs.

"I can't straighten these axles," Earl said thoughtfully as he inspected the damage. "I can start on the front end now, but for some of the rest I'll have to get new parts."

"You'll have to order them?"

"I'll go down to the salvage yard." Any ordinary mechanic might scrounge for months through that jungle of rusted metal and busted glass and maybe never find another Dodge Truck to get the axles from, but Earl could take the engine from a John Deere tractor and fit it in a Pinto. "What happened?"

"Sarah McAllus happened," Daisy said, squishing nondairy whitener against the sides of her cup with a spoon to keep it from clumping in her coffee. "Lucky me and Rodney saw her headlights on the bedroom wall. She was supposed to be in Chicago, but she came back early on purpose to surprise us. I heard her smash into my Dodge, then a gun go off four times. 'You got to get out,' Rodney kept saying—like I needed to be told that. I couldn't leave till I got my things off the floor, could I? Why I ever fooled around with that no-good Rodney McAllus in the first place is beyond me.

"Anyways, I heard the front door slam and Sarah yell out she knew I was in there, and I wasn't going nowhere on four flat tires. I took off down the hall—she has one of them houses that's got a hall from the front door to the back—which gave Sarah a clear shot, but I expect she hadn't expected to flush me out so soon, because she hadn't reloaded." Daisy stopped and sipped, recalling her night of terror. "She was right behind me, though. As I come around the back side of the house to my truck, I saw her on the porch stuffing in fresh shells.

"You can drive a truck with four flat tires, but not fast. The gun goes off again, and glass goes down my neck. She's hit the window. Sarah was mad enough, and I was driving slow enough, she could've outrun me all the way to town, but she couldn't reload, aim, *and* run all at the same time, so I got away. I finally saw her in my rearview head back to the house, but I didn't stay to see if she was going back for Rodney or just getting more ammo."

Daisy sat and drank her coffee, rocking back and forth on the sofa, which was too worn out to even squeak. "What would make me do Sarah that-a-way? She never did me no wrong. You hear women got needs, but don't nobody need a no-good like Rodney McAllus. Fooling with him was just pure orneriness. I don't blame Sarah for what she done, no, I don't." Warm salty tears of self-recrimination flowed down her cheeks.

As Earl worked on Daisy's front end, Daisy worked herself up to such a state of contrition that the very next Sunday she went to Goshen Baptist, and got down on her knees to Sarah McAllus, weeping like a child and begging her forgiveness for fooling around with Sarah's husband. Sarah was so moved, she began to cry too, and forgave Daisy with all her heart, and they hugged and cried, and everyone in the church praise-Jesused, and Sarah and Daisy left the church embracing like sisters.

About a week later, Daisy and Sarah were in court suing each other, but everyone agreed the peace was a plain miracle while it lasted.

Other people told Earl things just as personal, all of which demonstrates the reputation you can get as a good listener when all you really are is not much of a talker. All the time his customers talked, Earl made "uh-huh" noises under the car, but he was really thinking about Ellen. Whenever he was with her, he huffed up her shampoo smell, pressing his face against her neck and into her hair, inhaling vigorously, trying to get Ellen's molecules way back into the top of his nasal cavities, where they would hang on, to keep some of her with him while he worked. She sometimes came and helped him with the Endless Corvette in Jimmy's shed, handing him tools like a surgeon's assistant.

Not many people knew about Earl and Ellen even though secrets usually don't keep in Humble County; for example, years later when Troy Badcock let Edgar Tooley know he'd found

Confederate treasure at the bottom of Sloppy Floyd, word leaked within minutes to Judge Hathorne and Sheriff King as if by mental telepathy. Not that Earl and Ellen were trying to hide anything, but they were so private by nature, the county as a whole never learned they were an item. Ruby knew, and the Raleys, Jimmy, T. J., and Daisy, but that's all. Somehow or other, Earl and Ellen managed to reveal their romance to perhaps the only six people in Humble County who weren't natural gossips.

Earl and Ellen liked to neck at Good Hope Cemetery. Earl lay beneath a tombstone on a blanket they had brought, with Ellen in his arms. Another good place was the shed at Jimmy Wiggins' Used Cars. Ellen admired the beauty of the Corvette and wanted to memorize every piece of its body just as Earl wanted to memorize every piece of hers. The littlest things delighted and surprised her, and Earl saw them through fresh eyes when she was there: that a hose clamp tightens by eating its own tail like a mythical snake, that a wing nut exactly fits its name and looks like a little silver moth that's alighted on the oil filter, that every part nestled so exactly into and against every other part, fitting together like spoons or those wooden Russian dolls that each has another doll inside it and another doll inside that. He would turn his head to kiss her while they worked together, but before they really got to serious kissing, she made him clean his hands with white Goop until he got the oil out from under his fingernails.

With one arm around her shoulder and the other at the small of her back, they pressed their bodies together and she opened her mouth under his. In learning to kiss, at first Earl attempted the athletic approach, straining to reach her back molars or glottis, but he soon learned love should not be so strenuous.

Sometimes he watched to see her eyes turning beneath closed lids, lashes resting on her cheek, while she curled her tongue up so he could taste the velvet underside, or placed her own sweet tongue in his mouth. After he could stand it no longer, Earl gently undid the top buttons of her blouse, and touched her breasts, as softly as a shy boy in a petting zoo.

I hope I don't bore or offend you by going on and on about the mechanics of kissing, but kissing was of great importance to Earl and Ellen. Even today, if you made them swear on a Bible, they would have to tell you that those kisses in the late winter and early spring of '74 were the best they ever had. True, each of them had only one other person for comparison, but those other people—Troy Badcock in Ellen's case, and later on Barbara Allen in Earl's, were experts. Barbara brought a degree of professionalism and attention to detail when it came to kissing that few could match. And you shouldn't let Troy's jocular references to kissing as "swapping spit" or "tongue wrestling" fool you into thinking he was a bad kisser. Through wide experience he had mastered techniques of applying and withdrawing pressure and exploratory probing that Earl never guessed at. Troy and Barbara both gave good kisses, great kisses, but they didn't give themselves to kisses.

Together, however, Earl and Ellen learned something that not many people know: kissing, done properly, makes you dizzy. Not dizzy sick, like on a merry-go-round when your eyes and stomach insist you're still moving even after you get off, and if you trust your wobbly legs, they're likely to walk you slam into the nearest wall. Getting dizzy from kissing is partly an excited feeling in your stomach, as if you're rushing down a long hill, going faster and faster, but not at all afraid of what will happen at the bottom. Mostly, though, it's what happens in your head, and that part is impossible to accurately describe. The closest way to put it is that your brain rotates up and back, clean out of your skull, which sounds scary and horrible, but is wonderfully pleasant, and makes you feel like you've floated out of yourself. The whole time, though, you're fully there in your body, and all at once in the other person's body; you're all lips, mouth and tongue, and simultaneously, the other person's lips, mouth and tongue, and up above it at the same time. It's not something you can understand if you've never felt it, and I made a hash out of it trying to describe it, but there it is.

Every evening when he got off work, in spite of his friends' advice, Earl took Ellen walking to the cemetery. Ellen and Earl didn't say they loved each other, but they held hands, and in the shadow of a big marble obelisk named "Price," Ellen leaned back in Earl's arms and let him taste the softness of her mouth. Then one night, talking to Ellen, Earl fell in love with her.

He'd sort of been in love with her before, of course, or thought he'd been—but at first that didn't amount to much more than admiring the way she looked reading a book in her cut-off jeans and baby-oiled legs. And after that, it was mostly just the nice surprise that a girl he liked, liked him back. But then one night Ellen told Earl about a book she'd just finished.

She and Earl were sitting leaning their backs against an oak tree as Ellen talked. "Through most of the book, the boy thinks he's being set up to marry this rich girl because even though his family's poor, someone keeps slipping him money and getting him things. He figures it's the rich girl's aunt, who is this crazy lady who always wears a wedding dress because of being jilted years ago."

"I know a story like that," Earl said, nodding his head. "There's a ghost on Green Street that throws herself off the

91

balcony in her wedding dress every night at midnight, just like clockwork."

"Well, this is more a love story than a ghost story," Ellen said, "but it's not really a love story either. It turns out the person slipping the main character money all that time isn't the crazy lady but an escaped convict the boy had befriended years and years ago but forgotten."

"So do the boy and the girl end up together?"

"No. The crazy lady was raising the girl all along to break someone's heart, and it turns out she did a good job of it. Years later the boy and girl meet up, but it's too late. He loved her, but she wasn't for him." Ellen turned away to look at a gravestone in the distance.

Earl was thinking how it sounded almost worth reading, since it had a crazy lady, a pretty girl, and an escaped convict all in the same book. Then noticing Ellen had fallen silent, he touched her shoulder, and she turned back around. Her chin was shivering, her eyes large and moist. She leaned against Earl and bawled. It seems the book hadn't had much effect on Ellen right away, but had had a delayed reaction. All day long, while she'd been waiting for Earl to get off work, the sadness had been sneaking up on her, and now sitting in the graveyard, it hit her all at once. She cried and cried.

"I'm afraid it's like that with us," she cried. "Like the book."

Earl held her until she wasn't shaking anymore. When she was done, she stood up straight, and wiped the tears from her cheeks, and blew snot from her nose. To Earl, who'd already decided she was the most beautiful girl in the world, she seemed even more beautiful—she'd entered into competition with angels now. No man on earth can feel a girl cry in his arms and the warmth of tears on his shoulder, and not fall in love, especially not if she's crying over something great and beautiful, like Art.

～

At that time sad stories were not the only things that upset Ellen; many things worried her, great and small. One Sunday morning Mrs. Raley discovered that even going to the bathroom seemed to provoke her daughter.

Mrs. Raley knocked on the door and asked, "Honey, are you done in there?" and knocked on the door again.

"Just another minute, Momma."

"Your father's in the pink bathroom with a *Time*, so you know he's not coming out for another forty minutes. And I'm not sure I want it when he's done. We had spaghetti last night."

"Just a minute."

"Well, I had to hold it in all during church, is all. This morning you were using the bathroom then, too." Mrs. Raley had started fixing Sunday dinner early, and when Ellen had awoken to the smell of boiling rutabagas, she had become suddenly nauseous. "But I'm not complaining. Are you going to see the Mulvaney boy today?"

"Yes, Momma." Ellen wiped and looked. Just yellow and white.

"That's nice," Mrs. Raley said uncertainly.

I'm not going to worry yet, Ellen told herself, there's no point worrying yet.

"It's nice you're dating," Mrs. Raley said. She brought the side of her head close to the bathroom door. "Whatever happened between you and that nice Troy Badcock?"

At least another ten days before I worry. "I broke up with him."

"Oh." Disappointment. "I hear Troy's getting a football

93

scholarship to UGA. His father owns a plumbing business, you know."

Make it twenty. "Yes, Momma."

"And what does Earl do? He's a mechanic, isn't he?"

"You know he is, Momma." I won't worry for twenty days.

"That's nice he's supporting himself. Bless his heart, I don't know how he makes ends meet with that sick mother of his. I just worry you're making him spend money he can't afford taking you to the movies and things."

Flush.

"He's a sweet boy, but I worry if it's fair to be asking so much attention from him right now when he must have so much else on his mind."

Ellen washed her hands in cold water and deliberately dried them on one of her mother's peach-colored guest towels with the fancy embroidered "R". Twenty days. She opened the door.

"You know," Mrs. Raley said cheerfully as her daughter came out, "I bet Troy would just love to invite you to the prom, but he won't while he thinks you're seeing the Mulvaney boy."

"The bathroom's all yours, Momma."

"I just hate to see you miss your prom, is all."

"I'm not missing the prom," Ellen said with sudden decision, "I'm asking Earl."

"Well, you don't have to be so snappish about it," Mrs. Raley said. She closed the bathroom door behind her and realized with sudden pique she didn't have to go anymore.

Earl's being invited to the prom meant as much to Ruby as it did to her son. The peculiar ethics of the foot-washers dictate they must take all life's trials with cheerful fortitude, and all life's blessings with humility. Ruby had plenty of experience with the cheerful fortitude part, but she'd had so few blessings, she didn't quite know how to bring off the humility. Accordingly, when she spoke to Edna Edwards, one of her friends at Sanctified Tongue, her attempt to sound as if she were complaining was unconvincing at best. "Oh, Earl is such a whirlwind, go, go, go! It wears me out just thinking about it," she fanned herself vigorously with her Howell's Funeral Home Fan to demonstrate the whirlwind of Earl's social life. "He's going to the prom, you know."

Edna waved her fan to hide her mouth, which twisted briefly as if she'd just eaten a persimmon. The two women stood at the foot of the steps as the congregation flowed out and around them. Edna suspected Ruby had chosen this setting to mention the prom in hopes of being overheard. Not taken in for a moment by her friend's pretense, Edna stood ready to provide some spare humility to anyone lacking it. She smiled, so Ruby wouldn't be able to hear the frown in her voice and said, "The prom! Oh, dear, what are you going to do about the tux?"

"The tux?"

"Yes, the tuxedo. Earl can't possibly go to the prom without one. You don't have a tuxedo, do you, dear?"

"No, but—He can just wear his Sunday clothes, can't he?"

"Heavens, no, he'll look like a hick. Well," Edna said, as if reconsidering, "I suppose he could wear his Sunday clothes. People would understand."

When people in Humble County *understand* something, it's bound to be something along the lines of Vernon Lice's bleary eyes and whiskey breath Sunday morning, or the purple finger-shaped bruises that Cathy McCay has on her arms whenever her boyfriend comes home on leave. Above all else, you do not want to do something that will be *understood* in Humble County.

"Where do you get a tux?"

Edna couldn't help a genuine smile at the desperation that flavored her good friend's voice. "You rent them. The boys drive into Milledgeville and there's a place to rent them."

"Oh." Relief began to dawn. "How much are they?"

"About fifty dollars."

"Fifty dollars!"

"Some are as much as seventy-five. And then, of course, there's the corsage."

"Oh, dear, fifty—and the corsage. Oh, dear. How much is a corsage?" Ruby mumbled, deflating like a punctured tire. Her Howell's Funeral Home Fan wobbled weakly in her grasp.

Edna pretended not to hear what Ruby was saying. "Mr. Thigpen!" she called out, as the minister left the church, "lovely sermon, oh, lovely. Those Philistines certainly had it coming."

"Where do you get a corsage?" Ruby asked. "Is that in Milledgeville, too?"

"What? Oh, yes. You have to go to a special florist where they'll dye one for you."

"Dye it? I thought a corsage was a flower."

Edna attempted a tinkling laugh, like a wind chime in a summer breeze, but the effect was hoarser and brassier than she would have wished. "Oh, dear, yes, a corsage is a flower, but you have to dye it to match the girl's dress." Ruby's vacant stare said she still did not understand. "Go to Ellen's house and find out what color dress she's wearing," Edna explained. "Then you'll know what color to have them dye the corsage."

"Is that very expensive?" Ruby asked, and hated herself for asking.

"Well, it's not cheap," Edna said merrily. "But you only go to the prom once, you know."

Ruby walked to the Buick and sat behind the driver's wheel. In spite of the chilliness of the air outside, the harsh winter sunlight had heated the inside of the car, filling it with the stink of hot vinyl upholstery. Ruby did not start it up right away because she couldn't see to drive through the hot tears that filled her eyes.

Ruby got home, grateful that Earl was out walking with Ellen. She did not want him to see her sad. She had driven home in a kind of stupor. Except for bowling shoes, she had never rented clothing in her life, nor heard of such an unlikely thing being done. And she had never paid more than ten dollars for an entire outfit. For the first time she foresaw the unthinkable expense of high living. She clenched her real hand until tears rose in her eyes again.

She washed and dried her face, and dabbed on a little sweet-smelling face powder to cover the tear tracks. She studied the result in the mirror over her dresser. "Whatever else, this ain't going to turn out like Santa Claus," she said, pleased that her reflection looked back with an expression of serene determination. "Now, first thing to do is see about that corsage."

She had some white gloves that she put on to make a good impression on Mrs. Raley, and from the top of the closet got a tiny pink purse, which was highly impractical—too small to carry much more than a Kleenex—but very elegant. She did not have high heels, but she wiped her black flats with WD-40 to make them shine.

She took four deep breaths before she opened her front door to cross the street. "One for the money," she said, "two for the show, three to get ready, and four to go." With that, she opened the door and strode to the houses on the rich side of the street.

"Ruby, hello, what can I do for you?" Mrs. Raley said when she answered the door.

"Hello," Ruby began, suddenly flummoxed to realize she could not for the life of her recall Mrs. Raley's first name. She clutched her tiny pink handbag in front of her.

"Thank you," Mrs. Raley said, about to close the door. "But we're quite happy with the church we already attend."

"No, it's not that. I've come over about Earl's corsage."

"I beg your pardon?"

"I mean," Ruby said, attempting a tinkling wind-chime laugh, but succeeding no better than Edna had, "I want to see what color Ellen's prom dress is. We need to get a corsage to match it."

"Oh, of course, Ruby. Come in." Ruby followed Ellen's mother past the Raley's fancy avocado kitchen smelling of Top Job with its up-to-date Sunbeam appliances to the back of the house. Imagine living across the street from someone for twenty years and forgetting her name! A sewing machine sat open in Ellen's bedroom with cloth and supplies at the ready. "We just started on it. We're using a Butterick pattern, and we got the fabric from Milledgeville." Mrs. Raley held up a bolt of blue cloth.

"It's pretty—" Ruby said, still trying to recall Mrs. Raley's name.

"It's Quianna."

"Of course! I must've gone through a tunnel, there. Quianna, that's right. Well, it's very pretty, Quianna."

"This is the pattern," Mrs. Raley said, somewhat uncertainly, handing Ruby the pattern in a white package.

Ruby lay down her purse and studied the picture on the

label. "It don't—doesn't have straps, Quianna," she said. "It's going to be hard to pin a corsage on that."

"Well—"

"But I don't suppose it wouldn't take but a second to sew on a couple of straps," Ruby suggested. "Well, I know the color of the fabric now. I'll be heading back home, but sometime you *must* come over for tea." Ruby improvised the crowning remark of sophistication from something she'd heard about fancy English ladies enjoying tea and biscuits together. The custom had struck her as marvelously luxurious, to sit drinking cool, refreshing tumblers of iced tea while eating hot, fresh biscuits and waiting for the men to come home from hunting with a nice plump fox for supper.

That wasn't so bad, Ruby told herself as she headed across the street. And I'm sure I made a good impression on Quianna. What a lovely name. I bet Earl won't have to get a blue corsage, anyway, a white one would match well enough. And as for the tuxedo—She'd nearly reached her house before she realized she'd left her elegant pink handbag at the Raleys'.

This time, she didn't knock, but opened the front door slightly and stuck her head in, and was about to call out "Quianna," when she heard a tinkling, wind-chime laugh, exactly the sort of laugh Ruby and Edna had attempted earlier that day; she was on the phone.

"—by Mulvaney," she laughed, "dressed up as a cross between Jackie O and Aunt Bea. She had these white gloves on, and this pink handbag, honestly, it was the funniest—" Ruby stood there, frozen in the open doorway. "I thought she'd come over to give me a pamphlet. She said—she said—" Mrs. Raley could not speak for laughter, "I could sew some straps on a strapless gown, like it was a pair of overalls. Can you imagine?

And wait—on top of that, I was telling her the cloth was Quianna Knit, and she thought my name was Quianna! She called me Quianna the whole time!"

—

A week later, when she was driving the Buick home from the grocery store, Ruby saw that Deborah Howell, the undertaker's wife, was a having a yard sale. Ruby's eye fell on the most elegant frock coat she'd ever seen, hanging like a dignified crow from an aluminum rack by the driveway.

Deborah, in orange pants that very nearly matched her hair, sat in a folding chair, a Virginia Slim in one hand and a Tab in the other. "—so anyway, Sam still hasn't gotten back from his Friday night poker game," she told a potential customer. This was ten o'clock Saturday morning. "And I said to myself, I might as well have myself a yard sale and clear out some of this junk." She gestured with her cigarette at the souvenir ashtrays from Daytona Beach stacked on a card table.

Ruby examined the coat. It not only had tails and fancy pointy lapels, but a matching pair of pants. She admired the sheen of the black stripe that ran down the sides of the pants. "How much is this suit?"

"Twelve-fifty."

Ruby's shoulders slumped. Purchasing canned vegetables— what had possessed her to go to the extra expense of *LeSueur* Peas?—and frozen fryer parts had given her precisely a dollar and three cents left over. Another customer came up to Deborah pointing at the price sticker on a clock radio, "You want four-fifty for this? That seems a little high for a clock radio."

"It's the new kind," Deborah explained, justifying the price, "you don't have to figure out what the hands are pointing at to tell what time it is. The numbers flip over by themselves."

"I know how to tell time," the customer huffed. "Four-fifty still seems steep."

"Could you come down a little on your price for this frock coat?" Ruby asked.

"All prices are firm," Deborah said, answering them both at once. Being married to the undertaker had made her a stiff negotiator.

Ruby got back in her Buick and drove home. "I'm going to make this happen, I'm going to make this happen, I'm going to make this happen," she said to herself. Thanks to Earl's job and her envelope stuffing, there was just enough money to pay current bills, old debts, and a little left over for Earl to take Ellen to the movies once in a while, but the Mulvaneys still didn't have twelve-fifty all-at-once money. She was so desperate, she even thought of getting in touch with Harry Holton, but no. When she got home, she thought of a way to make it happen.

The Mulvaney Buick pulled up to the Howells' yard sale for the second time that day. "Have you sold that suit yet?" Ruby asked, though she could see it still hanging from its rack. The sun shone more brightly than it had earlier that day, and the ashtrays on display glittered like rock candy.

"Not yet. Are you interested?" Deborah asked, a flip-flop dangling from the toes of one pedicured foot. She noticed Ruby was holding a brown paper bag.

"Might be. But look here. I got a clock radio just like the one you're selling," Ruby extracted a clock from the bag, "—only newer—and I'm letting it go for three dollars."

The heads of two other yard-sale browsers turned.

"Ruby Mulvaney," Deborah Howell whispered angrily, "are you trying to undersell me at my own yard sale?"

"I'll trade it for that suit."

"No deal."

"OK, then, I'll sell it to you for two-fifty. That way you got two clocks you can sell for four-fifty and make an extra two dollars." Deborah considered this offer. "Or I'll trade it for the suit."

"I'll just buy it," Deborah said. She put her cigarette in her mouth and held her Tab between her knees as she reached into her purse. "Can't believe I'm doing this," she said through clenched teeth.

Ruby counted her money. "How much is that suit again?"

"Twelve-fifty."

"You couldn't come down a little bit?"

"How much?"

"Three fifty-three?"

"Not for that suit. My first husband was buried in it."

Ruby tapped her foot and considered her next move. Deborah saw a look of eerie determination flash in Ruby's face. She could have sworn she heard Ruby mutter something angrily about Santa Claus.

Then an idea came to Ruby, a terrible idea probably from the devil himself. What happens next is kind of shocking, and the only explanation I can think of is that between her love for Earl, Edna Edwards' prodding, and the humiliation at the Raleys', some gear or flywheel or spring got bent inside of Ruby, and she went off. Anyway, she got in her car, drove into town and then out to the county's edge, where Stump Road dead-ends at a culvert. Her tires scrunched against the gravel and sand as she parked between the Sheriff's patrol car and a familiar dirty Pontiac. Sam Howell's hearse was already there, and a late-model Lincoln. Even though she'd never been to Mort's place before, she'd known just where to find it.

Over the edge of the bank and down a little rabbit trail sat a slightly cockeyed single-wide with mildew growing up its sides in pointed fingers, as if it had been scorched in a fire. A heap of bald tires, crushed beer cans, and naked chicken bones lay conveniently close on one side, and on the other side a neglected bass boat grew a mimosa sapling in its stern. Ruby didn't step down into the musty dark air below for a little while. Did she really have the nerve to go through with this? Thinking back on the Quianna episode, it really seemed funny instead of embarrassing. Earl could wear an ordinary suit to the prom, couldn't he? A little voice warned her, "Don't do this. You're making a mistake." But that voice was in the passenger seat; the voice on the driver's side had made up its mind already.

While she was still standing in the bright sunlight of the gravel road, looking down at Mort's trailer, she said, "I know You can forgive anyone who asks. Only they got to really want forgiveness, be really sorry for what they did, wish they hadn't done it and be willing to take it back." She bit her lip. "But I can't be sorry for this thing. I know it's a sin, but I ain't sorry, and I ain't going to take it back. Some things you just can't help." She took one step onto the rabbit trail. "But forgive me anyway, if You can."

Careful of her hip and knee, she made her way down the rabbit trail, as scrabbly loose rocks slid under her sensible shoes. She knocked at the trailer door until Mort opened it, blinking his bleary eyes in the shady light. The sleeves of his v-neck T-shirt did not quite reach the tan line on his arms. "I'm sorry, missus," he said, and Ruby took a step back from a gust of beer breath. "I don't know where your husband is."

"It ain't my husband I'm looking for," she said, unable to keep her voice from shaking. "I'm looking for a card game."

Mort's eyebrows rose in surprise. "Well, we got a card game in here."

"Hello, hello," Ruby said shyly as she entered the wood-paneled room that served as dining room, living room, and kitchen combined. The other players—Jimmy Wiggins, Sheriff King, Judge Hathorne, and Sam Howell—sat around a dinette. Limp potato chips partly filled a communal Murphy bowl on one side of the table. The remains of other chips lay strewn under the chairs, ground into Mort's ratty brown carpet. Empty beer cans were everywhere: on the table, under the chairs, balanced on the pile of dirty laundry on the duct-taped vinyl recliner in front of the TV.

Money wads of various sizes sat in front of each of the players.

"What are you playing?" Ruby asked.

"Five-card stud," Mort said. He introduced Ruby and said, "She wants to play cards."

"You got any money?" Jimmy asked.

"Three dollars."

"Deal her in, then," the judge ruled. "Dollar to ante."

"Any wild cards?" Ruby asked.

Some questions are just too dumb to answer. The sheriff dealt two cards down, and flipped the last one up. Ruby had a two of clubs showing. "I'll bet two dollars."

"It's Mort to open," Jimmy explained. He could not peel his eyes off Earl's mother. She was much prettier than he'd imagined. "He's got the high card."

"Oh."

"Check," said Mort.

The house smelled of sour dishrags and mildew. Even the air seemed dirty. "I'll bet two dollars," Ruby said.

Everyone called. The sheriff dealt the next card face-up. Ruby had a five and a two. The judge had two fives.

"Five dollars," the judge said.

"Call," the sheriff said.

"Raise five," said Mort. "That's ten to you, missus."

Ruby began to shake and could not stop shaking. "I don't have any more money."

"That's why they call it gambling," the judge philosophized. "Ten to you, Jimmy. Are you in or out?"

"Wait," Ruby said. It came out in a squeak; she said it again, and this time it came out in a squawk, "Wait. I ain't done yet." She looked at her cards. The moment had come to prove just how much Earl's happiness meant to her. "Where's your restroom?"

Mort pointed to the short hallway past the vinyl recliner and the TV with its aluminum rabbit ears. There aren't many places to tuck away a bathroom in a single-wide.

"I'll be right back," she said. "Don't go on without me." She got her purse and took two steps toward the bathroom, but then paused, turned around, and picked up her cards. "I'm taking these with me."

The men looked at each other in surprise.

"Now, wait a minute," the judge said, "you can't—"

"I am not having you look at my cards while I'm gone," Ruby said, summoning as much frosty dignity as she could to her trembling voice.

"Oh, go on, let her," Jimmy said. "What do you think she's going to do, cheat us? Go on, ma'am."

"I don't know how she thinks she's staying in the game," the judge said after she left, "unless she's going to pull money out of the toilet."

Two minutes later she returned to her seat and put her bet on the table. "Call," she said.

Stunned silence for a few beats, then someone said, "Ma'am, that glass eye ain't worth nothing here."

"It ain't the glass eye," Ruby said. "It's what I'd have to do to get it back." Her voice was as cold and hard as the eye itself.

The men exchanged glances of amazement. Jimmy said, "I'm folding. This ain't fitting."

The sheriff folded, too.

Judge Hathorne considered. Was she bluffing? Ruby's blue eyes—one in her head, and one on the table—returned his stare. "Are you in, Judge?" Mort asked. "It's five dollars to you."

"Call," the judge said.

The last card was dealt facedown. Mort and the judge checked. There was no way to increase the size of the pot any more than Ruby's glass eye had already done. And so they turned over their cards. Judge Hathorne had tens and fives. Mort had three sixes. And Ruby, shaking and crying, as she retrieved her eye with one hand and swept her winnings toward her with the other, had four twos.

And that's how Ruby got enough money to buy the frock coat, along with her clock radio, and still give Earl money to buy Ellen a corsage.

But as it turned out, Earl and Ellen never went to the prom.

CHAPTER SEVEN

arl had come over to Ellen's house just about every day for nearly two months in a row, and they'd walked every day to the cemetery, and there'd been other dates at the movies—without Mr. Raley—and Ellen had grown accustomed to having Earl around, but one Wednesday in early Spring, even though Ellen sat patiently reading on her front stoop, Earl didn't show up from drilling with the Volunteers. She'd just begun a new book, but because she constantly looked up to see if Earl's Buick were coming down the street, she seemed unlikely to ever finish it. She'd turn her attention to the page and read determinedly for a while, only to discover that she'd begun again at the second paragraph. Mr. Dashwood, having had a son by a previous marriage, had him again. And the current Mrs. Dashwood, who had given him three daughters, seemed unable to do anything besides give him the same three daughters over and over again.

Finally, leaving the Dashwoods to their endlessly recurring offspring, Ellen walked across the street and rang Earl's doorbell. She knew Earl wasn't home because the faded blue Buick wasn't parked in the driveway, but maybe Ruby could tell her where he was. She rang a second time and waited for an answer without result, so she tried knocking. Still nothing, so she went to the front of the house and peered through the dusty-smelling window screen into the living room, her hands cupped over her eyes. Two end tables guarding a vacant sofa; the silent TV facing away; a large box of unstuffed envelopes waiting on the floor; a few lonely stuffed envelopes on the coffee table. She satisfied herself the house was empty, so wherever Earl was, he was with his mother.

The next day when Ellen visited Earl's house, she learned where he'd been. Earl, who'd stayed home from work that day, grinned—his first smile in forty-eight hours—when he saw Ellen at the door. Ruby, one foot wrapped in dry white gauze, the other bare and wet, sat on the couch, and sitting in a chair beside her with a large black Bible in his lap, a man Ellen had never seen before overfilled an armchair. A basin of soapy water sat in a puddle on the floor, and the knees of Earl's jeans were soaked.

"I hope I'm not—" Ellen began, and before she could finish, the large man was out of his chair, saying, "Come in, come in."

Ruby, who did not get up, waved her bandaged foot at Ellen. "Hey, honey. Come on in. You ain't interrupting. We was just finishing up some foot-washing."

"Are you okay, ma'am?" Ellen asked.

"Yes, Lord, yes," Ruby waved her foot again. "Two of my

toes had to come off. No circulation. Don't you worry about it, though, just more room in my shoes," she laughed. "Have a seat, honey. Have you met Mr. Thigpen? He's our minister."

"Reverend," said Ellen, shaking his hand.

"Just 'mister,'" said Mr. Thigpen. "We don't believe no one's 'reverend' but the Lord."

"Oh."

"Ellen," said Ruby, "I sure am sorry to keep Earl away from you yesterday. That boy thinks an awful lot of you." Earl's face got as red as a flannel shirt and nearly as warm, but Ruby didn't seem to notice. "Well, I'm going to go to bed, now. I'm tuckered out." She rose to her feet and got on her crutches, and Earl assisted her back to her room. "Don't you fret about me," Ruby called back for Ellen's benefit, "I'll be turning cartwheels before you know."

When Earl returned, Mr. Thigpen regarded him with an earnest stare that immediately made Earl uncomfortable. "Your mother is a great woman, Earl. I truly admire her," Mr. Thigpen said. "I'm sure she is glory bound, but sometimes, you know, I'm not so sure about you. I've been praying for you."

Earl fidgeted under the itchy sensation of having been prayed for.

"You know, Earl," Mr. Thigpen said. "Your mother knows something you may not know. I wonder if you know what it is."

"No sir," Earl said uncomfortably. Earl braced himself for the hard sell; Mr. Thigpen was preparing to make his Best Offer. Unlike Jimmy, who had a different car for every taste, Mr. Thigpen had only one thing on his lot, and he pushed it with the grim tenacity of Mr. Moss.

"Your mother's suffered many tribulations, but they've taught her one thing. Nothing in this old world can last. There's only one outcome with everything you love in this world; you will lose it. Everything you love," Mr. Thigpen repeated, "whether it's a fancy car, your pretty girlfriend," he nodded at Ellen, and Earl's face heated again, "or even your own dear mother. You have to lose it all one day. You'll either outlive it, or die first and leave it behind. That's the only two things possible that can happen. Doesn't that thought break your heart?"

"No, sir."

"Of course it does. But sometimes the only way Jesus can find room in a heart is if He breaks it open. That's what your mother knows. I wish you could learn that."

"Yes, sir."

"Because in my heart," Mr. Thigpen touched his chest, "I don't think you've learned it."

"No, sir. Yes, sir." Earl wanted to please Mr. Thigpen, but he figured he'd never learn what the minister hoped he would. Earl was too much his father's son to have any hope in the next world if it required giving up hope on this one. It seemed a much more sensible policy to keep picking black and doubling his bets.

"I just want you to think about it. No, I want you to pray about it. Will you do that for me?"

"Yes, sir."

"I'll be praying for you."

"Thank you, sir."

After Mr. Thigpen had left, Earl showed Ellen the frock coat his mother had gotten him for the prom. "Do you like it?" he asked.

"Sure."

"Are you sure?" he asked. She didn't seem pleased. "You don't mind that it's used, do you?"

"No, I like it."

"Really?"

"I like it. Quit asking."

Earl walked Ellen home. Through the sweet air birds called to each other from the trees, which were just then breaking into leaf.

They kissed. "Thanks for coming by," Earl said.

"Oh, that's okay. I wanted to see you," Ellen said.

Earl kissed her again without asking permission, and Ellen pulled away. "Earl, could you drive me into Milledgeville tomorrow when you go to work?"

"Well, I'd have to get up extra early. But tomorrow's a school day."

"I know. I'm skipping class, so you can't tell anybody." Earl read Ellen's discomfort with her own dishonesty in her face; she couldn't hold her eyes up to meet his. "Belks is having a one-day sale, and I need to get some shoes. I've got it all figured out. I'll tell Mom you're driving me to school and I've got Beta Club in the afternoon. That way she won't be suspicious. You can pick me up at Belks when you get off work. Will you do that?"

"Sure." In a wrestling match between Earl's natural honesty and his eagerness to please Ellen, honesty got pinned in a second flat. They kissed again, and she hugged him a long time.

The next morning Earl picked her up as arranged. She stowed her textbooks on the vinyl floor mat behind the passenger seat of the Buick, and they drove into Milledgeville. Earl noticed that the prospect of getting new shoes did not inspire Ellen to lively conversation, and so they drove most of the way without talking. He dropped her off in front of the Belks at the Milledgeville Mall, and said, "I'll pick you up here about an hour after I get off work, OK? It'll take me a while to get here."

"That'd be great," Ellen said, making a big smile.

"I don't think Belks is open yet."

"I don't mind waiting."

"Well, okay. See you."

"See you."

As soon as the Buick was out of sight, Ellen walked up to the corner, where she turned right. The air smelled of car exhaust, and the day already promised to be unforgivingly warm, but it was only a two-mile walk along the grassy verge of the road to the side of town where all the doctors were. The blue hospital sign told her she was heading in the right direction.

Being an avid reader of books, Ellen often imagined her life itself was a book, and she the main character. At one time she used to speculate whether the book of her life would turn out to be an interesting one or a boring one, but more recently she'd begun to wonder more if it would be happy or sad. Maybe it was working out to be a quirky romance where the hero discovers that the one person on earth who truly appreciates her unique and special qualities is the boy next door, a knight-errant disguised as a car mechanic in red coveralls and broken glasses. On the other hand, the book of her life might turn out to be one of those stories you almost couldn't bear to read, where the author takes a cruel satisfaction in dumping a truckload of consequences on top of a character for making just one mistake.

As she reached Walnut Street, and crossed the corner to the Family Practice Center, she felt as if she were opening the chapter that would let her know which kind of book she was in.

That afternoon, Earl picked her up at the Belks as pre-arranged. "Didn't you buy no shoes?" he asked.

"They were sold out," was Ellen's answer. So improbable that Earl didn't even challenge it.

Ellen had seen the doctor first thing in the morning, and it was a good job she had, because it gave her plenty of time to compose herself and dry her face before Earl came to get her. Now all she needed to do was to master herself to keep back the tears burning behind her eyes. Thinking he must have done something wrong—it's that frock coat, he told himself—Earl didn't say anything. And Ellen didn't say anything, and so the three of them rode home in silence.

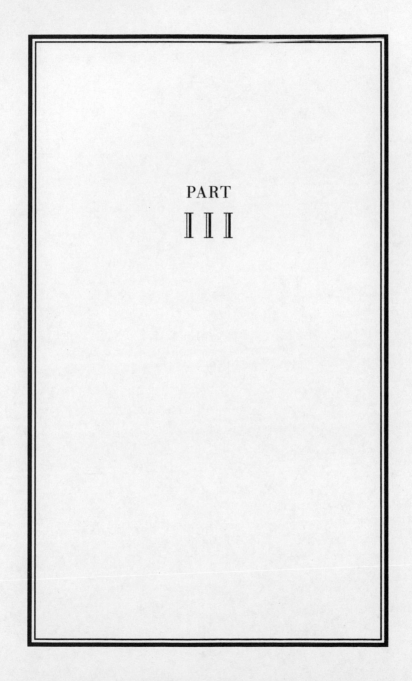

PART

III

CHAPTER EIGHT

T he next afternoon Jimmy noticed Earl seemed out of sorts. He was still everything a good mechanic should be—if not more—but he wielded his torque wrench with a heavy heart and when he drained a crankcase, he did so joylessly. It being Saturday, Jimmy Wiggins saw no harm in doing something to cheer up his favorite employee. He said to himself, "This damn gasoline shortage's got everybody spooked anyway." Prices had recently soared to seventy-five cents a gallon. "There ain't been a prospect on the lot since Tuesday. I expect I might as well close early, and give the customers a chance to grow back." So he gave Mr. Moss and Wayne the other mechanic the rest of the day off, and found Earl and T. J. talking in the garage. "Boys," Jimmy told them, "I'm taking you to Daisy's Diner for a beer."

"I need to see Ellen," Earl said. "I think she's upset about something."

"Boy!" the word came out of Jimmy's mouth as an explosion. "What have we told you about clinging to that girl all the time like a sandspur?"

"That's right," T. J. averred solemnly, "you've got to make a girl—what?"

"Wait," Earl said.

"Wait," T. J. said.

And so it was settled—Earl told himself he'd leave after just one chili dog and go see Ellen. As they entered Daisy's, T. J. greeted Roy King, Humble County's Sheriff. Sheriff King looked up from a corner table, where he had been studying a bug moving around on the grease-stained kraft paper.

"Hey, T. J., Jimmy. Things slow at the car lot?" King wore a perpetual hound-dog gloom, as melancholy as only an idealistic lawman can be in when he's in a place like Humble County where official duty and moral principle run in opposite directions.

"Slow?" Jimmy said. "They're petrified! Things couldn't be slower if you nailed 'em down with a hammer."

Daisy came from the kitchen, her full face glistening with sweat. "Here you go, Sheriff, I counted it twice to make sure," she said and handed Sheriff King a fat envelope labeled "Hathorne." He took it with a look of disgust and put it in his hip pocket.

Jimmy dragged a chair back from a table and sat. "Daisy, could you whip us up some onion rings and three Polish sausage dogs? And do you have any venison chili to put on those?"

"My pickup hit a three-pointer just yesterday afternoon," Daisy said, her plump dark hand writing down the order on a green pad as she smoked her cigarette.

"Deer take their lives in their hands when they move to Humble

County," Sheriff King said sourly, lifting his gaze from the bug in front of him, which Earl now saw was a bee. The sheriff was referring to the way Daisy got her venison. Some years back he'd cited her for hunting out of season; the Humble lawmen might be willing to close an eye on a bent liquor law, but they were dead serious about hunting season. In jail Daisy realized that while it was illegal to hunt deer in June, no one ever went to jail if a deer died of natural causes, for example in a car wreck. Since then, Daisy's rusty Dodge had been involved in numerous accidents, accidents invariably fatal for an unlucky deer and which always seemed to occur, Sheriff King noted, when Daisy's freezer ran low. He never voiced his suspicion that she used her truck because it was cheaper than ammo, but every time the subject of Daisy's chili came up, he was full of dark mumblings about ordering an autopsy for the next deer who went home to Jesus.

The door opened and let in an out-of-town man in a blue suit, blue pants, and a blue tie. If you need to ask how the patrons knew he was from out of town, it isn't worth explaining. "Do you know," he asked the gathering, "the way to State Road 12 to Warthen?"

"There ain't no State Road 12 into Warthen," Jimmy said helpfully.

"I saw it on a road sign," the man in blue said.

"It's a lot easier putting up a sign than building a road," Sheriff King said, tilting his head to one side like a quizzical dog. "That road was planned, but never completed."

"And the county never got around to removing the signs," T. J. said.

"Daisy, hand me a map so we can show this fellow how to get into Warthen," King said.

"I ain't got no maps," Daisy said. She set a tray of sausage dogs and onion rings on the table between Jimmy, T. J., and Earl; Earl's glasses fogged with steam from the venison chili.

"Toss me a grease pencil, then," Sheriff King said. "I'll draw a map on the tablecloth."

"Would you like a beer while you get directions?" Daisy offered.

"I never drink it," Blue Suit said sweetly but without being uppish. "I know Jesus himself drank wine, but personally I would have respected him just a little bit more if he didn't."

"Now this here is West Haynes." The sheriff drew a black wiggle on the kraft paper. He stopped to brush aside the bee. "Damn bee is getting in my way."

"Don't kill it," Blue Suit said. "I love bees. We used to keep them when I was little."

"No kidding?" said the sheriff. "This one's drunk. He's just been going in circles."

"Strange." Blue Suit bent so close to the bee, one good snuff and he'd have inhaled it. At length he said, "This bee isn't drunk. He's dancing." Sheriff King gave a half-laugh, unsure if Blue Suit was joking. "That's how bees communicate," Blue Suit explained. "Their dance is a code; in the hive it's how they tell each other where the good flowers are."

Through a mouthful of onion ring Jimmy pointed out, "But that bee ain't in the hive."

Blue Suit admitted this and pondered. "He must be trying to tell how to get back home."

"What?" two voices, Jimmy's and the sheriff's, said at once.

"Don't you see? He's flown too far to get back, and he's trying to tell us where he lives."

Daisy's was silent as everyone considered the bee's strange predicament.

"Too bad no one here can understand bee-dancing," Jimmy said, almost hopefully.

"But I can understand it," Blue Suit said. "It's simple when you know how."

Jimmy looked at the others. Their gazes answered his. Wild honey! Granted, honey could be had at Miller's Grocery—honey in jars with the wax comb inside, honey in squeezable bears with yellow hats—but nothing beats the taste of honey earned by right of conquest.

Everyone in Daisy's gathered around the little table. "What's this bee here saying?"

"See how slow he's going?" Blue Suit said. "The slower he goes, the further away it is. I'd say the food, in this case the hive, is at least thirty-five yards off. Look how he cuts straight across—there now! See that? That's pointing to the hive." T. J. ran to a window and looked out over the trestle in the direction the bee had indicated.

"Earl," Jimmy said, "go help him look. Two people can see twice as far as one."

"That's no use," the sheriff said. "He just said the hive's more than thirty-five yards off." Then he sketched a rough map of the upper side of Humble County with the grease pencil. "The hive must be past the trestle off Old Stump Road." He x-marked the approximate location.

"We're going to need something more precise than that," Jimmy said.

"The bee can give us more directions when we're there," the sheriff explained. "What've we got to carry a bee?"

"I got this." Daisy produced an empty quart mason jar from behind the counter.

King unscrewed the lid and carefully pushed the bee into the jar with the heel of his hand. "We'll need to punch some holes in this." Daisy reached into the cleavage behind her yellow blouse and brought out a bowie knife. The sheriff jabbed three gashes in the lid.

"But now if someone could direct me to Warthen—" Blue Suit said.

"You're coming with us," Jimmy said. "You're the only one who understands the bee."

"But I need to get to Warthen."

"It'll be easier to tell you how to get there from the Stump Road," the sheriff said, rolling up the kraft paper map with a brisk crackle, into a brown tube. "Daisy, we're taking the tablecloth."

"Sheriff," Daisy ordered, "you all bring me back some honey, too."

"Okay, but how will we get there? I can't use my patrol car except on official business." A brief discussion revealed they couldn't fit in Jimmy's truck, and Daisy's had a busted headlight.

Blue Suit quivered as all eyes turned to him. "Let's take my car," he said finally.

Earl, Jimmy, and T. J. squeezed in the backseat, which was already crowded with a mauve binder, satin, silk and lace strips, and a cylindrical pink-and-white striped box. "I'm carrying that box for a friend who's in ladies' hats," Blue Suit said. Sheriff King got in and closed the door. "I'm in ladies' underwear."

"Personally, I don't mind," Sheriff King said, "but that's not something I'd broadcast."

Earl opened the binder. It was full of women in brassieres and panties. This was before the Sunday paper began running those risqué Sears lingerie ads, so Earl and T. J. examined the pictures with understandable absorption all the way to Old Stump Road.

"God did the first surgery in history," T. J. said, "and did it without antiseptic, too. Put Adam to sleep and pulled a rib off him, that's right. That's how he made Eve. When Adam woke up, he took one look and said, 'Whoa, man!' And that's why we call them a wo-man."

The car pulled onto the shoulder of Stump Road and they piled out. Sheriff King unfolded the map on the hood. "I calculate the hive's in this general area," his said, waving his hand at the pinewoods stretched out beneath them. "We need further instructions from the bee."

Earl imagined the faint beep-beep-beep warning of a truckload of consequences backing up toward him. But it was too late; he'd made his decision. He told himself Ellen would be pleased with some wild honey as he upturned the jar over the map. Landing on its back, the yellow and black navigator righted itself and at once obliged them with a dance.

"Yes," Blue Suit exclaimed, "We're much closer now! It looks like—" The bee lit off.

"Stop!" the sheriff ordered, but it was too late, and they took off down the hill after it.

The flight path of a bee to its hive will encounter no solid obstacle whatsoever, if you're a bee. If you're larger than a bee, however, it intersects every bramble bush, muddy sinkhole, and sharp-toothed stump in the region. Except for T. J., who arrived without a speck of mud on his tangerine-colored shirt, the little band looked as if they'd taken turns sliding down a twenty-foot cheese grater into a tar pit. But the journey was worth it, caked with filth and lashed by branches as they were, when they crested a hill and saw on a high branch of a tree below them the great thrumming hive! For a moment, as the poet says, they stared at each other in wild surmise.

"There it is!" and "There it is!"

Wild surmise became tamer, however, as they weighed the problem of getting at a hive hanging on a fifteen-foot-high branch. Humming filled the air with a low continuous threat.

"I've got an idea," Blue Suit said. "Find some good-sized rocks while I go for supplies." Using sticks to chop into the red clay of the hillside, they gathered a pile of fist-sized rocks. Blue Suit returned with the striped hatbox and several samples of merchandise. "I brought a couple so we could see what worked best. I figured a C-cup for greatest range and a D-cup for maximum payload."

⁓

Earl, T. J., Sheriff King, and Blue Suit rode back shrouded in grim contemplation. Jimmy, however, was effusive.

"We're heroes! Heroes! Men," he said turning around to Earl and T. J., "I'll never forget the sight of y'all drawing back that slingshot and letting those bees have it with both barrels! And putting the hatbox under the hive to catch it!" Jimmy said, looking at Blue Suit, "Genius!" The hatbox in Earl's lap buzzed only faintly, but pure insect fury bristled through the sides, and he could almost feel their stingers pricking through the pink and white stripes.

"It would have been even more genius if it'd worked," Sheriff King muttered.

"Only missed by an inch, and Blue Suit snatched it up like a football player. He had the lid slapped on before the bees hardly saw him coming! You are a hero, man!"

"Fangs," Blue Suit managed to say between swollen lips.

By unanimous decision, the heroes did not bring the hatbox

inside Daisy's, but left it on the black railroad ties just outside the door.

"Where's the hon—Oh, Jesus." Daisy said when they entered. Blue Suit's face looked as if tiny moles had been at work underneath it. "I'll get some meat tenderizer."

"It's good for bee stings," Jimmy said, answering the panicked look in Blue Suit's eyes.

"Now we got to figure out how to get the honey out of the hive," Earl said.

"I vote we throw the hive in the river and buy some honey in the store," the sheriff said.

"Lean back, and close your eyes, sir," Daisy instructed and began sprinkling white powder over Blue Suit's face. "Where is that honey, anyway?"

Just then, Judge Hathorne, tired of waiting for his monthly envelope, drove up. Determined to give that derelict sheriff a piece of his mind, he walked across the trestle, and was about to open the door when he noticed a pink and white striped box sitting near the entrance.

"It looks like someone's dropped off a package for Daisy. A hat, I expect." The judge picked it up with the kindly intention of completing the delivery. "This is just like Christmas." He lifted the lid to take a peek as he went inside.

⁓

Earl escaped with only a few stings, having fled through the backdoor along with Jimmy, T. J., Daisy, the sheriff, and Blue Suit. Six bees managed to fly into the collar and up the cuffs of Earl's coveralls, and so relieved themselves of needing to keep up. Passengers in his clothing, they picked their spots and stung him at leisure, as he stumbled out the backdoor, tripped trying to run on the railroad ties, and limped away on his sore knee. Their dying act was leaving stingers in two parallel lines running diagonally down his back—leaving marks like something had walked across him and left little red footprints. Their fuzzy corpses rolled around in the folds of red cloth until Earl shook them out of his coveralls that night.

For his part, Hathorne showed considerable presence of mind in dropping the hatbox as soon as he saw what was in it and running back out the front door, thereby getting stung only a few times himself. Once the hive was safely shut inside, Daisy wrote "Closed for Bees" on the back of one of Sheriff King's citations, which she safety-pinned to the screen door until the fumigator could come out. Understandably, Earl did not visit Ellen the afternoon of the honey-hunt, but the following afternoon he dropped by.

Mr. Raley answered the door; his eyes were red-rimmed and swollen. "I'm sorry, Earl," he said, sternly, but not unkindly. "Ellen can't talk now. Let me tell you about this later. OK?"

Something in Mr. Raley's voice sent a handful of lug nuts to the pit of Earl's stomach; the disastrous bee chase, already half-forgotten, boiled up in Earl's mind on a sudden wave of shame. Earl looked over Mr. Raley's shoulder through the kitchen door. Ellen and her mother sat at the table with Troy Badcock and his parents. Ellen lifted her head and met Earl's eyes with a forlorn face he couldn't read. Earl went back across the street mystified, scarcely noticing his sore knee or the stings he'd gotten from his passenger bees, but fearing some unknown doom. Some crucial thing had happened in Ellen's life without his being there. If you've ever gone gallivanting when your better angel warned you against it, and then found out that while you'd been off amusing yourself with friends and honeybees, you'd left your sweetheart to face the cross alone—if you've ever done that, as I say, and I hope you have not—you'll know just how Earl felt: a mixture of nausea and heat—as if his whole body was blushing—an echoing silence in his ears, and the weird sensation that the world wasn't real, that if he walked over to touch that line of trees on the horizon, he'd find they were expertly—but unconvincingly—painted on a backdrop of sky.

"Sugar, don't let the door slam behind you," Ruby said when Earl came in the house.

Earl sat on the couch beside her and stared at the wall above the TV. Every last wall in their house had chipped paint, he realized for the first time as he looked around, every last wall. It was true. Roy Mulvaney, no master craftsman, had unwittingly painted latex over oil without applying the proper primer. The walls, which had once been bright white, but were now the smeared gray of a bad tooth, had chipped away from corners and ceilings, revealing the duller darker yellow wall beneath, which had originally been painted in something optimistically called "Daisy Land" but had long since faded to old nicotine-stain color.

Earl stood up and began to peel.

"Earl, what are you doing to that door?"

"This paint," he began, unable to explain further why the sight of it so upset him. Starting from the upper corner of the hall door, Earl peeled back a loose tongue of dull white and slipped one finger under it, stretching a dead layer of paint away from the door. Working at the freed corner, he'd soon torn off a long rectangular slough of paint that hung from the door like dead skin peeled away from a sunburn. Earl kept at it, pulling the loose latex flesh by the handful off the door's drab skeleton.

"Earl, what are you doing?" Ruby asked. "Stop that. If you pick at it, you know it won't heal."

"Daddy put latex over oil," Earl explained, peeling back a strip. "The whole house needs to be peeled and redone."

"Why don't you go see Ellen?" Ruby suggested before he could do more damage. "I thought you'd gone over to see her."

But her words only seemed to make him more determined; as Earl worked at it, a strip of paint rounded the corner of the hinge and led to the molding. Now a little open mouth of freed paint lifted from the frame. Earl contemplated the monstrous task of pulling the paint down throughout the entire house, each torn shred opening the way to the next.

~

Had the conference across the street at the Raleys' house occurred a decade or even five years later than it did, it might have had an entirely different character. *Roe v. Wade* wasn't old enough to institute its own vocabulary. The Raleys and Badcocks did not know how to use words like "fetus," "reproductive rights," or "choice" when discussing such matters; instead they naively said things like "baby," "responsibility," and—if they'd been able to bring themselves to say the word at all—"abortion." Which shows what a difference knowing the right vocabulary can make.

~

The Raleys and Badcocks set Ellen's and Troy's wedding just a few weeks later. Ellen hadn't mustered the courage to tell Earl what had happened, and her parents didn't make her. It was Mr. Raley who came over and broke the news to Earl. They sat together at the Mulvaney dinette. Earl's heart felt like it had dropped out of his chest, leaving him behind, a hollow swaying tube as Mr. Raley explained the situation and then rubbed his hands together. Mr. Raley said, "Earl, you understand?" It seemed to Earl that Mr. Raley said this over and over again.

The morning of the wedding Mrs. Raley saw Earl coming across the street and opened the door before he could raise his hand to knock. "I know who you came to see, but she's already gone to the church," she said. Ellen, standing in the foyer, just out of sight behind the door, heard the lie and gave a guilty shudder. At that moment, Ellen could have made it right; she could have pushed past her mother and told Earl she was sorry, that she still loved him, and she didn't want to marry Troy, and so forth. She thought about doing that, and maybe that's what she should have done. Maybe if you'd been in her shoes, that's what you'd have done, but I doubt it. Instead she touched her nose to the curtain lace beside the door, and through the gauzy white filter watched Earl's slumped shoulders as he walked back across the street.

"It's a good thing your daddy didn't get the door," Mrs. Raley said to Ellen's back. "Lord knows what he'd have said. That boy ain't going to go to church looking for you, though, I expect. He'll leave well enough."

Mrs. Raley was right. It being Sunday, Earl, who had the day off, could have gone to First Methodist if he'd wanted, see if he could find Ellen there, but he'd guessed Mrs. Raley had lied and Ellen really was at home. The wedding was at 5:00 to allow the church to finish its regular business, and it was only 10:15—far too early to arrive, even for the punctual Earl. He did not blame Mrs. Raley for lying.

Instead of going to Church Street, he walked down Warthen

and to the town square. It was a sunny morning in early spring; the morning birds sang. Earl bought a Dr Pepper from a machine in front of the Deepstep Drug Store; at the last second he thought of getting a Coke instead, but he'd already mashed the button. Back at home, Ruby Mulvaney—too miserable to attend Sanctified Tongue—did an uncharacteristically poor job at stuffing envelopes; her real hand and her plastic one seemed unable to work together. The creases came out crooked and the letters sat unevenly in their envelopes. Behind the door of the hall closet, Earl's frock coat, the money for which she had won in a poker game, silently accused her of the pending catastrophe.

Apart from hearing her mother lie, Ellen had two other bad moments that day; the next one was when Troy rang the doorbell at 11:15.

"It's bad luck to see the bride before the wedding," Mrs. Raley protested.

"That's just if she's in her wedding dress, Momma," Troy reassured her and gave her a kiss on the cheek, which she returned by kissing the air near his ear. He'd already begun addressing his future in-laws as his parents. One thing Mrs. Raley did not want—two things, really, but Earl Mulvaney had already been taken care of—and that was for Troy and Ellen to spend any time together before the wedding, but adroit at slipping through lines of muscley tackles and tight ends, the Humble Tigers' fullback had already gotten past her into the foyer, and Ellen stood in plain sight in the living room, so there was nothing she could do about it.

"Hey, Ellen," Troy said.

"Hey, Troy," she responded.

"Hay is for horses," was Mrs. Raley's normal correction for such casual greetings, but under the circumstances she just fluttered her hands with a "well," then said, "Do you want to stay to dinner, Troy? We got leftover pot roast and I'm warming up some butter peas."

"No thank you, ma'am. I just needed to see Ellen is all."

"Hello, kids, uh." Mr. Raley got up from the couch with his *Time* and went back to the pink bathroom to leave Troy and Ellen alone when they came into the living room.

The affianced couple sat on the Raley's plaid couch and Troy held Ellen's hand. It was about as tender a moment as they'd ever had. "Ellen," Troy said, leaning his head forward and speaking so softly that Mrs. Raley had to stretch uncomfortably to stir the butter peas and still hear him. "Did you see anyone else while we was apart?"

A loud crash came from the kitchen along with Mrs. Raley's exclamation, "God bless America!" the closest to profanity she ever came, then a few seconds later an apologetic, "Don't worry about me, kids, it's just the butter peas fell off the stove."

"I wouldn't mind if you did, and I'm not trying to get out of this," Troy explained. "I ain't angry. It's just—they said at school you had bought prom tickets, and I—" Troy studied Ellen's eyes, red from crying. He felt he deserved to know exactly what he was getting into.

Looking over Troy's shoulder, Ellen saw her mother's face framed by the kitchen door; two blue eyes—as bright and hard as marbles—stared warningly. "No, Troy," Ellen lied. "There wasn't anybody else." And so she got through her second bad moment.

Her third bad moment didn't come until the minister asked if anyone had any objections to this union, and Ellen braced herself, half-hoping, half-fearing, that Earl would burst in and abduct her. But he didn't. At the time, Earl was standing under the Deepstep water tower, wishing he had another bottle to throw, and wondering what would have happened if he'd never chased that stupid bee halfway across the county. Would she have married him instead of Troy? Would Earl have asked her to? Impossible to say; different futures branched off in every direction from the joint of that one decision.

About halfway between Ellen's second bad moment and her third, Earl had passed the courthouse to Jimmy Wiggins' Used Cars. The lot was silent on Sunday except for the flapping of multicolored flags. In the privacy of the weedy patch behind the sales office, Earl shouted "Goddamnit!" and hurled his empty Dr Pepper bottle where it struck the cinderblock base of the sales office and shattered gratifyingly into pieces. He opened the double doors and Simonized Jimmy's Corvette, rubbing it until it shone like a pearl. He used upholstery cleaner and made the red seats gleam. With each furious rub, Earl thought *Ellen, Ellen, Ellen.*

He went outside and sat Indian-style, his head in his hands. "Daisy was right," he said, "it don't pay being nice with girls. I got to start being more mean." He resolved to do just that. Then he worried someone might step on the glass from the broken bottle. He knelt and carefully retrieved each bright shard from the high weeds before throwing them into the trashcan.

The courthouse clock facing Earl, though he couldn't have seen it from where he picked glass slivers from the dandelions, said 8:17, which by coincidence was the actual time that the newlyweds checked into a Macon motel that evening. Exactly twelve hours earlier, Troy's father was still giving Troy a little last-minute advice.

"I expect you've made some mistakes, son. Ain't no shame

132

in that, we all make mistakes. But a real man faces up to his mistakes and works them out," Mr. Badcock took a slurp of coffee. "I've worked in the plumbing business twenty-five years, Troy," Mr. Badcock said, "it's taught me a lot about life. For example," Mr. Badcock said, his hands knobby and hard around his coffee cup, "if you have a pinhole leak in a pipe, you can plug it by breaking off a pencil tip in it. It'll just hold a little while. But sometimes a temporary fix is all you need."

Troy and his father sat at the kitchen table drinking coffee and picking over the remains of their eggs and grits. Outside the spring birds sang. The room was middling dark since the windows faced away from the sunrise, toward the side of the courthouse that read 12:05, which just so happened to be about the time that Earl would later pick pieces of his broken bottle out of the weeds.

After Earl had picked up all the glass and thrown it away, he wandered a side street and stood under the Deepstep water tower. As he walked, he imagined that maybe Ellen would have second thoughts, and might be wandering the streets herself, looking for him, maybe dressed in her wedding gown like the crazy lady in the book she'd told him about. She didn't want to marry Troy, she'd explain; it was Earl she had loved all along. Wasn't that her in fact, right now coming toward him in her wedding dress? No—it was just a woman in a white shirt—no, not even a woman, a man, an old man. But wait—that was her sitting hunkered behind a bush, in fact, he was certain of it— no—it was just a piece of paper caught in the branches.

Earl saw a movie where the hero interrupts the wedding at the last possible moment, to the stunned amazement of the congregation. The bride seems rather stunned herself, but overwhelmed by his bravado, takes his hand and runs up the aisle with him. They improvise a bolt for the front door using an enormous crucifix lying handy, trapping the outraged wedding party in the church, and the pair make a getaway on a crosstown bus.

Earl pondered doing something along the same lines—he would have to work quickly, though; the afternoon had flown, and although he didn't own a watch, he could tell by the angle of the sun over the water tower that it was nearly five. When the clock on the north side of the courthouse was right, Ellen Raley would be Ellen Badcock, and the newlyweds would be on their way to Macon for the honeymoon. Earl began walking to First Methodist.

He did not have a concrete plan, just a general idea he might see Ellen. Maybe Ellen would drive by on her way to church, and see Earl walking alone by the side of the road. She didn't. Earl did not intend to watch the wedding—he hadn't been invited and wasn't dressed for church anyway. But he thought he might catch sight of the happy couple entering or leaving the service. As he approached Church Street, the possibilities of what might happen when he saw the couple grew and forked into branches.

On one branch, Earl shook Troy's hand and said something that sounded ordinary and polite, but was secretly sarcastic underneath. Troy, who was more full of himself than usual, didn't pick up on it, but Ellen did, and her eyes filled. Troy asked Earl did he want to kiss the bride, and Earl curtly declined.

The next branch over, Earl shook Troy's hand and said something that sounded like ordinary politeness but underneath was secretly noble. Troy was too full of himself to pick up on it, but Ellen did, and her eyes filled. Troy asked Earl if he wanted to kiss the bride, and Earl politely accepted, brushing his lips to her tear-wet cheek like he was kissing his cousin.

On yet another branch, Ellen impulsively turned her tear-wet cheek away, instead pressing her lips to Earl's for one last lingering kiss, as a strangled sob broke in her throat. Full of himself, Troy was looking away at the time and didn't notice.

Had the distance to First Methodist been far enough, Earl's imagination might have produced the one branch that showed the scene that actually occurred—a scene without Ellen or Troy or kisses either on the cheek or elsewhere—but just Earl alone in the empty oil-stained parking lot of First Methodist. It's impossible to know the right time without a watch, you see, at least in springtime. Earl had arrived after the wedding had ended, and the bride had been kissed by all who cared to do so. The offering of pineapple-juice-and-club-soda punch and stale Danish wedding cookies in Fellowship Hall hadn't enticed the guests to linger. Five minutes after the vows, everyone but Troy and Ellen themselves had gone home to get ready for Sunday supper.

On the drive out of town, the new Mrs. Badcock asked her husband if he ever considered that the way people thought about time might have anything at all to do with their digestive system, and he reassured her not to worry, that they would have time to stop for supper at a Shoney's and still get to Macon well before 8:30. Then to have something to talk about, Troy told her an interesting remedy for a pinhole leak.

Maybe you would have done what Earl didn't, and go rescue your true love from her wedding. But you wouldn't have gotten away with it. An oversized crucifix smelled too much of popery for First Methodist to keep around in the lobby, and the outraged wedding party would just let themselves out the back-door through Fellowship Hall and circle around to catch you instead of just hammering uselessly at the bolted front door like they did in the movie. Besides, Deepstep didn't have any cross-town buses to get away on.

⁓

The fall of 1974 marked Earl Mulvaney's one-year anniversary at Wiggins' Used Cars. On that day Jimmy asked Earl into his office. "Earl, you know what day this is?" Earl looked at Jimmy's calendar; the Clik-Tite Girl wore a strawberry-red miniskirt and shiny black thigh-high boots. "What I mean is, it's one year exactly since I took you on. Congratulations. This calls for a raise, I think." Earl's unsmiling face did not move a muscle. "I might be able to squeeze out an extra buck an hour for you. How's that sound?"

"Good, sir. Thank you, sir."

"You ain't been coming to Daisy's for a while," Jimmy said. "We've been missing you. Is everything going all right?"

"Yes, sir."

"And your mother? She good?"

"Yes, sir." This last was a polite lie; Ruby had gone into a steep and rapid decline following the disappointment of the prom. She had not only lost all her hair, but wasted away to such an extent that when she turned sideways, she just about disappeared. Jimmy did not mention Ellen, and Earl didn't say anything about her. Earl Mulvaney never spoke about Ellen Badcock.

Trying to maintain a cheery voice to lift his mechanic's spirits was a strain on Jimmy; he had a splitting headache just then, but he persevered gamely. "You know it's a funny thing, I thought I saw you putting a padlock on the shed the other day."

"Yes, sir, I don't want no one going in there right now."

Jimmy considered telling Earl to remove the padlock, but thought better of it. "How is—how is that, uh, Endless Corvette coming?"

"Real good, sir. I got enough leftover parts now to start putting together a new car."

"Really?"

"It's not enough for a whole car, you know. Just enough to get started."

"You don't say."

What Earl did not say was that Jimmy's original Corvette, the source Corvette, was beginning to fatigue. Steady removal of parts seemed to have diluted its vitality; it still started up without hesitation, but to Earl's trained ear a resigned rumble had replaced the vigorous purr of the Blue Flame.

It so happened that Wayne the other mechanic had spoken to Jimmy just that morning about Earl. "You're going to have to talk to that boy," Wayne had said. "He's getting strange. The timing belt in his head was always slipping to begin with."

"Strange how?" Jimmy asked. He'd already seen the padlock on the shed and was beginning to harbor vague doubts of his own. Moreover, Deborah Howell, whose blue Camaro had needed work, asked Jimmy if his young mechanic had trouble with his eyes. "He gave me the funniest stare—like he'd forgotten how to blink. Has he been to see a doctor? It's like his eyelids have gone numb."

And now Wayne had some other disturbing news to share, "This morning before we opened up, Mr. Bell dropped his LeSabre off for a tune-up. Mind you, he left it before any of us came in, so we didn't know what it needed. He wrote a note and dropped it with a key into the door slot."

"Yeah, yeah."

"As soon as Earl came in, he said he was going to fix the brake pads on the Le Sabre. He hadn't even looked at it."

"Maybe he saw the note."

"The note just asked for an oil change and to clean the spark plugs. Earl's trying to diagnose engine trouble—I don't know how, by ESP, or something."

"Did the LeSabre need new brake pads?"

Wayne didn't answer for a moment. "That's not the point. That boy has thrown a rod."

"Did it need new brake pads?" Jimmy repeated.

"Well, yes. Okay, we got under it, and it needed new brake pads. But that's not the point."

Jimmy sighed, "I'll talk to him about it."

And Jimmy had meant to talk to Earl about his behavior, but now facing his earnest stare behind his taped-together glasses, he couldn't find a way to lead up to what needed saying. Jimmy couldn't bring himself to suggest that perhaps Earl was no longer firing on all cylinders. As he considered what to say next, Jimmy sucked on his Macanudo, taking in a contemplative mouthful of smoke, and blew it out into the already foggy office air. Of course, Earl had always been half a bubble off level, like all great mechanics, or anyone else of genius. Jimmy suspected Earl had been born out of plumb; Roy's scientific researches had become notorious all across the county. With a father like that, it had only taken some outside shaking to skew a boy completely out of kilter, and Earl had had more to shake him up than most.

"Listen," Jimmy told Earl. He rubbed his closed eyes with his fingers. "You and me need to set aside some time for another conversation. It can't be right now, I've got a doctor's appointment in about thirty minutes. But we'll have to have a conversation later, OK?"

"Yes, sir," Earl said.

"Well, that's settled," Jimmy said, forcing a smile. He closed the door to his office and set the little plastic hands on the cardboard clock that said "I had to step out!" to 1:00. As Jimmy left the sales office, the blue Volkswagen drove by, slowing slightly as it always did when it passed the car lot. A shudder of nameless dread ran down Jimmy's back. A week would go by without seeing the VW, and he would begin to hope it had ceased to haunt him, but then for no apparent reason it would appear three times in one day. What was it up to? And what did it want with *him?*

CHAPTER NINE

During the summer of 1974 Richard Nixon shocked the folks not just in Deepstep but all of Humble County by resigning from office. Local loyalty to the president was strong, since the majority had voted for him. The county took collective pride in knowing the majority of its citizens had voted for the winner in every presidential election since FDR. Many people could not have told you what Nixon stood accused of, and even more felt that he hadn't done anything much worse than any other president. The new president, Gerald Ford, pardoned Nixon a month later, which fact Sheriff King took as proof that Humble County's political system was pretty much typical right on up the line to the White House. That same year the city fathers floated a bond to break the earth dam that held back Sloppy Floyd Lake based on information that the bell, organ, or gold and silver pigs had been sunk there. They ran into unexpected opposition, however, from environmentalists up in Atlanta; it turned out Sloppy Floyd was within the range of the American alligator. The environmentalists filed an injunction in State Court against draining the lake, and so matters stalled.

Ellen and Troy, meanwhile, settled into married life. No one made any disparaging comments about Ellen's wearing white at her wedding, or the fact that her dress fit just a bit tight across the middle. If the bridesmaids didn't scramble to catch the bouquet when Ellen threw it, they didn't scatter like pigeons either. Everyone concerned had been determined to do the right thing, so all in all matters could have turned out worse.

Unless you're already familiar with the breed, you would be amazed at the generosity of the Methodists. I can't speak for other regions of the country, but the Deepstep Methodists do not scorn sinners—in fact, they prefer them. Unregenerate sinners receive unfailing courtesy and curiosity and are recipients of incessant behind-their-backs being prayed over. And penitent sinners, such as Troy and Ellen, find themselves on the receiving end of such bounty they must feel like grand prize winners on *Let's Make a Deal*. No deed of kindness is too great to extend a penitent sinner, at least until the new wears off. The young couple got a two-bedroom, one bathroom fixer-up on the county line at a give-away price. The loan officer of Farmers and Mercantile asked only the collateral of personal salvation and Mr. Badcock's co-signature. From as far away as Macon, somebody offered Ellen's father a used car for sale at a Reformed Sinner Discount. Troy took one look at it and swore he would never get in "that little thing," so Ellen only drove it when she came to town alone. Whenever they came to town together, they took his truck.

While Troy worked at his daddy's plumbing business, Ellen

spent the day replacing missing shingles in the siding and repairing broken tiles in the bathroom with the help of a home repair manual. Saturdays and Sundays Troy and Ellen worked on the house together and in the evening had supper with the Raleys or the Badcocks. Mrs. Raley and Mrs. Badcock gradually transmitted, by written directions, telephone, and personal instruction, almost all their culinary secrets, and by the time Jennifer was a babe in arms, Ellen could, when she wanted to, lay out a complete Sunday dinner in the southern tradition with fried chicken and livers, sliced homegrown tomatoes, fried pimentos, fried cornbread, fried eggplant, black-eyed peas with Vidalia onion, mashed rutabagas, turnip greens with side meat and spoon bread, and for dessert cat's tongue cookies, chocolate pie, or on really special occasions, fried apple pie. Troy, being a modern husband, also willingly helped with the cooking during the week, so long as it meant grilling outside. He loved dropping a match into the Weber after dousing the coals with lighter fluid, and feeling the heat against his face as the flames rose up with a mighty "whoom!" He always threw the old coals in the garden, claiming they were good fertilizer for the tomatoes.

You might expect me to tell you Troy beat up on Ellen, or ran around on her, or made her so desperately unhappy she decided to kill one or the other or both of them. But that's not the case. Their honeymoon in Macon was not as festive as other honeymoons have been, and they didn't start their marriage with that giddy rush of puppy love that most other couples experience, but all that might have been to the good. They had no expectations to disappoint. It did not particularly upset Ellen, for example, that her husband developed into a prodigious and chronic farter. Troy released farts only around Ellen, but these were of such astounding stench, they had to roll down car windows even in midwinter. Ellen even claimed that one of his farts set off all the smoke alarms in the house, and though Troy swore this was pure coincidence, he did go through later and remove all their batteries.

On Troy's part, it was probably lucky that circumstances forced him to go back on personal rule number three for selecting a wife. Had he married an idealized woman such as he had imagined, it would have later appalled him to watch her six months pregnant, sitting on a toilet, mouth agape while she flossed her teeth, and pausing to study from time to time the wet meaty gobs hanging on the thread. As it was, the sight produced no reaction from him at all, except he asked could he please use the floss when she was done and did she think she would be much longer because he had to take a leak.

If Troy could have changed one thing about Ellen, it would have been a certain look of serene seriousness she wore that told him she thought she was smarter than he was. He knew she was brighter than anyone else in the county, himself included, and would have been the first to admit it—proudly. But when she got that look, he could tell she was thinking how she was smarter than her husband in particular. And that rankled.

Once she said something that put him in a stew for a week. It was before Jennifer was born; they were at Sunday dinner at his parents' when Ellen mentioned the theoretical cat.

"I saw an interesting thing in a magazine," she said as she cut herself a bite of country-fried steak. A feeling of collective dread settled over the Badcock table at the mention of anything that interested Ellen. "It was an experiment about a cat." She noticed Troy across the table looking grimly at his mashed potatoes, but she determined to plow ahead. If Ellen could have changed one thing about her husband, it would have been to make him curious about something in this world besides plumbing and the Atlanta Braves. Sometimes, between the newlyweds, silences stretched out that were longer than those between couples married for decades. Troy rolled his eyes and turned on the TV whenever Ellen wanted to talk about a book she'd read or if to a sea cucumber time might move backward instead of forward. Eventually Troy stopped rolling his eyes and just turned on the TV, and in time Ellen stopped mentioning books and sea animals. But the cat came before that.

"The idea is you shoot a subatomic particle through a box. The sides of the box are just dense enough that this particle has exactly a fifty-fifty chance of getting through," Ellen said. Troy's dad, Bill, listened to his daughter-in-law intently; there was just the off chance that this experiment might have something to do with plumbing, in which case he'd be on familiar territory. Troy's mother smiled and passed the boiled cabbage and did not listen at all. Troy solemnly lifted a forkful of potato to his mouth. "If the particle goes through, it breaks a cyanide bottle inside; if it doesn't, nothing happens. And there's no way to tell if the particle went through the box without opening the lid. In that box you have a cat, but until you open the lid, there's no way to find out what happened.

"And this is the part that's really amazing," Ellen said, and with that Bill Badcock turned his attention to his fried steak, seeing that no pipes or wrenches would come up in the discussion, while Mrs. Badcock, sensing the story was near its close, listened for a little bit, "until someone opens the lid, the cat isn't alive or dead because there's no observer to see and make him settle down on being one or the other. So he's neither one. He can't be alive or dead unless somebody knows what happened. Isn't that amazing?"

"The things some people do to their pets," Mrs. Badcock said disapprovingly as she reached across the table for the squash.

"That's not the point," Ellen said. Troy chewed his mashed potatoes as angrily as it is possible to chew mashed food; he could see Ellen was right. The point was for scientists to make up something so football players and plumbers and everyone else could feel stupid. Troy took a bite of steak, but it had no more flavor than sodden cardboard. Troy could see the cat-in-the-box theory itself was like a subatomic particle. It bounced harmlessly right off his mother because she was so dense, but it penetrated just a little way into Troy's head, making it feel swollen and hot.

For the next week Troy fretted over that cat's predicament every waking and sleeping moment. Was a cat neither alive nor dead if no one was there to check on it? Was there even a cat at all? On some cardboard packing for a ballcock, Troy wrote,

> Every Cat is either alive or dead.
> No Cat is both alive and dead.
> No Cat is not one or the other.

Troy grinned after he wrote that, thinking he'd settled the matter. But then it came to him that *Every Cat* couldn't possibly be in the box, but it was possible that what was in the box just might be a *No Cat*. Then his perplexity started again. Sending a snake down the Bells' tub drain later that week, he said to himself, "It don't make no sense. Things don't need someone to see them for them to happen. The end of that snake's still there even though I can't see it. It don't go away. I just can't prove it, is all." Then to try to prove it, Troy pulled the snake back out to demonstrate to himself it was completely intact. "It still don't show nothing," he muttered. "It might have come back all at once out of nothing. I don't know what it's doing when I can't see it." Mrs. Bell, who happened to peek in the door during the last part of Troy's monologue, suspected he'd played a few too many football games without his helmet on right.

When Troy lay beside Ellen at night, he stared in the darkness toward the ceiling, frustrated to think that if he couldn't see it, he had no way to be sure the ceiling was still there at all. When he finally did fall asleep, fretful dreams haunted him of staring at a deck of cards through closed eyelids, trying to see what they looked like when no one was looking; when he opened his eyes to check himself, he found that while he wasn't watching, the deck had swirled around and muddied like cream poured into hot coffee, so now it had weird never-before-seen cards like the Seventy-Two of Clubs or the Jack of Cats. He jumped out of bed in alarm and opened and shut his sock drawer several times to assure himself that while he wasn't watching, his socks hadn't turned into garter snakes or elephant trunks.

Then one afternoon, the solution he'd been looking for came to him out of the blue, right in the middle of wrapping Teflon tape around a pipe thread. He left the tape dangling there from the galvanized pipe, left the customer's house without an explanation or running water, and drove out to his house off Old Eighty-Five.

"The cat knows!" he said, when he found Ellen in the living room repairing a crack in the drywall. "You said the cat ain't alive or dead till somebody knows what happened. The cat knows!"

Ellen held a can of spackling in one hand and a putty knife daubed with white in the other as she considered this. Then she smiled, and it was a beautiful smile. "You know, you're right.

I don't think anyone else has ever thought of that before." Troy couldn't help but grin. Then Ellen said, "The baby's moving. Feel." Beneath Troy's palm, Jennifer changed her position, pulling her elbow in a slow circuit across Ellen's belly. A little Not Jennifer, knowing herself, even if nobody had ever seen her.

~

Earl, in a mammoth effort, pulled all the latex paint from the walls. At first he tore small strips, then sheets, and finally he got so adept, he could peel an entire room at one go. Working his way patiently around each bedroom, he removed the paint from the walls and ceiling in an unbroken sack, and pulled it through the door like a collapsed lung. When the walls sat coldly skeletonic in their original thin coat of faded yellow, Earl went back with a suitable white primer that smelled like fingernail polish, and as soon as that had dried, he covered it with a vivid white satin. The result, although she didn't say so, was not much of an improvement to Ruby. The house, instead of looking like a neglected boneyard, resembled the white of an unblinking eye. She didn't care to be alone in that staring white house if she could help it, but it saddened her that Earl didn't even stay out with the Humble Volunteers anymore.

Fridays they stuffed envelopes and watched TV. "Son, ain't there girls where you work?"

"No, ma'am. Not really."

"Maybe you could start going to church. There's some nice girls there."

"Mmm," Earl said.

"'Mmm—'" Ruby said. "I hate it when you get nonresponsive." After Ellen's marriage, Earl's nonresponsive moods had become frequent. They were silent. On TV, Ted said something stupid and Murray said something sarcastic. Mary rolled her eyes. "I let you down, son," Ruby said. "I was prideful, and I let you down."

"Mmm. Momma, do you ever think about toothpaste?"

"Toothpaste?"

"Like how much there is in a tube. I've been using the same tube for eight months now, and I still ain't run out."

"We got new toothpaste. We just got a new tube of spearmint."

"I know. I just ain't been using it."

"Son, you got to brush your teeth," Ruby said, an image rising in her head of her son's mouth full of rotted stumps.

"I am brushing my teeth. That's my point. I've been using the same tube of toothpaste for eight months and it still hasn't run out."

"You got to use enough toothpaste. It don't do no good if you just use an empty brush."

"I do brush. I do use enough. It gets harder and harder to squeeze out a full toothbrush full every time, but there's always enough left for one more brushing. That's the thing."

"I don't think I understand you, sugar," Ruby said. Actually, she was sure she didn't understand him.

"If it turns out a tube never runs out of toothpaste, then a car might not ever run out of spare parts. That stands to reason, don't it?"

"I don't know, sugar." Trying to think about things she didn't understand tired her out. But then, she tired out so easily these days. A dull ache pressed the back of her head just above her neck. "Will you put me in bed, honey? I'm wore out."

"Sure, Momma, but don't you want to stay up for supper?"

"No, son, I ain't hungry. But you know how much I like your scrambled eggs." Earl did the cooking those days: scrambled eggs, grits, and bacon every night for supper, the only meal he knew how to fix. Earl lifted his little mother from the couch, and carried her into her bedroom. "Sugar," she said after he laid her in the bed, "I don't understand all that you were saying, but toothpaste ain't going to keep you from getting lonely."

"I ain't lonely, Momma," Earl said and kissed her on the forehead. Having no hair, she no longer smelled of hairspray, but of Ivory Soap. Her skin was soaplike, too, as white and translucent as a bar that's been washed to a sliver.

"I've been whittling away for a long time now," she said. "I've already mostly left. You've got to think of when I won't be here anymore."

"Yes, ma'am."

"I'm sorry I let you down, son. I love you."

"I love you, Momma. And you didn't let me down," Earl said, turning out the light.

"And don't forget to brush your teeth," she told the darkness.

"Yes, ma'am."

～

In 1975, if you had seen Ellen Badcock with her straight red hair falling to touch the little denim backpack she took with her to carry wipes and Jennifer's blanket, wearing her favorite flare-leg jeans and mirrored sunglasses, as she expertly loaded Jennifer's car seat into her blue SuperBeetle (A point of some delicacy that she hadn't bought it at Wiggins' Used Cars; her father bought it for her secondhand from a friend of his in Macon.) you could be forgiven for speculating that she might even be a Hippie Chick.

Had circumstances been different, had Ellen and Troy been allowed to idle in extended childhood a little longer instead of shifting straight into responsible adulthood, one or the other or both of them might have turned out cool. If Ellen had gone on to UGA, she would no doubt have fallen in with intellectuals, free-thinkers, and maybe even dope-smokers, and become one of them herself, trading her favorite Brontë and Austen for Sontag and Friedan. She might have even burned incense; it's hard to say.

If Troy, used to being a football hero in Deepstep, had gone on to the University, he would also have blended in, in time. He would never have let his hair grow longer than Paul McCartney's had been back in 1965—that would have been sissy, but, in spite of the fact that his drug of preference would have always remained beer, he no doubt would have become a social marijuana smoker, although even then only as a way to get hippie chicks, secretly all the while still holding fast to his four rules. When the curtain came down on the seventies, Troy would have gone into business becoming a Yuppie or a Yorpie (YOung Rural Professional.)

As for Earl—well, Barbara Mandrell and George Jones recorded a duet, "I Was Country When Country Wasn't Cool"—but even that didn't describe Earl. Earl had never owned a pair of cowboy boots, and although James Dean or Marlon Brando might have sanctified wearing white T-shirts and jeans, no movie star ever made hearts throb in red coveralls with the name "Earl" stitched above the pocket. Even when the fickle wind of fashion temporarily decreed it was acceptable to put peanuts in Coca-Cola, it did not have the power to make Earl cool. A more fitting song for Earl would have been, "I Wasn't

Cool When Not Being Cool Wasn't Cool." Earl couldn't have been cool, not if you'd nailed cool to his head.

But circumstances prevented even Troy and Ellen from being cool. Ellen's chief diversions were Jennifer, the tomato garden, and reading. Troy's were Jennifer, the tomato garden, the Braves, and the Falcons. Once a week Ellen went to town to buy groceries and ask me what was new at the library. Maybe Ellen took the circuitous route she did because a Volkswagen engine was one of three sounds—along with rain or a vacuum cleaner—that made Jennifer fall asleep. Coming from Old Eighty-Five into Deepstep on the Kaolin Road, Ellen got on Warthen Street, drove *past* Miller's Grocery to turn right on Suggs, went clear around the block, slowing down in front of Wiggins' Used Cars, in case she caught sight of red coveralls leaning under a car hood, before turning left back onto Warthen and approaching Miller's from the other side. She made the same loop heading from Miller's to the library, and once again when she finally headed home.

Judge Hathorne brought in his Town Car for an oil leak. "I told my wife, every night let's put a pan under it to catch the oil, and in the morning, just pour it back in. Heh-heh." One of the judge's rare jokes. The judge huddled in the couch cushions and brought his coffee under his nose, checking if it were cool enough to drink. Outside was a regular cloudburst; the garage door stood open letting in the chill, and the seed and feed store across the street looked as if it were behind a sheet of wax paper. "I understand your mother's very sick. I'm sorry to hear it."

"Thank you," Earl said manfully. All the judge could see of

him were two tennis shoes pointing East and Nor' Nor' West, and the wrinkled legs of his coveralls sticking out from under the Town Car. The squeak, crrritch, squeak of a socket wrench said Earl was loosening the plug.

"Don't know her personally. Only met her once. By all accounts she was a good woman. Maybe even a Christian woman, and that's a high compliment."

"Yes, sir. Thank you, sir."

Silence except for rain. It would be untrue to say you could have heard a pin drop, unless it was a bowling pin, but still it was pretty quiet. "You don't waste a lot of breath flapping your jaw, do you?" the judge finally said. "I respect that. Still waters run deep." A long silence except for the pounding rain. The judge inhaled the sweet rain smell and took a sip of coffee. "I think you and I might just be the only ones around here that have a clue what's going on and which end is up."

"Yes, sir."

"Look around you sometime and you'll see what I mean. All these Bible-thumping hypocrites, and not one of them who isn't crooked as a dog's hind leg. The difference between them and me is they all think they're Christians, and I know I'm not."

The judge regretted saying that as soon as it left his lips, but Earl's reply was another calm, "yes, sir," without any judgment or surprise, and the judge felt reassured.

"A real Christian, if I ever met one, has to give to anyone who asks, do favors for anyone who asks, and never ask for anything in return. A real Christian can't worry about winding up poor and associating with a lot of no-accounts, whores, and white trash, figuring he deserves a higher class of friends. Don't go quoting me to anyone. I have a certain reputation to uphold in this county." A gust blew through the open door, causing a notice to flutter on the pegboard on the back wall—Do Not Accept a Check from this Man.

"Yes, sir. No, sir."

"People think being Christian means going to church. But look into it. How many times did Jesus himself go to church? Twice. Once as a child when he back-talked the grownups, and once as a man when he beat up the money changers. If you saw Jesus in church, you'd better give him a wide berth; everywhere else he was as sweet as pie."

"Yes, sir."

"As I said, I don't claim to be a Christian. But if you tithe, and go to church, and pretend to love your enemies just so you can get into heaven, that's not Christianity either; it's a swap. Real Christianity means giving everything and asking nothing. There's nothing Christian in going the extra mile if you're pulling down time and a half for overtime."

"No, sir."

"You know Pascal?"

"Does he own that Italian Restaurant in Tennille?"

"Maybe. The one I'm thinking of said having faith is like betting that there's a heaven. If you're right, and you win the bet, you get eternal bliss as your payoff. On the other hand, if you're wrong and you lose, you're just worm food like everyone else and no worse off than you would have been anyway. So if you're religious, you stand to win everything without risking losing anything. That makes sense, doesn't it?"

"Yes, sir."

"Too much sense." The judge leaned close and spoke to Earl's knees protruding from the Town Car. "Faith is faith. You can't make up your mind about God just because it don't cost nothing and might pay off later. If faith doesn't have any more to it than beating the odds in a casino, it's just shit." The judge leaned back again, slurped his coffee, and studied the falling rain outside the garage door. "A lot of people in this county do just that, though. Put a chip on eternity and say, 'let it ride.'" A chill ran down him, and he took another slurp. "Like I say, I'm not a Christian and never claimed to be. Everyone here thinks he's a Christian, and he's not. But me, I know I'm not."

We'll never know how the judge's philosophy would have twisted Earl if he'd listened to a word of it, but, as so often in the past, while Earl pretended to listen, he had his mind on other things. On this occasion he was planning how he was going to turn mean. I know that disappoints you, having a high opinion by now of Earl's character as you naturally do, but if you'll try his shoes on for a while—the girl you love turning up pregnant by someone else and dropping you to marry him, a thing that's bound to wound your pride if you've got any pride to wound at all—then maybe you can understand how Earl would feel that the only thing to do was take that wound and pass it on to someone else: find a girl, get her used to loving him, then dump her down the road and move on to someone else. Earl, with hard-won insight, saw love as a ladder, with everybody trying to climb up and stepping on the fingers of everyone beneath. If someone stepped on your fingers, it just made you a tougher climber, and better able to step on someone else when the time came.

Earl had high standards for the girl he was going to hurt: he wanted someone pretty because he wanted to dish a little pain to Ellen, too, which shows you just how mean he'd determined to become. But he also wanted someone he didn't really like too well to start with, which would make it easier when it got down to the hurting part.

Anyone who knows a thing or two regarding meanness will

tell you it requires first of all a knack for reckless flirting, which some boys are born with, and some like Earl must gain by patient study if at all. Earl's early tries at this maneuver had not met with much success. Deborah Howell, the undertaker's wife, had not responded to the suggestive leer he'd given her while working on her manifold. Candy, the cashier at Miller's Grocery, stared blankly when he told her how sweet he thought she looked in her new retainer. In fact, until he ran into Barbara Allen one afternoon as she waited for some carryout at Daisy's, he'd begun to doubt if, when it came to being mean, he'd have any aptitude at all.

"Hey, Barbara," he said. "What are you doing?"

"Me and Grady Cook are going to the fair. He sent me in to get some chicken."

Earl leaned close to her, one elbow on the counter. "Do you want to go to the movies with me sometime?" Mean and daring, to move in on a girl with her boyfriend sitting right outside waiting for chicken, but if you're serious about turning mean, you've got to be prepared to go the whole hog.

Barbara did not meet his eyes, but stared over the counter. "You got a car?"

"Sure."

"What night?"

"How about Friday?"

"I got something Friday."

"Thursday?"

"What movie?"

"I don't know. What's at the Pastime?"

"I seen it. They got *Towering Inferno* in Macon, though."

Daisy came in from the kitchen holding two large mason jars filled with translucent amber liquid and a brown grocery bag with a grease stain already spreading across the bottom. "Here's your chicken and your—sauce," she said.

"Get me at five-thirty," Barbara said, gathering her purchases in her arms.

"Are you going out with her?" Daisy asked when Barbara left. "I guess."

"Mmm-mmm," was all Daisy said, lowering her face in a frown and wiping her hands on her apron.

⟶

Earl borrowed the Corvette for his date, and at exactly five-thirty, walked up to the Allens' door between the white-painted half-buried tires lining the driveway. Across the street, three-year-old Donny Garland, wearing a cowboy hat, stained striped shirt, and nothing else, briefly aimed a bow with a suction-cup arrow at Earl, thought better of it, but continued staring at him with a doubtful expression. Blackboy, the Allens' dog, barked a hysterical greeting, pacing the circle of lawn the length of chain had allowed her to worry bald.

"Well, Momma, you said you wanted me to find a girl," Earl said to himself, lifting his finger to the doorbell.

"Come in," Mrs. Allen greeted him at the door; she couldn't have been happier to see Earl if he'd been her date instead of her daughter's. "It's so nice Barbara's finally dating a decent boy. Now be careful, here." She helped him thread his way between stacks of old magazines that formed a maze on the floor. "I keep asking to Nolan to throw out these *National Geographics*, but he won't do it. Barbara! Earl Mulvaney's here! Why don't you have a seat? Nolan, make Earl some room."

Nolan Allen, a tall man with thick dark hair and deep-set

dignified eyes, shifted a pile of *National Geographics* to the floor, and cleared a space for Earl on the couch beside him.

"Barbara! You work at Jimmy Wiggins' Used Cars, don't you?" Earl said he did. "It's so nice Barbara's dating a boy with a job. Some of these boys!" Her hands flew up in exasperation at the mention of "some of these boys," the fat under her arms waving like curtains. "Do you want some iced tea?" Earl said he did not care for any, thank you. "It's good to have a job. Do you like where you work?" Earl said he liked it very well as he accepted the glass of iced tea she'd brought him anyway. "That's nice. Barbara's father is on disability," she said regretfully, "but if it wasn't for that, he'd be looking for something all the time, wouldn't you?"

Nolan Allen nodded that were it not for his disability, he would indeed be looking for something all the time, hocked up something deep in his throat, and took a sip from his Pabst.

"Bar—! Oh, there you are."

"You didn't have to holler, Momma."

"It ain't polite—isn't polite to keep your date waiting."

Earl escorted his date through the channel of *National Geographics*. Outside, Barbara put a Virginia Slim between her lips and lit it as they walked up the drive. "Are we going in that?"

"'53 Corvette," Earl said proudly.

"I'd've thought a mechanic could get hold of a newer car."

Earl let her in and got in on his side. It is a strange thing that when Jimmy or anyone else drove the Corvette, it could be counted on to break down within ten miles, but when Earl himself was behind the wheel, she seemed content to run indefinitely without so much as stalling, and, as far as I can make out, without even needing gas.

"Your dad sure reads a lot," Earl said as they drove off.

"He ain't really my dad, I'm adopted," Barbara said. "Which shows they must have really wanted me, more than if I'd been their regular baby, because they went to so much trouble to get me."

"That's nice."

Barbara blew smoke through her nose and nodded. "And I also got a sister somewhere. I never met her, but she might come in handy someday if I ever need another kidney or something."

The movie was about a lot of rich and famous people at a party in the top floor of a skyscraper. Everyone is drinking and having a good time, but all along there's a fire spreading in the floors below, which started mainly because the building was too tall in the first place. The fire cut the rich people off from the ground, so they were trapped by the very fact they were so high up. It was a familiar story to Earl; a Class B electrical fire becomes a Class A.

Dating Barbara was different than dating Ellen, Earl soon learned. Barbara had many marks of superior sophistication, such as knowing how to "French inhale." Dragging on her cigarette, she'd fill her mouth with smoke, then breathe in through her nose and let her jaw hang slack so smoke poured out, a thick cloudy river across her upper lip, and into her nostrils. Earl tasted smoke whenever they kissed, and the taste of Virginia Slims remained on his tongue.

Barbara was also very forthright. When they went out together, Barbara always chose where they went—Earl did not even attempt to walk her to the cemetery—and she made no bones about how much he should spend. The chili dogs at Daisy's were superior, but Barbara insisted on sophisticated dining, so Earl had to drive her all the way to the Sonic Drive-In in Milledgeville. Standing at the candy counter at the movies, she surveyed the choices behind the glass and said, "I want Sugar Babies, butter popcorn, and a big grape soda." Being mean, Earl discovered, was much more expensive than being nice.

Barbara also went in for long-range planning more than Ellen had. Ellen had general plans about getting a degree from the university, and then a job somewhere—plans which had fallen through when she got pregnant—but Barbara had very detailed plans that reached all the way from the current moment to her deathbed. "I'm going to be a fashion model," she confided. The subject had arisen when Earl compli-mented her on how she could eat a twelve-inch chili-cheese dog without getting so much as a dab of grease on her lips. "Grady Cook says I'm good-looking enough. I'm saving up my money to go to Atlanta. I know a man there. And then after I get rich and famous and really old, I'm going to repent so I can get into heaven. The minister says it's a big risk to take because you might die any day when you least expect it, but I figure it's worth the chance. And anyway I don't think I've had time enough yet to do anything bad enough to go to hell for."

Unlike his courtship of Ellen, which had remained secret, the Earl Mulvaney/Barbara Allen affair was public knowledge. Judgments differed on its suitability. The white Corvette left a wake of snickering and winking neighbors whenever it passed by with Earl and Barbara in it. Had these same neighbors known that Earl planned to split up with Barbara one day and break her poor heart, they would have guffawed and slapped their knees. Ruby was mortified—torn between gratitude that Earl had found a girl, and shame that it was Barbara Allen. The Badcock vote was split: Troy uncommitted and Ellen foursquare against it. The Corvette drove by Bells' Seed and

Feed as she and Troy were loading twelve-foot lengths of quarter round into the back of Troy's pickup.

"What did you say?" Troy asked. Too busy contending with the quarter round, he'd missed her comment. Quarter round, if you've ever had to wrestle with it, combines all the worst habits of two-by-fours and red wigglers.

"What?" Ellen asked.

"I thought you said something just now."

"Someone ought to tell Barbara Allen to quit hanging on Earl Mulvaney like he was a handle."

Her husband shrugged and looked down the street toward the receding tailpipe of the Corvette. "Earl doesn't seem to mind," he observed. "Hey—! Take it easy with that toe molding, Ellen—it's already paid for!"

For all her self-assurance and sophistication, Barbara often shocked Earl with her flagrant disregard for ordinary manners. Once, coming to get her for a date, he met Grady Cook at the front door. Grady gave Earl a big grin on his way out, and Earl said hello and goodbye. Nolan Allen was in his customary spot, the TV on. His eyes widened when Earl came in, and then he turned back to his show with a half shrug. "She's in there," he said, nodding to Barbara's room.

Earl went in. "Hey, Earl." Barbara sat on her unmade bed, doing up the top four buttons of her shirt. "Let's go," she said. "I want to go in to Milledgeville and get a Sonic Dog," and getting up, slipped on her sandals and picked up the twenty from her dresser top.

Earl didn't know quite what to say, and so didn't say anything, although he really felt he should. He could imagine how mistreated Grady must've felt that when he came to visit; Barbara hadn't even bothered to get out of bed. He wanted to let her know that wasn't any way to treat a guest, but Earl felt great reluctance criticizing anyone, and besides, improving her manners was hardly consistent with his mission to break her heart.

~

After Earl went on his first date with Barbara, Wayne the other mechanic came into Jimmy's office. "That boy of yours took the Corvette."

"He'll bring it back." Jimmy was the only one in town, with the possible exception of Mrs. Allen, who was one-hundred percent behind the romance. He not only permitted, he encouraged Earl to use the Corvette on dates. Guilt continued to sting Jimmy like his own private squadron of bees; after Ellen's marriage he had begun seeing an ominous blue SuperBeetle that seemed to pass—slowly—by the car lot three times every Wednesday, its little 1285 cc engine mumbling vague accusations.

Wayne pursed his lips before telling his boss what he'd really come to say. Finally, he came out with it. "Earl's been unbuilding and rebuilding that same Corvette almost two years now. I actually think—" It had taken Wayne a long time to figure out what Earl was up to with that '53 Corvette, but little by little he pieced it together—"he might be crazy enough to think that if he keeps tinkering on that car, and saving up the leftover parts, sooner or later, he's going to have enough for a brand-new Corvette and still have the original car left over."

Jimmy sighed, cocked his head and looked at Wayne. "So you figured it out, did you? And once he's got two Corvettes to work with, he'll have breeding stock, and the third one will come even faster." Talking to Wayne, Jimmy had not even looked up from the jumble he was working, but now he put it away in the top drawer of his desk, and fumbled for a cigar. He bit off the tip, and spit it into the trashcan. After he'd lit it and taken a few thoughtful puffs, he said, "And who's to say he couldn't do it?" What Jimmy said next didn't come out fast, but in such a steady flow that for a time Wayne couldn't have squeezed a word in sideways with a pair of calipers and a ball-peen hammer. "There's a lot more things in heaven and earth than you ever dreamed of," Jimmy said. "Says so in the Bible. We don't know nothing except the back of our hands, and we don't know much about that. You know, Henry Ford said, 'History is bunk,' but if you go looking into it, you'll find he didn't say that at all, but only 'history is more or less bunk,' which I guess at least goes to show he was right, that history really is bunk, more or less, which I guess proves even further that we don't know half what goes on in the minds of geniuses—like I always suspect in one of them big universities that's trying to figure what time's made of, someone's going to up and say time really *is* money and be done with it."

"Sooner or later, he's going to run out of parts," Wayne said stubbornly. "There's only one distributor cap in a car."

"You can cut off a crab claw and in another year he'll have a new one."

"A crab is alive."

"That's my point exactly," Jimmy began, thinking of his pet idea about cars evolving, but then realizing that was crazy talk, steered the conversation a different way. "But who's to say how many parts a car has? I've been looking through the *Clik-Tite Manual.*" Jimmy got the heavy *Clik-Tite* down from the file cabinet, along with the massive hardbound companion work, *Laeder's Guide.* He began flipping the pages of *Clik-Tite* until he came to spark plugs. He pointed to a diagram that took up a quarter of a page. "It says a spark plug has four parts: connector, ceramic insulator, center electrode, and ground electrode. But *Laeder's Guide* says a spark plug has twelve parts. Look here." He flipped pages again, this time through the gray hardbound manual, opening it at another illustrated sparkplug. "Terminal, insulator, resistor, spring, shell, gasket, insulator tip, side electrode, gap, center electrode, threads, and center socket. Now, I don't know myself how many parts a spark plug has, but anyone can see the more accurate guess is the bigger one. And *Laeder* left out some of the parts in *Clik-Tite!* Twelve parts—and that's just one spark plug—I don't think there's anyone who knows how many parts there might be in a whole car!"

"But you can't take a spark plug apart, and anyway, a gap ain't even a part—it's just an empty space between one part and another."

"Just an empty space! That empty space is the point of the whole thing! If there wasn't no empty space, there wouldn't be no spark, then what'd you have? Just a plug. And *you* might not be able to disassemble a spark plug, but I wouldn't put it past that boy to take apart a lock washer if he had a mind to. And by the way, gaps and empty spaces are most of the extra parts he ends up with. The other day he showed me—well, I can't tell you that."

"What?"

"No offense. Being a pessimist you just wouldn't understand."

"Now you have to tell me."

Jimmy rubbed his jaw and considered. "The other day Earl was showing me his leftover parts, and one of them was one side of a muffler."

"He sawed a muffler in half?"

"I didn't say half—I said one side, I saw a muffler on the floor that looked just about like you said. It looked like someone'd cut a muffler in two lengthwise—if you looked at it from one side. Earl was rooting around for something, and tipped it over. And on the other side it wasn't there no more. I was just looking at bare concrete where a minute ago there'd been a muffler—or at least part of one. Now nothing but oil stains. That muffler only had one side. The other side was still in the car."

"Oh, bullshit," Wayne said as he left. At the time he ignored what Jimmy said because he thought he was fooling; later he chalked it up to the tumor.

CHAPTER TEN

That'll be the Volunteers, Earl thought in the wee hours when the phone woke him up from a dream in which he had just introduced Ellen to Barbara. The Volunteers were the only ones who called so late. "Jimmy?" he answered the phone.

"Someone spotted a fire off Old Eighty-Five. I'll be by directly."

Earl let his mother sleep, and went to wait on the front step. Minutes later Jimmy picked Earl up. There wasn't any need to study a map because everyone knows Old Eighty-Five. They turned left off Warthen onto Elm, then right onto West Haynes, which forks south of town to become Kaolin Road and Old Eighty-Five. Headlights played on the blacktop; over a line of pines an owl glided. Behind a web of silhouetted trees, the pale yellow brightening the horizon said dawn was on its way. The coffee Jimmy poured him warmed Earl's hands, and as he sipped it, he inhaled the steamy fragrance. "Now, remember, boys," Jimmy warned them. "I don't want no one trying to be no hero."

"Did you remember to bring the fire axes?" T. J. asked.

"Damn!" Jimmy slapped the steering wheel.

It was silent for a while except for the sound of the tires on the road; then Earl spotted the fire. "There it is."

At the end of a long driveway of gravel and sand, in the woods behind a frame house, a fire was well under way. It later turned out that the owner had dumped out some old charcoal briquettes into his backyard, only one or two of them still had a live coal. As the Volunteers pulled up, they saw flames had spread to the back side of the house, and could even now smell the scorched siding that perfumed the darkness.

"Now, I know that house," Jimmy said, fumbling uselessly for a hazy recollection. "Who lives there?" Earl knew whose house it was, but said nothing. Had Jimmy noticed the blue VW parked around back, he would have been alarmed, but in the darkness, and later in the hustle and bustle of dealing with the fire, he managed to overlook it.

"Damn," T. J. said, "what a time to be without our fire axes. Jimmy, I'm running up there and see if I can't break the door down."

"You're doing no such thing," Jimmy said, calm in the crisis. "You go up and ring the doorbell and see if anybody's home. Earl, you go around the side door and see if it's open." As Jimmy spoke, he brought the truck to a stop in the front yard. "I'll poke around and see if they got a garden hose."

T. J. pressed the doorbell, pounded on the door and waited,

as Earl went around to the side door, and finding it unlocked, let himself into the kitchen. Meanwhile Jimmy felt along the rough shingles behind some shrubs planted along the front, until he felt the cold wet galvanized metal of a spigot attached to a garden hose. Troy Badcock came to the door, having taken only long enough to get his jeans and a shotgun. He was not entirely surprised to find a black man standing there, but he hadn't expected him to be wearing a fireman's hat.

"You got a fire," T. J. explained to the shotgun, grateful that he hadn't broken the door down after all.

In the darkness Troy spotted the owner of Wiggins' Used Cars straining at the garden hose to stretch it around to the back of the house. "You got an extension for this thing?" Jimmy shouted. Troy looked around the side of the house. Trails of yellow fire spread south through the underbrush toward the spur from the old Nancy Hanks. He could taste the smoke in the air. "Ellen!" he shouted. "Get out here!"

By this time Earl, guided by a shaft of moonlight coming through the back windows, had left the kitchen and headed to the bedrooms. Ellen should have bumped into him on her way to the front door, and the only reason I can think of she didn't is that Earl must've already passed her bedroom and nearly reached the end of the hall before she got out of bed, so when she came out, and turned left to see what the matter was, her back was to him. In any case, when Earl tried the door at the end of the hall, he found it was just a linen closet, and so turning left, he found himself in the baby's room. Jennifer was sound asleep in her wooden crib, curled up like a roly-poly under a pink fleece blanket.

Earl scooped her up, and with Jennifer tucked against his stomach like a football, ran down the hallway of blinding black smoke as red embers dripped from the ceiling, fire curtained every doorway and window, and sudden blazes erupted underfoot. Reaching the front door, which was not only burning but closed and locked, Earl lowered one shoulder, increased his speed, and smashed into it; the door, already in a weakened state, burst open in a shower of splinters and cinders, as Earl ran clear off the stoop and did a tuck-and-roll in the front yard. Meanwhile, a pursuing fireball, which Earl had outdistanced by mere inches, gushed from the open door as if in impotent fury that its prey had escaped. Gasping, and nearly unconscious, Earl lay back on the grass, and unwrapped his uniform from his precious cargo; Jennifer, safe and in fresh air at last, let out a lusty wail to the relieved applause of a crowd of onlookers that had gathered. Earl placed Jennifer in Ellen's arms; Ellen hugged him in gratitude, her face wet with tears, and Troy clapped him on the back.

The Humble Progress ran the full story the next week. The front page said, "LOCAL MECHANIC HERO SAVES BABY." It showed photos of Earl and Jennifer and what remained of the Badcocks' house, a few charred supports sticking out of the ground like blackened teeth. Numerous eyewitnesses, whom the paper had neglected to interview, also confirmed the dramatic account.

Now it will show you what bitterness will do to some people when I tell you that Wayne the other mechanic—out of pure spite—had the audacity to say none of that ever happened. According to Wayne, at the time Earl removed Jennifer from the house, he was in no more danger than he might face carrying any baby down any ordinary hallway. Because the Volunteers kept busy digging firebreaks and the garden hose didn't help very much to quell the flames, eventually the house did burn down, but that happened hours after Earl already rescued Jennifer.

"Wake up and smell the coffee," Wayne told anyone who'd listen. "If you believe all these so-called eyewitnesses, then half the county must have been out in their pajamas on Old Eighty-Five at five in the morning. Forget about asphyxiation, I'm surprised the baby wasn't trampled. And Earl couldn't have busted through a locked door unless Ellen turned around and locked it herself, which don't make no sense. And if things was so all-fired desperate, where did Troy and Ellen get time to take every stick of furniture out of the place?"

This is indeed a mystery; for not only the Badcocks' chairs, sofas, and tables, but every personal possession they owned— right down to Ellen's Brontë and Troy's Shakespeare fishing rod—wound up lined high along the upper end of the driveway, well out of reach of the flames. Wayne insisted that while the fire worked its leisurely way up the back side of the house, Ellen and Troy had plenty of time to remove all their possessions through the front door, returning several times to make sure nothing had been missed.

But although the Badcocks could not recall how their furniture and appliances made it to safety, they had very clear and definite recollections that grew, if anything, more vivid with time, of Earl bursting through the door, the fireball, and all the rest. And while Wayne the other mechanic had not been present, T. J. and Jimmy, who had been, along with the numerous eyewitnesses already mentioned, all upheld the fireball story. Earl himself, who did not weigh in on the controversy, lent support to the dramatic version of the rescue with that manly silence so typical of heroes.

The other outcome, apart from suddenly finding himself a

hero, was that Earl finally gave up being mean. The moment he'd felt Ellen's grateful tears against his neck, he'd known that he'd never be able to carry out his transformation, but the last straw came the morning after the fire. He and his mother had just sat down to breakfast when the doorbell rang. Mrs. Raley stood on the stoop holding a cake. Ellen and Troy had spent the night at her house after the fire, so she'd heard the whole story, although in the excitement she'd gotten the facts a little embellished in her head, and thought Earl had escaped the inferno by jumping through a window, shielding Jennifer in his arms from the flying shards at the risk of his own skin. An exaggeration, of course, but an innocent one not worth correcting.

"It's pineapple upside-down," she said. "Just to say thank you. I'll set it on your table."

"That's a pretty cake," Ruby said, admiring it from her chair.

"I'm worried it's a little dry," Mrs. Raley said. "I just hope it's fit to eat." A Southern lady never accepts a compliment on her cooking. "How are you feeling today, dear?"

"I'm just fine, Mrs. Raley," Ruby said, the second polite lie of the day—Mrs. Raley's cake was perfectly delicious, and Ruby was about as far from being fine as a person can get. You could've just about read the classified ads through Ruby's skin, and her hands trembled so badly, she had to eat her scrambled eggs with a tablespoon.

When had this sweet woman become so frail? For a moment Mrs. Raley couldn't bear to lift her eyes for shame, and she scrutinized the coffee table with its feet on the worn blue throw rug. Then she said, "Please call me Dorrie, after all, we've lived next to each other for—we live next to each other."

"Thank you so much for the cake, Dorrie," Ruby said.

"You know," Dorrie said more cheerfully, "it's been too long since you and me had some girl talk." A strict accounting would have revealed they'd never had any girl talk. "I'm going to bring over dinner this afternoon, and you and I are just going to have some good old-fashioned girl talk."

"Oh, you don't have to bother," Ruby said.

"I insist," Dorrie said, "I don't want to hear another word about it." Once she'd put the cake down, Dorrie Raley turned to Earl and squeezed him. "You were always so good," she said. "You are so sweet to us."

After Earl and Ruby ate their scrambled eggs and bacon, he cut them each a slice of cake. Ruby took a bite, pronounced it delicious, but said she was really too full to have any more. Earl ate his slowly. His neck was moist. Mrs. Raley's eyes, like Ellen's, had been wet. He knew then that he would never get over Ellen Badcock.

He made up his mind that he would go straight over to Barbara Allen's and break up. A sad thing and a hard thing it was to do, to go and break Barbara Allen's heart, and especially ironic because he did it after giving up on being mean. Earl didn't know how much it would hurt her, but the sooner it was over with, the less pain there would be.

Accordingly, right after work the next day he pulled up his Buick at Barbara's house. Nolan Allen sat in a lawn chair, smoking a cigarette and not reading *The Humble Progress* in his hands, but watching his adopted daughter wash the car. She had on cutoffs, and her t-shirt, knotted over her bellybutton, had gotten soaked when she reached across the hood to lather it with a soapy sponge. Blackboy raised her head indifferently when Earl got out of the car.

"Barbara, I need to tell you something," Earl said.

Barbara studied his face. Something in it said this needed to be a private conversation. "We'll go around back," she said.

"You ain't done washing the car," Nolan said.

"And you ain't paid me," Barbara said. "Keep your shorts on, I'll do it when I get back."

In the backyard, Earl stared at the boxer shorts flapping on the Allens' clothesline as he marshaled his thoughts. He had to say this right. "I can't see you no more," he said. He wished he'd been more delicate, but it just came out that way.

Barbara reflected. "Does that mean you ain't taking me to the movies?"

"Yes. I'm really sorry."

Barbara's eyelids fluttered closed, and for a moment Earl worried she would cry. When she opened them, she said, "Okay, I figure it's three-fifty for the ticket, and another four for grape soda and snacks. Give me seven-fifty and we'll call it square."

Earl reached into his wallet and settled up with her.

~

A few days after breaking up with Barbara, Earl came into the Humble County Library and told me, "I want to check out a book."

The appropriate response to such a dumb remark would have been, "I'm afraid we don't do that here," but Earl's face was so earnest, I just couldn't make a sarcastic reply, so I just said, "What's the name of it?"

"I don't know. Not any particular book, just a book."

To say the least, I was nonplussed, but I'm one of those librarians who loves a challenge. "Well, can you be more specific? What kind of book did you have in mind?"

"I don't know. Literature, I expect. I want to read a thick

book." From his parents Earl had inherited an infinite capacity to hold on to hope. His resolution to go against his nature and turn mean hit a sprag after the fire, and he realized he might as well be nice after all. Under ordinary circumstances, you can get over a girl by getting another girl, but in Ellen's case it was like trying to put out a Class C fire with water, not only useless, but foolhardy. After breaking up with Barbara, Earl reasoned that he loved Ellen, and that Ellen loved books. He made up his mind to start reading and see what came of it.

"Well, okay. Literature, huh? Do you have a library card?" I studied his face. *The Humble Progress* hadn't run his story yet, so I didn't know he was a hero, but he didn't look the sort to steal a book or write dirty words in the margins.

"No, sir."

"Fill out this form, and I'll see if I can't fix you up with a good book of literature. A thick one." I slid a white card across the desk to Earl and went to select him a book. The Humble County Library primarily houses fat romances and detective stories, but years ago spread itself to buy The Classic Literature A–Z by Classic Books, Inc. These were stored on the Literature Shelf, and this is where I went. Earl asked me for a thick book, and he got one, as thick as anything he'd ever seen Ellen read. When I handed it to him, he looked discouraged by the heft of it, but that very night he began doggedly plowing through it page by page. It turned out better than he'd hoped, and a few weeks later he came back and checked out another.

—

Earl was still reading the first of the books I'd lent him when his doorbell rang. It was Troy. "I just stopped by—oh, that looks like one of Ellen's momma's upside-down cakes. Those things are great. Afternoon, Mrs. Mulvaney."

"Good afternoon, Troy. Tell Ellen's mother I had a fine time with her this afternoon."

"We spent the whole day toting stuff to Ellen's folks's place," Troy told Earl. "I'm taking a break and going fishing at this place I know. You can come, too, if you want to."

Few fishing invitations are harder to turn down than one coming from a man who doesn't suspect you're in love with his wife. Earl looked toward his mother for permission.

"You go on, son," Ruby said. "I just want to rest here on this couch and close my eyes a spell."

So Troy generously took Earl to his favorite fishing spot—past Daisy's diner and the county line, past the spot where Pinebark Creek joins Gumm Creek, a cleft between two granite boulders that pinch the stream, really almost a small river by that point, into a very pretty waterfall that has dug out a deep bowl in the sand beneath, eddying out in a peanut shape about four yards long and three wide. At the upper end of this peanut, where the water is the deepest, and where little fish drop over the waterfall like manna from heaven, larger fish—perch and catfish—circle with all the watchfulness and unsatisfiable appetite of a Mr. Moss waiting for a customer.

Troy did not mention Earl's saving Jennifer's life, but spoke on a number of other topics. "See that bank right over there?" He pointed to the opposite bank with a cast; the line whirred out and landed—ploop!—his bobber in the water. Earl cast his bobber nearby. "That's a good spot to dig for shark teeth. Daddy used to bring me here when I was a kid, and we found about a bucketful. This whole place was under water about a million years ago back with the dinosaurs." Troy stared at his bobber; the red underside flashed up briefly, indicating that a fish was investigating the bait. Troy wiggled his pole to impart a semblance of liveliness to his worm.

Thinking of shark teeth led Troy to another topic, "You know the Confederate gold everyone's looking for?" Troy asked. "I got an idea about it. The reason no one's found it is because they're looking where somebody would have buried it. But it ain't going to be there any more. Wherever it is now, it ain't where it started out. It's been *moving*. Way to go, Earl!" Earl's bobber flashed red, then sank under the water's skin; Earl jerked back his pole, and yanked out a plump perch. After Earl landed it and Troy put it on a stringer, Troy continued. "Ellen was telling me that it turns out how islands and continents and all that don't sit still. They shuffle around, like, jostle and shove—only so slow you can't see it. It's like electronic supper plates. So like a long time ago, Humble County might've been way over next to Bibb, or Bibb might've been on the other side of Lincoln. So that got me thinking—if that treasure was buried such a long time ago, it wouldn't stay put. Like with shark teeth. There'd be like an underground current—only made out of dirt and rock instead of water, and the gold would wind up 'downstream,' if you catch my drift. What do you think? You think that might be right?"

~

Troy Badcock fell in love with his wife the day of Jennifer's baptism.

That day Ellen's parents, Troy's parents, and Ruby shared a pew as well similar views. "It's about time is all I can say," Dorrie Raley whispered to Ruby.

"Amen to that," said Mrs. Badcock, who'd overheard.

The Raleys were Methodist, the Badcocks, Baptist, and Ruby, True Gospel—they would have disagreed whether baptism should be accomplished by sprinkling, pouring, or dunking— but they would have said with one voice that baptism—like changing diapers—was not something that could be long postponed. It so happened, however, that Dorrie was referring not to the baptism, but to the official recognition of Earl as Jennifer's godfather.

Earl stood between Ellen and Troy as water was sprinkled on Jennifer's head, and when the minister asked if he would help see to it Jennifer was brought up in a Christian household, Earl said, "Yes."

Originally the minister had made a fuss about permitting Earl to play a part in the service; the church stipulated that godparents be Methodists, but Dorrie Raley, not a woman to be gainsaid, had prevailed, and so the minister pretended not to know Earl's denomination while performing the sacrament. The scripture that day was also Dorrie's choosing, from Paul's letter to the Galatians, "There is neither Jew nor Greek, slave nor free, male nor female, for you are all one in Christ Jesus." When this was read, she looked around eagle-eyed for any objection. She needn't have worried, though; by this time Earl's heroism was so well known, he'd have been welcome in any church in the county, even if he'd dressed like Harry Krishna himself.

But I was forgetting the point of this story, which is to tell you how Troy fell in love with his wife. An odd thing, I know, for Troy to do it this way. Most men fall in love with women while they're still girlfriends, and then if they're lucky, remain in love with them after they're wives. A lot of times they fall out of love with their girlfriends once they become wives, but that's not how it was with Troy. The first few weeks of Troy's marriage, he was frequently overcome by a feeling not unlike raw panic. He knew nothing about this woman with whom he shared a bed, and later, a daughter. He'd made a terrible mistake, ruined his life and the lives of any number of others, his one misstep sending out waves of misery through the entire world.

A trapped raccoon will debate with itself on the advisability of chewing off its own foot. An unappetizing task, he'll think, but on the other hand, when I'm done I'll still have three perfectly good feet left over, and my situation certainly isn't going to get any better on its own; that's just how Troy reasoned with himself as he weighed different methods to make the quickest and most painless possible exit. But Coach Fuller trained his men not to run away from trouble, but directly into it; and Troy stuck around. Gradually the panic subsided, and he found himself not in love with Ellen, but on cordial and even affectionate terms. But the day of the baptism, when he saw Ellen pick the wild violet, he fell in love.

In the Junior Midget league, Troy had learned his fourth rule. Already a star player, he'd not yet taken the importance of proper posture to heart. But on a beautiful Saturday when the leaves had just begun to change and the air was cold and sweet as a Red Delicious apple, the quarterback handed off the ball to Troy and WHAM; Bob Cook knocked Troy on the hard green ground. Troy lay stunned in the grass, the no-longer delicious breeze blowing across the numb throb that was his body. His coach's face, not Coach Fuller, this was before that, Coach Martin, appeared in the little window frame created by his helmet. "Stay low, knees bent, legs wide," he repeated. "That'll learn you, I expect."

It had learned him, and the rule had served him well from that day to this.

But before the service that morning, Ellen in the white muslin dress she'd worn for the baptism, the dew still on the church lawn and a thousand little spiderweb hammocks stretched between the blades of grass—reached down to hand a wild violet to Eddie Cummings's daughter. The sight struck Troy's chest hard as Bob Cook had all those years ago. Ellen stood legs straight, bending down from the waist, one arm cradling Jennifer against her chest, the other reaching out the flower toward Candy Cummings's dimpled hand. How could anyone be as beautiful as Ellen? There were a hundred things Troy loved about her, like the way that when something touched her heart, she'd do the same: hands against her chest, elbows out. He couldn't have told you why he thought of that just then, or why he wanted then to touch her heart, or hold her hands in his against his own heart.

Now, you'll probably say that one moment—white dress, dewy grass, wild violet—couldn't in itself be enough to love someone, and love must have been sneaking up on him a little at a time and he just hadn't noticed up to then, and I expect that you'd be right. Chances are the same phenomenon accounts for how Ellen fell in love with Troy, one night years later, after learning always cook beans *thoroughly* before you put them in tomato sauce, otherwise they never will get done. On a steamy August night when they just couldn't get cool, and both the window units were on the fritz, Ellen was wiping out the Crock-Pot with a rag, and Troy was watching the Braves, when they heard their daughter's sudden cry.

They had seen prettier sights, I can tell you.

It would have been bad enough if Jennifer had merely upchucked the two bowls of chili she'd had for supper, but her parents had decided to put an oscillating fan by her bed to keep her cool. Weeks later Ellen was still finding stray kidney beans behind the dresser, under the bed, jammed in the crown molding. Jennifer, who looked as if she'd been dipped in chili, knelt in her bed and wailed—the most terrifying experience she'd ever had, first getting sick and then finding herself in a cross-fire of ricocheting kidney beans. Ellen began wiping chili off the baseboards before it could harden, while Troy gingerly lifted his chili-caked daughter from the bed, keeping her at arms' length, considering whether to put her in the bathtub, sink, or just hose her down outside.

But Jennifer would not stop crying, and she reached out with her splattered arms. "Daddy," she cried tremulously. That's when Ellen had her moment. Troy Badcock, who in his prime had knocked the toughest linemen in the state flat on their ass, tenderly pressed his puke-caked daughter to his chest, and said "there, there," hugging her and kissing away her tears.

—

Troy and Ellen stayed with the Badcocks while their house was rebuilt. Their worldly possessions were stored at the Badcocks' and Raleys' carports in exactly the condition they had been jumbled together any which way during their retrieval the night of the fire. Knickknacks and high school yearbooks were stuffed in the vegetable crisper of the refrigerator, which stood, door slightly ajar to prevent a stink, next to the dinette, on which chairs sat upside down, beside which was the sideboard containing among other things, Troy's spare fishing tackle.

Inside, Troy and his father sat in armchairs, and Ellen sat on the sofa. Troy had *The Humble Progress*, and Ellen had a book. Jennifer lay curled in Ellen's lap with a sippy-cup and heavy eyelids, slowly moving toward sleep, but for all the world, seemingly intent on the incomprehensible lines of print in front of her. The TV was tuned to an Andy Griffith rerun. In the kitchen Troy's mother prepared one of her massive suppers; steam drifted into the living room promising two meats, four vegetables, and dinner rolls. Ellen had given up on offering help to her mother-in-law; Mrs. Badcock wanted no one in her kitchen but herself. Ellen made do with the menial task of doing the dishes.

"I read somewhere that it isn't good to let babies fall asleep with juice," Mrs. Badcock called helpfully from the stove. "It rots their teeth."

"I don't think she's really drinking any," Ellen said. Jennifer let the cup fall from her lips and rested her face against Ellen's breast. Ellen adjusted to nestle Jennifer closer to her side; as her daughter breathed deeply, falling asleep, Ellen felt the comforting pressure of Jennifer's little chest grow and shrink against her.

"I don't want to interfere," Mrs. Badcock said, "just something I heard."

"Ellen? What're you reading? Ain't you already finished that one?"

"I'm rereading it," Ellen told her husband. Actually, she was no more reading it than the now-sleeping Jennifer had been. She was mulling over the mystery of finding Earl Mulvaney's name beneath her own when she'd slid the library card out of the envelope pasted in the back of her favorite book.

"Hey, y'all want to hear a joke?" Mr. Badcock suddenly volunteered. "The Japanese came out with a transistorized septic tank." He paused for effect. "It's this big across," he finished, holding his hands a football's width apart. His wife laughed dutifully from the kitchen, although like most professional in-jokes, its humor was not readily evident to an outsider.

The next morning Ellen came to the library and stood with Jennifer on her hip in the dust-moted light from the big windows, pondering the literature shelf. She'd gone there to conduct an investigation of her own. Ellen's love for difficult reading was so well known, if people saw her name on a book's checkout slip, they wouldn't even bother with it. Mrs. Price, the science teacher, was even more widely read than Ellen, but she stuck to the Reader's Digest versions in the interest of efficiency. So once "Ellen Raley" or later "Ellen Badcock" appeared on one of the little blue lines, it was the only name that appeared until she checked it out again. But there was Earl Mulvaney's name, written beneath two consecutive "Ellen Raleys" in the meticulous copperplate script of someone who doesn't write very often.

She took down other books and examined their cards. Sure enough, Earl had already checked out *Pride and Prejudice*, *Jane Eyre*, and *Don Quixote*. *Great Expectations* was not on the shelf. She deduced he was reading that one now. It didn't take Ellen more than a second to figure out my system for recommending books to Earl. The next one he'd come to would be *The Mill on the Floss*. An impulse struck her; she wrote, "I hope you like this. It's very sad." on a piece of paper and slipped it inside the cover and replaced the book on the shelf. She reconsidered a few moments, then removed the book again and added a little picture. It would have been wildly inappropriate to add a heart, but what she drew would have special significance for the two of them. She didn't need to sign her name because if Earl had any doubts, he could always check the library card to see who had it last.

Weeks went by as she waited for Earl to return *Great Expectations* and check out *Mill on the Floss*. When he had, she wrote a message in *Tom Jones*, the next book along: "This one's happier. Did you like my picture?"

When Earl returned *Mill on the Floss* a long time later, under her original message he'd put, "I did like it. It was sad. Aren't there any happy books? What does the Swiss cheese mean?" Ellen realized their communications were out of phase; necessarily she already written her next message before she got Earl's reply.

"It isn't Swiss cheese," she wrote in the next book along, *As I Lay Dying,* "it's a sponge."

When Earl finally got around to checking out the next book, he understood at once the significance of the sponge. Time for sponges swirls around and around instead of going in just one direction the way it does for people. If Earl and Ellen were sponges, they would still have happy days of their past to look forward to just like the future.

At this point you might ask why if they felt that way about each other, they didn't just do something about it. The reason is Ellen wasn't the type to go back on her wedding vows, and Earl wouldn't have loved her if she had been. And Earl wasn't the type to take advantage of a married woman, and Ellen wouldn't have loved *him* if he had been. So each decided to go on loving the other, but at the same time knowing they could never be together. It sounds far-fetched, but there are historical precedents. The closest parallel is probably Dante, who saw Beatrice just one time on her way to convent school, fell head over heels, and wrote her an epic, using a rhyme scheme so complicated it would have driven a lesser poet insane, even though she never let him so much as smell behind her ear. Of course, the poem he wrote was all about Hell, which gives you some idea what Earl had let himself in for, to spend his whole life loving Ellen, but never to tell her.

At night, if Ellen held her hands in a certain position on Troy's back, she could make believe Troy's large square body was Earl's small skinny one. It wasn't exactly cheating on her husband, but whether it made her predicament more or less painful would be hard to say. As for Earl, unsatisfactory as he found it, but necessary for survival whenever his mind drifted to 1973 and those lingering kisses at Good Hope or Jimmy's shed, he followed the advice in Ecclesiastes 9:10.

They never signed their letters, nor wrote, "Dear—" because both of them knew without saying whom each letter was from and to. The following letter was evidently written late at night. Although it's clearly Earl's handwriting, the customary careful print is just a tad uneven. Anyone who'd never seen one of his letters would be surprised by how voluble soft-spoken Earl could be when he sat down to write, after they'd gotten over the shock of Earl Mulvaney writing a letter in the first place:

I saw something that made me think of you—early in the morning in your momma's yard—a little deer. It didn't run but came right over into our yard. I had got out of bed to pull the shade, as I had been woken up by the full moon. When I saw it I stopped and stayed and watched it from my room. Coming into my yard wasn't anything to do with me, I know she was just passing through but it did me a world of good to see something as beautiful as that little deer. Then she smelled me and ran away, I just stood there still a little while before I remembered I had to pull the shade.

Next morning you could trace her steps. Every foot left behind a pair of hollow teardrops like this:

It was on the exact spot I played pirate once and hid a buried treasure that I lost. I got the idea from something on TV but pretending my front yard was a pirate ship was not much use—there wasn't ~~no oth~~any other kids to play but me. I had a silver heart without the chain that was supposed to be the treasure. Which I buried. I kept singing "Three thing-things on a dead man's chest, yo-ho-ho and a thing-thing-thing." A pirate song—I didn't know the rest. I pretended I was Captain Earl till dusk but when I went to go and get my treasure some low-down town dog had got there first. I dug and dug all afternoon till supper. I'd lost it for good through being careless but all in all it served me right, I guess.

Remember Mrs. Love back in English class? The one who gave us chalky candy hearts on Valentines and used to wear those pointed glasses? She read us this peculiar poem one time I will never forget that I can't remember. At the time it didn't make a lot of sense. It said to everyone who was a hunter, the best hind ever was marked off limits. It was really about a man who loved a woman but they couldn't be together. Mrs. Love said you had to keep in mind the deer symbolized a lady to get it—but I was too busy laughing at that one word "hind" so I never really got it but I regret it. I

think I see a little now what that poet said. I wasn't
really listening then but now I wish I had so I could
remember more.
    Tonight I just couldn't sleep even when I got to bed.
My head was too full of deers, and poems, and treasure.
And writing you this letter.

All in all, Ellen's letter in response in the next book along
doesn't seem to have much of anything to do with Earl's. If you
didn't know better, you might think maybe she was about half
a bubble off level when you read her opening question, but
wondering about car faces is just the kind of speculation that
came naturally to her.

Incidentally, a couple of years back, the Badcocks had a yard
sale, and rummaging through a table of children's things, I
came across an old water-stained toy that I think may be the
actual one mentioned in this letter. Maybe you've seen one like
it: it's a telephone on wheels that you pull along on a string. As
the wheels turn, little eyes in the telephone's face move back
and forth and it makes a quacking sound. It really is the
damnedest amalgam of things—you wonder what sort of distorted image of reality kids grow up with.

Ellen's former high school teachers would have been disap-
pointed at all her comma splices, but after all, she didn't write
it for them. She claims in the letter she wrote it while cooking,
which is corroborated by a little greasy stain that appears to be
butter, over the words "I'll write you."

    Did you ever notice that cars look just like they have
faces? That's the sort of thought I'd associate with you.
It came to me while I was looking over recipes for bread.

Might as well bake, I decided, Jennifer is taking a nap, the forecast today is rain, it's something I can do alone.

Don't misunderstand, though—I'm not lonely!

Jennifer's favorite toy has a little face, I realized I can't tell what it's supposed to be when I brought from the rain. Maybe you can tell me if it's a car, telephone, or animal—next time you're here, I'll show it to you. I dried it off so Jennifer can play with it when she gets up from her nap, and then after she's done playing, we can have a nice slice of bread.

I'm cooking honey-whole wheat-wheat germ bread, a recipe I half-invented on my own, you should see how domestic it looks rising in a Murphy bowl covered with a red-and-white checkered napkin! I just took a break to rinse the flour from my face and I found myself thinking about you—I remember how you always liked to listen to the rain.

I think it would be nice to sit and watch the rain if I could have a nice hot pot of Earl Grey and a buttered slab of bread, I'd write a letter just like this to you, while I was sitting curled up in my couch, my favorite comforter fluffed up by my face and the cup and saucer in my lap.

Jennifer's old enough now she doesn't normally take naps, but she always gets drowsy when it's raining. When she's asleep like this, I can put my nose right up to her face and breathe in her quick warm breaths that smell like bread, but that only makes you feel more alone, and wishing I could talk to you.

I wish I could go on writing this to you, but I think I hear Jennifer finally getting up, she doesn't get up well

if she's alone, and she's out of sorts whenever it rains,
stop by if you ever want to try some homemade bread,
It'd do me good to see you.

Thank goodness, Jennifer's up from her nap, and it
finally stopped raining. I gave her bread and jelly—you
should see her face! Next time I have some time alone,
I'll write you.

Earl and Ellen carried on lengthy conversations through their letters, although these entailed considerable lag time between writing and getting a response. For example, by the time they finished their entire exchange about car faces, it had taken them all the way from Faulkner to Hemingway. Ellen said that cars don't really have faces, but people are so used to finding faces everywhere they look, they just imagine a car's grill is a smile and its headlights are eyes. As Earl saw it, however, cars really do have faces, but they were put there by engineers. He imagined the first carmakers hunting around for a hint to how the front of a car should look. How should the headlights go? In a line? In a circle? All over like a Christmas tree? What about the bumper? Top, bottom, and middle? Should the windshield wipers go up and down, side to side, or around in circles? Finally they settled on an already familiar design, the human face. "No one comes up with anything really new," Earl wrote. "Everything we make is out of something else we found already lying around."

Troy, although by now a successful plumber in his own right, had higher aspirations than just following in his daddy's footsteps. Mostly these dreams consisted of getting rich from finding the Confederate treasure. "And when we find it, you and me are going to split it right down the middle," Troy promised Earl.

"You don't have to do that," Earl said.

"That's what best friends do," Troy said simply, and settled the matter. If they ran into a stranger when they went fishing past the county line, Troy would introduce Earl, "Not only is Earl a volunteer fireman, who saved my baby's life," a pause to allow the impressiveness of this to sink in, "he is the greatest—and I mean, the greatest—mechanic who ever picked up a wrench. If your car ever needs fixing, take it to Earl Mulvaney."

Earl found himself reciprocating, "Not only is Troy a star football player," Earl always used the present tense, although Troy's fullback days were far behind him, "he is the best plumber who ever lived. Any troubles with your pipes, and you call Troy Badcock."

The stranger would smile glassy-eyed at this, his reel hanging limp in his hand, nonplussed to be in the presence of such entities.

Earl was habitually quiet around his best friend, but when he did talk, Troy leaned his head forward in that way he had and listened as if he'd been lying awake all night wondering what Earl would say that day. Troy and Earl went fishing together in Sloppy Floyd or prospected together with a Techtronic Metal Detector Troy had ordered from Edmund Scientific.

"They also had a personal flamethrower for sale," Troy said the first time he showed his Techtronic Metal Detector to Earl, waving the head of his device slowly over a half-dollar he'd dropped on the ground to test it. It identified the prize with a triumphant beep-beep-beep. "Think of that. Said it would be useful melting snow and ice off your sidewalk. We don't get much snow and ice around here, though," Troy said, the disappointment evident in his voice. "Still—your own personal flamethrower, think of that!" It was something he intended to buy for himself when they found the treasure.

Troy was an inveterate believer in the existence of the buried pipes, pigs or bell, and constantly following new hunches or leads where they had been buried or dumped, or where they may have likely drifted. The fact that he and Earl had searched so long, indeed the entire county had searched so long, without success, only confirmed in Troy's mind the existence of the treasure.

One time Troy took Earl prospecting in the pinewoods below a familiar stretch along Stump Road. Earl recognized the spot with a little dart of pain; it was where, years earlier, he had gone chasing wild honey when he should have been with Ellen. Earl had noticed that as he got older, there were more and more locations that brought painful memories: this stretch of road, the parking lot of First Methodist, Good Hope Cemetery. Earl imagined his heart was gridded off in a map of Humble County, and a white spot, dry and chalky like kaolin, marked each painful location. When someone's heart was covered all over with white, the time had come to die. There would simply be nowhere left to go without feeling sad.

"It stands to reason," Troy said, as they waded through a thicket of blackberry vines; the metal detector had given a strong signal on the shoulder of Stump Road, which had proven to be only a missing chain from someone's locket, but Troy had insisted this meant they had stumbled across one of the junctures where the Electronic Supper Plates of Humble and Hancock Counties converged, meaning that all buried valuables might ultimately deposit themselves nearby. "They would have buried it in the last place anybody would think to look. And *so*," he concluded with unanswerable logic, "we're going to find it in the very last place we think of. That stands to reason, don't it?"

"Uh-huh," Earl said.

Troy waved his metal detector over a clump of sweet-smelling ferns uncurling on a promising-looking mound of dark loam. Not so much as a beep rewarded his efforts. "I ain't so sure this thing ain't broken," Troy said, and he whacked it judiciously against the base of an oak between the yellow awnings of mushrooms growing from its side. "I sure am getting hungry. I can hardly wait for supper tonight. Ellen's Momma said she'd fry you and me up that catfish we got the other day." Earl was aware of a blackberry vine stretching taut over one foot and then the ground rushing up toward his chin. "Hey, Earl, you OK?"

"I'm fine," Earl got up, and wiped off two dead leaves clinging to his pants. The fall hadn't hurt him, but he wished it had, the same way he sometimes wished a few more bees had flown up into his coveralls that time. Writing Ellen letters and reading and rereading the ones she'd written him, thinking about her the way he did—he had worked up a terrible debt to Troy and figured it might balance things out a little if he, Earl, could just really suffer bad just one good time. He wished the thought of seeing Ellen that night at supper didn't make his chest hurt with anticipation. He wished some personal angel of retribution would fly down from heaven and beat the snot, just beat the ever-living snot, out of him for being so in love with Troy Badcock's wife. That might balance things out a little.

Every day at noon, while Earl was at work, Dorrie brought her friend Ruby a little tray and they had lunch together and watched soap operas and game shows.

Of course, Dorrie only began doing this for the sake of Earl, who had rescued her granddaughter, but over time she became genuinely devoted to Ruby. Which is often the way things are; when you start to care for someone, sooner or later you start to care *about* them. A similar case I know of was when Betty Horton's mother-in-law, who was in declining health, moved in with her son. The Elder Mrs. Horton was mean—Lord, she was mean; she had a tongue on her so sharp it could peel potatoes, and she used it unsparingly on her poor daughter-in-law, who naturally had to bear up without complaint, and who all the while was emptying bedpans, changing pee-wet sheets, and sponge-bathing that scabrous mean-mouthed old lady. But then, Mrs. Horton up and died, and at the funeral, it was Betty Horton who was inconsolable. If someone can come to love a bitter old bottle of snake spit and spite like Mrs. Horton, imagine how close Dorrie Raley would grow to a sweet, gentle, grateful soul like Ruby Mulvaney.

A typical meal of Dorrie's was chicken potpie, pimento cheese sandwiches with the crust cut off, and fruit cocktail in a cup, but Ruby could only manage a few bites. Some afternoons they had tea and biscuits, one of Ruby's suggestions, but even then Ruby could only manage a little.

"You have to eat, honey," Dorrie remonstrated, but Ruby only smiled softly and said, "I just ain't hungry. That lunch was plain delicious, though."

Once every other week or so, the Raleys invited Earl and Ruby over for Sunday dinner. Earl helped his mother assemble herself and rolled her across the street in the wheelchair Troy had given them—it had once belonged to Troy's grand-mother—for one of Dorrie Raley's feasts: two kinds of meat, five kinds of vegetables, bread, and biscuits, not to mention dessert. Troy, Ellen, and Jennifer rounded out the guest list. Troy would recount his and Earl's latest exploits in trying to recover the fabulous Confederate treasure of Humble County, or repeat something funny: "Did you hear the Japanese came out with a septic tank this small?" holding his hands apart to indicate something the size of a loaf of bread. Everyone around the table waited expectantly for the punch line as Troy sat in mute perplexity, realizing he'd waded into the joke from the wrong end.

"Don't you want some more?" Dorrie asked Ruby, looking at her still-full plate.

"She's just saving room for dessert," Mr. Raley suggested hopefully.

"No, I just ain't hungry," Ruby said with a smile. "It sure was delicious, though."

Earl always insisted on reciprocating after one of the Raleys' meals, and so invariably a few nights later the Raleys and Bad-cocks found themselves crowed around the Mulvaney dinette, passing around big bowls and serving themselves the *spécialité du maison Chez Earl.*

"These are the best, I mean the best, scrambled eggs I ever tasted," Mr. Raley said as he dug into his third plateful. "I can never get enough of them. Why can't you make eggs like this, Dorrie?"

Dorrie didn't mind her husband's enthusiasm for someone else's cooking; she just said, "Earl, you have to tell me your secret for cooking these delicious eggs."

"There ain't no secret, really," Earl said modestly.

"Aren't you going to eat any more, honey?" Dorrie asked her friend. "You're letting your son's delicious eggs go to waste."

"I just ain't hungry," Ruby apologized with a smile. "They sure are delicious, though."

But nothing could induce Ruby to eat more than a few bites at any meal, and her downhill only got steeper as time went on. She was still as sharp as ever, when she wasn't taking one of her increasingly frequent naps, and though Earl took care of all the housework, she insisted on handling the bills—feeding monthly payments into the empty belly of debt from Roy Mulvaney's research and her various illnesses. After her luxuriant hair fell out, she got a wig. Always slim, she thinned down even more, and her petite dresses hung around her like loose husks. Mr. Thigpen came over frequently, bringing his Bible, basin, and soap. Earl often found them together when he came home, Mr. Thigpen's Bible opened to its favorite chapter in Ecclesiastes, and Ruby wiggling her eight remaining toes, her feet glistening and damp.

"I have something terrible on my conscience," Ruby finally admitted to Dorrie and Mr. Thigpen one afternoon when all three of them were alone together. Ruby lay in bed, from which she had not risen from all day. Sunlight made the quilt sweaty and uncomfortable. She felt if she didn't get out of bed that day, she'd die. "It's so terrible, I don't know if I can bear to say it."

"The Bible says to confess our sins," Mr. Thigpen said. "There ain't nothing the Lord can't forgive."

Ruby patted his hand, grateful for the wisdom of a simple answer. "You're right. Honey," she said to Dorrie, "I want you to go to the hall closet. There's a coat on a hanger. Will you bring it to me?" Dorrie brought the black frock coat, dusty but still elegant. "Lay it on the bed." Dorrie did, and Ruby ran her

195

trembling real hand over its glossy lapel. "Oh, Lord, this room is so hot. Would someone bring me a glass of ice water, please?"

"Sure, honey," Dorrie said. From the kitchen came the crunching sound as she pulled the lever of the ice tray, freeing the cubes from their little cells. Then ice crackled and popped as the thawing tap water poured over it. Dorrie came back after a minute.

Ruby was too weak to hold it without spilling, so Dorrie held it to her lips.

"I stole that coat," she said, just as the tumbler reached her mouth. She sipped, smelling the bristly promise of cooling release. Dorrie and Mr. Thigpen exchanged a look—neither of them believed Ruby any more capable of stealing a coat than of bench-pressing an engine block. "That is the best-tasting water I ever had," she said when Dorrie lifted the cup away. "It's too complicated to explain how I stole it, but I did. It was my pride that made me." She stroked Dorrie's hand as it lay on the white chenille bedspread. "I am so sorry, Dorrie. I am so sorry. Only, I ain't been able to ask forgiveness the right way. You can't ask forgiveness unless you're really sorry for what you did."

"You know what happened between Earl and Ellen," Dorrie said, "it didn't have anything to do with a coat."

"I know it looks that way," Ruby said, "but we don't understand the ways of Providence, how things really happen. I don't expect Noah's neighbors thought their antics had nothing to do with the weather, either."

Mr. Thigpen nodded in solemn agreement; the congregation at Sanctified Tongue had a firm grasp on the concept of God's wonders and the mysterious ways by which he performed them.

"Ruby, you are not responsible for Earl and Ellen—" Dorrie began.

"But you're sorry for what you did?" Mr. Thigpen interrupted.

"Yes, sir."

"Really?"

"Oh, yes."

"Well, Jesus says if you're truly sorry, He'll forgive you. I expect you can ask for forgiveness now."

Dorrie shot the minister a look of blue-eyed fury, but neither he nor Ruby noticed it.

"That's right, I can," Ruby said, and smiled. "I am sorry, I am truly sorry, and I will make it right. Can I have another sip of water?" Dorrie raised the glass to her lips, and she felt the cool relief flow like a river through her.

"We'll go now and let you rest," Dorrie said. After she and Mr. Thigpen were on the other side of the Mulvaney's front door, she let the minister have a little piece of her mind. And that's just how it came out too, in pieces. "How dare you let that sweet woman—! How dare you—! That sweet woman—after all she's been through!"

Mr. Thigpen remained unperturbed, but patted the heavy black Bible he held against his stomach. "We're all sinners, missus. Jesus don't see a speck of difference between the worst rascal whoever crawled and the sweetest woman," a nod toward the Mulvaneys' house, "ever lived. And pain don't make things balance out. Ain't nothing we can do can pay the debt. Jesus pays it for us—for all our sins. If we ask."

～

"Son," Ruby told Earl when he got home from work, "will you take that frock coat by Howells' Funeral Home tomorrow?"

"Yes, ma'am," Earl said.

"Promise me?"

"Yes, ma'am. First thing tomorrow."

"Good," Ruby said, feeling she had finally begun to settle up accounts. As soon as the coat was returned to its rightful owner, she'd also tell Earl about Mr. Holton.

Then late that night Ruby woke up to the sound of someone gasping loud and harsh. The faint rectangle of light of her bedroom window told her where she was. But who is that breathing so loud? Then she realized the gasping was her. Another thing I have to see the doctor about, she thought, oh well.

As Ruby lay there, she began thinking about the Bible and going over something that had always puzzled her, but she'd never gotten around to asking Mr. Thigpen. In Matthew and Mark, Jesus says "My God, my God, why hast Thou forsaken me?" but in Luke He says, "Into Thy hands I commend my spirit," and in John He just says, "It is finished."

Now that's something you'd expect the Gospels to get straight, Ruby thought in the darkness, something as important as the Lord's last words. Of course, she thought, He could have said all of that, He was up there a long time with nothing much else to do. But still, His exact last words, what he said right before He died. Maybe there wasn't nobody close enough to hear, Ruby said to herself, those crosses were pretty high up.

That might explain things, Ruby thought. After all when Jesus said, "Eloi, Eloi,"—that's Jewish for "My God, my God," someone thought he was calling for Elias. So maybe no one really heard him straight.

I wonder who was standing closest. That might give us the answer.

Probably Luke. He's the only one who overheard the conversation with the two thieves. You'd have to be pretty near to get

all that. Luke. I bet that's it, Ruby thought, but I know there's
something more to it than that. I just haven't figured out what
it is. She thought about getting her Bible, which was on the
nightstand beside her in the darkness; she could almost smell
its worn black leather cover, feel its familiar onionskin pages.
But she couldn't lift her arms, and so she just lay there.

Ruby's bedroom fell completely silent. She figured she
must've closed her eyes, because she couldn't see the rectangle of light anymore, but then she thought, no, my eyes are
wide open. She realized her breathing had stopped. Well,
darn, she thought, first breathing too loud and now not
breathing at all; the doctor isn't going to like this. She felt
herself drifting back off, the darkness soft around her as a
fleecy blanket, as she wondered about Jesus's last words. Her
mind really was getting funny, not only had she forgotten the
different things He'd said in the Gospels, she couldn't even
recall the names of the Gospels themselves. Let's see, there's
Matthew, Mark—*Something*—Luke, and John. Funny, she'd
known the names of all the Gospels since she was a girl. The
leather-smelling onion-skinned Bible was right beside her, and
she was certain Jesus's actual words were in the one between
Mark and Luke, but what was the name of that Gospel?

Then all at once she remembered it, and with it Jesus's
last words.

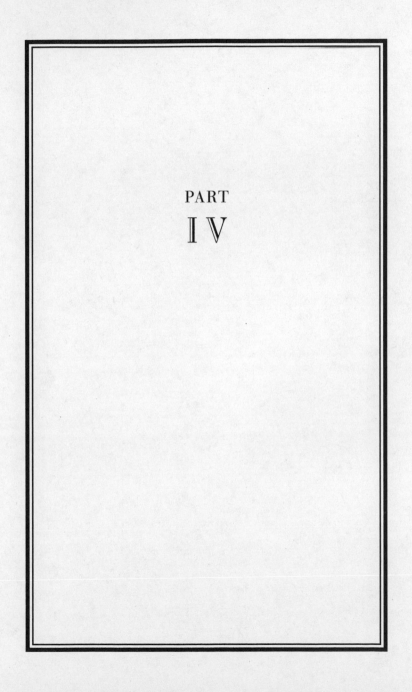

PART

IV

CHAPTER ELEVEN

The next morning Earl let Ruby sleep in while he made his breakfast. After he'd eaten, Earl went in to ask his mother if she was ready for her egg. He knew at once she was gone. He sat on the edge of the bed beside her and touched her cool forehead, and closed her eyes. Even with her eyes closed, she did not look like she was sleeping. She didn't look like his mother at all; she looked like a very, very accurate wax copy of his mother. And Earl did not feel as if he'd really found her dead; he felt as if he were rehearsing to find her dead at some later date.

Yes, he thought, this is probably exactly how it will be when it finally happens for real. The gray blankness outside the window was overdoing it a little, perhaps, but otherwise everything was a very realistic simulation.

He went back in the living room and sat on the couch to

think. He swallowed and thought, well, so it's finally happened. I guess I knew it was coming. He swallowed again. There was a dull rushing sound in his head. I'm not very upset about it, he thought, I must not be much of a son. What would people think if they saw me taking it so calm? He swallowed again. I sure am doing a lot of swallowing, he thought. He knew he needed to go ahead and clean up his breakfast dishes, but there didn't seem much point in doing that. Nor did there seem any particular point in getting dressed or parting his hair.

He wondered who he should he call. Howell's Funeral Home seemed an obvious choice, but as Earl thought about it, funeral homes didn't seem likely to pick people up directly from their houses, like TV repairmen taking sets back to the shop. So he called work to explain he would not be in that day, and why. But when he heard Jimmy's voice, and got out the words, "Momma's gone—" Earl lost control and began sobbing, shaking as if he were sitting on a paint-mixer.

Soon the Mulvaney house had more people in it than any time since Roy's disappearance. Sheriff King, the Medical Examiner —a short, fat man who smelled of body odor and cologne, and constantly ate sen-sens—and Jimmy Wiggins, Troy, Ellen, Jennifer, and Dorrie Raley were all there. "There are too many of us here," Jimmy said, "Earl don't need this many people around." There was general agreement at this, but no one volunteered to leave. Ellen went in the kitchen and made coffee and brought it in to Earl, who was sitting on the couch. Earl could hear the sheriff and the M.E. talking in the other room.

"Cause of death?" the sheriff asked.

"Take your pick," the medical examiner said, his words distorted by the sen-sen in his mouth. "Everyone knows they made Ruby Mulvaney on a Monday. Heart failure is what I guess I'll put it down to. But you could probably add failure of kidney, liver, and chitterling on top of that. Only thing that didn't go wrong was a wall safe falling on her."

"I'll help you bring the stretcher around," the sheriff said.

"If Momma was here," Earl said, pouring milk into his coffee, "she'd want me to get the creeper." He began giggling and spilled some of the milk on his sleeve. Earl felt bad laughing on the very day his momma died, but later as he thought about it, he realized it isn't strange to feel bad in the middle of a good time, so it shouldn't be strange to feel good in the middle of a bad one. Ellen sat beside him and put her soft, cool hand over Earl's. Earl wished he didn't savor that touch as much as he did.

"Son," Jimmy offered, a hand on Earl's shoulder, staring into his eyes as if he were trying to find a VIN number. "Do you want us to handle the arrangements?"

"Yeah," Troy agreed. "You got enough on you without dealing with that, too."

"You shouldn't try to take on too much at a time like this," Dorrie concurred, in a steady, helpful voice. "We can take care of Ruby." And then, at the mention of her friend's name, Dorrie burst into tears. There being no one else to comfort her, Ellen sitting holding Earl's hands, and Troy holding Jennifer, the sheriff awkwardly put an arm around her shoulder.

Earl thanked everybody for their offers of assistance, but said, no, it was something he wanted to take care of himself, but he would appreciate it if someone would go with him to Howell's. A few hours later, Earl took along the frock coat, which Deborah Howell accepted with a grateful, if puzzled look, then Sam Howell took them to a lemon-oil-scented showroom and let them see several models displayed along the walls.

Surprisingly to Earl, wooden coffins, which he would have thought would be less expensive, cost more than the metal ones. And even the metal ones were pricey.

"Shoot," Jimmy muttered as they studied the prices. "I got a '67 Skylark on the lot that'd be cheaper to send her out in. But when my time comes, that's the one I'm getting," Jimmy pointed to a mahogany coffin with brass handles called "The Elite." The dark wood gleamed so, you would have expected it to have a keyboard.

"Don't think you need to spend a lot of money on this," Troy whispered to Earl. "Your momma don't need something fancy to know you love her."

"Look here," Sam Howell said, putting a dollar bill on the lip of the Elite and closing the lid so one end of the bill was sticking out. "If you can pull that dollar out without opening the lid, I'll let you have it." Neither Earl nor Jimmy tried, but Troy did, once, before Sam Howell gave the bill of few tugs himself, uselessly, before opening the coffin again. "Now that's workmanship."

Jimmy thought that if he ever went out of the car line, he might go into coffins, imagining a business with high markups, motivated buyers, and no trade-ins.

They went into the office and the three of them sat across the desk from Sam Howell. The funeral director offered them mints from a green glass bowl and then showed them an itemized list of expenses.

"I don't have much money," Earl said thickly. A more accurate statement would have been he didn't have *any* money. Somehow his weekly paychecks always disappeared faster than water down a shower drain

"I can help you out," Troy began, "if you need—"

"Well," Sam said, "have you ever considered the possibility of crema—?"

Deborah Howell appeared behind Sam, in the doorway to a back room, and mouthed a solemn "no," and shook her head slowly. She came forward and touched her husband on the shoulder. "Sam, we got to talk," she said, jerking her head for him to follow her to the back room.

Earl and his two friends could hear the Howells arguing about something behind the closed door. At first it was just indistinct voices, but gradually Deborah's voice grew louder, and they could pick out phrases, "everything he's been through . . . not going to cheat him . . . Sloppy Floyd . . ."

Then there was silence, and when Sam returned red-faced a few minutes later, he had a manila folder in his hands. "Some good news. We—uh—looking through our files it turns out your mother's funeral expenses are prepaid." And so they were. Earl's grandparents on his mother's side had long ago paid for Ruby's and Roy's funerals with all the fixings, fearful that their daughter would die an early death and hopeful their son-in-law would. They'd sworn the Howells to secrecy, foreseeing that every known asset the Mulvaneys had would sooner or later be sold or double-mortgaged to finance Roy's scientific research.

Earl got to look through page after page showing the most beautiful, richly appointed coffins from a big glossy album. "You can pick any of these you want," Sam reassured him. "It's all been covered."

Smiling and shaking his head at his mechanic's unexpected good fortune, Jimmy told Earl, "You must feel just like a kid in a coffin store."

~

207

Even though she didn't get out much, there was a fair-sized crowd at Ruby's funeral: the Raleys, Mr. Thigpen, of course, her fellow church members, some nurses who knew her well, Jimmy and the others from Wiggins' Used Cars, Ellen, Troy, and little Jennifer. The main service was at Sanctified Tongue, and then the mourners drove out in a line of cars to the gravesite. Even Kaolin trucks turned on their lights and slowed to a stop as they passed, as a sign of respect. A few white puffs of cloud trailed slowly across the sky; it was a blustery winter day, but with sunshine as bright as any day in August. Wind whipped around the green canopy under which the mourners sat, flapped the men's jackets against their thighs, and ballooned and ruffled the women's skirts. The pallbearers couldn't have gotten much exercise that day; Ruby was a frail thing to start with, and a good twenty-five percent of her had been donated to a charity that takes leftover artificial parts.

Mr. Thigpen's eulogy took as its text, John 10:10: "The thief cometh not but for to steal kill and destroy; I am come that they might have life, and that they might have *it* more abundantly.

"Thieves come to kill and take; that's what thieves do, it's their job," Mr. Thigpen explained, standing under the green canopy in the wintry sunlight. "But God comes to give and bring life." At this there was a great whoop of unrestrained grief from Dorrie Raley. Mr. Thigpen paused and continued, "See, that's the whole difference between God and a thief right there. And God don't just give life, He gives it abundantly. Heaven ain't just eternal life, it's abundant life. It ain't just long, it's wide," and he stretched out his hands as far as he could to demonstrate was Ruby was in for.

Earl did not cry that whole day until he walked away from the grave; then it struck him that he was heading home, but his mother would stay behind. He began bawling so hard, Jimmy had to prop him up to keep him from falling.

"Your momma loved you, son," Jimmy said, his right arm around Earl. He seemed to want to add something else, but he didn't.

"She still loves you," Mr. Thigpen said, putting his left arm around Earl, "She always will. There ain't no such word as love*d*. Don't cry. The funeral of a Christian ought to be a time of rejoicing."

"Yes, yes," Dorrie said, her face shining with tears.

Mr. Thigpen and Jimmy went to Earl's house, as did some of Ruby's church friends. The church friends brought covered dishes, and Mr. Thigpen brought the Holy Word. Mr. Thigpen urged Earl to take the opportunity of his mother's death to consider the destiny of his own soul, and the church friends wanted Earl to try their casseroles.

Thankfully, for Earl's sake, Jimmy drew Mr. Thigpen aside to discuss the philosophical conflict between evolution and the Bible. Now, an inexperienced oyster shucker, not knowing to stick the knife in the hinge in back and twist to pop it open, will go at an oyster from the front, trying to pry it open at the mouth, and work and work at it without accomplishing anything more than scraping off pieces of oyster shell and knuckle skin, and that's just the way Jimmy cornered Mr. Thigpen and tried to bring him around to an evolutionary perspective.

"The way I see Christianity," Jimmy said, "and I ain't putting it down, is like something you'd come up with if you was a thirty-year-old bachelor who never had a steady job or a mortgage. You take Jesus; now, I ain't trying to put him down or nothing, but from a purely scientific perspective, he don't make sense. For starters, he didn't reproduce. Now right there

Darwin would say, 'Hold on!' First job you got to do is reproduce. Otherwise everything dies out, and you got nothing.

"But it ain't just that he didn't reproduce; this thing about
turning the other cheek just ain't e-vo-lutionary. If you go
around turning the other cheek every time someone slaps you,
after a while the cheek-turners will die out and all that will be
left will be the cheek-slappers. How would that be?"

Mr. Thigpen was not persuaded, but could not find a
foothold in Jimmy's argument to respond to, so sat there with
a plate of yellow squash casserole cooling in his lap, tight-
mouthed, except to say, "That ain't the way things are. You just
want to believe things are a certain way to suit yourself."

In spite of the fact they spent so much time around each
other, you might have gotten the impression that Earl and
Ellen didn't like each other much—they had to be careful, and
seldom spoke more than ten consecutive words to each other.
But the funeral allowed special dispensation; while Jimmy had
Mr. Thigpen cornered, Ellen permitted herself to hug Earl and
even kiss him, and Earl permitted himself to kiss her back. Jennifer was in Ellen's arms as a chaperone. But she'd gotten so
used to speaking to him mainly through letters, that even then,
Ellen only said a few words.

"I just wanted to tell you how sorry I am," she said.

"She lived a full life," Earl said, as he'd been taught to.

"That's not what I meant," Ellen said. "That's not all I meant."

Earl swallowed. He'd been doing a lot of swallowing lately,
he noticed.

Troy came forward and put an arm around his wife. "I'm
sorry about your loss, man," he said.

"She lived a full life," Earl said.

One by one everyone left until it was down to Mr. Thigpen,

one church friend, and Jimmy. When the three of them finally left, Earl escaped the stuffiness of the house, which smelled of grease and too many people, to go into the backyard and breathe the star-filled night air.

The day after his mother's funeral, he returned to work. Grief for Earl came in different flavors. Mostly it was a numb itchy feeling accompanied by a dull rushing in his ears as if he were walking around town under an invisible blanket. There was another background experience beneath that, however, a fluttering sensation in his stomach that felt a lot like stark terror. Sometimes the sensation of terror would overwhelm him and he would fall out sobbing. Other than that, grief was mostly boredom. Earl felt bored with cooking, cleaning, washing, and dressing. At night he was too bored to go to bed, and in the morning he was too bored to get up. Everything seemed so unimportant; he wondered why he had ever bothered with it at all. He was even bored with himself, but with other people he was both bored and annoyed. He learned to dread the friendly, eager, concerned look in peoples' eyes when they came up to tell him they heard his mother had "passed," and how sorry they were for him, and if there was anything they could do—all the while staring in his eyes as if they'd seen a piece of bark in them, or Earl's face might hold some clue about what happens after death or the location of a buried treasure.

Little by little, Earl improved, took more interest in dressing and feeding himself. The dull itch, the boredom, the terrified feeling, all faded, and except for a dry white spot on his heart where his mother's voice had been, he was back to normal.

CHAPTER TWELVE

I t would have been so much easier for Ellen and Earl if
they could have talked openly about their letters. If they
had, it might have become a public joke between them,
and would have been innocent. But they didn't, and so whenever they were near each other, they both burned with the
conscious shame of keeping a guilty secret. What made things
worse, they followed an unwritten agreement never to mention
in their letters anything that actually happened between them,
never to continue any of their public conversations in writing.
So Ellen never got to tell Earl how much she missed his mother
or how much she loved him for making the green eggs.

You see, even early on Jennifer was shaping up to be as big
on books as her momma, and loved nothing better than to curl
up in someone's lap and be read to. Her favorite book at that

time was *Green Eggs and Ham*, which I'm sure you're familiar with, and I won't comment on it, except to say everything comes out right in the end and teaches a very good lesson about not being afraid to try out new things. Anyway, Jennifer just loved that book, and, well, who wouldn't?

One night when the Badcocks came to Earl's for supper, he put a few drops of blue food coloring in the scrambled eggs and turned them the most gorgeous shade of green. And instead of bacon, that night he served fried ham. Jennifer's eyes lit up like she'd just had the bulbs replaced.

Earl didn't serve green eggs the next time they came, explaining that they were hard to come by, but he'd keep his eye out, and the next time he saw some at Miller's, he'd be sure to snap them up. From then on every once in a while, just often enough to keep the enchantment from wearing off, Earl would dish out green eggs and ham just like in Jennifer's favorite book. Jennifer thought magic hung on Earl and everything he touched. And so did Ellen, but she never got to tell him.

Maybe Ellen should have said more to Earl at the funeral, but Earl and Ellen had too much to say to each other to talk much. And their letters worked so hard at not saying certain things, they weren't much help either. But in spite of that, reading Ellen's letters and the books he knew she loved meant more than anything to him.

Earl's coworkers enjoyed hearing about the stories Earl read, and they sometimes discussed the philosophical implications of them.

"Now you take that Don Quickoats," Jimmy said one December morning during a meeting with his staff, returning to the subject of one of his favorite characters. Jimmy sat behind his desk, the first cigar of the morning unlit, but promising luxurious and satisfying smoke. T. J. And Earl sat in folding chairs in front of the desk, T. J. Erect, eyes bright, barely touching the back of the chair, looked like a minister—which he was, part-time—waiting for the choir to finish so he could stand up and testify. Earl sat, his hands clasped between his knees. Wayne slouched against one wall. Mr. Moss stood half inside the doorway, one eye on the lot outside in case of an early customer. "No matter how many times he gets beat up by them townpeople—and they are always beating him up—I mean, that fellow is a walking encyclopedia of ways to get your own ass kicked. But no matter how many times it happens, he just gets back on his horse and sets off again. That fellow don't give up for nothing, and see, that's a moral we could all live by."

Wayne the other mechanic said, "Well, that's part of it I guess, but don't forget Donald's crazy in the first place, or he wouldn't be getting in all them scrapes. And what drove him crazy? Reading books. There's the moral for you. No offense, Earl. If you think a windmill's a giant, you got it coming to you. Donald's an old man riding around getting whupped instead of sitting at home and taking it easy. I don't know how he takes it, being beat up all the time. And every time he says it was the fault of these enchanters. Whoever wrote it couldn't think of nothing else. It ain't realistic. No one has a one-track mind that way. It was sort of funny at first, but after a while it just gets depressing. Like I said, it ain't realistic. Thank goodness life ain't really that way. Ain't there any happy literature?"

"No," T. J. said, his lavender shirt so stiff with sweet spray starch it fairly crackled when he turned to face Wayne, "that ain't the point. He's crazy—right—according to other people. But what he sees is real for him. And he's luckier than we are living in the world he makes up on his own than just settling for where he finds himself. And who's to say who's crazy? Them townspeople is crazy in their own way."

"Y'all are getting off the whole point," Jimmy said. "The whole point I'm trying to make is perseverance. I brought it up to motivate y'all to sell more cars. I'm trying to make you see I don't want you to give up. For example, if someone looks like they ain't going to buy a car, you can't give up on them no matter what. Just like Don Quickoats. You got a story like that, don't you, Mr. Moss?" he asked, trying to steer them onto the subject of perseverance, thinking Mr. Moss's unending search for his dog's fate would provide an example.

"Uh-uh," Mr. Moss said, in between sucking on a cigarette. So lively were these literary discussions, that even he ventured a topic besides the loss of Digger. "But I ain't so sure Donald even fought windmills in the first place. I think maybe he imagined even them. Who ever heard of a windmill in Mexico or Spain or wherever it is? Windmills is in Dutch, that country with all the dikes. Kind of overdoing it having dikes and windmills all in one country but that's the way they do it there. On top of that, they wear wooden shoes there, which, Lord knows, must make a terrible racket. Their big claim to fame is their tulips, which are supposed to be so pretty, but I wouldn't pay a plug nickel to see them if it meant putting up with all them wooden shoes and leaky dikes."

Earl had his own ideas about the don, which, like so many of his ideas, he did not say aloud, and which he was not sure he could have been able to put into words if he wanted to. Earl couldn't have told you the difference between karma and Kmart, but it had something to do with the idea that Don Quixote kept getting beat up trying to balance accounts for every little petty, thoughtless, or mean-spirited thing he'd done before he went crazy—all the little badnesses we do just to get through the week, things we don't take back or make up for, but just stop thinking about, which build up a tally on the wrong side of a ledger sheet, and maybe Don Quixote thought by being a general punching bag for every innkeeper, mule driver, and yokel with a pair of fists, he might help pay something on the arrears and balance things out a little.

It was a pretty gloomy philosophy, but the more Earl looked into it, the more he found that books with happy endings were few and far between. He told everyone at Daisy's Diner about one of Ellen's favorite books, the one about Jane. For a full fifteen minutes, as Earl told about Jane, the millionaire, and the crazy wife in the attic, Jimmy and T. J. ate their sausage dogs, Daisy stood hands on hips, sometimes shaking her head, and Sheriff King and a stranger in a string tie sat at separate tables, all listening in silence to the story. But no one seemed to like it very well.

"That's a happy ending?" T. J. asked. "Is that the best she could do?"

"She does marry Rochester," Earl pointed out.

"Who would want him?" Daisy said. "What did he do to get the other wife so riled up in the first place, that's what I want to know. Jane don't know the whole story behind him if you ask me. Trying to get a second wife while the first one's still in the attic."

"But the crazy wife dies at the end."

"Yes—that's right. In an accidental fire," Sheriff King pointed out, judiciously wiping brown grease from the corner of his mouth with a napkin's edge. "Ain't that convenient? What that book needs is a first-class detective in it. There's a few questions I'd like to see Rochester answer."

"I don't think there's no foul play," the large man in a string tie at the next table reassured the sheriff. "It might seem unbelievable, but that fire could be just a coincidence. Ain't nothing wrong with a story having at least one unbeliev- able coincidence. Unbelievable coincidences happen all the time. A story without one wouldn't be believable. By the way," the stranger said, extending his hand, "your name is Earl Mul- vaney, ain't it?"

Earl said it was and shook the stranger's hand. It was as hard and callused as a prize-fighter's.

"See? There you go. A coincidence right there," the stranger said. "My name is Harry Holton. You don't know me, but I used to work with your daddy before I went into business for myself. I came to town just to see you and your momma."

"Momma's passed on," Earl said.

"No! You don't say." Harry frowned and ran a hand through his white hair. His face was sunburned with few wrinkles, but those ran deep. "I'm sorry to hear that, son. I wondered if something like that had happened because I hadn't heard from her in so long. It wasn't like her." He stared at his hands as he sought words to say. "Listen, I know this is a lot to ask, but would you take me to her grave? I'd like to see it for myself."

Harry's El Dorado followed Earl's Buick to Good Hope, where they parked, and Earl led Harry up the low hill to Ruby's grave. The big man knelt beside the tombstone, and ran his fin- gers over her name and dates, reading them aloud. It had rained that morning, one of those anemic winter drizzles that seems like it will never peter out. But Harry did not seem to mind kneeling on the wet grass. "Oh, Ruby, looks like you're finally out of this world of pain and suffering." He sighed. "I thought something like this might've happened because you ain't written me in so long." Harry stood up and brushed some of the mud and grass from his knees. Then he turned to Earl. "I got to drive back to Macon today, but first, if you don't mind, I'd like to come by your place. You and me got some things together."

When they reached the house, Earl asked his guest if he'd like something to eat and drink. "What you got?" Harry asked. They looked into the refrigerator and saw Dr Pepper, Kool-Aid, eggs, and bacon. In the freezer were casseroles left over from Ruby's funeral. "Let's put one of these in the toaster oven to warm up," Harry said. "I'm always hungry. I'm a growing boy." He patted his belly with a laugh. While the casserole was warming, Harry and Earl went out on the back stoop and sat. "You and me got some things together, but before we do that, I want to tell you a story," Harry said. "It may do you some good; it may not, but I want to tell it. Do you mind?"

Earl leaned against the unpainted wood rail. A limb broke off a pine tree way up high, and fell, hit, and fell, hit, and fell—knocking its way through layers of branches down through the air to the ground. Harry took Earl's silence as consent and began. "I was always getting into fights when I was little. I wasn't afraid of nothing or nobody." He laughed. "Anyway, one time I got sent home from school for fighting, and my mother sent me to bed early. Now this was about three o'clock in the afternoon, and Momma told me not to dare get out of my bed or there'd be you-know-what to pay. I lay there in that bed, it was broad daylight, you understand, and I was about eight or nine years old without a living thing to occupy me."

Harry took out a can of tobacco and rolled himself a cigarette. When he'd licked it into shape and lit it, he took a puff and went on, "So what I started to do—out of sheer boredom—was just say my own name over and over again: 'Harold Everett Holton, Harold Everett Holton, Harold Everett Holton, Harold Everett Holton, Harold Everett Holton, Harold Everett

Holton, Harold Everett Holton, Harold Everett Holton, Harold Everett Holton, Harold Everett Holton,' just like that, over and over, like a kid can do, just say the same words over and over without stopping. 'Harold Everett Holton, Harold Everett Holton.' And after a while, my name didn't have no meaning no more—but see, that name was *me*, but after I'd said my own name maybe a thousand times, I couldn't tell anymore what *me* meant. Harold Everett Holton, Harold Everett Holton, just like that, I didn't know if Harold Everett Holton meant the ball sitting in the glove in the corner of the room, or the lightbulb hanging on a string from the ceiling or the sunlight coming in through the windows. Do you understand what I'm saying to you? It's hard to explain. It was like I was hypnotized."

Earl stared at Harold Everett Holton as if hypnotized himself. In spite of his gray hair, Harry's sunburned face was surprisingly youthful and vigorous, and his green eyes sharp; Harry gestured with powerful leathery hands.

"I'd repeated my own name—Harold Everett Holton, Harold Everett Holton—I don't know how long—maybe an hour, and all of a sudden I realized that one thing I would never ever be scared of, and that was dying. This was when Harold Everett Holton might have been a catcher's mitt, or a lightbulb, or the sun in the sky as far as I could tell. And not only would I never be scared of dying, dying was such an impossibility, thinking about it made me laugh out loud!"

Neither of them spoke for a little bit. Earl said, "Do you think I could do that?"

"I'm not sure. I don't think so," Harry Holton said, and blew out a thoughtful stream of smoke. "You have to do it when you're young, or I don't think it'd work."

"Oh."

"Now what say we eat some of that casserole?" Harry suggested. "That cheese and yellow squash I believe is calling my name." They went inside and Harry dipped their paper plates high with yellow squash casserole. "You take these," he told Earl, giving him the two buckling plates, "and I'll be out directly." He came out with soft drinks in two big tumblers of ice. After he set these down, he reached for his back pocket and asked, "Are you a whiskey drinker, Earl?"

Earl said he wasn't.

"Well, I expect you're going to be one today anyhow," Harry said, extracting a small flat bottle and unscrewing the lid. He poured a generous gurgle in each of their tumblers. After swirling his glass around to mix it, Harry took a taste. "Ugh. Jack and Dr Pepper is a taste sensation I little dreamt I'd encounter." His whole body shook, as if trying to clear the flavor from his internal organs; then he took another sip and said, "I expect I could get used to it, though, if I had to."

They ate, and Earl decided Harry was right about the casserole tasting better with little ice crystals still in it and that even though Dr Pepper and Jack Daniels tasted nasty, it was something you could probably get used to if you had to. The sun went down behind them, and darkness crept over the trees. Town dogs started up.

"The way I see it, Earl," Harry said, "God put each of us here to do a certain job, and we all just have to find what it is and do it the best we can. For instance, you're a mechanic, right?"

"Yes, sir."

"Well, that's an important job. And you can't go deciding, 'well, I don't want to fix this here car because—because—well, because I don't feel like it,' because fixing cars is your job. It's the job God chose you for. And a car you didn't fix—you don't know why God might need that car. It might be going to take a woman to the hospital who's about to have a baby. And that baby might grow up to be president or solve world peace or something. You never know. God's the only one who sees the big picture; each of us just got to do our job. Did you ever think of that?"

"No, sir, I didn't."

"See, a man can't refuse to do his job. It's like a big assembly-line where you just have to tighten your bolt and pass it on down to the next one. 'Cause we all got a job to do, but none of us knows the big picture."

"No, sir."

"Only God knows the big picture."

"Yes, sir."

"Now you take my job," Harry leaned back and stretched. "My job is helping people out. When the bank won't help them, when the church won't help them, when their own friends and family won't help them, they come to me. What I do is give them money and get them back on their feet." Harry put aside his paper plate and rolled himself a cigarette. "Of course, they got to pay the money back or pretty soon I'd be out of money myself and then I wouldn't be able to help no more people, and then where would I be?" Harry put his cigarette to his lips; the other end glowed hot red in the sinking light. Earl felt his insides grow clammy and cold; whiskey, Dr Pepper, and squash rose in his throat. "I wouldn't be able to do my job. So when you stop and think about it, giving money out is only half my job. Getting it back is the other half. And here's the thing," Mr. Holton said, picking a stray piece of tobacco from his teeth, "before he ran off, your daddy borrowed a lot of money from me."

"Yes, sir. Excuse me, sir," Earl said. He got up and walked stiff legged as quickly as he could to the bathroom, where he upchucked a mustard-colored bellyful in the toilet. He rinsed his mouth in the sink. A sweaty, wide-eyed face in the mirror stared back at him. He returned on wobbly legs to the back stoop, where Harry Holton waited for him.

"Are you all right, son?"

"Yes, sir."

"Now, like I was saying, after your daddy left, your mother would take some of your paycheck every week and send it to me. Kind of paying on the interest. Well, I came here today, Earl, because we got to settle up accounts."

"I ain't got much money, sir. I ain't got no money, really."

Harry nodded and put out his cigarette, pinching the lit end between his fingers. "I figured that, boy. And if you did have any, you sure ain't got enough to pay off what you owe. But I'm ready to close the book on this one. You see, in my business we got a special provision for folks that just can't pay up. What I do is take it out of their hide. It don't get my money back, but when word gets out what happens to folks who don't pay, it makes everyone else work their dead level best to pay me back. See, a person can't live without self respect, and paying me off is part of how people get their self respect back, so it's important to do everything I can to encourage that. Do you understand what I'm saying?"

"Yes, sir," Earl stammered.

"So I'm going to take it out of your hide now."

"Yes, sir."

"You understand this ain't personal. It's only business. I'm just doing my job the best I know how."

"Yes, sir." It's finally here, Earl thought.

"Let's stand up." Harry lightly placed his hands on Earl's shoulders as if balancing him. "You ready?"

"Yes, sir."

"Here we go, then." The first punch went to Earl's stomach, causing him to bend over, and the second, an uppercut to the chin, sent him to the ground. Earl did not try getting up after that, and Harry Holton, who had more experience beating people to encourage payment than to accept in lieu of payment, regretted his efficiency, foreseeing that he would be able to get limited satisfaction at best. Harry made do with kicking Earl thoroughly and from all sides.

Earl lay on the cool moist dirt, his mouth filled with the warm saltiness of his own blood; through the one eye not already swollen shut he saw a ruined paper plate lying in the grass, sodden with greasy remains of squash and cheese. A white glare lit the world up three times; Harry Holton was taking pictures with a pocket flash.

"I am sorry about this," Harry said, wiping the toe of his boot with his handkerchief. "Just business, like I said. You sure deserved a better father than what you got."

—

Earl lay on the ground for a while before he tried to get up. Nope, nope, nope. That hurt too much. He was lying on his side and managed to roll onto his back. He folded his hands across his stomach. He could feel dirt and twigs clinging to his cheek and chin. I need to get up and go inside, he thought, but I'll lie here a little longer until it stops hurting so bad. He either closed his eyes or they swelled shut. He dozed off and had a dream that he had decided just to keep on lying there until daybreak.

The Bridges, who lived on a street perpendicular to Warthen, were raising chickens that year, and that's what woke Earl. If you don't know a thing or two about roosters, you might think they only crow at dawn. The fact is that as long as the sun's out, they crow more or less constantly all day long, although it is true that they don't start crowing until first light. So the scratchy caw of the Bridges' rooster was Earl's alarm clock that morning.

Earl opened his eyes. The sun hadn't cracked the horizon yet, nor color returned to the dark trees in the corners of his vision, but the sky had brightened. Swelling, cuts, and the cold night air made getting off the ground a multistage process. He rolled onto his stomach and pushed up to get on all fours. He experimented with bringing a knee to his chest so he could stand. It felt like he was ripping his thigh out of the hip socket. He panted through clenched teeth, his ribs too sore for him to draw a full breath, and sweat popped out on his trembling face. He waited for the dirt and crushed chickweed below him to come back into focus.

Standing up was out of the question, but he could move his knees and arms a little, so he began to crawl stiffly without lifting his head, stopping every once in a while to gather his breath. Slow, slow, sliding a knee, a hand, a knee, a hand, like the world's most arthritic dog. If someone saw me, he thought, I bet they'd just laugh and laugh. I must look a sight.

At last the bottom of the back steps came into view under him. He reached up blindly for the wooden rail post he knew was there, and when he'd grasped it, he pulled himself upright, putting his free hand on the bottom step to help push. He couldn't straighten his legs all the way, raise his head, nor bear to bring his arms down to his sides. He stood half crouched, like a paratrooper who'd just touched down or a ninja waiting to spring. He held that pose for a minute or two and then tentatively raised his neck to reconnoiter. The sky had gone from luminous blue to hazy white. Color had returned to the world, and a thin layer of yellow light lay on the eastern side of every surface. Earl let his head drop again and considered his next move.

A gopher turtle dumped on its back flails its legs to its utmost ability and abruptly pauses; its reptile eye assumes a distant thoughtful expression as it works out a turtly puzzle of geometry that would have stumped Archimedes. How do I, positioned as I am, constrained as I am, and dome-shaped as I am, fulcrum myself in such a way as to turn the world right-side up again? The legs flail afresh, and the turtle neck cranes back and forth, less in expectation of righting himself, than in the hope of gathering more data. Having conducted the experiment, the turtle pauses to weigh the new information and see if it sheds any light on his predicament.

That's how it was with Earl. Visually he measured the distance from the ground to that first step, attempted a leg lift. Stopped and reconsidered. In his imagination he rotated his body in various attitudes and degrees, imagined angling himself toward the step and lifting his leg sideways, or falling forward in such a way that one foot would leave the ground and somehow land on that step, coming at the steps butt-first—but that required backward-bending knees like a grasshopper's. He gave a half try at each of these procedures, and each time the pain stopped him. Then he lifted his head, measured distances and angles again, and recalculated.

The day wore on. Inside the house, the telephone rang and rang, then stopped. Earl took a few steps forward, sumo-wrestler style, and then back. Finally he stopped, too sore to move further, even to lie on the ground. Earl might be there yet if Dorrie Raley hadn't seen the Buick still in the driveway and, realizing he hadn't gone to work, dropped by to investigate.

Earl heard the doorbell ring inside the house, ring again, and Dorrie's voice singing, "Yoo-hoo, Er-herl!"

"Here!" Earl said as loud as he could through gritted teeth. He was unable to open his swollen jaw farther. "Here!"

Dorrie heard him and came around the back of the house. She screamed at the sight of this gory monster crouching in Earl's coveralls but with a swollen head like a black pumpkin. Then she saw it was him. "Oh dear, oh dear, Earl what hap— Earl, we've got to get you inside!"

"Can't."

She put one of his arms over her shoulder, and with her support, he made it onto the first step. But the second step was too much even with her help, and so Earl had to wobble there holding onto the rail with one hand until she'd gotten her husband, Troy, and Ellen. Mr. Raley and Troy draped Earl's arms over their shoulders and gingerly lifted him in by the thighs, Earl crying the whole time in pain, relief, and gratitude. Once inside, his friends discussed how to proceed.

"We ought to call an ambulance," Mr. Raley said.

"That's too long," Troy said. "And I don't want him bumping around in no car when he's this way."

"We'll start him here," Ellen said.

They peeled off his coveralls, carefully working them loose where dried blood had bonded them to his sores. Soon he was stark naked in front of two men and two women, but love doesn't always leave room for modesty.

Ellen ran a bath, and they helped him into the tub. He could not lie down in it, but they tenderly sponged him down as he stood there in his half crouch. The warm water soothed him, and soon he was able to stand nearly straight. They determined that Harry Holton had not broken any bones, nor beat him bad enough to put him in the hospital—not quite. But there was not a single unbruised, unbloody spot on his whole body.

The Raleys and Badcocks cleaned him, patted him dry as gently as possible with cotton towels, put Neosporin and white gauze on his cuts, dressed him in the softest terry robe Dorrie owned, and gently lifted him into his bed and drew a clean white sheet up to his chin. Earl's head sank into his pillow, his eyes stinging with tears he was too tired to cry.

For two days he did not get out of the bed except to pee, and only then with assistance. Until his jaw stopped being too sore to chew, Dorrie brought him thin, thin Cream of Wheat for breakfast and warm noodle soup for dinner and supper, and Ellen stayed by his bed night and day, sleeping beside Jennifer on a pallet on the floor. She may have taken the opportunity when they were alone to brush her lips against his purpled puffy ones, but I couldn't say. The swelling subsided, and on the third day he arose and went to the bathroom by himself. He felt a little better the next morning, and even better the next. But if his experience taught him one thing, it was that Don Quixote was wrong; suffering doesn't do anything to balance things out.

Jimmy got the final diagnosis shortly after New Year's. At first, when the doctor told him, Jimmy did not react. As he left the office, Jimmy marveled at how unperturbed the news had left him.

"That's funny," he said to himself, as he unlocked his car door. "I would have thought I'd take it harder than this, but I don't feel so bad about it. I guess I knew I had to die sometime, we all do. And it's not like I'm going to die tomorrow." He drove through downtown Deepstep, under one of the weary red, green, and silver Christmas banners still hanging over West Haynes, leoN xueyoJ, numbly congratulating himself on how well he was taking it.

When he got to the lot, T. J. asked him, "What'd the doctor say about those headaches?"

Jimmy put a hand on his star salesman's shoulder, "In another six months he guarantees I won't have another one ever again."

Back in Jimmy's office, he took the little plastic clock—"I stepped out!"—off the door. The Clik-Tite girl saluted him with a glass of champagne. She had dressed for a formal party in a top hat, cane, tuxedo hot pants suit, sheer black stockings, and high heels. Behind her waited a full-sized customized stretch Lincoln. Jimmy put his feet on the desk and lit a meditative cigar. "It's Donna that ain't going to take it good," he said aloud. "She's a lot younger than me. She ain't going to understand." Leaning back, he cradled the back of his head in his hands. Somewhere in that bristly bowling ball was a thing the size of an avocado pit, gradually getting larger. "I just wish I'd had a son, or even a daughter," Jimmy said. "I wonder if he would have had extra fingers."

Jimmy's mother had had twelve fingers, an extra one on each hand growing next to the pinky finger, about the size of your little toe, complete with a fingernail and wrinkled knuckle. These had never prevented her from playing piano for First Baptist, and may have even improved her. She told Jimmy she had them because of some gypsy blood way up in the high branches of her family tree. When five-year-old Jimmy told her once he wished he'd had extra fingers, too, because he thought they'd have come in handy, she said he'd been born without them. Jimmy always suspected, however, that really he had been born with extra fingers, but the doctor had sliced them off in the delivery room. He had two tiny scars, one on the edge of each hand just below the pinky, which he could never remember having gotten. As a child he'd found in the bottom of one of his mother's dresser drawers, under one of the clove-stuffed oranges she used for potpourri, the heavy brown parchment birth certificate, which bore his hand- and footprints; he studied the prints for evidence that he'd originally had twelve fingers. The little baby handprint only had four fingers and a thumb, but that really proved nothing; they might not have pressed the extra finger onto the ink pad, or the certificate could have been made after it had been removed. The foot only had five toes, but little Jimmy had never wanted an extra toe. After he grew up and developed his scientific abilities, he would have told you that unlike having twelve fingers, having twelve toes just didn't make evolutionary sense.

Jimmy remained completely calm most of that day, only troubled at how he would break the news to his wife and that he'd never fathered a son, twelve-fingered or otherwise. It wasn't until almost evening, in a smoky basement room of the courthouse at a meeting of the Concerned Citizens Committee, that the enormity of the diagnosis struck him. Several of Humble County's most prominent business and civic leaders sat around a table in the courthouse to discuss, among other things, the draining of Sloppy Floyd.

"If it's a court order, can't you just overrule it or something?" the mayor asked Judge Hathorne, "You're a judge ain't you? Check."

"I can't overrule an appellate court if I'm just a circuit judge," Hathorne explained testily. "It doesn't work that way. Check."

Sheriff King said he would open for a buck, and dropped a folded dollar bill onto the polished tabletop, where it sat like a green pup tent.

"I'll fold," Jimmy said, and it was at that moment it occurred to him that he really would fold one day, and one day soon. The old gambler's metaphor for death, "cashing in his chips," slapped him with unexpected force. The room seemed to grow dark.

"I don't like it," said Sam Howell, who not only owned Howell's Funeral Home but also managed Good Hope Cemetery, which abutted the lake. "I don't think even back in the Civil War they were dumb enough to sink a chest of gold or silver to the bottom of the lake. And don't that lake belong to the Calhoun brothers anyway? Anything we find in there would belong to them. If we did find anything, that is." Sam's dollar fluttered to the table alongside the sheriff's.

"It's got to be there," the mayor said. "Everybody knows we can't find that Civil War treasure, and the only place we ain't looked is under that lake. It's got to be there. It's just a pure mathematic certainty." The mayor's dollar joined the other two on the table. Jimmy watched the poker game as if creatures were playing it on another planet; he could scarcely imagine he'd ever participated in such an unlikely activity—everyone would take turns throwing crumpled pieces of paper in the middle of the table, and at the end, one of them would pull all the paper out. What did it all mean? What did anything mean?

"In any case, I don't have to overrule anything," Hathorne said. "It's another buck to you, Roy. I can't overturn an appellate court, but if someone, on his own, mind you, acting without our authority, were to dynamite the earth dam, well. The lake would just drain on its own, and those people in Atlanta could turn blue trying to get a court order to make the water go back in. I'll raise a dollar."

Sheriff King did not comment on Hathorne's idea, but put

in another dollar. Through the black mist rising before his eyes, Jimmy watched the betting go around again. Sam Howell, the undertaker, and Judge Hathorne, whose skull-like face had not aged a day since Jimmy was a teenager. Then came the flop, which was a two, jack, and queen. Jimmy foresaw that he too, would soon flop, like the jack and queen, and that the play would go on without him, each one calling and raising as he had before, and Jimmy would never see the end of the hand.

"I ain't having any part of it," Sam Howell said. "And I have half a mind to blow the whistle on all y'all if it goes any farther. Y'all are talking about defying a court order."

Sheriff King looked up at the unexpected burst of honesty from Howell.

"What's gotten into you, Sam?" Hathorne asked. "You never used to be such a panty-waist. I thought you'd be glad to get that lake drained. Wasn't it last year that *The Humble Progress* ran a story about what happens every time the lake rises? It said after a heavy rain, bodies in the lower graves bob in their caskets like corks."

The mention of graves caused a rabbit to run over Jimmy's, and he shuddered violently.

"Well, that's no never mind," Howell said. "A court order is—"

"Say, Jimmy, are you OK?" Judge Hathorne looked over with concern at the car dealer, whose eyes were suddenly full of tears.

"They cut off my goddamn fingers," he burst out, unable to control his voice. Through watery eyes, he looked down at his upturned hands, "I never even got to keep my goddamn fingers." Without further explanation Jimmy rose and left the room. The door slammed. Whatever would be decided about Sloppy Floyd would be decided without him.

CHAPTER THIRTEEN

Some miscreant, whom Sheriff King was unable to identify, dynamited the earth dam holding back the lake. People halfway across the county claimed to hear the blast. Mrs. Price's china saucers rattled against each other behind their glass doors, and one of the Calhoun brothers swore he saw a pair of skyborne alligators, twirling end over end in a cloud of smoke and debris.

In spite of the mayor's reassurances that the excess water would all drain harmlessly into Gumm Creek, several people feared that the low-lying parts of the county would soon be underwater.

As Judge Hathorne had predicted, the appellate court and sundry environmental groups found injunctions useless to push the water back in the lake once it had begun flowing out. Sam

Howell swore and fumed and vowed to blow the whistle on the whole city council. He said he was closing up shop at once and moving to north Florida where people still had some ethics.

Meanwhile as Jimmy's illness progressed, his personality underwent a series of dramatic changes. Formerly Jimmy had maintained that charity begins at home: as he put that motto into practice, charity not only began there, it stayed there and never budged. After the diagnosis, however, the car dealer became remarkably open-handed; it seemed like every week *The Humble Progress* carried a front-page headline saying Jimmy Wiggins had made yet another anonymous donation to something or other. He rented Legion Hall and laid out a banquet for all the poor people of the county: turkey and dressing, green bean and sweet potato casseroles, cranberry sauce, and pumpkin pie. It wasn't anywhere near Thanksgiving, but since he was doing all this for their benefit, he naturally expected the poor people to be, well, thankful. In spite of the ad he placed in *The Progress* and the banner he put in front of Legion Hall, "Poor People Welcome!" no one showed up except one stoop-backed old lady who filled up the Styrofoam containers she'd brought with victuals before driving off in a green sedan that looked suspiciously like it did not belong to a poor person. Then Jimmy bought a new bouncier diving board for the county pool; sad to say, the city fathers had already closed the pool following integration, having a horror at the thought of black and white bodies in the same water. Since then, the pool has filled in with leaves and dirt, so as far as I know, the board is as springy as ever. *Roots* had come on TV a couple of years back, so Jimmy sponsored a Martin Luther King Coloring Contest to promote civil rights. Deciding who would get the grand prize—a one-hundred-dollar savings bond and three cans of cranberry sauce—proved extraordinarily difficult. Owing to a limited selection of crayons, all the drawings came out looking pretty much the same: like a chunk of coal with startled white eyes and glowing red lips.

Jimmy's charitable phase gave way to an angry phase. Jimmy started talking a lot about God, whom he referred to as "It." Listening to him, you could infer Its general characteristics in Jimmy's view: a paradoxical being—a blind, deaf, and dumb bully, utterly careless and indifferent, and yet a meticulous craftsman piecing together by raw trial and error a painstaking creation which was an endless tower reaching nowhere. "It don't care nothing about us," he said. "It don't know nothing about us. It couldn't care less if we're happy or miserable, but in most cases keeping us miserable makes us do our jobs better. Our job is just reproduce and get out of the way. And what's it all for? Nothing."

This phase was followed by another outpouring of charity, which was followed in turn by Citizen Jimmy railing against all rascals and mischief-makers in high places. He began telling anyone who would listen that there was no bell, organ, or pigs, and that there never had been. Jimmy claimed the decades-long search Humble County had undertaken for Confederate treasure was a wild-goose chase, on top of which the city fathers were frauds and cheats. Judge Hathorne received Jimmy's special ire. "Why this county keeps voting in that god-damn crook is what I'd like to know," Jimmy said one after-noon in Daisy's Diner. Beside him sat a fifty-pound sack of lawn food, which in his gathering dementia he'd purchased months out of season from the seed and feed.

"Because he's *our* goddamn crook," Daisy said, coming to the judge's defense.

"Why are you sticking up for him?" Jimmy asked. "Didn't he cheat you and fine you fifteen hundred when Sarah McAllus took you to small claims for running over her flower bed?"

"That wasn't his fault," Daisy said as she swept trash down the hole in the middle of the floor, sending it tumbling it into Gumm Creek far below. "He miscounted and thought I short-changed him. He thought I only gave him sixty because the first ten bills were all fives, so he thought they all was. He just didn't notice the faces on the last two was Grant. As soon as I showed him he'd got his full hundred and fifty all along, he was just as sorry about it as he could be. So when I came back and sued Sarah for shooting out my tires, he awarded me two thousand, and that's the most he can give out in small claims. Fifteen hundred for what I lost on the first case, and another five hundred for my trouble and to apologize for not trusting me in the first place. On top of that, he told me later that my next case was on him, free of charge. You can't be fairer than that. I'm making up my mind now whether to go back and sue Sarah some more or save up for something bigger like manslaughter."

In spite of Daisy's and others' reasoned defense of Judge Hathorne, Jimmy continued publicly denouncing him. In particular Jimmy seemed to find it offensive that the judge never seemed to get any older. "Thirty years ago, he looked the exact same as he does today, like he was about a hundred and twenty years old," Jimmy told T. J. one time. "He used to drive around this old Model A he said his dad gave him. But I'll bet if you look into it, you'll find out he was the original owner." This was the rawest calumny; Judge Hathorne was not much older than Jimmy; he just had one of those faces that age prematurely and then stay put. His high school yearbook picture showed the same hollow-eyed hairless face that he had in his fifties. Eventually the mayor responded to Jimmy's erratic behavior by disbanding the Humble Volunteers, and hiring in their place a pair of honest-to-goodness professional firefighters, virtual Yankees having come from as far away north as Charlotte.

Jimmy, however, felt his judgment had been vindicated the time Judge Hathorne tried to cheat the county out of a fortune in Confederate treasure.

＊

As the Sloppy Floyd drained, fishermen descended like flies, braving the Calhoun brothers and alligators to bring home record catches, the ratio of fish to cubic foot of water increasing rapidly after the earth dam's destruction. By the end of the month, Earl and Troy could scoop out bream and perch by the net full, not even needing to cast a line, the shallow water was so thick with fish.

Troy came by Wiggins' Cars to pick up Earl after work, and they'd go straight to Sloppy Floyd to "fish." By that time the lake had drained too low for boats, so Earl and Troy pulled on their waders and went to the middle of the lake, where they could see supper flopping around in the shallow water.

"You know what your boss did?" Troy asked as he slogged across, the mud and water slurking around his foot each time he drew out a wader. "He gave Jennifer a Bible Stories Coloring Book and a full set of crayons! Gave the same thing to every kid in every church in the county!" Earl raised his eyebrows at this. There was no guessing on any given day whether Jimmy would be engaged in bitterest warfare with the Almighty or trying to make peace with Him and doing everything in his power to sweeten the deal. "But you should see the way Jennifer goes at

coloring them Bible pictures. Purple, black, green, orange—
there ain't a color in the box she ain't put to use. It's as good, I
think, as any modern art they got these days. Ellen says—"
extracting his wader from an extra-deep pool of mud made Troy
pause "—it's only scribble-scrabble, but I can see she's got
talent. Now of course, we'll want her to go to the University so
she'll have something to fall back—" Then Troy's toe caught on
the edge of something hard, and the next thing he knew, he was
lying stretched out in the muck.

"Are you all right?" Earl asked, running toward the scene as
quickly as it was possible to run through calf-deep mud.

Troy lifted his face from the goo. "I tripped over something."
Whatever it was, it was at least as long as a grown man because
he'd painfully jammed his elbow landing against the other end
of it. Troy pushed himself up, and realized the obstacle was not
only hard and long, but *smooth*. Even under the cool sludge, it
was unmistakably metallic.

"Earl, get over here, quick!" Troy called. "Help me out with
this!" Together they scooped and scraped mud away from the
thing, and succeeded in revealing the slightly rounded top what
was undeniably some sort of enormous metal trunk, but it was
too heavy and too deeply sunk in mud for them to extract. Troy
looked up and surveyed the March sky, which, though still
bright, showed an ominous purpling on the western horizon at
the approach of dusk. "We got to get this out before nightfall.
If we leave it here until morning, someone else is bound to find
it first." Troy held his face in one hand as he pondered.

"We could use a tow truck," Earl said. "Ed Tooley."

Troy nodded solemnly. "I didn't want to split this three
ways, but I expect we got no choice. Maybe we'll give him a
smaller share."

This was in the days before cell phones, so they went back to Troy's truck, leaving behind their nets and fishing tackle, and one of Troy's waders, which was lodged irretrievably in the mud.

Ellen's greeting as they came in her kitchen door was less than cordial, "What are you doing! Have you lost your mind! Troy! What are you—? Troy!" Ellen continued, her remarks unheeded.

Later she would marvel not just at the amount of mud the two men brought into her house, but at how they had succeeded in distributing it so equally and so broadly and across so many surfaces. On the floors, of course, that went without saying, nor did it surprise her that they left fat layers of dried mud insulating not only the walls on the left side of the room, but the cabinetry on the right, even though these were separated from each other by a good six feet, allowing anybody with any sense to navigate between them without touching either one. It did not even strike her as particularly blameworthy that they fouled her refrigerator door—when was that surface ever not a mess after Troy had been through?—although it was an unaccustomed novelty to scrape off complete mud castings of her husband's hands?—so detailed they looked as if they belonged in a crime lab. But how could you explain the mud inside the knife drawer and the vegetable crisper? They hadn't even opened any drawers. And what of the crusty mud oval on the ceiling, overlapping the fluorescent lamp and the drywall? What short of a miracle could account for that, unless they had emerged from out-of-doors into her kitchen so encased they had lost any distinct human shape, but were mere grime-caked tubes, needing her kitchen's friction to slough off their three-foot layers of mud skin?

"Look up Tooley," Troy said, his mud-fat finger poised over the rotary dial of the kitchen phone. "I'll call."

Earl awkwardly flipped to the "T's." He felt as if he were wearing gloves made of drying concrete. Later that phone book swelled fatter than any in the county, even the one the Kellys dropped in the bathtub. It bore Earl's handprint on all its pages, and rattled and dropped brown crumbles whenever it was handled.

"Ed, you got a tow truck, don't you?" Troy asked. "And chains—All right—Bring them to Sloppy Floyd, me and Earl Mulvaney'll meet you there—No, my truck ain't stuck—" A long silence fraught, as the poet says, with weighty meaning. "All right, I'll tell you what for, but can you keep a secret?"

When Earl and Troy arrived back at Sloppy Floyd, they discovered one thing Ed Tooley could not keep, and that was a secret. "Dang it!" Troy swore. "Dang it, dang it, dang! After all our work!" Not only was Tooley's tow truck there, but so were the sheriff's patrol car and Judge Hathorne's black town car.

Tooley later swore, vehemently swore, that he hadn't told a soul, and tried to place the blame on Ellen. "Three ways to spread news," Tooley remarked, "telephone, telegraph, and tell-a-woman." Ellen was many things, but not a gossip; moreover, even the most casual observer of Ellen Badcock's character would have known she wouldn't have put that phone to her ear until it had been cleaned, disinfected, and possibly boiled in water. Neither the sheriff nor the judge ever revealed who'd tipped them off, but perhaps if Tooley didn't tell and Ellen Badcock didn't tell, they'd gotten wind of it through some subtle psychic vibration in the air. In any case Sheriff King deputized Troy and Earl on the spot to help search the mud banks and muddy pools of the lake bed for more sunken chests while Ed Tooley studied the first one and considered the engineering problem of hauling it out.

"I can't find a hold on this thing to drag it out by," Tooley called, kneeling by the chest and feeling along it under the mud. "It's about as smooth as a baby's butt, only it don't even got a crack. Wait a minute—here's a handle. Reach me that chain." The judge threw the hook about a yard, where it landed with a soft glup in the mud. Tooley retrieved the hook and slid it into the chest's handle. He got back to his truck and threw up the long lever in the back. Edgar and the judge watched from the back of the truck; the chain tightened and the winch strained as it pulled against the sunken chest. Beneath the winch's whine, another softer noise could be heard, something that sounded ominously like metal tearing.

"Stop it," Judge Hathorne commanded. "You're going to break that handle. Turn it off." Edgar complied. "You don't have enough torque or pull or horsepower to get that thing. You're going to need to get down there and dig out along the sides to loosen it up while we pull."

"We found another one!" Earl called out from the lake bed where he and Troy had been searching, forgetting to be mad at Tooley in the Easter-egg-hunt excitement of looking for hidden treasure chests.

"And another one!" the Sheriff yelled. "There's one here, too!"

"Why don't you get down there and dig it out?" Tooley said to the judge. "I'll run the winch."

Judge Hathorne ran his eyes down Tooley's overalls. From the middle of the bib down, he was the color of a chocolate-dipped ice cream cone.

"There's no sense both of us getting muddy," the judge said. "You get down there. I expect I know how to turn on a god-damn winch."

So back Tooley went as the judge waited by the tow truck.

"I ain't got no shovel," Tooley complained.

"Scoop with your hands," the judge shouted. "I'm starting the winch."

"It smells like I'm digging shit," Tooley yelled as he lowered his knees into the suddenly stinking slime, and dug up and slung out foul-smelling fudge-colored gluck fistfuls as winch groaned against chain up on the bank.

"Keep going, it's coming loose!" Sure enough, the chest budged, stuck, bumped forward slightly from its spot, then with a ponderous slurp, it slid suddenly free, and Tooley pitched face-first into the rectangular gulch it left behind. As the chest surfed slowly across the muddy bed, its handle began to pull off, and finally tore loose, leaving a jagged rend in one side, and then the hook with its separated handle went bouncing over the mud, across the bed, and back to the truck.

"Well, anyway, we know it ain't no bell or pipe organ. These've gotta be pigs," Troy said. "I wonder what three chests are worth." Witnesses later claimed when Troy said this, you could see the judge's nostrils flare from as far away as twenty feet. He high-stepped the remaining distance between himself and the exposed chest, ignoring the damage done to his linen pants and his saddle oxfords, and flung himself lengthways in the mud alongside, his curious fingers reaching at once into the hole, trying to pull back the jagged metal. "This is just like Christmas," he laughed.

"What are you doing?" Sheriff King asked.

"Maritime law," the judge said. "Phew, these damn Confederates weren't much for cleanliness, I can tell you. In deep-sea salvage—I got hold of something! It feels like a bowling ball—the first person who, ugh, brings an artifact from a sunken ship to the surface—I can't get the whole thing through the hole—

has a legal claim to the entire boat—I'll have to break off a piece—and everything on it."

"This ain't deep-sea salvage," Sheriff King pointed out.

"Notwithstanding," the judge said. He'd bloodied his hand against the metal edge, but managed to remove a precious mud-covered scrap. "Same legal precedent."

Earl and Troy hadn't even needed to hear this much; they'd already found rocks and begun pounding desperately at the other chest.

"You boys stop that," the sheriff ordered ineffectually. "Ain't none of this belongs to you! This here's county property! Including that nugget you got, Hathorne!"

"Tell it to the judge," the judge said. He hocked up a generous mouthful and spat on his find, then rubbed the mud off with his necktie.

"We got a hole!" Troy shouted triumphantly. Red streams ran over the brown slime that reached to his forearms. Herculean battering had opened a hole big enough to stick in a man's fist. He extracted a piece of treasure from the chest and stood up to study it in the failing light. "What is it? It looks like a stick."

"That ain't your stick!" the Sheriff warned.

"It's something white," the judge said in puzzlement.

"Kaolin," ventured Earl.

"Who'd go to the trouble to bury kaolin?" the judge said. "Unless—oh, my God," awe spread over his bony face, "this is ivory! This chest is full of it! Hot damn! You know how valuable this is? This stuff isn't even legal!"

"Ivory?"

"Ivory—ivory for gun handles, ivory for piano keys, for cameo jewelry. Elephant ivory, whale ivory, I don't know, but it's worth a fortune," the judge said, pushing his hand back in for more.

"Uh-huh," Sheriff King said, who'd meanwhile gotten a closer look. "Someone carved Troy's piece of ivory into the shape of an arm bone."

This observation somewhat cooled the ardor of the ivory hunters. Troy dropped his piece as if it were red hot, and the judge, whose hand was even then back in the first coffin, made a face as though he'd found his mouth suddenly full of bad oysters.

—

Sheriff King developed a confident swagger thanks to his successful resolution of the Case of the Sunken Coffins. He'd sent samples all the way to a laboratory in Atlanta, which discovered the identity of the corpses, corpses which records inexplicably showed had been cremated years ago. It fell to Sheriff King to make the inexplicable, explicable.

It transpired that fifteen years ago when the parsimonious Keys children decided to cremate their mother to reduce funeral expenses, the nearest crematorium had been temporarily closed for maintenance. Sam Howell, ever the resourceful one, therefore, placed the late Mrs. Keys in the least expensive coffin in stock, The Standard, sank her in the lake, and presented the survivors an urn of white powder in lieu of ashes. By the time the crematorium had been restored to working order, Sam had realized by disposing of the bodies his own way, he could save the crematorium fees and pocket the difference. Twice more he had done so—the departed David Bell and Henry Hogg. The white powder he'd given the bereaved might never have been identified except that the Bell family never bothered to empty their urn, which meant the "ashes" could be analyzed. They turned out to be Quikrete. The Keys, who had scattered what they believed to be their mother's remains over the surface of Sloppy Floyd—a notable coincidence because that's exactly where she ended up—recalled their astonishment when the white dust hit the water and instantly congealed into a lump that sank like a stone.

During the sheriff's investigation, Jimmy's moods settled through various strata of generalized rage to silent despondency and from there to noisy despondency. Worse still, was Jimmy's undercurrent of hideous, bowel-twisting uncertain dread that the tumor had driven him crazy—that even the Theory of Car E-vo-lution was a delusion, (No, not that, it was too eminently sensible.) or else that he only imagined a blue Volkswagen Super-Beetle was spying on him, or that the blue Volkswagen SuperBeetle itself was an hallucination. Volkswagens had been around for decades, but Jimmy had never given them a thought before, and now, when he wasn't looking, they'd come out with a SuperBeetle! Even the name portended the apocalyptic appearance of some invading species. It reminded Jimmy of the poem, or at least it probably would have reminded him of it if he'd known it, "What rough beast, its hour come round at last, slouches toward Deepstep to be born?"

One day T. J. came into Jimmy's office and found him particularly low. "I got an offer on that green Barracuda," T. J. said.

There had been a time when any car named after a fish, particularly if it were a green car, would have had Jimmy enthusiastically discussing the evolution of cars. It indicates his great gloom that he did not even stir at the mention of a Barracuda, let alone that it was green. Instead he looked at the contract with half an eye and wrote in a counteroffer with a ballpoint that leaned so lazily, it looked like it just wanted to find a place to lie down.

"Oh, man," T. J. said when he saw the figure Jimmy had written down, "you ain't going to let it go for that, are you? Give me that pen. Is this thing erasable ink?"

"All my contracts are written in erasable ink," Jimmy said defensively. At least he still had that much pride.

T. J. erased Jimmy's offer, brushed the pink eraser crumbs away, and wrote in a higher number. "This ain't like you. You can't let this get to you."

Jimmy's face was an uncanny sight, managing to appear both bloated and gaunt at once. His whiskers revealed an uncommonly slipshod application of the Norelco—a smooth stripe of skin crisscrossed bristly areas that remained unmowed. "This cancer," he said. "Oh, God, T. J., some days it just seems like everything's going down. I look around and all I can see is just swirling blackness. Everything's just black."

T. J. did not take offense. "Jimmy, you got to take your troubles to the Lord."

"I tried that. You don't think I tried? Weeks now I been talking to the Lord night and day, trying to get Him, or It, or Whatever to make an offer, give me a sign or something. My knees got blisters from praying so much, and I just about emptied my bank account doing good works." Jimmy's bleary bloodshot eyes locked with his salesman's clear bright ones. "You know how good I am at keeping shut. My saying is 'He who speaks first, loses.' I say keep your mouth shut and let the other fellow mutter and mumble until he works himself around to your price. Well, God can teach me and you and everyone here a thing or two about not talking, I can tell you. At first I just said, show me a sign, and I'll try to be a better person from here on out. I'm not asking for a crowd of angels or nothing, just something to show we ain't so far apart. Nothing. So finally I came around and said, 'Well, I'll start doing some good works first'—it's like earnest money, you know—'and *then* You can show me a sign.' I'm going to church on Sunday and Wednesday, too, and that collection plate always leaves my hand heavier than when they passed it to me.

"Nothing.

"He don't say a word. I start to get desperate. That Bastard's got me by the short hairs, and He knows it. Finally, I say, okay, I'll give it all away, everything. I mean it, I won't hold nothing back. A regular Saint Francis the Sissy. And I'm not going to ask You for a sign or nothing. I'll just give out of the goodness of my heart. But if You want to, and it ain't no bother, maybe You could just give me a sign just anyway." Jimmy banged the desk with his fists, making the ballpoint jump in the air. "Nothing! Nothing! Damn! I was sure He'd go for that! I'm giving it all away! It ain't costing Him nothing, but He won't come across for shit!" His outburst exhausted him, and he sagged forward.

T. J. put his hand on one of Jimmy's. "You can't talk that way. Don't lose hope, now." T. J. looked over his shoulder at Jimmy's door, "My Door is Always Open," which T. J. had closed behind him. He rapidly calculated how much longer the customer would be willing to wait. "There is a God, Jimmy. I know it for a fact. Did I ever tell you about the time I sold my soul to the Lord? You always hear about people selling their soul to the devil, well, I sold mine to the other one. Here's how it happened.

"Before I moved here, I drove a pulpwood truck in Washington

County. I was on my way to this farm down South Georgia off Four Forty-one, so I figured there'd be no harm stopping in to see this girl I knew in Dublin. Well, when I got done, I was way behind schedule, so to make up time I took this shortcut I knew. My boss had already warned me about screwing up and said if I did it again, he'd fire me. Next thing you know, I got— what?—lost, that's right. I was driving up and down and up and down this two-lane blacktop looking for this one road, Floyd. I knew it had to intersect somewhere, but I couldn't find it. I was sweating bullets by this time, I can tell you; I knew if I didn't find that farm soon, I could kiss my job goodbye. Now I was an atheist in those days—or I thought I was—but right there in the truck I prayed. I said, 'God, I don't know if You even exist or not, but if you'll make this next road coming up be Floyd Street—' Now mind you, I knew good and well it wasn't Floyd because I'd been by it six times already, but even so I wasn't going to say something dumb like, 'I'll serve you forever and go to church every Sunday'—so I made it little, I just said, 'If You make this next road be Floyd, I'll look for You and try to seek You out.' That's it. Right when I said it, I felt all of a sudden relieved, and sure enough when I came up to the next road, it was—what?—Floyd, yes it was."

"That ain't a miracle," Jimmy said, but there was the slightest lifting in his voice that suggested he was hungry to believe it was. "You probably was just too nervous all those other times to read the sign right. It was probably Floyd all the time."

"I thought of that, and I wouldn't put it past Him to get me all scared and flustered, so I'd be asking for a miracle when there wasn't no need. But on the other hand—if I drove past that road one time, I drove past it six, Jimmy—on the other hand maybe God rearranged geography all over middle Georgia, because you can't just twist around one road without twisting around a whole bunch of others, and not just geography but time, too, because once He made that road into Floyd Street, He made it so it had *always* been Floyd Street—so maybe He rearranged space and time just to get my one soul. But however He did it, whether it was an honest-to-God miracle, or just a trick, He had my name on a contract, and wasn't letting me turn loose. But I've been in here long enough. I got to get back to that customer. I'll come back in a little and tell you the rest."

T. J. left, and Jimmy waited, staring at the open door without so much drumming his fingers until the salesman returned. When T. J. came back, Jimmy said, "That still wasn't no miracle."

But T. J. saw he had the car dealer's interest, which is all any good preacher needs. "That's not the whole story. Did I say it was the whole story? After the Floyd Street thing, at first I was all religious, but little by little I backslided, and figured it was just a coincidence, like you said, and there wasn't no God after all. But all that time, He had my name on His contract. Eventually I lost my job with the pulpwood company, and that's when I came here looking for work. I was standing on West Haynes sort of at sixes and sevens, out of work, wondering what to do next, when I saw this sky-blue Mercury LeSabre parked under this humongous oak tree. I was just thinking to myself how I'd like to have a car like that, and how the owner shouldn't've parked it right under that tree that way when blam! This big old branch falls off the top of the tree and slams into that car. I mean it demolished it, that branch was as big as a whole 'nother tree by itself.

"The next thing I know, I'm called up in court as a witness. You see, the insurance company don't want to pay up, and I'm the only one who saw what happened. So they make me swear on the Bible and tell exactly what I saw."

"Did the insurance company pay up?"

"I don't know, and it don't matter. The thing is what the judge said." T. J. allowed an impressive silence to fill the room until the air was fairly humid with it. "He ruled. What I saw. Was an Act. Of. God. That's right. You can ask Judge Hathorne if you don't believe it. Somewhere in the Humble County courthouse there's my legal sworn testimony and a judge's official verdict that I witnessed an Act of God. I couldn't deny Him no longer. That's when I became a minister. And when I couldn't make money enough doing that, I came to work here as a sideline.

"Now look at this here offer," T. J. said, pointing to the contract. "He still wants to counter. He's already bending, though. Let's get in there, so you can say, 'We ain't so far apart.' Throw in a fill-up and knock off an extra twenty bucks and I think we got him. Let's go." And taking his boss by the elbow, T. J. led Jimmy out of the office.

CHAPTER FOURTEEN

E arl," Jimmy said, late one afternoon, "you're the only one I can talk to about this."

Jimmy and Earl were sitting in lawn chairs in front of the shed, viewing the amber glow of the water tower through the telephone wires as the sun set over Deepstep. The first town dogs were just starting up. They were both drinking Dr Peppers, and Jimmy was smoking a cigar. The good thing about a brain tumor is it means you don't have to worry about lung cancer.

"About what, sir?"

"My cancer. The Big C. I expect you know I'm pretty sick."

"Yes, sir," Earl said. Suddenly Jimmy began trembling so violently you'd have thought there was an earthquake from the way the lawn chair was shaking. He looked down in his lap, his face deathly pale.

"Jimmy, are you OK?"

"Just look out in the street," Jimmy said in a strangled voice. "Try to act natural. Don't act like you're looking for nothing. Now tell me," Jimmy hesitated and then in a gasping whisper, "you see a blue SuperBeetle out there?"

Earl looked up. "Yes, sir."

"Oh, thank God. At least I'm not imagining that." He brought his cigar unsteadily to his whitened lips for a reassuring drag. "You're the only one I can talk to who ain't going to try to sell me on believing something or other. I been trying to get right with Jesus. All my life, I've pretty much looked out for number one, but now here I am facing the Big C."

"Yes, sir."

"I never did tell you how sorry I was things didn't work out between you and your girlfriend all them years ago. I always sort of blame myself for that. You two was a sweet couple."

A memory of bee stings along his back caused Earl to shift uncomfortably in his lawn chair. "I don't think you had nothing to do with that, Jimmy."

"Well, I just wanted—I'm trying to make amends for things. Thing is, I'm trying to negotiate with God. I need to strike a bargain for a miracle cure or, at the very least, heaven, but you know, I can't get nothing from Him. He don't give no indication which way he's leaning."

"Sir?"

"I have done everything I know to close this deal. I've been praying, going to church, and good works—don't get me started on good works. Did you know this year every kid going to school is getting a free pencil box and a pad of paper—absolutely free? Courtesy of—" Jimmy pointed a thumb at himself. "And Botswana; I have adopted a regular swarm of kids over there. It's that thing where the lady says for the price of a cup of coffee you can feed a kid every day? Well, I'm shelling out enough for an entire Waffle House breakfast three times a day seven days a week and hash browns scattered, smothered, and covered, and enough to tip the waitress, too. And mind you, all of this is on top of a regular tithe at First Baptist. You think God would be glad of all that."

"I'm sure He appreciates it, sir."

"Well, you wouldn't know it from any reaction. I'm not asking for a crowd of angels to come down or nothing, just a sign. Something. Something to let me know me and God ain't that far apart." The sun hit a red streak in the sky and turned three skinny clouds all pink underneath. A little bird hopped into the dust at Jimmy's feet and gave itself a dirt bath and sang two satisfied notes before flying to its nest in a crepe myrtle and tucking itself into a ball to sleep.

"Tell you the truth, I was never much for religion before I got this damn tumor. I was gone on e-vo-lution from the moment I heard about it. Bible says we're all brothers, which is a nice thing, but the theory of e-vo-lution says that crepe myrtle over there is a cousin of mine. I always liked that thought. And I always hoped I'd have a son to carry some of my genes, and he'd have a son, and so on, and they'd be mutating just a little on down the line, until one day a million years from now, one of my descendents would have mutated into this super-duper car man. Like he could swap out a Pinto and get back a Cadillac. But I never had a son. And even if I had, it don't add up to nothing. It's just a big dog chasing its tail, and going faster and faster. Even the fittest don't survive; they just survive a little longer than the un-fittest. And if car salesmen are mutating, the customers are mutating, too.

Everything's changing and dying, but it's just blind. There ain't no purpose in it."

"Mm-hm."

"I've been thinking about faith and all that." Jimmy paused for such a long time Earl figured he wasn't going to say anything else. Another bird lit on a telephone wire in front of them and then flew off again. "The Bible says we've all got Jesus inside us. But it won't do to go looking for Jesus inside me. I've looked—" Jimmy was losing control of himself, starting to sob, "there ain't nothing in me but a big hollow—and this goddamn cancer!" Jimmy composed himself with an effort. "I'm reading a book called *Life After Life*. It's kind of interesting. It's interviews with all these people that were clinically dead— their hearts stopped beating—and they all say the same thing. They saw this bright light, and they went toward it. Some of them say they even saw their relatives who'd died before coming to meet them. It's like there's proof of heaven. Kind of makes you hopeful."

"I guess."

"Do you think there's any truth in that?"

"Maybe."

"I just wish I knew for sure. Signs," Jimmy said with a sigh, and exhaled a plume of white smoke. For a few moments he was coughing and couldn't speak. "Do you believe in signs?"

"You mean like from God?"

"Yeah, or like an angel. Some people say they've seen angels."

"I've never seen an angel," Earl said after a thoughtful sip of Dr Pepper. "That don't mean they're not around. I've heard of a lot stranger things than angels that turned out true."

Without mentioning Ellen's letters, Earl brought up the subject of car faces, and, as you might have expected, Jimmy had an evolutionary explanation. According to Jimmy, the reason is that as cars evolve into fish, they're developing similar anatomies. Headlights are so the car can see, just like eyes are so a fish can see; it would be surprising if they *didn't* look the same. The grille looks like a mouth because it lets in air to cool the engine just like a fish's mouth lets in water.

"The Studebaker had three headlights," Jimmy pointed out, jabbing the air with his cigar, and forgetting the Big C as he warmed to his topic. "And the middle rotated, which you think would be real practical, but the design died out. And do you know why? It just wasn't adaptive e-vo-lutionarily. You ever see a three-eyed fish? Now if you want to get real scientific about it, you'll see that the radio antenna does the same thing for a car that whiskers do for a catfish, which is why antennas are long and skinny and stick out like whiskers. And you might think side-view mirrors shouldn't look so much like ears, since fish don't have ears, but if you research into it, you'll find out fish really do have ears, and you know where they are? On the sides, right where the side-view mirrors would be if fish was cars, and of course, fish really are cars, or vice versa, which is my whole point."

Jimmy sucked on his cigar and reflected. Car lights flashed on the windows of Miller's Grocery across the street. Fryers 49¢/lb. "This is the best I've felt in a long time," Jimmy said. "It's a funny thing to be so happy in the middle of being so miserable."

Leaving out the parts about the antenna and the side-view mirrors, Earl later wrote down Jimmy's theory about car faces in a letter to Ellen, and it seemed so reasonable, even she had to agree it was the most plausible explanation.

Jimmy and Earl talked into the early evening that day, and after dusk settled, Earl unlocked the shed to show Jimmy his progress on the Endless Corvette. Later, Jimmy would contradict himself about what he had seen in that shed. Sometimes he said there was nothing in it but his original white '53 Corvette. Other times he claimed he'd seen another Corvette, nearly complete, sitting beside it. The second Corvette, according to Jimmy, was shimmery and vague, and disappeared or reappeared depending on how you looked at it, like a hologram.

"The clearest way to see it," he later told T. J. and Daisy when they came to see him in the Baldwin County Hospital, "is to look at it sideways, out of the corner of your eye. If you look at it straight on, it ain't there."

"Medication and fear done got to that man," Daisy said as she and T. J. waited for the elevator. "If that don't beat all. A see-through Corvette. They must have him on enough THC for a whole 'nother Woodstock."

"I don't know," T. J. said. "I've seen some weird things happen around that boy. Some weird things. If there's anyone could make two Corvettes out of one, it's Earl Mulvaney."

∼

Ruby Mulvaney had died in dribs and drabs, shedding parts here and there, until what was left of her just quit entirely, but Jimmy was different. He died in two stages. There was a rapid decline, but for a time after that he floated near the surface, twirling around, but going no deeper. When he did go, he went under all at once in a rush.

During his twirling-around phase, he ran his business and gave considerably to charities, but as time went on, Jimmy spent more and more time at the hospital. For a while, whenever Jimmy was absent, T. J. would take complete charge of approving all deals, sitting behind Jimmy's desk, much to the resentment of Mr. Moss. It was a small car lot, however, and neither salesman could be spared, so T. J. had suggested that Earl become the "we ain't so far apart" man. Wayne the other mechanic disapproved of this imposture, ostensibly on the grounds that everyone in the county knew Earl was a mechanic, and would not be taken in to see him do a walk-on as a sales manager. Wayne managed to partially convince Mr. Moss that the scheme was sure to backfire, and the hunchbacked salesman in his roundabout way suggested to T. J. that they might want to think of another plan. Ultimately, however, selling cars, especially the "we ain't so far apart" part, is just theater, and in a small troupe, such as this one, anyone may be called upon to play two parts.

When T. J. or Mr. Moss got an offer, he'd walk it over to Jimmy's vacant office, look up the car in the gray metal file cabinet and see the actual bottom price Jimmy was willing to take. (Jimmy himself had never needed to look up any cars; he knew them all by heart.) Then the salesman would write a counteroffer in different color ink and walk it back to the customer. On receiving the second offer, the salesman would go outside as if rechecking the VIN number or something on the car. This was the signal for Earl to spring into action. He'd take a handful of Goop to wash the grease off his hands, slip from his red coveralls into his Sunday clothes and clip-on tie, put his taped-together glasses in his pocket, and run around to the far side of the building to approach the salesroom from the direction of Jimmy's office.

"This is our sales manager," the salesman would say to introduce Earl.

Earl would come in, give the customer two firm handshakes

as T. J. had taught him, and say, "We ain't so far apart." Then Earl would pretend to study the proposal, although without his glasses he couldn't see much more than a blurry white rectangle, and pretend to write in the Final Offer—the salesman had already written it in—presenting it to the customer, saying "This is the best I can do."

Usually that was all it took, and the customer signed the papers right there; the acid test, however, came when a prospect of Mr. Moss's had the audacity to counter the Final Offer.

"Well, I don't know," said the customer, who'd selected a plaid blazer for his day of negotiating with the salesman. In other words, he'd come loaded for bear. "I still need you to come down a couple of hundred dollars."

Earl was dumbstruck. T. J. had never coached him for any point beyond "This is the best I can do," the performance at that juncture requiring too much subtlety and depth for a walk-on player. Unscripted and unable to ad-lib, Earl did not know whether to get up, say something, frown, smile, or shake his head, so he just sat there silently, wishing unhappily he could get back to the transmission on that Pontiac. Mr. Moss, who had never thoroughly approved of T. J.'s scheme, stood with his lips twitching in disgusted vindication.

The tableau only lasted a few seconds by the Clik-Tite clock on the wall, but to the prospect, it felt long enough for continents to shift and stars to cool. He, Mr. Moss, and Earl stared at one another with the creeping awareness that unless someone spoke, archeologists in some future age would dig them up, frozen in exactly those positions. In desperation, to answer the yawning gulf of silence, the customer finally stammered, "Never mind, I'll take it," and so the deal was closed.

So grateful and impressed was Mr. Moss, and so contrite for ever having doubted Earl, Earl the genius mechanic who had years ago fixed the unfixable starter on his Rambler, that he later revealed to Earl the letter, which, of all the sacred things he knew, was most sacred. He came shyly into the garage one day soon after with a sheaf of yellowed notebook paper, as fat around as a muffler, just as Earl had unwrapped the wax paper from the bacon-and-scrambled-egg sandwich he'd brought for his lunch. Mr. Moss coughed softly and sat beside Earl on the greasy wooden bench at the back of the garage. He looked down at the papers in his hands, making up his mind whether he should share them with another living being. He gave them to Earl, and Earl's hand dipped down under the weight.

"The envelope come nearly covered up with ten-cent stamps," Mr. Moss said, "but even then, I had to pay a quarter extra postage due. It come from Pam one month later to the day that she run off with Dwayne, postmarked Perdido, Nevada." Mr. Moss paused and raised his trembling Camel to his lips. "She's supposed to say in here what became of my dog, Digger."

Earl opened it respectfully and began to read the crowded lines:

Dear Mr. Moss,
   I know you may never forgive me for what I did,

Yes, even his fiancée, strange as it must seem, called him Mr. Moss. The man was born, as far as I can tell, without a proper name, unless he was christened "Mister" by his parents. And if you doubt it, you can find his gravestone and see it's carved there, too. At any rate, the letter went on unnumbered pages; I'll only print as far as Earl could stand to go, which wasn't

very far—and I won't blame you if you choose to skip ahead
and pick up later on.

Dear Mr. Moss,

    *I know you may never forgive me for what I did, and
I can't blame you if you don't, but I had to write this
letter to explain myself and tell you what happened to
your dog, Digger—starting with the night before our
wedding when the doorbell rang—I already had the
wedding dress laid out (It was pink crinoline, you
remember, with a sash across the waist (Some people
said it was bad luck to wear pink instead of white, but I
always said it wasn't like I was getting married in black
or something, and anyway my shoes and veil were
white, and besides it shouldn't have mattered what I
wore—it was my wedding!!))—which you never got to
see me in, but it fit real nice except the sash was tight
across the middle, (which Momma said was because I'd
eaten too much for dinner and swelled up and I
shouldn't of gone for that second helping of pot roast,
(only I said pot roast don't swell my stomach, it's onion,
(only she said there was onions in the pot roast, (only I
said I don't mind cooked onions, it's only when they're
raw, and Momma said the swelling would go down
before morning anyway, so long as I didn't have no
more pot roast, and I said I was hardly liable to eat pot
roast for breakfast or raw onions neither,))) but we still
had to decide what to take (You know a bride's supposed to take 3 things—I can't remember the first one,
but the last 2 are something borrowed and something
blue) and Momma said for the borrowed part I could*

use daddy's wristwatch, and for the blue thing I could
wear this turquoise bracelet she got in New Mexico, and
I said I didn't think it would be right to wear something
Mexican to a wedding, and anyway, it wasn't blue, it
was turquoise, and Momma said of course it's turquoise,
that's what it's made of, and I said turquoise isn't a
rock, it's a color, and Momma said no it wasn't so we
asked Dad, (he said he believed turquoise was a rock
and a color, but anyway, turquoise was a type of blue,
(and maybe I should take some Kao-pectate for the
swelling, and I said Kao-pectate don't help swelling,)
and Momma said your daddy was always color-blind
anyway, and Dad said let's stop fussing about it—this is
like the time we all stayed up till ten o'clock arguing
about the right way to spell mosquitoe—and we all
laughed at that)—but then I got worried about the
watch—(Oh, I just remembered what the other thing
was—something old and something new (which is really
2 things) but for the old thing I had the veil that I'd got
in Macon way back the last part of May, and for the
new thing I had the shoes I'd only just got the first of
June)—because I thought a man's watch would look
funny on me—(especially next to a Mexican bracelet)—
and Momma said you wouldn't have to wear it, just
tuck it in under somewhere, and Daddy said he wasn't
having any watch of his tucked down in anyone's
underwear, and Momma said she doesn't need to put it
in her underwear, just tuck it in her sash is all, and I
said the sash is tight already, (Momma said that's what
you get for eating all that pot roast, (but anyway one
watch isn't going to make that much difference)), but

*Daddy said he didn't even know where his wristwatch
was, he hadn't seen it in a week, (and I thought maybe
in the basket by the kitchen door, and he said no, he'd
already looked there twice, (besides he never put his
watch there anyway, but always on*

This is where Earl stopped reading, and if you didn't want
to bother with the letter, you can pick up here.

"It just goes on and on that way," Mr. Moss complained.
"I tried reading till my eyes got sore, but if she ever gets
around to Digger, I can't find the spot. I never can read the
whole way through."

"Maybe you could take a break partway through and later
on pick up where you left off," Earl suggested.

"I tried that; it don't work. There ain't a single period I can
find in the entire thing. If I start in the middle of a sentence, it
don't make no sense. You got to get a running start at it to get
anything out of it."

"Maybe if you started at the end, and read it backward."

"I tried that, too." Mr. Moss shook his head and blew an
emphatic jet of cigarette smoke. "It didn't do no good. As far
as I can tell it's wristwatches, pot roasts, and sashes from start
to end. I ain't sure she ever mentions Digger at all."

—

As Jimmy declined, eventually winding up at the Macon hospital, it was Troy who rode over with Earl every day to visit.
Troy did this without asking, showing up one day at Wiggins'
Used Cars after work one afternoon and saying, "I hear you're
going to visit your boss today."

"Yes."

"I can ride over with you if you like."

And that settled it. They began driving every afternoon in Troy's truck to visit Jimmy. It was just the crack of spring, so on the long scenic trips into Baldwin County they saw the pollen blowing off the pine trees in heavy yellow puffs, the morning that all the dogwood blossoms popped and suddenly the woods were flecked with white, and all the wisteria came in and hung the pine trees with purple. It's a real brief time, and you have to be there on the spot, or you'll miss it, because the next thing you know, the first hard sweet rain will fall and batter all the white petals to the ground, and the wisteria will fade, and the only thing that can hang on are the azaleas.

Troy was easy company; he didn't do a lot of talking or try to make Earl cheer up, but the ride back home with the image of Jimmy's wasted body pasted in Earl's retinas was a lot easier to take with someone in the seat beside him. One time Earl even told Troy about the Endless Corvette. They were sitting in the hallway outside the room while Mr. Thigpen visited Jimmy inside. Troy listened, then nodded thoughtfully and said, "That makes sense."

That happened to be the night that Jimmy died. Neither Troy nor Earl knew at the time that Jimmy would die that night, and when they left, he was still there, but it was clear even then he wasn't ever going to leave that hospital bed on his own. Mr. Thigpen had come in earlier that day to console Jimmy and was still there when Earl and Troy arrived. I hate to say it, but I do believe Mr. Thigpen had been waiting ever since Ruby's funeral, when Jimmy said all those things about Jesus and evolution, to see Jimmy get his comeuppance from the Lord.

"I just need a sign, is all," Jimmy said, "I just need to know God's out there and He cares about me."

"He cares about you!" Mr. Thigpen exploded—more in fury than reassurance. "What is all this if it ain't caring about you?" Mr. Thigpen waved his Bible around the room at the hospital bed, the medical charts, the clear bag of morphine dripping into Jimmy's arm. "You're standing right in front of God's billboard, and you're asking for a sign! God *chastises* those he loves! Why you probably ain't suffered one day in your whole ornery life, and now you're complaining because God's kind enough to give you this here wake-up call, let you know what you're in for if you don't repent? And instead of being grateful for God's message, you just bellyache." Mr. Thigpen pretended to rub tears from his eye with a balled-up fist, and spoke in a high-pitched little-girl voice, "'Oh, I got cancer, oh, I'm going to die, oh, boo-hoo, God is so mean.'" Abruptly, Mr. Thigpen snapped out of it and spoke in his normal gravelly baritone, which was something like the hoarse rumble of a Mustang when you rev it up just before burning rubber, "Whatever made you think God'd go any easier on you than He did on His own Son? And He *crucified* Him! Life is hard, that ain't news, and I tell you, whatever heaven's like, I don't expect even it's going to be any easier. God's trying to toughen us up for something, mark my words. In the meantime, you got to learn some patience; you got to learn some faith and humility. God wants something with you, that's why He's doing you this way. There's your sign. Why you take Ruby Mulvaney; what you're going through a few months ain't a patch on what she endured her whole life. And she never doubted God's mercy not one minute or ever turned her back on Him!"

By this time Mr. Thigpen was roaring, stomping around the little room like an angry bear in a too-small cage. But when the door opened to let in Earl and Troy, Mr. Thigpen fell abruptly

silent, dropped his arms, and turned his back in embarrass
ment, wiping spit from his chin.

"Oh, sorry," Earl said, "I didn't mean to interrupt nothing."

"I'm just leaving," Mr. Thigpen said, not meeting their eyes.
His voice was hoarse and trembling. His hands were shaking,
too. His outburst had taken a lot out of him.

"Well, it sure was wonderful, you taking time out to come
and comfort Jimmy," Troy said.

Jimmy did not look wonderfully comforted. He looked dead;
he skin hung on him like soggy newspaper. He was shaking
almost as much as Mr. Thigpen. "Ruby Mulvaney," he managed. His quiet voice was serious and seemed freighted with
something of awful import. His three guests looked at him.
"Ruby Mulvaney," he said again, and after a pause in which he
seemed to make up his mind about something, "Ruby Mulvaney loved you, Earl."

"Loves," Mr. Thigpen corrected.

Jimmy closed his eyes and nodded, his head sinking even
deeper into the white pillow. "Loves."

Jimmy had just made a difficult choice; he dearly wanted
to rebut Mr. Thigpen's tirade, and had the perfect comeback,
too, but he decided not to use it if it came at the expense of
hurting his friend Earl. In all of Humble County, Jimmy was
the only person who knew the whole story of how Ruby'd won
that card game years ago, and what a terrible risk she'd taken
on behalf of her son. When she'd shown her hand with four
twos, Jimmy had been sitting there with a pair of twos himself. He hadn't said anything at the time, and had gone home
completely stupefied at how she'd accomplished it. Finally
he'd figured it out.

On the way to Mort's trailer, Ruby had stopped at the Five

and Dime and bought two decks of cards, one red and one blue, so she'd be covered either way. She'd had them in her purse when she'd gone to the bathroom, and fished out the extra twos she'd needed to fill out her hand.

That was Jimmy's secret, and if you've ever felt the tremendous pressure of holding back an interesting secret, you can understand what a relief it would have been for Jimmy to let it out right then, knowing, as he did, this was his very last chance. Especially after the browbeating he'd gotten from Mr. Thigpen and how Mr. Thigpen had compared him so unfavorably to Ruby Mulvaney. It would have been so easy, and satisfying, to spill the beans just then. But he didn't do it, and took the secret to his grave.

It would sadden you to hear that some readers might actually question how I came to know a secret that Jimmy never shared with a living soul. Such petty, thankless quibbling naturally angers a generous, fair-minded person such as yourself —imagine doubting a narrator who has shown nothing but the utmost candor and goodwill! But while your honest outrage does you credit, remember that those few wretched skeptics— and there can't be many—are more to be pitied than blamed. I know that from the kindness and goodness of your soul, you will forgive them in your heart as I do.

Now, there are a lot of people in this story who give various opinions on life and death, and what it's all about, and I've tried my best to be even-handed and not put my oar in or come down on one side or the other. But without my endorsing or repudiating it, Will Buran had an interesting idea that seems like it fits here.

Buran isn't in this story; he was an auto maker before the stock market crash in 1929. Actually he made more stock certificates than cars, and there's some question whether he was entirely on the up-and-up. But when the crash came, he lost his money along with his investors' and he wound up owning a bowling alley.

Buran's idea was that heaven or hell is whatever goes through your mind the moment you die. He thought you never really die, you just get closer and closer to death without ever reaching it. Time stretches out more and more the closer you get, so that the last moment is eternity. Your last thoughts before you die are your eternity; if they're good generous thoughts, you're in heaven; if they're bad, it's the other place. I'm not saying that's so, but if it is, that moment decided whether Jimmy would go to heaven. He had to choose whether to satisfy the little mean bone we all have inside us and tell Ruby's secret even though it meant hurting a friend.

"Your mother loved you very much," was all Jimmy said, that and the word, "loves," and those were the last words he said to Earl, maybe the last words he said to anybody. So I expect if Will Buran was right, Jimmy went to heaven. But as I said, I'm not coming down on one side or the other about death. Anyway, it's an interesting theory.

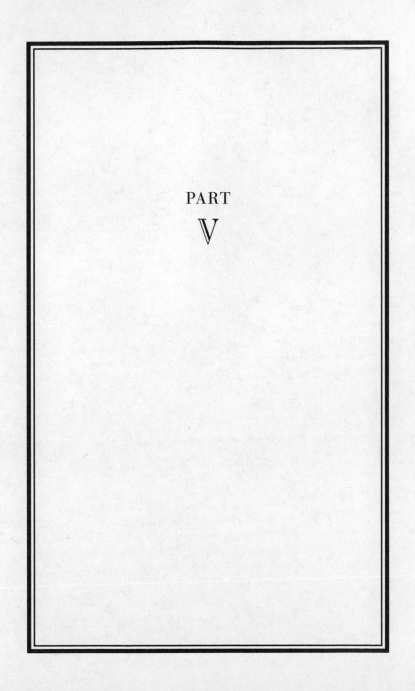

PART

V

CHAPTER FIFTEEN

S ince Sam Howell was still serving time for fraud, public endangerment, and littering, Jimmy's funeral arrangements had to be handled by a funeral home in Milledgeville. Jimmy's widow gave him a good funeral, but not a great one. While frugal on the coffin, her parsimony in the matter of flowers was more than compensated for by arrangements donated by various groups and individuals Jimmy had benefited. Floral sprays, bouquets, and other displays overflowed the sanctuary of First Baptist, the graveside, and the Wiggins home. Guests of the funeral ended up taking excess flowers home like party favors. I myself got a very nice arrangement of white and blue roses shaped to resemble a telephone with the motto, "Jesus Called." Every little stir of air carried on it the soft fragrance of blossoms, so if you closed your eyes, you would almost think you were in Hawaii instead of the chapel of the First Baptist Church.

T. J. came up to Earl and Wayne during the reception before the service. "Did you take a look at Jimmy?" T. J. asked, nodding his head toward the room that held the burnished gray metal casket.

"No," said Earl, who didn't care to look at people who couldn't look back. It was like sneaking up on them.

"Well, he looks real natural," Wayne said.

T. J. snorted, or came as close to it as it is permissible to snort at a funeral, "He looks like his wife is sending him out in a Chevette instead of a Cadillac is what he looks like." T. J., who was an ordained minister, knew a thing or two about the price of a good casket. He told Earl and Wayne that instead of springing for "The Elite," the cherrywood, white-satin-lined number that Jimmy himself would have preferred, Donna Wiggins had gone for "The Standard," the gray metal job in the other room that stood out among the colorful flowers like a horsefly on a wedding cake.

Earl felt bad for Jimmy because he knew his former boss would've wanted to make his last appearance in style, but in his heart, he did not judge the widow. He figured he didn't know her circumstances.

A good crowd came to the funeral, but most of them were the sort who evaporate immediately after the service, and so only Earl, Troy, T. J. and his wife, Mr. Moss, and Wayne the other mechanic went to Donna Wiggins's house. They wound up sitting in her living room trying not to stare at one another. T. J. shared one of Jimmy's favorite stories, one about two brothers and a gold pocket watch. A chuckle ran through the room—that was Jimmy all over—and then the pressure to say something else was so great that the engine flooded, so to speak, and conversation stalled out. Troy thought about saying that Donna should please call him if there was anything at all he could do for her, anything at all, but then he remembered he'd said that twice already and remained silent. T. J., having told his anecdote, thought about how *white* Jimmy's house was, and that you could always tell white people's houses, but you couldn't explain exactly how, and that you could have laid out doilies and antimacassars and bric-a-brac a foot deep in his own house without getting it half as white as Donna Wiggins managed to do just putting out a few coasters for their iced tea. T. J.'s wife, Gloria, was thinking something along the same lines. The mention of pocket watches reminded Mr. Moss irresistibly of Digger, and he sank into a private reverie on the history of his loss.

Earl asked if he could use the restroom.

"Why sure, honey," she said. "Just down the hall and first door on the left. You can't miss it."

While he was gone, there was a general shuffling and getting up and commenting that it was probably time to go. Earl returned and said, "I see your bed fell through the frame. I can fix that for you."

"You don't have to do that," Donna Wiggins said. "I'll get someone to take care of it later. It fell last week and with one thing or another I just haven't been able to get someone out here."

"I don't mind," Earl said. "I'd be glad to help out."

"Thank you, Earl, you are so sweet," she said and kissed him on the cheek.

Troy, T. J., Wayne, and Mr. Moss exchanged a regular crossfire of glances, but neither Earl nor the widow caught it.

Earl showed up on the Wiggins' doorstep the next morning holding a brown paper bag.

"Oh, thank you for coming out, Earl!" Donna said. "I don't know what you must think of me! I'm not even dressed yet!" She pulled a strand of brown hair away from her forehead and cinched her short robe a little tighter, squeezing her chest into a Y. An early success in business, but late to marry, Jimmy had chosen a wife ten years younger and a good deal better looking than himself.

"I think you look pretty, ma'am," Earl said, which was only the simple truth, but Donna Wiggins smiled and blushed.

"Call me Donna."

"OK, Donna. I'm sorry for coming so early, but I've got to get into work today."

"That's okay."

"Well, let's take a look at the bed." Earl followed her down the carpeted hallway to the bedroom.

"I didn't make it yet."

"That's OK; I've got to take it out of the frame anyway."

The phone rang. "I'll go get that in the kitchen," Donna said. "Are you OK here?"

Earl nodded, and she left. He lifted the mattress and box springs, and leaned them against a wall. A black-framed picture of Jimmy Wiggins on the dresser caught his eye, and he stared at it for a moment. Then he took his tools from the paper bag: a hammer, nails, needle-nose pliers, a pair of turnbuckles, and a loop of picture-hanging wire. After he'd attached wires to the sideboards, he could hear Donna talking in the other room: "Yes—yes—Thank you—Yes—Oh, I've got it taken care of. There's a man in fixing it right now. Earl Mulvaney, one of the mechanics down at the lot—yes—yes—Oh, he's an angel."

Earl had never heard himself referred to as "a man" before, especially not by a woman. His face got hot, and he focused his attention on tightening the turnbuckles. Soon all he could hear was the reassuring squeak-squeak of the sideboards pulling closer together.

By the time Donna returned, the mattress and box springs were replaced, and the bed was made up. Earl was just then putting his tools back in a paper bag.

"You did it; oh, you're marvelous."

"I'd better go, I've got to be at work."

"I've got to go to work, too. I'm the new boss now."

"Oh, yeah. I guess you are. I hadn't thought about that." During Jimmy's illness, the car lot had basically been running on cruise control.

"We might as well drive in together. Wait here a sec while I shower and change."

—

On the drive to the car lot, Earl wished uncomfortably that he hadn't gotten in the car with Donna. Had he only imagined it, or had she acted a little surprised when he got in on the passenger side? He wondered if he'd misunderstood her suggestion. When she said "drive in together," did she mean "in the same car" or just "at the same time?"

The widow smelled lightly of perfume and herbal shampoo. She'd chosen a floral print top with a flouncey collar. Earl had to keep his eyes trained forward to avoid catching sight of her left breast in profile. He sat carefully, wishing he had something to do with his hands besides rest them on his knees. Like his father, he was afflicted with not knowing what to do with his hands. He tried to visualize himself as that statue of Lincoln in Washington, D.C., sitting in that big chair, and always looking so calm and unselfconscious.

"I noticed your door swings closed," Earl said to fill the silence.

"What?"

"Your bedroom door swings closed."

"Isn't it supposed to do that?"

"If you hang it right, it won't swing one way or the other." Then, "I could fix it for you if you'd like," and immediately Earl wished he hadn't said it.

"Oh, that'd be great."

And it was settled.

That afternoon Donna Wiggins had a meeting with the employees. She sat at Jimmy's old desk; the Clik-Tite girl had disappeared, leaving a white rectangle where she had been. The cardboard clock, "I stepped out!" useless now because its red plastic hands had gone missing, lay in the bottom of the metal trashcan beside the desk. Aside from straightening some papers, those were the only changes Donna had made.

"I want you all to know I've decided to keep the car lot open. And I'm going to keep all of you on. You may have been worried that I was going to close it, or sell it to somebody, but it isn't going to happen. Jimmy built this business up from scratch, and he'd want it to stay with the family. This is Wiggins' Used Cars, and it's going to stay Wiggins' Used Cars." She waited after that as if she expected applause or at least a murmur of appreciation, but there was none, so she continued, "Wiggins' Used Cars. Because that's the way Jimmy would have wanted it. And I plan to run things pretty much the same way Jimmy did in his day, so you can rest easy about that."

The next morning, Donna watched, leaning against a wall with a thoughtful frown, as Earl tightened the screws on her newly adjusted door hinges. She asked him, "Do you think the guys will respect me?"

"Yes, ma'am."

"Really?"

"Well, it may take a while at first. They're just not used to working with a woman is all."

"I need you to help me out, Earl, fill me in on everything," Donna said. "I've got to make a go of this. Jimmy gave away just about everything that wasn't nailed down," she explained. "Every hard-luck case in the county had his hand out near the end. Jimmy may have found Jesus, but it cost me a fortune."

Earl stood up and brushed the wrinkles from the knees of his coveralls. He opened the door and left it slightly ajar to show it wouldn't swing shut. Donna admired it. He closed the door to show it wouldn't swing open. Donna admired that, too. "Thank you, Earl. I'm fixing breakfast, do you want some?"

"Wel—"

"Please—? There's plenty, and it'll keep me from eating alone. I'm having oat bran."

Oat bran is not much of an inducement to share breakfast, but Earl couldn't have let her eat alone, could he? After eating, as he was helping Donna put up the dishes, he saw a silver pearl grow under the faucet, drop, and be replaced by another. "Don't your faucet turn off?"

"Not all the way. It's always been like that."

"It's easy to fix. Just a couple of washers is all."

"Really?"

"Easiest thing in the world."

"Why don't you come by tomorrow morning? I'll have breakfast for you."

After that Earl and Donna began carpooling to the car lot

every day, which only made sense because Earl always went by Donna's first thing in the morning and also after work.

~

Humble County observed these goings-on with mixed emotions. Mr. Moss endorsed the match wholeheartedly and stood ready to serve as best man if called upon. T. J., Judge Hathorne, and Daisy looked on the matter with bemused approval. Wayne the other mechanic, to anyone not asleep or otherwise incapable of smelling coffee, swore with righteous indignation that the whole thing was a shame and a disgrace, and only a person lower than a snake's belly would try enriching himself by going after the boss's widow and that right at that moment poor Jimmy was probably spinning in his cheaply made casket.

The Badcock household was divided on the matter. Troy did not think it was any of his particular business one way or the other, but would stand by whichever choice his friend made. Ellen was dead-set against it. Ellen and Troy had never discussed Donna with Earl, although Earl would sometimes mention needing to get a part to fix some little something or other around her house.

"I'm not saying anything against her," Ellen told her husband one night on their way to Earl's house to enjoy one of Earl's scrambled-egg suppers. "But she's got a lot to deal with right now—entering a man's world, running a business, losing her husband and all. I don't think he should be taking up her time right now." Jennifer, in the seat between them, playing with a Barbie wearing a gold lamé vest and nothing else, listened with all the rapt attention of a foreign spy inadvertently admitted to the inner chambers of the Pentagon. A pimpling of raindrops gathered on the windshield, and the wiper dismissed them with a wave of its narrow hand. "Besides she's so much *older* than he is."

But Ellen's imagination, whenever it turned with disgust to thoughts of Donna Wiggins and how inappropriate she was for Earl, did not dwell on her advanced age—Ellen did not, for example, picture Donna with sagging basset-hound eyes and bulldog jowls, brittle graying hair, trembling age-spotted hands, and false teeth clacking between cracked lips. Instead, she conjured up Donna exactly as she was—only more so. Smooth skin, a trifle too made-up, arched eyebrows, a trifle too plucked, a good figure, a trifle too good and a trifle too emphasized by clothes a trifle too revealing. Donna's breasts did not jut so far out you could stack supper plates on them, nor was her blouse cut *quite* as low as the women's in *Li'l Abner* or *Hee-Haw*, but—Donna Wiggins wasn't actually so much a crone as a sort of gaudy butterfly, pretty in a vulgar way, and fatally attractive to any unwary little— Here the metaphor deserted Ellen, and she stared angrily at the stupidly persistent raindrops gathered like gnats on the windshield, and felt an angry triumph when the wiper's thump pushed them away, as if she'd done it herself.

Troy's truck pulled into Earl's driveway behind an unfamiliar LeBaron. Ellen got out and unfastened Jennifer's seatbelt. Earl's front door opened and he and Donna Wiggins stood together in the lighted frame. Donna was wearing an apron. An apron! Ellen's eyes shot a laser signal to her daughter, "We don't repeat anything Mommy and Daddy say in private." But Jennifer only had eyes for Ms. Wiggins. She stared thoughtfully at the widow as if trying to picture her in a gold lamé vest.

An unfamiliar aroma, an aroma not of scrambled eggs, filled the house.

"Aren't we having scrambled eggs?" Ellen asked Earl.

"Not tonight. I told Earl, please! We can do better, I think," Donna replied, even though she hadn't been asked. "I made curry." On the dinette sat a large casserole: pallid lumps floated like swollen drowning victims in a white semisolid sauce. "Chicken," Donna explained in a bright voice to Jennifer, bending over with her hands on her knees to make eye contact.

"We really like scrambled eggs," Ellen said. "Sometimes Earl makes green eggs and ham. It's something between us friends. You wouldn't understand."

"The chicken looks good," Troy said. "I like scrambled eggs, too, though," he added impartially.

"Do you want me to go in the kitchen and make you some eggs?" Ellen offered Jennifer.

"I want chicken," Jennifer said decisively. "And I want to sit next to her."

"Why sure, honey," the widow said. "You sit right here by me."

Donna made much over Jennifer, and Jennifer, won over, stuck by her the entire night, hugging her neck and wanting to sit next to her, if not actually in her lap. This pleased Donna, of course, but Ellen was not in the least taken in. If I told you that Ellen did not stop smiling the entire night, it might sound as if she'd enjoyed an evening of high hilarity. In reality, she felt as if the corners of her mouth were held in place by fishhooks. Her smile was about as unbending and sincere a grin as Albert the Skeleton's and a good deal less appealing.

Sheriff King's deductive powers had not enabled him to solve a mysterious act of vandalism that manifested itself during the time of the Case of the Sunken Coffins. Whether the act of some vengeful ghost whose rest Judge Hathorne had disturbed or else some mundane agency, patches of grass on Hathorne's carefully maintained lawn suddenly blackened and died, spelling out the words, "F—k You." The judge reseeded the affected area, and the grass took hold about the time of Jimmy's funeral, but when it did, it spelled out the same words only in vivid luxurious green.

"Hello, stranger," Sheriff King said to Earl, seeing the mechanic come into Daisy's one afternoon after a long absence. "Long time no see."

Earl said hello and ordered a venison chili sausage dog, rings, and a Dr Pepper.

"How's Donna Wiggins?"

Earl said she was fine.

Daisy and the sheriff laughed, and Daisy said, "Now, don't you tease him."

"So have you all set a date?" the sheriff asked.

"A date?" Earl asked.

"Well, I expect if you play your cards right," the sheriff said with a wink, "after a while they're going to change that sign to Earl Mulvaney's Used Cars."

"What do you mean?"

"I know you've been keeping company with her," the sheriff said, revealing his investigative powers. "Hey, I'm not dogging you. Donna Wiggins is a pretty woman. Still, not a bad move, I guess."

"Don't you tease him," Daisy repeated, and playfully slapped the sheriff's head with a white envelope before giving it to him and sending him on his way.

Earl considered the sheriff's words as Daisy went to bring

his order. Did Donna Wiggins have matrimonial objectives? It did not do to ignore the opinions of someone who'd cracked the Case of the Sunken Coffins.

"Do you think there's anything between me and Mrs. Wiggins?" Earl asked when Daisy returned with his food in a red basket.

"Ain't there?" Daisy asked. She looked at Earl's face and seemed to find the answer there. "Oh, Jesus." She dragged a chair out from the table and sat down with him. "If there ain't nothing on your side, there sure is on hers. Ain't you noticed in all the time you've been going over there, she's started treating you different?"

Earl thought back; though he thought nothing of it at the time, the last several days Donna had met him at the door in a black slip, black camisole, and a sheer black chemise. When she served him breakfast, she now leaned over his shoulder and dipped grits onto his plate rather than letting him dip his own. Once she had asked him to help her with a zipper. At the time he had taken these things as natural indications of her growing comfort around him. He now saw in them something more portentous.

"I didn't mean to lead her on."

"Oh, Jesus. You ain't leading her on. I don't expect you could lead a woman on if she came up to you wearing a dog collar and a leash. But you've got to look after yourself. Donna Wiggins is a fine woman, and any man'd be lucky to have her."

"But I don't love her."

Daisy blew through her lips, making a sound like a horse shaking off flies. "Aw, sugar, that ain't important. People make too much of that anyway. In the end a marriage comes down to three little words, 'How much money?' and Donna Wiggins got it. Not as much as before Jimmy went on that charity binge, but she's still got it." Daisy saw her sales pitch had not convinced Earl. "Earl, you got to do what's best for Earl. Donna Wiggins's a good-looking woman, she's got money, and she wants you. And let me tell you; she ain't going to take it too good if you turn her down now."

Earl bit an onion ring and considered this.

He asked Troy's opinion about it as they sat together on the wet sandy bank of their favorite fishing spot. "I didn't think it was anything between us that serious."

"You and her ain't—?"

Earl said, "I just didn't think it was that serious." Silence reigned as they watched the dark green pine trees reflected in the water, waiting for the silver ripple of a fish coming to the surface or plucking down their red and white bobbers. "Daisy thinks I ought to go through with it. Sheriff, too, I expect." A gnat buzzed in Earl's ear and he brushed it away. "What do you think?"

Troy took one of his High Lifes out of the cooler as he thought about what he thought. The pop-top popped and spat, and Troy took a thoughtful sip. What did he think? "I think," he said, "you shouldn't marry nobody," he leaned his square head to Earl, "if you don't love them."

Earl decided that the next time he spoke to Donna, he would bring up the possibility, as remote as it might seem, that she might have romantic designs on him. He went over the very next morning to change out her two-prong outlets for three-prong ones. He lay stretched out on the floor, and whirred out screws with a power driver. The replacement outlet lay ready near his shoulder. Donna stood nearby, in a peach-colored chiffon robe that would have, had Earl chosen to tilt his head just a bit to the right, given him what you might call full visual access.

"Donna, is there anything between us?" Earl said, in his direct fashion.

She fought back the urge to say, "Not much, sugar, but this chiffon," and instead said, "What do you mean?"

"Do you want to be, like, serious?" This was at the dawn of the eighties, before the more sophisticated word "relationship" had entered the vernacular. "Partner" was still a word reserved to address a cowpoke or someone who shared the profits of a business.

Donna had been hoping and waiting for Earl to bring this up, but now that he had, he'd done it in such a way she had to proceed very carefully. A fisherman, seeing his bobber twitch under the water, must decide in an instant if it means that a fish in the cool darkness below is chewing at the bait or only nudging it, and whether to jerk back tightly to sink the hook, or give the fish more time to investigate, knowing that if he pulls back too soon or too late, the fish will be lost either way; that's exactly the way Donna measured her response. Too eager and she would frighten him off; too reserved and he would move on. Above which, there was that in Donna Wiggins that shamed her to be caught holding the pole. It took only the flutter of an eyelash for her to decide what to say.

"Do *you* want to be serious?" she asked right back. The words needed to come out precisely balanced between playfulness and scorn to be equally consistent with her acquiescence should he suddenly stand to his feet and take her in his arms or if need be later telling herself she'd never really been interested in the fool all along if he rejected her. And you can't really blame her if she didn't bring the line off, if a tinny note from her laughter echoed hollowly back from the crown molding; the greatest actress who ever lived could not have performed that line any better.

"I can't be really serious about anyone," Earl said. "There's already someone." He began reaching in his back pocket for something.

Donna felt her skin grow cold then hot; her teeth chattered at a sudden shiver. She saw with a sudden shock how homely and skinny Earl was with his goofy haircut and taped-together glasses. And those coveralls. Jesus. What had she been thinking? She had already composed herself in distaste for him by the time she reached out for the snapshot he handed her from his wallet.

From what seemed like a long distance away, Earl's voice floated up to Donna, telling her about Ellen, and she looked at the trembling photo in her hand, and the heart drawn on the back. "You'll keep this secret, won't you?"

"Sure, Earl," Donna said, putting on a smile. She hadn't recognized Ellen from the picture. "But she's very young for you, isn't she?"

"It's an old photo."

She handed it back to him. "I think you need to be careful. You don't want to get in the habit of throwing yourself at women who aren't available."

"I'm not. We don't even see each other, really. And I don't want nothing from her. I just love her."

"Oh, Earl," Donna gave a friendly sigh and spoke from the depths of mature experience. "Having a bunch of romantic ideas is only going to let you down. You have to be practical about the opposite sex."

"I hope I didn't hurt your feelings."

"What are you talking about?"

"Saying that I really didn't want to be serious."

Donna's smile grew increasingly uncomfortable as if she

were balancing a teacup in front of her nose by holding the saucer between her teeth. At that moment, however, Donna would have maintained that smile if it had meant holding up a cast-iron skillet. She knew better than to attempt a laugh, but she made sure to keep her tone as light and cheerful as she could manage. "I'm really sorry if you got that impression, Earl. You mustn't go reading into everything. That's what I mean by all these romantic ideas, Earl. Really, you should be more mature than this by now, to go imagining every attractive woman you meet—" here Donna cinched her chiffon tighter and stepped back out of easy visual range, "—I mean that's just not mature, Earl. And I'm not sure it's healthy."

Earl twisted a cap on two exposed wires and wrapped them with electrical tape. "We're still friends, aren't we?"

"Definitely," Donna said, relieved that Earl had finally turned his back so she could drop the lead weight of her grin into a deep frown. "We'll be just like before." Donna turned and walked to her bedroom for the purpose of slipping into something a little less comfortable, then reconsidered. "Actually, Earl, after you finish up that outlet, leave the other ones alone. I've decided to leave them the way they are. *You* can just go on home."

⌇

In the morning sunlight a few days later, just as the lot was opening, some men came with a truck and a big yellow ladder to take down the sign that said "Jimmy Wiggins' Used Cars." Wayne, T. J., Mr. Moss, and Earl stood in a semicircle in front of the office watching the always-intriguing sight of a sign removal.

"Ms. Wiggins already got a new sign on order," Mr. Moss said. "It's going to say Donna Wiggins' Used Cars."

There was unanimous but silent agreement that the name was not an improvement.

"And I'd watch myself if I was you," Mr. Moss said. It surprised Earl to realize Mr. Moss was talking to him.

"What?"

Mr. Moss sucked on his Camel and blew the hot white smoke through his nostrils. He studied the remainder of his cigarette, holding it between two bony fingers with nicotine-yellow fingernails. Five decades of searching for Digger and sucking Camel butts had gradually transformed Mr. Moss into a cigarette. He was a skinny white tube of a man, stumped out in the ashtray of life and bent like a question mark. "I'd watch myself, is all," Mr. Moss repeated. "That Ms. Wiggins is looking to fire you."

Earl looked at the others for confirmation. He met T. J.'s sympathetic eyes and Wayne's cold and indifferent ones.

"Why would she want to fire me?"

Mr. Moss shrugged. "Prove she's boss. You're the newest one so you'd be the first to go. Also, there's something else. Wasn't she sweet on you?"

Earl's face got hot and his breathing came out in a huff. "No."

"A woman might not like an old boyfriend hanging around."

"But I never—"

Mr. Moss said, "I'd watch myself if I was you, is all."

～

That afternoon as Wayne was draining oil from a Carolina Blue Chevette, Donna came over and sat down beside him.

"Hey, Wayne," Donna said. "So where's your partner in crime?"

"Huh?"

"That other mechanic. Earl Mulvaney. This isn't his day off is it?"

In the darkness beneath the car, Wayne watched the black, dark-smelling worm of oil braiding into the pan. He rolled out from under, and sat upright, resting his palms on the cool gritty floor as he studied her.

"So where is he?" Donna asked with a friendly smile that didn't fool Wayne for a minute. Should Wayne answer the question honestly or give Earl an alibi? Complicated counter-weights, flywheels, springs, and pulleys went to work inside Wayne's head, to settle the delicate balance between dislike and loyalty toward Earl, and distrust and duty toward Donna Wiggins. The flywheels stopped turning, and the counterweights came to a rest: "You'll probably find him in the shed."

"The shed."

"Out back." The clarification was not strictly necessary. The gap-boarded building with flaking paint was the only structure in a quarter-mile radius that could qualify as a shed.

"Yeah, what's in that? I can't find a key to the lock."

"No one does. Just Earl. He's working on this old Corvette used to belong to Jimmy."

"So that's all that's in the shed. That Corvette."

"Yeah, it's mostly in pieces. Earl has this weird idea that if he keeps working on it, he'll end up with two Corvettes."

"You were in the shed?"

Wayne looked at Donna, deciding how much he should tell her as the flywheels and pulleys in his head went spinning again. Finally he said, "I picked the lock."

Donna nodded, not disapprovingly. "So, has Earl been able to make a second Corvette?"

Wayne didn't think some questions were worth answering; he rolled himself back under the car.

That very afternoon Donna called Earl into the office. She hadn't repainted the office yet, and the Humble Volunteer plaques left rectangular ghosts of brighter paint on the wall. Other than that, it did not much resemble Jimmy's old office. Donna Wiggins kept her desk much neater than Jimmy had, no cigar smell lingered in the air, and the Clik-Tite calendar girl had been replaced by a kitten in an awkward predicament, and the slogan, "Hang in there, baby!"

"Earl, I got to let you go."

"Yes, ma'am," Earl said, forewarned by Mr. Moss that this was coming, and turned to go.

"That's it? You aren't going to say anything?"

Earl turned and tried to think of something of something else to say. He couldn't. "No, ma'am."

"This doesn't have anything to do with—well, I don't want to you to think it's because of—"

"No, ma'am."

"It's that Corvette you're always wasting time with. It's like you're stealing time from me."

"Yes, ma'am."

"Time is money."

"Yes ma'am."

That damn ma'am. Why does he keep calling me that? Well, if that's how he wants to play it, that's how we'll play it. "Your time, when you're here, isn't yours. It belongs to me. Whenever you're not here, you can do what you like."

"OK."

"Do you want another chance?"

"No, thank you."

"I'll write you your last check." Donna tried to open the top drawer and found it jammed. "This is one of the things I keep meaning to fix around here."

"That's okay," Earl said. "I can get my check later."

"No, I need to do it." Donna tugged at the stupid drawer, which stubbornly refused to open up. A final terrific yank and it came loose with a bang, sliding all the way off its guides. Freed pens and postage stamps flew out of its metal mouth like captive flies. Earl came around the desk and stooped to help her retrieve the things scattered on the carpeted floor. "Don't help," Donna said hotly, "just don't help. I'll get it myself." She wrote out Earl's last check, ripped it out of the big checkbook, and gave it to him, spelling his name in her consternation, "Earl Mulvulvaney." That would have been the last transaction between Earl and Donna, had it not been for a later accusation of theft.

It was a tough break for Earl, not just losing his job, but losing access to Jimmy's Corvette as a source for leftover parts. But Earl wasn't licked yet. He reasoned he had enough leftover parts to work on that he didn't need a source Corvette anymore. And anyway, if Jimmy were right about automobile e-vo-lution, then car parts must have a kind of DNA, and even the most insignificant oily black rubber gasket holds inside itself the potential for the pistons, pipes, and sun-reflecting chrome of an entire car. Earl called up Troy and asked to use his truck to load up all his tools and leftovers from the Corvette. As the two carefully stacked hose clamps, various castoffs from the engine block, and rattling jelly jars of assorted shiny wing nuts, machine screws, and lock washers into the back of the pickup, Earl told Troy about getting fired.

"Oh, man, that's a tough break. I'm sorry—I expect that advice I gave you—"

"No, it's okay. I got a plan worked out," Earl said. He handed Troy a business card he'd already hand-lettered.

"Going into business for yourself, huh? That's a smart plan. Do you know what my daddy told me?"

Earl said he did not.

"We was working on Mrs. Price's septic tank." Troy banged the gate on the truck closed and continued the story as they got in the cab. "The dang thing had completely collapsed—don't know why—probably bad construction—Anyway, Dad and me was working on this tank, we was down in the ground, you understand, in hip boots, knee deep in—" By this time Troy had started the truck and they were backing out of the lot, "—well, knee deep, and it just hit me how important my job is. I mean, nothing against car mechanics, Earl, but us plumbers get people out of some real shit, and that ain't just a figure of speech. Well, Dad and me was standing in this stuff, and the same thought must've been going through his head that was in mine. I was just thinking how important our job was and how proud I was to be doing it. He looked at me with a big smile on his face and said, I'll never forget it, he said, 'Son, if you love what you do, every day's like being on vacation.' Ain't that something?"

Earl said it was something.

"If you love what you do, every day's like a vacation," Troy repeated and stared out over downtown Deepstep toward the water tower. "And when it comes to your business, I don't want you coming to nobody but me if you need start-up money." Troy would have reached into his back pocket for a checkbook without waiting another moment or gone to the bank with Earl then and there, but Earl refused. He figured he'd be able to start up a business the same way he repaired cars—out of spare parts.

CHAPTER SIXTEEN

T he day after Earl lost his job, Wayne went to Donna's office and asked his boss a question. "You know when that Earl Mulvaney left, he took about half of Jimmy's old Corvette with him, don't you?"

"What?"

Wayne wiped his greasy hands with a chamois as he spoke, pulling grime from each finger in turn with the soft brown rag. "He went to that shed back there to get his tool box and came out with that plus about half of Detroit City, it looked like. Gears, cams, shocks, the works. His buddy Troy Badcock came over to help him get it. Took an hour and the whole bed of his truck to unload the shed. Mr. Moss saw it, too. I doubt there's much left of that Corvette but the sidewalls."

Donna's face got hotter than a manifold, and she went at

once to the shed to see for herself. The door stood ajar, the lock no longer in its hasp. But the '53 Corvette inside looked just the same as it ever had. During the subsequent investigation T. J. denied even knowing that Earl had removed anything, leave alone that Troy had abetted the theft with his truck. Mr. Moss confirmed having seen Earl take "a few odds and ends" but said they filled up no more than a croaker sack and would have gone on to explore the intriguing batrachian etymology of croaker sack, had not Donna turned on her heel and left.

The next morning, while an egg-coated skillet, dish, and fork still waited in the sink to be cleaned, Earl looked up from the dinette table and the business cards he'd been hand-lettering, at the sound of car tires scrunching into the gravel driveway. He watched, concerned, as Sheriff King's patrol car pulled to a stop with an irate Donna Wiggins in the passenger seat.

Donna later said she saw enough leftover parts piled beside Earl's house to build two or three Corvettes, but Sheriff King's official report makes no mention of this. Instead, it says that when asked if he had unlawfully removed any parts, the suspect maintained that complainant's vehicle still had all its original pieces, and that he had only taken what was "left over" as per a verbal agreement between himself and his former employer, complainant's deceased spouse.

Sheriff King asked Earl would he mind coming along to the car lot to see if they couldn't clear this matter up, and Earl said he would be happy to, leaving for later the rest of the poster-board rectangles he'd carefully trimmed into business cards with his mother's old red-handled sewing shears. After they arrived at Donna Wiggins' Used Cars, in front of several witnesses —Donna, the Sheriff, Mr. Moss, T. J., and Wayne—Earl went to the shed, took the key from its hiding place behind the

Corvette's left front tire and started her up on the first try, bringing the Blue Flame Special into purring life.

"Case," said the sheriff, taking out his notebook, and beginning to draft his report, chewing the cap of his Bic as he wrestled with the spelling of "complainant," "closed."

~

One afternoon not long after that, T. J. sat by himself at Daisy's eating a polish sausage dog with venison chili, drinking a beer, and thinking how things had certainly changed for the worse at Jimmy Wiggins'—no—Donna Wiggins' Used Cars since Jimmy's death. The fact he was eating alone was only one symptom of this transformation—in the old days he, Jimmy, and Earl would have been sharing a meal, but if leisure had lost its savor, work had become downright distasteful. As T. J. saw it, there were two kinds of people: good guys and bad guys. At first Wiggins' Used Cars had been evenly split between good and bad: T. J. and Jimmy on one side, and Mr. Moss and Wayne on the other. Then, after Earl Mulvaney had come on, the good guys had outnumbered the bad three to two. Those odds had suited T. J. exactly fine; there were just enough bad guys around to make things interesting but not enough to ruin things. But then Donna Wiggins had replaced Jimmy, and gone and fired Earl. Now T. J. counted himself as the lone good guy remaining in a car lot overrun with Mr. Mosses, Donna Wigginses, and Waynes. And so, as T. J. meditatively chewed his venison chili dog, he weighed his options vis-à-vis his career and pondered the ominous upwelling of bad guys in the world.

"Hey, T. J.," Sheriff King said, letting the screen door slam behind him. Sheriff King also divided the world into good guys and bad, but as far as he could tell, the relative proportions always remained about the same, with the bad guys always having the upper hand by a comfortable margin. "I saw your old partner in crime the other day."

"Who's that?" T. J. asked.

"Earl Mulvaney, he's gone in to business for himself. He runs a tow-truck business. Well, sort of. Anyway he advertises himself as a tow truck."

"What do you mean?"

"I was off duty last night, driving home when my Crown Victoria stalls out near Green and Montgomery. It's about eight o'clock, you understand, so I'm thinking 'damn, I've got to get Ed Tooley's number and call me a tow truck.' I find a payphone, and there's a business card stuck to the glass with Scotch tape. Only it ain't a business card either, it says 'Need a Tow?' over a picture of a tow truck, a phone number, and the name 'Aardvark's Auto Emergency,' hand-lettered and drawn as neat as you please on a piece of cardboard trimmed to business-card shape.

"I call the number, and when Earl shows up in that old Buick of his, I ask where his tow truck is, and he says, he ain't got one, but he's saving up to buy one as soon as he can. Then he explains a regular tow truck is going to cost me about twenty-five dollars, plus whatever my mechanic asks for, and on top of that I'll have to wait at least a day to get my car back. Earl says, 'I can get your car running right now, and I'll only charge you twenty-four ninety-nine.' In no time flat my Crown Victoria's purring like a kitten, and Earl's closing the hood and putting some leftover pieces in a little brown paper bag he's got with him.

"So I gave him twenty-five and told him to keep the change, but I had half a mind to run him in anyway. Something smelled fishy. At first I thought he might have arranged it for cars to break down at Green and Montgomery, but I can't figure how even Earl Mulvaney could have done that. So I asked, 'ain't it false advertising saying you got a tow truck if you ain't got one?' But Earl explained his card don't say he's got a tow truck, just that people should call if they need a tow. He's just providing a better alternative. Well, I can't argue with that, so I ask him why he's calling himself Aardvark's Auto, instead of something like Mulvaney's or Earl's. He says he looked it up in the dictionary at the library. He wanted to be the first name in the Yellow Pages." King accepted the fat white envelope from Daisy, and said, "It don't hit me until I'm pulling up into my own driveway; he ain't in the Yellow Pages!"

T. J. mulled this conversation over for some time and at last made up his mind to speak to Earl in person. As a used-car salesman and ordained minister of God, he could see that a man like Earl Mulvaney was likely to get himself taken advantage of by the first smooth talker that came around and offered to manage his business. T. J. was determined to prevent that.

The next day T. J. parked outside Earl's house. He had chosen his wardrobe with extra care for this interview and did not regret having done so. He would cut an impressive figure in his peach shirt, cut just slightly puffy at the cuffs, the matching tie, knotted just so, the white vest, cut to accentuate his trim torso, and the creased flare legs that broke exquisitely over his glossy stacks.

As he raised his hand to the doorbell, T. J. took a moment to survey his surroundings. Earl's familiar old faded-blue Buick sat in the yard. Behind it, under a carport that Earl had added on to the house, lay piles of odds and ends stacked and arranged in such a way as to suggest the outline of a sports car.

But as T. J. approached, and his perspective shifted, the illusion vanished, and it became just an ordinary pile of junk.

"Hello, Earl," T. J. said when the door opened. "I haven't seen you in a while; I just thought I'd drop by."

"T. J.," Earl responded, not seeming in the least surprised to see his former coworker.

T. J. hadn't set foot in the house since Ruby's funeral, so he was understandably curious about what he might find. Knowing Earl had shown no signs of recovering from his first love, T. J. expected to find the room nearly empty: a TV dinner tray, fossilized mashed potatoes hardening on its sides, a single chair with a permanent hollow in its green vinyl cushion from unnumbered hours of occupancy, the wall covered from toe molding to crown molding with pictures of Ellen at work, Ellen at play, Ellen in repose.

But that was not the case.

The living room was neat, if bare, a shabby but perfectly clean couch sat in front of a TV, a model that T. J. knew had gone out of production a decade ago. On top of the TV sat a picture of Ruby and Roy on their wedding day. This ain't so bad, T. J. thought, I half expected to see the boy had flipped his lid.

"So, T. J., can I offer you something to drink?"

"Oh, a beer would be great, thank you."

"Sorry, I don't have no beer. Do you want some Dr Pepper or cherry Kool-Aid?"

"Cherry Kool-Aid?"

"C'mon in the kitchen," Earl said hospitably, "if cherry don't suit you, I can whip you up any other flavor."

"No—no—cherry's good." T. J. followed Earl into the kitchen. Earl poured T. J. a big plastic tumbler of Kool-Aid and a Dr Pepper for himself. T. J. got only one brief glimpse into Earl's refrigerator, but that was enough. In the drying rack next to the sink sat a skillet, a single clean plate, and another tumbler. To confirm a suspicion, T. J. peeked in the garbage can; it was filled with eggshells, dented Dr Pepper cans, and greasy bacon wrappers.

"Earl, you can't live this way," T. J. said, taking the Kool-Aid from Earl's hand. They went into the living room and sat on the sofa. "You live alone tsoo long, you're going to start going crazy. People need someone around to straighten them up when they start to go out of alignment and say, 'Now you're starting to get crazy,' and steer them back from the edge."

"You're right," Earl said. He, too, had begun to worry about the effects of his solitary life. "Do you think I've gone crazy, T. J.?"

"No," T. J. said, slowly and with deep consideration, "if you was, you wouldn't ask such a smart question like that. But I've got to tell you, I do believe you're heading toward crazy. You may not be there yet, but you can definitely see it from where you're standing."

Earl thought about that as he drank his Dr Pepper. "I don't know what to do about it."

"Well, to start with, let's talk about what you've been eating. Am I right in thinking that you haven't had a single meal since your momma died that wasn't scrambled eggs, bacon, and Dr Pepper?"

"Sometimes I go to Daisy's."

"Good."

"Ellen and Troy invite me over for dinner sometimes."

"Good."

"There were some casseroles left over after Momma's funeral. But they're gone now."

"OK. But mostly just eggs and bacon, like I said," T. J. noted.

"Yes."

"Earl, do you know what the Bible says? 'Man does not live by'—what? Bread alone, that's right. Now what that means is you've got to mix up your diet some. If you go eating all that grease and nothing else, it's like running a car without no oil, sooner or later your parts are just going to lock up solid, and you won't even be good for scrap."

Earl nodded. T. J. made good sense.

"Now also, I understand you're running your own car repair business here."

"That's right." Earl reached in his back pocket and gave T. J. one of his business cards. On one side it said, "Aardvark's Auto Emergency," in Earl's neat handwriting, and on the other a self-confident looking character with a yellow lightbulb for a head raised one of his lightning-bolt arms in a wave. "Sparky Sparks, Electrician, Macon, Georgia."

"See, that's what I'm talking about," T. J. said. "This proves you ain't all the way crazy. If you was, you wouldn't know how important it is to advertise. And Aardvark Auto Emergency is a fine name."

"It comes first in the phone book," Earl pointed out.

"Exactly," T. J. said. "But here's where I come in. You're developing a tendency to pull to one side, like I said, and you need someone around to get you back in alignment from time to time. That's me. I'm going to be your general business partner because I've got some ideas to make this thing run a whole lot better. We'll start with these business cards. I'll go to a printer in Milledgeville and we'll print you up some real ones. No point of having a business card if on the back it's just advertising someone else's business. Next thing is the phone book; we're going to call the Yellow Pages and have them put you in there. And not just a little ad, either, but a box."

Earl leaned forward in rising excitement at T. J.'s business plans. T. J. set his bright red drink on the coffee table, leaned back, and stretched his long arms over the back of the sofa as he let his eyelids fall over his eyes and dreamed of the Aardvark Auto to come. "And we're going to put a picture in it of an aardvark to help people remember. What is an aardvark anyway? A kind of a penguin?"

"It's a kind of anteater."

"OK, we'll have one on there. My cousin Bobby knows how to draw, and he can make us one. We'll have him holding a wrench or something."

"That's good."

"You got money to pay for all this, right?" T. J. asked. "I expect eating nothing but eggs and bacon, you've saved up a good bit of cash by now."

"Oh, some, sure."

"That's good, too. And I'll be your accountant to take care of the counting. You've got to keep records and stuff. If you don't pay taxes at least every few years or so, the government's likely to come for you. Also I'm going to put my wife Gloria in charge of your diet. You won't have to pay her much, but she'll make sure you eat more balanced food, not just scrambled eggs and bacon but green vegetables and sunflower seeds and things. Now, when folks come in for repairs, we're going to do triage, like they do on *M*A*S*H*, when someone wants something major, that's you. If it's a little thing like spark plugs or an oil change, I'll do it. Later on, we'll hire someone on to do oil changes and that. Before you know it, I expect we're going to have more business than you could shake a stick at.

And I figure we could mail out cards to people and let them know when it's time to change their oil."

"Those are good ideas," Earl said, excited to have such a smart partner.

—

Soon Earl had bona fide business cards, two hundred fifty of them sitting in crisp, stiff, uniform virginity, packed into their box and smelling tantalizingly of ink and opportunity from a Milledgeville printer. When the new Yellow Pages came out, Aardvark Auto had a big block ad. The card and ad featured the same design: a picture of a penguin, who looked a lot like the Kools penguin except he was holding a monkey wrench instead of a box of cigarettes. Underneath ran the words, "Aardvark Auto Emergency" in big black letters along with T. J.'s and Earl's names, a phone number, and address. T. J. was right about doing a good business; customers began bringing their sputtering or oil-burning cars to Earl's house from as far away as Sparta.

Many of these customers got a look at the junk pile Earl claimed was his Endless Corvette, but no one seemed to agree on its state of completion. Some said it was a heap of the merest scrap, and that even a mechanic of Earl's undoubted genius would be unable to put it together; others claimed the car was nearly complete but for a few missing parts of the chassis; however, even this subset of witnesses could not agree which parts were missing; some said it was the passenger side door panel, others it was the red dashboard, others the rearview mirror, and so forth.

Humble County has an anti-liquor law, a law against dancing on Sunday, and a law that says if a motorcar and a mule come to an intersection at the same time, the car has to pull off into a ditch, but the county fathers have never seen fit to enact any sort of zoning ordinance, so on a residential street there was nothing illegal about Earl's running a car-repair business, or for that matter, a pig farm, if he had so chosen. Nevertheless, nothing could prevent Earl's neighbors from voicing their displeasure.

Mrs. Smith, whose house sat just to the right of Earl's, gave Mrs. Raley a piece of her mind while standing in line at Miller's Grocery. "It's nothing but cars, cars, cars, night and day. That business is overflowing out of Earl's yard onto both sides of the street. One man was about to park in my driveway, and I told him flat out, 'You can just move your car back on out, this ain't no Indian Appleless.' I've got a good mind to call the judge and see if can't something be done. There's a colored woman coming there to cook, which ain't so bad, but he's also got working there a bee-el-ay-see-kay man, so we got one of them coming in the neighborhood every day on top of everything else. I've got a good mind to call the judge like I said."

Mrs. Raley's eyes narrowed to little blue points. She did not have a butcher knife handy, which was a lucky thing, but she made do with pointing a can of crushed pineapple at Mrs. Smith's chest in a most threatening way. "If you do one thing— If you do one thing to hurt that boy's business, Emma Smith, or anything at all to hurt him, I'm going to turn my house into an all-body restoration shop, and I'll tell you what else, I'm going right over to Earl Mulvaney's this very day and tell him if he's got extra customers, they can feel free to use my driveway. They can park their cars in my front yard if they want to, right on the grass!"

Fortunately for all concerned, Aardvark Auto soon had enough money to move into a regular business location. Daisy was all for letting them open up next to her diner, figuring that she could serve people sausage dogs and onion rings while they waited on their cars, showing she was both a helpful person and shrewd businesswoman. But as it turned out, the place they ended up buying out was Tooley's Texaco on West Haynes. T. J. and Earl pulled down the old sign, and from somewhere T. J. found a secondhand light-up sign with a picture of a sleepwalking bear. Using Glidden semigloss exterior, T. J.'s cousin Bobby painted out the nightcap and changed it into a baseball cap, and changed the nightshirt into red coveralls. He painted the bear's eyes wide open and then in one paw added a monkey wrench. In the remaining area of the sign, he fit in "Aardv. Auto Em."

T. J.'s marketing program proved effective, but left some people perplexed. "Why is that bear holding that wrench straight out in front of him that way?" Daisy wanted to know. "It looks like Frankenstein's coming to work on your car. And why's it a bear? The phone book's got a penguin."

"That's just smart advertising," T. J. explained to her. "We're too smart to have just one animal. If we had just the bear, it would only remind customers of us every time they saw a bear. And how often does that happen? This way anytime folks see a bear *or* a penguin, first thing they're going to think about is Aardvark."

～

In the early part of 1979, Humble County saw a few signs that civilization had finally headed back from the deep precipice that had threatened it during the rest of the decade. Jimmy Carter, a decent churchgoing Georgian, whose initials, J. C., coincidentally were the same as Jesus Christ's, was in the White House. An editorial in *The Humble Progress* praised a group called The Village People for writing two successful songs about good American values that everyone endorsed, *YMCA* and *In The Navy*, which just showed, thank goodness, you didn't have to make songs with a lot of nasty lyrics about sex or drugs or even stuff a person didn't even understand to have a hit record.

In 1980 the government gave Lee Iacocca a loan for one and a half billion to bail out Chrysler. As far as Sheriff King was concerned, this was yet one more example of the corruption that stretched from Humble County all the way up to the top levels of the government. Iacocca was the same man, King reminded people, who concealed the fact that Ford Pintos tended to explode on impact, reasoning it would be cheaper to litigate the occasional wrongful-death suit than spend $11 per unit to adjust its faulty engineering.

T. J., however, saw the loan in a more favorable light. Chrysler alone employed about thirty thousand people, but those were just the ones in the actual factories. The number did not include teachers to take care of their kids, contractors to build them houses, short-order cooks to make their hamburgers, not to mention farmers to raise the cows to make the meat to turn into hamburgers. It didn't count the folks on rubber plantations making tires, or steel workers making engine parts, or highway departments pouring out tar for roads, or the Philco people making car radios, or Country and Western singers making music to play on those car radios, or people with drive-through windows and drive-in movies making places to drive cars to. "If you really looked into it," T. J. speculated, "it would probably turn out everybody on earth one way or another is working for Ford, GM, or Chrysler.

"And on the Pinto thing," T. J. said, "Jimmy and I disagreed on the subject of e-vo-lution, but I know what he would have said. By saving money not fixing all them cars, not only did Ford have more money, but car buyers and stockholders, too. They all came out ahead. And who died in them explosions? People who had accidents in the first place. The reckless drivers was dying out, leaving all the careful drivers to—what? Survive and reproduce. That makes everyone better off. It's what you call a win-win proposition."

~

Earl was adjusting a Pontiac's timing one Wednesday morning when he got the news about his father. T. J., who was sitting on a stool beside him drinking coffee and cream and reading the *Wall Street Journal*, had just finished saying, "Options. What we need to go into next is options. Puts and calls," when the phone rang. "Aardvark Auto." T. J. listened, saying, "Uh-huh, uh-huh," at intervals, and then with a worried expression handed the phone to Earl. "It's for you, it's Gloria," he said, and gave the phone to Earl. "She said the Fulton County Sheriff called. I think you need to call Grady Memorial up in Atlanta."

After talking with Gloria, Earl called Grady Memorial, which had been trying to contact him about his father. Roy Mulvaney was in intensive care. "I'm coming right up," Earl said over the phone.

T. J. took Earl by the shoulders and stared him in the eyes as if trying to memorize his face. "You're in shock," T. J. said. "You ain't fit to drive. You wait here. We're going to call up your buddy Troy to drive you."

Obediently Earl sat on a wooden bench and waited, his hands on his knees. There didn't seem much point in starting back on the Pontiac when he was going to be interrupted any second. When Troy arrived, he and T. J. consulted briefly on the route to Atlanta, up Deepstep Road, dogleg to I 20, then west, and get off at the Grady Memorial exit. On the way there, Troy offered an interesting new remedy for a pinhole leak, but otherwise they said nothing. It was a silent drive and a long one. Pine trees filled the road on both sides.

The lady at Grady Memorial's front desk told them Roy Mulvaney was in ICU on the third floor. At a nurse's station on the third floor, they asked a doctor which room he was in.

"Family members?" the doctor asked.

"He's the son," Troy answered, and went on in perfect seriousness, "Earl Mulvaney, best mechanic ever touched a lug nut."

"And you are?"

"Troy Badcock, my friend," Earl said, and went on automatically, "World's greatest plumber."

"I'm Dr. Grisham," the doctor said, having no one to introduce him. "Mr. Mulvaney, if you could come with me."

Troy and Earl had pulled out of Aardvark Auto at 10:00 A.M. and arrived at Grady Memorial at 1:30. Roy Mulvaney's death certificate, which had not yet been made out, read 12:45. They had been driving through that endless canyon of pine trees when Mr. Mulvaney had died. It had been years since Earl had seen him, but even so, though his father's face was swollen, though his nose was pushed to one side, his ear partly detached, and his mouth and eyes strangely crooked-looking, like a Mr. Potato Head with the parts in all the wrong holes, Earl was able to identify his father at once.

Dr. Grisham told Earl how when the police arrived at Roy's hotel room, they found his assailant taking a rest from his labors, drinking a beer in front of the TV among the scattered

Bicycle cards and broken hotel furniture. In the doorway to the bathroom, the victim lay struggling for breath with smashed ribs and a fractured jaw. Roy Mulvaney identified himself during a brief period of consciousness on the way to the hospital, and the ambulance drivers had confidently expected he would pull through because there was so little blood. They discovered at Grady, however, that Roy had done considerable bleeding, except all on the inside, filling up his chest cavity, which in the end killed him just as surely as if his blood had gone to fill up the motel bathtub.

Troy and Earl spent the entire day in Atlanta, and ended up in the hospital cafeteria eating a late, late dinner of red Jell-O, wilted salad, and something calling itself Salisbury Steak before driving back. Before they left the hospital, a nurse gave them a shoebox. "This stuff belongs to you, I expect. Anyway, I don't expect anyone's going to fight you for it. And I don't expect you need to fill out a receipt or nothing."

Earl lifted the lid. The sum total of his father's personal effects: a partly full pack of Fruit Stripe gum, a pencil stub with a broken tip and damp eraser, a little flip book with a series of arcane mathematica such as— "1, 2, 3, 5, 8, 13 (13!) 21, 34, 55 (52 + 2 Jokers + Instruction card = 55!)" And an unfinished letter home:

> *My Dearest Ruby,*
> *How can I express all that is in my heart?*

That was as far as his father had gotten.

When the gate lifted to let them out of the parking lot, Earl looked back to see dark clumps of storm cloud towering behind the hospital, hiding the rising moon.

Earl and Troy drove a long time, again in silence. It grew darker. Just outside of Covington it struck Earl that he was an orphan now. His mother had died, his father had died, and Jimmy Wiggins had died, who had been more of a father to him than his actual father. The best friend he had left in the world was Troy Badcock, who was driving him back to Humble County, and whose wife Earl had loved since high school. Earl shifted uncomfortably in his seat.

"There's something I got to tell you," Earl said.

"If it's about Ellen, don't bother."

"What?"

"You two love each other. I know that."

The heat rose up in Earl's face. "How long have you known?"

"Since the fire. Before. I seen the way she looks at you. And then there's those messages you been sending each other in books."

"Oh."

"But she's my wife, and you know that. And I expect she knows that, too. And Jennifer is my daughter, and I'm sure of that. If I wasn't sure of that—well, that'd be a different story. But like I say, all of us know where we stand. And I love Ellen, and she loves me. Maybe not the same way she loves you, but she loves me. We been through some things together that you wouldn't know about. Bills and diapers, and leaky faucets. We depend on each other and we're going to stick together. If you two want to write notes to each other and make cow eyes once in a while, I guess I can put up with it so long as no one else knows about it and it don't go no further than that."

"It won't."

They drove in silence. Two monstrously large dragonflies chased each other across the blacktop through the high beams.

From the west, thunder played a low, continuous timpani. You could smell rain in the distance. Earl thought about how much Troy had changed since high school. His face had gotten heavier, and bags had begun to form under his eyes. His hair, though thick, had already begun to recede. Of course, they had all changed.

"I saw a movie on TV with a situation sort of like this," Troy said. "Two men in love with the same woman, but she's married to one of them. Anyway, one of the men says, 'We're both men of the world.'" Troy's hand flinched, sending the truck onto the shoulder, and he snatched back the wheel to bring them back onto the highway. "They were both Frenchmen or something." Troy gripped the steering wheel with both hands, his knuckles white in the glow from the dashboard instruments. "If you go calling me a man of the world, I swear to God I'm going to whip your silly ass black and blue." They drove a quarter mile further, and Troy said, "Sorry, man, I wasn't thinking about your dad."

The first big pelting drops of a downpour fell on the windshield.

CHAPTER SEVENTEEN

Roy Mulvaney was buried in The Standard next to his wife. It was the most sparsely attended funeral in county history. Mr. Thigpen gave the eulogy. His text, Deuteronomy 5:9, was not one anyone could recall having been read at a funeral before: "I the LORD your God am a jealous God, visiting the iniquity of the fathers upon the sons to the third and fourth generation." Mr. Thigpen did not explain his purpose in selecting such a peculiar text. Instead he said, "Roy Mulvaney was a man who spent his life pursuing the wrong things. Maybe in the last few minutes of his life, Roy realized his mistake and turned to Jesus. Maybe he finally found the one thing that would bring him peace. We'll never know. In any case, it's too late for Roy Mulvaney. But it ain't too late for us." Here Mr. Thigpen looked meaningfully at Earl from under his

311

bushy eyebrows. For Mr. Thigpen, Jesus was as definite and substantial as a Briggs and Stratton engine, and a good deal less mysterious.

After the funeral, Earl was walking down the gravel lane to his car when a slight-built man with a shock of white hair came running up to join him. "I'm Willie," the stranger said. "I'm one of your daddy's poker buddies. I was with him." Earl stopped to listen. "At the end," Willie said. "I was with him."

It was a warm breezeless day, too hot for any birds to sing. Willie flapped his sportcoat to fan himself. "It all started when your daddy started drawing flushes," he explained. "I never seen nothing like it. Four flushes in a row. He was winning every pot." Willie wiped his mouth nervously with one hand. "Naturally we started to get suspicious. I ain't saying your daddy was cheating, but it ain't natural getting that many flushes. Spud, he's the man who beat up your daddy, had called him on every hand—and lost—so of course he was madder than even we were. On the fourth hand, he got out of his chair and said he was going to kill your daddy for cheating.

"We tried to calm him." Willie saw a piece of gravel had strayed onto the grass. He began to push it back to the pathway with his toe. "We told him, Spud, that Roy'd give us our money back for those four hands, and we could start over, and he would promise not to draw any more flushes. But your daddy wasn't having it. He said something about the laws of probability and that things was finally swinging just now back into balance. He said he expected he was going to draw at least a hundred ninety-six more flushes that night, and he was going to play every one of them. That was all Spud needed to hear. He sailed into your daddy like a windmill, and me and the others saw it wasn't no use to interfere, and cleared out. Before

I left the hotel parking lot, though, I found a pay phone and called the police." Having at last returned the rock to its proper location, Willie looked up and met Earl's eye. "That's how they knew to come."

~

Aardvark Auto continues to prosper, and I can recommend it if you ever have engine trouble. Just about all the folks in the county and the next county over bring Earl their cars and troubles. Thanks to Earl, cars last longer than they used to and in fact there was so little business in used cars that Wayne would have wound up unemployed except he finally married Donna Wiggins shortly before the car lot went under for the third time. Wayne went into real estate, so they're doing quite comfortably now.

By the way, Barbara Allen, whose heart Earl had broken all those years ago, got over her distress, married Grady Cook, who finally got a job in the chalk mines, had a baby, which Grady swore was not his, then finally divorced him and went up to Atlanta where she knew an agent, and for all I know, she has since become a world-famous model or actress.

In most cases Earl can fix your car while you wait, so people stay and talk with him as he works on their cars, telling him all sorts of things they wouldn't have told anyone else, such as Judge Hathorne's theory that the Rapture has already occurred, but there were so few real Christians, nobody noticed when they all disappeared and went to heaven, or Daisy's vow that no matter if people said you couldn't do it, she was going to take her worldly possessions with her. She had hidden the better part of her fortune in various nooks and crannies that she felt confident no undertaker would care to palpitate, so when her time came to go, she'd have it all right there in the coffin. Daisy's Diner has since disappeared, and the county lost track of her, so maybe she did take it with her after all. Hathorne is still judge, just as he seems to have been as long as the oldest resident can remember, and has little need to get his driver's-license photo retaken, because his appearance has not changed in all that time.

One of Earl's most frequent customers is Mr. Thigpen, and although he would never accuse the minister of dishonesty, Earl sometimes suspects that he might be deliberately disconnecting his own distributor, because he gets towed in for the same simple reason time after time.

"Each of us gots a Jesus-sized hole in him," Mr. Thigpen told Earl once. "We're just born that way. It's the exact size and shape of Jesus, and you can try and try to fill it with something else, but ain't nothing but Jesus going to fit. Anything else you try to fill it with—money, success, good times—you'll never get enough of because only Jesus can fill that hole."

Earl did not comment.

Another time Mr. Thigpen brought out his Bible, and said, "Do you mind if I read to myself while you work?" Earl said he did not mind, and forcing his heavy black Bible to open somewhere besides Ecclesiastes, the minister read aloud to himself as if completely at random, "that whosoever believe in me shall not die, but have everlasting life," then he looked up into the middle distance and said in a contemplative voice, "That's quite a promise." Mr. Thigpen is about as good at subtle salesmanship as Earl was at being mean, but he hasn't given up yet. He's confident Earl will find Jesus one day, but as far as I can tell, he hasn't found him yet.

T. J. is a good partner to Earl, bringing him customers on a tow truck, making sure customers pay, and making sure Earl eats a more varied diet than just eggs and bacon. Opinions continue to differ on the size and the state of completion of Earl's junk pile, which he calls his Endless Corvette. Some say there are barely enough pieces to spread out and cover the top of a picnic table. Others say the odds and ends stand knee-high and form the unmistakable outline of an engine block. There are even a few who say the Corvette has been completed, chassis and all, but like any classic sports car, she needs constant rebuilding to keep in running condition.

The original Corvette never ran again after that one time Earl started it up to show Sheriff King, and naturally Donna Wiggins had too much pride to bring Earl in to repair her. When the car lot had its last going-out-of-business, everything-must-go sale, the only car Donna could not get anyone to take was that Corvette. Years later when the car lot was converted into a church for the Jehovah's Witnesses, the shed out back was torn down, but except for some oil stains and old cinder blocks no trace was discovered of the '53 Corvette, so no one knows what became of her.

Earl has read all the way through Great Literature A–Z, and started over at the beginning. By Earl's count, Mr. Dashwood has had a son by a previous marriage, and the current Mrs. Dashwood has given him three daughters two times now. Earl and Ellen still exchange messages through library books, and Earl looks forward to rereading her first messages again, along with his answers, and sometimes he imagines it will be like swirling back and forth in time, just like one of those sponges she told him about so long ago. There are times when the library is quiet, and I fall to musing on Earl and Ellen, that I think the only place they'll ever be together is in the pages of the books of the Great Literature Shelf. Or in the pages of this book.

Sometimes in the evenings Earl parks out along Old Eighty-Five, brings along a Dr Pepper, and stares at shadows moving in the brightly lit windows of a distant house. Okay, it's the Badcock's home, there's no point being coy about it. Jennifer plays in the front yard, chasing fireflies if it's the season, and sometimes her mother brings a book on the front stoop to read by yellow bug light. Earl watches until Ellen calls Jennifer in, and then he finishes up his Dr Pepper and heads back home.

One night someone who looked a lot like Earl Mulvaney was seen driving something that looked a lot like a '53 Corvette in a wide circle around Humble County. I do not insist this really happened. Atmospheric conditions in Humble County in the fall have been known to play tricks on people. The combination of twilight, leaf smoke, September rain, in addition to the ever-present ghostly sound of town dogs barking in the distance, not to mention the feeling of a kind of general longing in the air, which is hard to explain if you haven't been there, is enough to make some people half-see and half-imagine many things. Nothing ever momentous, like ghosts walking around with their heads on fire writing out cusswords on someone's lawn, or anything like that, but just little things, pieces or hints that make you feel you might have seen something astounding if you'd looked up just a second earlier.

Once, just for an example, I thought I saw a brontosaurus stretching his long neck over the back of Miller's Grocery to get a look at something in the parking lot. I was not particularly surprised to see him because he seemed so natural standing there, and I felt like I'd known all along Deepstep was full of dinosaurs except that you rarely got to get a good look at one of them. And he wasn't surprised to see me, because as I said, he wasn't really looking at me but at something else that had caught his attention. It only lasted the blink of an eye, but I perfectly remember the expression on his face of goodwill and calm as he studied an oil stain on the blacktop far below him, and then my focus shifted after a second and he wasn't a brontosaurus anymore but just a light pole.

This was back in the '70s, and I later learned that it couldn't possibly have been a brontosaurus because there's no such thing, and it must've been a diplodocus.

But if you accept eyewitness accounts, however unreliable, of someone looking a lot like Earl Mulvaney driving a vintage sports car that looked a lot like a '53 Corvette, he tooled up around Prosser Road near the county line, came back down along Deepstep Road where it turns into West Haynes and goes straight through town. Mrs. Price, sitting on her front porch reading the condensed version of *Gone with the Wind*, had just finished the page about the Battle of Atlanta when she heard the throaty rumble of an engine and looked up in the gathering autumn twilight to see what she thought was a white sports car turning left onto Floyd. In the uncertain light and lingering smoke from burning leaves, it seemed to her the pearly car shimmered out of existence just as it reached Betty Key's mailbox, catty-corner across the street from hers, reappearing at the end of Floyd where it turned right on Back Boulevard.

From there he must have taken the Kaolin Road to Old Eighty-Five, but there was a considerable time lag before the next sighting. Night had fallen, and the first drops of a September shower had begun to come down before one of those wide-spaced houses on Ridge Road heard the sound of a Blue Flame Special along with the unmistakable voice of Johnny

Cash coming from AM speakers. The sounds grew gradually louder as he came down the road, and then fainter as he passed, and seemed to be heading north. That would have taken him to East McArthy, which, if they had turned right and patiently doglegged in an easterly direction, would have eventually brought them to Savannah, running parallel to the tracks of the Nancy Hanks. If he turned left, it would have brought them straight back into town and crossed Warthen Street, where East McArthy turns into West McArthy.

Again, I don't insist it happened any more than I would ask you to believe I saw a dinosaur in downtown Deepstep, although it *was* there.

And that, at the risk of frustrating you, is where the story ends. Part of me wants to assure you that Earl did build his Endless Corvette and the day after Troy's funeral, he showed up at Ellen's door, declaring his undying love and asking her to come away with him. By that time Jennifer would be married with children of her own, so nothing would hold Ellen back. So after embracing him, and letting her warm tears fall on Earl's cheek, she'd get in the car with him, and they'd drive off for some Dr Peppers down State Road 12 to Warthen, which would strike you as eerie and mysterious because you know full well that highway was never built, and I would write, just to add to the mystery of the whole thing, that on their way out of town they were spotted by at least one incorrigible—Wayne the other mechanic, say—who on seeing them happy together would suffer a pang of redemptive regret, and then just before the city limits, the car would become milky and translucent, and then disappear altogether.

But I can't say that.

Not that I don't hope it will turn out that way, and maybe it even will, but it hasn't happened yet, and in any case, that's not what this story is about. If I wanted to be harsh, I could end it like one of those books on the Great Literature Shelf of the Humble County Library, where the main character never gets the girl but ends up dead, and the green light or whatever it was that symbolized his desire goes on shining uselessly for everyone else. But I can't say for certain the story ends that way either. I'm afraid we're just not going to open the lid on this particular box to check on this particular cat. The story's not about getting or not getting, but just wanting and waiting. And so again, at the risk of royally ticking you off and with my profoundest apologies, I'm going to let you off here, pretty much where we started off.

Sometimes just before twilight Ellen comes out to read a book, and Earl comes out, too, to see her.

ACKNOWLEDGMENTS

Thanks to my teachers Sheri Joseph and John Holman for their feedback on the early stages of this manuscript. Thanks to my agent, Sorche Fairbank, and my editor, Keith Wallman, for sharing their insights and for their unflagging efforts to make this book a reality. Thanks to my wife Nancy for her continual support, encouragement, and love. And thanks to my sainted mother, to whom I owe all I am or ever hope to be.

ABOUT THE AUTHOR

MAN MARTIN was awarded the Flannery O'Connor Writing Scholarship at Georgia College and then earned an MFA in graphic design from the University of Georgia and an MFA in creative writing from Kennesaw State University. He is currently working toward a Ph.D. in writing at Georgia State University in Atlanta. He was the creator of the nationally syndicated comic strip *Sibling Revelry* that ran from 1988 to the mid-1990s. His writing and drawings have been published in *McSweeney's Online*, the *Kenyon Review*, *Atlanta Magazine*, *Marietta Daily Journal*, and *Carve Magazine*. He lives in Atlanta, Georgia.